The Forgotten Flapper

Sepia Stories Publishing

ISBN: 978-0-9947349-0-7

First Edition

The Forgotten Flapper

A Novel of Olive Thomas

Laini Giles

ALSO BY LAINI GILES:

Love Lies Bleeding

For Aunt Hopie, who would have approved.

OVERTURE

PROLOGUE

NEW YORK, NEW YORK, *today*

You know, it's really no fun haunting people who refuse to be afraid of you. When you say, "Boo," they're supposed to scream, not say, "Hi Olive." Just so you know, I'm not one of those chain-rattling, doom-and-gloom ghosts. It's not my style. Instead, I rearrange the scenery and materialize for the folks who work here. Keeps 'em on their toes.

I live at 214 West 42nd Street, New York, New York. That'd be the New Amsterdam Theatre for you non-showbiz types. I used to perform here back in 1915. In my day, this was the place to be. Bright lights, hooch, and the girls of the Ziegfeld Follies. The most lavish musical revue of its day, and I was there for it.

See those fixtures up there? Those murals? Fancy, huh? Decades ago, this was the biggest venue in New York. I was just a dumb appleknocker from Charleroi, Pennsylvania. The New Amsterdam was the most glamorous place I'd ever seen. I spent the happiest time of my life here, dancing, singing, and chatting with everyone. What a gay time we all had! Whether it was champagne and roses backstage, dancing 'til dawn at Bustanoby's or Murray's Roman Gardens, dining on oysters Rockefeller at Delmonico's or even the butter cakes at Childs, it didn't matter to me. I loved it all.

I went to Hollywood too. But that didn't turn out quite like I planned. I ended up back here on this ghostly plane, the century barely begun. I guess that was my problem. I was never happy with what I had. I always wanted something else.

In the 1930s, the owners turned this place into a movie palace. But with sound, we silent stars were forgotten when the new stars like Clark Gable and Greta Garbo showed up. It wasn't fair. We were just as glamorous as they were. I couldn't help thinking how I should have been up on that screen too. Instead I watched from the wings like I never existed. Goddamnit, I once had the world wrapped around my little finger. What the hell happened?

By the 1960s, life as a ghost at the New Amsterdam had definitely lost its luster. The dark corridors got a little drearier, the once-vivid red, green, and gold patterned carpet was nearly black with fifty years of wear, and the moisture and mildew seeped into every ornamented crevice. For the first time in my life, I wished I'd had a book to read. Any day the bulldozers would show up, and what the hell was I supposed to do when that happened?

In the 1970s, I sat twiddling my thumbs while the whole country went through its selfish phase. This place was a shithole, and it smelled even worse. The roof had leaks no one bothered to fix, and mushrooms were sprouting in the orchestra pit. They were hawking God-knows-what out on the street in Times Square.

My days and nights blurred together after years of boredom. From my perch in the mezzanine, I watched that dishy Chinaman in his "kung fu" movies. When it wasn't Bruce Lee double features, I had to sit through crap like *Beware the Blob* or Jacqueline Bisset in her wet T-shirt.

Disney arrived in 1995. I was intrigued when the suits showed up, pointing and planning. Then the hardhats arrived. They set up scaffolding, and the hammers and paintbrushes started flying. They brought in artists to restore the murals and the sculpted rosettes and sconces. When all the work was finished, I felt a huge lump in my throat. The old girl was beautiful again.

They threw a hell of a party in 1997 for the reopening, and the New Amsterdam was back to live theater—musical versions of Disney favorites. It was Broadway's newest showplace: refurbished electric, updated plumbing, commercial carpet, fancy paint job, and the murals like they were supposed to be—pictures of goddesses and muses and all that stuff.

The audience was full of conversations about the area and its "rebirth." The theater district sprang to life like never before, with families drawn to the shows, the shopping, and the restaurants. Now, theatergoers showed up with shopping bags from places like Aéropostale and Ann Taylor. Much different from the hookers and bums I'd seen the previous decade or two. The actors and actresses and musicians and prop people livened up my life more than anyone had in years! This was the place to be again, like it had been in my day.

The first few performances of a new show were always my favorite times. Even though I'd seen the players rehearsing for weeks, it was almost like being at the Follies again. Only in the audience this time.

Round about the twentieth performance, when I could sing "Hakuna Matata" or "Spoonful of Sugar" from memory, I'd climb up to the roof to get away from the music, and I'd reminisce about the old days.

I overheard one of the foremen say there were too many ancient problems up top and they couldn't bring it in line with modern building codes. So Disney sank all their cash into the ground floor and used the roof garden for air conditioning units. Why, we used to entertain the richest men in the world up there!

I can't stay on the roof too long or my eyes get misty. I have to go downstairs searching for company, like this poor sap Dennis in the hallway just now. Only a few days into this job, and he still hasn't met me yet. He's not like the pros who've been at the theater for years and gotten blasé about me.

He's a looker, ain't he? Reminds me of Tony Moreno when he was just starting out. Smooth, with fancy white caps on his teeth. But he lisps, and he wears too much gel in his hair. Definitely a *faygeleh*, as Lil Tashman used to call them.

If there's new blood, I like to parade down the hallway to see who notices me. I've been wearing this same green outfit and feathered headdress for years. When I got to the Great Beyond and told them I wasn't ready to wrap it up yet, they told me that if I planned on staying I'd have to pick something to wear. This was my favorite costume— velvet bodice, bare shoulders, and yards of flowered tulle for a skirt. *Why not make the most of it?* I thought. I hadn't considered how cold I might get in this drafty old theater—I just liked the reactions I got. Even the raccoon collar around my neck didn't help ward off the chill much.

Watch this. I'll do a little turn toward Dennis and give him the ole smile and wink. Then I'll slip through the wall.

His mouth is gaping, and the paintbrushes are clattering on the linoleum. Ha! His hands are shaking, and he's hotfooting it upstairs. Knocking on the manager's door, he doesn't even wait for an answer before stumbling in. That's usually how it works. Hear him telling the old guy about me? We can watch if you want. Sometimes people can see me, sometimes they can't. I haven't quite figured out the trick, but I love eavesdropping the way I never could in life.

The big guy at the desk is Mr. Wright. He's been at the theater since *The Lion King*, Disney's first big success here. I like him. He respects me and my paranormal clout. He'll let Denny jabber for a bit, then cut him off.

"Denny, relax. You've been on the job, what, four days? They should have told you when they hired you. She's very famous."

"Tell me what? Who's famous?"

"You said golden-brown hair and a green costume, right? You saw Olive, that's all. She's our resident phantom."

Phantom? A little overdramatic, don't you think?

"Who is she? Why is she here?"

Why am I here? I live here, son.

"She was a silent movie actress, but she was a Ziegfeld girl before she went to Hollywood. Died very mysteriously."

"She winked at me," Denny says.

"Yeah, that's Olive." Mr. Wright nods. "She flirts with all the guys. Come with me for a second."

Ooh, they're going downstairs. Come on, I love this part. Those pictures on the wall? All spit curls and expressive eyes and bee-stung lips? That's me Mr. Wright's pointing at. That's the costume I wore as Miss January.

"This was Ollie. Supposedly, her eyes were violet blue. You know, like Liz Taylor? You might notice that when we get to the theater in the morning, and when we leave at night, we always say hello and goodbye to her. It tends to keep the peace with the old girl, so she doesn't toss the scenery all over the place."

Old? Hmmph. *And toss?* I beg your pardon. I kicked a wooden tree over once. Okay, twice. I hate being upstaged.

"The only time she gets upset nowadays is if we have old vaudevillians attending tributes. That sort of thing. Doris Eaton Travis visited a few years ago, and Olive lost her mind throwing stuff around. She doesn't appreciate it when we rearrange the office either—desks and chairs and file cabinets. She likes things the way they are, thank you very much."

What can I say? I don't like change. And I'm more famous than Doris what's-her-name ever dreamed of being. I couldn't see why they were rolling out the red carpet for a wrinkled-up old biddy like her. People love me because I'm twenty-five forever, and because they think I never left. Like Dennis with his eyes glued to my portrait. He's interested now, huh?

Wright's going to tell him my whole story. You wanna hear?

ACT ONE

CHAPTER ONE

This may surprise you, but I didn't have a theatrical background when I joined the Follies. That Booth fellow who shot Lincoln? They always said he came from a "theatrical family." Same with my Jack. But nothing for me, unless you count my brother Jim putting on a scene every time he had to eat string beans. Now that was some entertainment.

"Ollie, what's your favorite thing about New York?" people used to ask me.

"The sun," I'd say. No hesitation at all. "And blue sky. The color it's supposed to be."

Black as a Hottentot's ass. That was the color of the sky in my neck of the woods. Like nighttime even during the day. And the air reeked to high Heaven. Like a sickening mixture of coal, sulfur, and skunk cabbage. Imagine the lobby of the New Amsterdam at intermission, and know that the smoke was a hundred times worse. When it rained, you swam through a foul paste. And the steel factories, beehive coke ovens, smelters, and Bessemer processing plants shook the earth for miles in every direction. The only other noise you could hear were the church bells, tolling for everyone who died working in those places.

Charleroi, Pennsylvania, is a little town not far from Pittsburgh by way of the Monongahela River. In my day, it was known for two things: its plate glass company, and the oh-so-respectable Mrs. E.C. Niver, governor-appointed Assistant Censor of Motion Pictures for Pennsylvania. Because God forbid anyone might go to a flicker and actually enjoy it.

"There's another city called Charleroi in Belgium," Mamma told me once. That town had to be much nicer than ours. There wasn't much to recommend our town (or Pennsylvania on the whole) that I could see. But it was still home.

As a little girl playing on the stoop of our house, I'd cringe when the men trudged home at the end of the day, their boots leaving deep pits in the yellow mud that served as a road. Their faces were covered in soot, and the eyes that peered out had lost all hope. I could sense it even then.

"Mamma, why are the men's faces black?"

She sat down on the porch with me, wrapping an arm around my shoulder.

"Ollie," she said, "those men have the hardest jobs in the world, pulling coal out of the ground to keep us warm in the winter, or baking it to make iron and steel. They deserve your respect."

They all looked like they'd tramped through Hell and come out the other side. In a way, they had.

Why, only two years before I came along, there was a huge battle up the river at Homestead. Mr. Andrew Carnegie owned a factory there. When the workers decided to strike, the factory goons tried to bring in scab labor and Pinkertons to rough them up. The whole town took up arms against them, and lots of people on both sides died. By fall, the bastards at the factory had broken the strike. Take it from me: you'd be hard put to find anyone in the Mon River Valley who'd set foot in one of Mr. Carnegie's libraries after that.

They say the first man a girl falls in love with is her father. I'm no different. My father, Michael Duffy, was a huge man, built like a stevedore, with legs like pillars and arms like a great grizzly bear. His work boots were the size of the tugs plying the Mon.

Da's parents came over on a boat from Ulster, so his blood was as Irish as a four-leaf clover, but he'd grown up in Ohio, so he was American through and through. He had a hearty laugh and loved my mother's homemade sarsaparilla. He was a mason, lifting massive hunks of rock and stone every day for the buildings in Charleroi. I was fascinated by his hands. They were huge, rawboned, and knob-knuckled, usually red from a full day's work. His work gloves, the most important piece of equipment he owned, were ragged and frayed from so much use. When I was very small, Da moved us to Pittsburgh where the work was better.

It was impossible to be blue about anything when Da was around. He'd scoop Mamma up in a big hug, lifting her off the ground as she giggled and squealed, batting at his hands.

"Rena, me darlin'! Tell me all about your day!" he'd say, setting her down and planting a loud, boisterous kiss on her in front of all of us.

"I've made us lamb stew and an apple pie," she'd answer, blushing and looking up at him affectionately as she adjusted her apron.

"And you three scamps," he'd say, grinning at us. "What mischief were you up to today? The house is still standing, so I've high hopes for the evening." He'd let out a hearty laugh and collapse into his favorite chair, his feet up on the hassock. Then one of us would bring his slippers.

My brother Jim was the oldest, and the smart one. Always with his nose in a book. Then came me, then little Spud. His real name was Bill, but nobody called him that. When he was little, he'd eat an entire plate of potatoes if you let him, so Da began calling him Spud. He'd been Spud ever since.

We kids all took after Da, with his red-gold hair and deep blue eyes, but Mamma said I was the most like him in personality.

"How's my little Rose of Tralee?" he'd ask as I crawled into his lap. I'd smile up at him and pat his face, then nestle against his side. His smell was comforting—flannel just in from the smoky air and tinged with sweat, Blackjack gum, and the blackberry tobacco he packed into his pipe.

We were poor, but not as poor as some, and Da saw to it we were fed, clothed, and had a roof over our heads. We never wanted for anything. Especially love.

PITTSBURGH, PENNSYLVANIA, *December 1902*

"God's teeth, this bastard is heavy!" Da said, stumbling in the door with a tall, lush fir. Its spicy evergreen scent filled the house.

"Michael Duffy, you hush with that talk," Mamma said.

"It's a fine specimen," he said, bracing it as he placed it into the stand. Then he stood back to admire it. "Took me an hour to chop it and get it back here."

"You're working too hard," Mamma said, wiping her hands on her apron.

Letting out a thunderous sneeze, he pulled out his handkerchief and blew his nose. He tucked it back in his pocket and then wiped his forehead on his sleeve. He'd been helping lay the foundation of a new building downtown when he'd caught a cold the week before.

"Mike, go lie down, please," Mamma said. "I'll bring you some of this chicken soup I made, and some Salada tea with a little lemon and a dram the way you like it."

"I am feeling a little tired," he said. "But there's wood needs chopping."

"I'll get it, Da," Jim said. He looked up from his copy of *Captains Courageous* and began pulling on his coat and gloves. "You go rest."

"There's a good lad," Da said, letting out a deep bark of a cough on his way to bed.

The cough went from bad to worse. Then the cold turned into pneumonia, and they admitted Da to Allegheny General. Mamma sat vigil with him for a week. Mamma's parents, my Grandma and Grandpa McCormick, looked after us, and they brought us to the hospital that last day, Jim and Spud and me.

I barely recognized my father. He wasn't the big strapping fellow I knew anymore. His ruddy complexion was a ghostly grayish-blue. And that cough—it was a hacking sort of honk that rattled from deep inside him.

Mamma softly sobbed into her handkerchief as Father Delancey sat near the bed saying prayers.

"Almighty God, look on this your servant Michael, lying in great weakness, and comfort him with the promise of life everlasting, given in the resurrection of your son, Jesus Christ our Lord. Amen."

Mamma put her arms around us and brought us closer to the bed, where Da could see us. He tried smiling but ended up wincing instead as he coughed. Pushing through the pain, he opened an arm to us, and we scooted closer.

We all stood there shaking and helpless, and he touched each of our faces, gazing deeply into our eyes.

"You're wee gems, all of you," he said, his voice a raspy whisper. Be good for your ma. And make me proud of you," he said. He gave a final wheezing breath, and then he was gone.

From that day on, I hated hospitals—the smells and the sounds of death. I never wanted to feel that fear again.

Family and friends gathered at the house and brought offerings of boxty and colcannon. Mrs. Szabo across the street brought goulash. Mrs. Gianelli next door made noodles and sauce. We would have eaten like royalty for a week if any of us had felt like eating at all. Then life got harder than I ever thought it could.

Mamma did her best, scrubbing floors, taking in wash, and selling baked goods to McBrendan's Bakery, but it never went far enough with three children to provide for. I was able to watch Spud, and I helped her clean house. We ate a lot of cabbage soup.

The day our landlord told her he was evicting us, I found her crying at the kitchen table, nursing a cup of tea that had long gone cold.

"Mamma, Mamma, what is it?" I said.

She tucked me into her arms, her warm tears soaking into my hair as we sat together. She held me there, rocking back and forth, whispering how everything was going to be okay, when she didn't know herself if it would be.

Mamma moved us in with my grandparents in McKees Rocks so we'd still have a home. I loved Grandma and Grandpa McCormick, but their house was stifling for a girl my age. My grandfather rarely moved from his Morris chair near the fireplace except to feed his chickens in the backyard. There were doilies on every single surface, and the portrait of Jesus on the wall stared at me accusingly. The place reeked of mothballs, and our evening meal was usually some form of potato and a cheap piece of meat from Halsey's Butcher Shop with all the flavor boiled out many times over. A year later, when she was returning from Halsey's, Mamma met a brakeman named Harry Van Kirk on Chartiers Avenue.

Harry was a mild-mannered man. Where Da had been outspoken and loud and fun-loving, Harry was quiet and respectful and would never have dreamed of frequenting a saloon with the boys after work. I was happy Mamma had found someone, but Harry and I had nothing in common. To me, he had all the personality of a communion wafer. It took a lot for him to raise another man's three children, and we were all thankful for that, but I couldn't wait to get away. On the positive side, he did love my mother, and the house he moved us into on Patterson Street didn't smell like camphor.

Harry seemed unable to form opinions of his own unless they'd been filtered through the other men he worked with at the Pittsburgh and Lake Erie Railroad Company. And while the P&LE was a huge part of life in the Rocks, I found it hard to believe that two men there knew everything there was to know about life and living it.

"Do you know what Mr. Dick Eberhardt told me?" he'd say, taking a bite of pot roast. "He said that the hospital is getting ready to add a new wing. The mayor told us there would be progress, now didn't he?"

When Dick Eberhardt was out, his second-in-command, Ernie Twitchell, provided the gossip for our dinner table.

"Ernie Twitchell said today he read about a couple who left California and drove all the way across the country in a horseless carriage. Took 'em thirty-two days! How about that? Used to take the pioneers months and months to do that. Look at the Donner Party. Guess all they needed was a Packard."

I was only a wisp of a girl, dumb as a can of soup, honestly. Back then, when you were young and poor and female, your options were limited. But I missed Da, and I was tired of Harry's secondhand opinions, tired of living at home, and tired of my life being decided by everyone else.

It wasn't that I hated Harry. He was a decent fellow, but he wasn't my father, was he? I'd barely begun to live, but I could feel myself dying a little more every day I was cooped up in that house. I despised the Rocks—the smoke, the hard winters, the smells of overcooked meat and potatoes, dinge and smoke, poverty and despair. I didn't care what I had to do to get out, but whatever it was, I'd do it. Everyone always told me I was too pretty to waste my life there, and they were right.

MCKEES ROCKS, PENNSYLVANIA, *early September 1910*

"Whatcha readin'?" a voice beside me said.

I held up my copy of *Theatre (The Magazine for Playgoers).* I was reading an article about Kathlyn Williams and having a chocolate soda at Goldsmith's Drug Store. At first, Snappy Powell put in a little extra seltzer because I asked him to. Now he just knew I liked them extra fizzy. Plus, he let me read the magazines—not like his boss, Mr. Goldsmith, who always said, "We're not running a library here, Olive." I think Snappy was sweet on me.

"Doing okay, Olive?" Snappy asked. His red polka-dotted bow tie distracted everyone from his buckteeth. They called him Snappy because he dished out drinks so fast.

"Great, Snappy, thanks," I said, stirring to mix the syrup as it settled to the bottom.

"Olive?" the fellow at my right said. "That's a pretty name."

"Thanks," I said, barely looking over. I laid five cents on the counter and gulped the rest down.

"See ya later, Snappy," I said and hopped off my stool. Placing the magazine back in the rack just so, I left Goldsmith's and continued strolling down Ocean Avenue.

Two nights later, my friend Helene Wise and I decided to go see a flicker at the Star Family Movie Theatre. It wasn't much of a place. Someone had set up a projector inside the fraternal hall. But it was a chance to escape for a little while. Hel and I both worked at Horne's Department Store in downtown Pittsburgh, and we both lived in the Rocks, so we'd gotten to be good chums.

As we paid our ten-cent admission, I heard a familiar deep voice at my side.

"Hello, Olive." I looked up to see the fellow from Goldsmith's. "Hi, Helene," he added.

"Hi, Krug," Helene said.

I remained silent but looked back and forth between the two, wondering who would be the first to do the honors. It was Helene.

"Do you know each other?" she asked a little tentatively.

"Not for lack of trying," he said.

"Oh. Ollie, this is Krug Thomas. He works for the railroad. Krug, this is my friend Ollie Duffy."

"What kind of name is Krug?" I said. "Sounds like something pirates tote treasure around in. Or a beast in the jungle somewhere."

The corners of his lips curled up in a grin. "It was my mother's maiden name," he said. "My real first name is Bernard."

I wrinkled my nose. "Yeah, I guess I'd go by Krug too if I were you."

"Ollie!" Hel said, obviously horrified.

I shrugged. What was I supposed to say?

"May I accompany you ladies in?" he asked. He hung back for a moment.

"Suit yourself," I said. At that, Hel gave my arm a pinch. "Ow!"

"Must you be so disagreeable?" she whispered. "Krug's a nice fellow."

"What business is it of yours?" I whispered back.

"You remember me telling you about the guy who won the Coney Island dance contest a few weeks back at the Norwood Pavilion?"

"Yeah, so?"

"So, that's him!"

"Really?"

On second glance, I noticed how lovely and thick his light-brown hair was. And how nice his gray-blue eyes were. The more I looked, the more I saw a little resemblance to my father. He wasn't as big, true, but he looked...dependable.

We sat through the flicker, Hel on one side of me and Krug on the other. I don't even remember it. Some Selig one-reeler, maybe. All I remember now was that little bit of chemistry Krug and I felt as we shyly smiled at each other in the darkness. When the lights came up and the tinkling of the pianist had stopped, the three of us headed for home. He said he lived in the Bottoms with his parents. Helene broke from us at Island since she lived on Stewart Alley, but he continued all the way with me.

"Miss Duffy, I'd be most pleased if you'd accompany me to the Pavilion this weekend for the West End Lyceum social."

I didn't even have to think about it. Kicking up my heels with the best dancer in the Rocks? Of course!

The Norwood Pavilion was up on the cliffs overlooking the town. Like an eagle's nest above the filth and stench, it gave you a gorgeous view of the Ohio River. Dancing up there gave me energy, and I had visions of what living outside stinky old Pennsylvania might be like—dancing somewhere glamorous. Broadway, maybe.

Krug was a great dancer, but when we weren't dancing, we didn't have much to talk about. He went on and on about railroad stuff—switching and brake yards—things I didn't care a whit for. And when he wasn't talking about that, he loved talking about President Taft.

"You know what Taft said the other day? 'I am president now and I am tired of being kicked around.' Now that is something I'd love to say someday," he said, taking a sip of his egg cream. We were back at Goldsmith's after seeing Rose Sydell and her London Belles at the Gayety Theatre in Pittsburgh.

"You're going to run for president?"

"Why not? In America, anyone can get rich, and anyone can run for president. This is the land of opportunity, Ollie. You can be my first lady."

"Okay. You can buy me some gowns and jewels then."

Snappy stood nearby, pouring some strawberry phosphate, and let out a little chuckle. Krug and I looked at each other and smiled.

We went out a few nights a week. Krug would collect me after I got off work at Horne's in the city, and we'd stay in town and see the military band play on the lawn at the Hotel Schenley, or go to a show if he could afford it. Sometimes we just strolled through the Jenkins Arcade, the giant market at 5th and Liberty, laughing at the season's new hats or browsing the sewing machines at the Singer store or the Kodaks at the Hambly Camera Shop. We'd imagine the picnic lunches we would make of the fresh loaves, thick juicy hams, and wheels of yellow cheeses, or he might buy me a box of cordials at the Old Virginia Chocolate Shop. If he'd just gotten paid, he might take me to dinner at Monongahela House or the Red Lion Hotel. Krug was attentive—a real gentleman, pulling out my chair and ordering my dinner along with his own.

Finally, in late March, he let me know he was in love with me.

"Then marry me," I said. "I can't stay in that house one more minute."

"Of course. I want to make you happy."

"All right," I said.

April Fools' Day, 1911, was the day I became Olive Thomas. And don't think I didn't feel like a genuine fool afterward. I mean, the first six months were great. Krug and I still went dancing, and Krug's mother, Stella, helped me with my cooking. Truth be told, she had the patience of a saint when I'd make a cake and forget the eggs, or fix a pie and leave out the sugar.

But then Krug told me he wanted us to settle down.

"We can't go dancing every night, Ollie," he'd say. "We're married now. And we'll want children soon."

We would? Jesus. I was sixteen, and nowhere near ready for that.

I tried to be good. But Krug knew all he had to do was take me to a show or out dancing for me to get amorous. One of the greatest nights we had as a married couple was when he took me to see Eva Tanguay at the Gayety. For a week after that, he'd come home to find me dancing with the broom and singing "That's Why They Call Me Tabasco."

Every month, Krug expected me to run the house on the seventy-five dollars he gave me, but I'd had to have this dress. Hel and I might sneak off to the flickers while he was at work, or we'd stop at Goldsmith's for a chocolate soda. Between the dresses and the sodas, pretty soon I didn't have anything left to pay the bills.

"Ollie, how could you be so careless?" Krug would say.

"I'm sorry, Krug. I meant to pay that bill. But then I saw this dress at Kaufmann's. Isn't it pretty?"

He sighed and walked away, not even looking at the lime-colored chiffon I was so proud of.

That was beginning to look like it for me—being a good little wife, learning to bake bread and do laundry, and eventually popping out babies once a year until my insides gave up the ghost. But a little voice in the back of my head kept telling me there was more out there. That I was wasting myself here. That I needed to be singing, dancing, or making my name doing something big. Something important. Da came to me in dreams, letting me know it was too early to settle.

"What are ye doing, Ollie?" he'd say, shaking his finger at me. And the dream would stay with me for days afterward.

One of those dreams woke me at 3:00 a.m., with cold sweat soaking my nightgown, but I still didn't know what to do. It was the next week that decided me. I'd overcooked some pork chops, and Krug picked at one as he told me about his day.

"They put me on a different crew," he said. "Met a couple new guys said they know Harry."

"Oh yeah?"

"Yeah. They invited me down to the tavern after work. Dick Eberhardt and Ernie Twitchell."

That was all it took. I saw a future full of the same secondhand stories, the same dumb jokes, and everything I never wanted to know about President Taft. I wrote to Mamma's sister

Elsie, and I got a letter a few weeks later, saying of course I could stay with her in Brooklyn. I filed for divorce before I left Pennsylvania. Then I packed up my little carpetbag, left Krug a note, and booked a ticket on the Pennsy to New York. I know I hurt his feelings, but I had to get out of there. Everyone else went to New York, escaping their Podunk lives. I decided I would too. To do big important things. I had no idea what. Da's voice guided me through the next few months, until he threw a gauntlet down and dared me to accept the challenge.

CHAPTER TWO

S. KLEIN AND COMPANY DEPARTMENT STORE, NEW YORK CITY, *March 1914*

"Miss Thomas, I think you'd be an excellent addition to Klein's," the woman said. Her name was Miss Bishop, and she was assistant supervisor of the men's section. "In light of your experience working in ginghams in Pittsburgh, I believe you'll do fine. Can you begin tomorrow morning at 8:00 a.m.?"

I had scanned the ads for a couple of weeks, and now an opportunity had arrived at last. Klein's dominated Union Square. Unlike many of the other stores that tried to outdo each other with marble columns, chandeliers, and a tasteful selection of men's and ladies' fashions, Klein's was a discounter. The front of the building was a haphazard collection of signs: *S. Klein on the Square—Dresses! Fur coats! Suits! Millinery! Values!* Most of my work was folding and refolding the shirts potential customers had set aside for a different size or design. The men flirted, but the close contact and the pinches on my backside were exhausting. From the younger, more attractive set, the attention could be flattering, but most of the old coots I helped were Harry's age or older.

This job does not pay enough for a black-and-blue fanny, I thought, massaging my most recent bruise from an old lecher in need of sock garters.

Aunt Elsie's was a dingy little place at Fulton and Hudson Avenue, under the clanking, hissing, elevated railroad, with a stop for the #1455 streetcar nearby and Fong's Chop Suey Palace a block away. It wasn't much, but at least I was in New York.

I loved reading the variety section of the *Tribune* advertising the latest in entertainment—Potash and Perlmutter at George M. Cohan's Theatre, or Maude Adams in *The Legend of Leonora* at the Empire. I couldn't afford to see any of the shows, but I loved imagining the excitement of the stage. I kept hoping something might change—like a stuffy old millionaire buying suspenders falling so madly in love with me that he'd leave mc all his gold—but as time passed, I realized the millionaires all shopped at Bonwit Teller or Bloomingdale's, not Klein's. I'd only exchanged one prison for another. If it wasn't living in a tiny house in the Rocks bickering with Krug, it was being chained to a cash register in the Klein's basement, folding shirts and being fondled by mashers. I couldn't tell which was worse anymore. How was I supposed to do anything big and important when I came home exhausted every night from escaping wandering, veiny hands? Even if I'd been able to save any money, I still couldn't afford to go to the theater.

I was standing in the stockroom one day, copping a secret smoke, when Pauline O'Connell joined me. She worked in millinery. Redder hair you've never seen in your life.

"Careful The Archbishop doesn't see you," she said, peering around the corner. "She sacked Katie Epstein last week for the same thing." We gabbed for a minute, and then she reached for a newspaper that lay on the stock table. "Ollie, have you heard about this?" She laid the copy of the *New York Statesman Examiner* down in front of me and watched my reaction.

"What is it?" Stamping out the cigarette, I kicked it under the table and picked up the page.

"It's a contest! Mr. Howard Chandler Christy, the artist, is searching for a shopgirl to draw. 'The Most Beautiful Girl in New York City,' they're calling it! The winner can get her picture in the paper, along with a photograph and some *money*." Pauline was supporting her mother and three little brothers, so anything that offered money appealed to her. Personally, I didn't give her a chance. Sweet girl, but too big boned, and her nose was the wrong size for her face.

Back in Pittsburgh, I'd strolled by the May Company druggist on my way to and from Horne's. The window always featured a display of chocolate boxes covered with paintings of dainty models, and I admired them any chance I got—the golden locks, the eyes of blue, and the deep ruby lips. I was every bit as pretty as those girls. This contest could be my proof.

"Are you going to enter?" I asked her.

She glanced away, her large nose obviously an embarrassment to her. "Oh, I couldn't. I'd never win." Then she turned back. Her eyes narrowed and she sized me up. "But Ollie, you have to enter this contest. I'll *die* if you don't!"

"I'll think about it," I said. "Can I take this?" At her nod, I took the *Examiner* and stuffed it in my bag.

On the trolley headed back over the Brooklyn Bridge, I pulled it out and stared at it.

"Are You the Most Beautiful Girl in New York?

Let an expert decide!

Award-winning illustrator Howard Chandler Christy, with sponsorship from the New York Statesman Examiner, *will be choosing Gotham's most perfect specimen from among its shopgirls.*

Interested applicants should present themselves at Mr. Christy's studio, Hotel des Artistes, 1 West 67th Street, on April 1 to win a specially painted portrait, a promotional photograph to appear in this paper, and a generous cash award."

Hell's bells. April 1st was a weekday, and I couldn't get out of work. But that whole night and the next day the contest taunted me. Wasn't this why I came to New York? Wasn't this what I said I wanted?

At the last minute, I sent a message to Klein's calling in sick. I dressed in my best skirt and least threadbare shirtwaist blouse, but I couldn't stop trembling. My fingers shook as I did up the buttons, and I spent extra time pin-curling my hair and applying powder and lip rouge. Then I pinched my cheeks for a rosy glow.

"Name?" An assistant with hair the color of autumn wheat was taking our names and making a list.

"Olive Thomas."

"Can you read and write?" he asked.

"Yes, sir."

"Then follow that group upstairs and fill this out. Mr. Christy is viewing you in small bunches. And hold up your number, please." He handed me a page full of questions, a pencil, and a paper where he had written a large *17* in black fountain pen.

In the case of the girls who had little education, Mr. Christy's assistant completed the information for them. Hell, half the girls barely spoke English, but at the thought of being discovered, it turned out we all spoke the same language—cold, hard cash.

The studio was an airy space, reeking of turpentine, with oak floorboards and huge windows overlooking West 67th Street and the buildings that lined it. Holding our numbers up, we paraded in front of Mr. Christy, who examined our faces and bodies carefully, walking among us and stroking a cheek or running his hand over a girl's hair. The assistant followed him, and from time to time Mr. Christy spoke to the young man, who made notes on a notepad. This wasn't the touching I'd experienced from the pigs at the shop. He was an artist studying his subjects, getting to know us better. A professional.

Mr. Christy had an elegant face, with graying brown hair parted in the center. It swept over a high forehead, and his eyebrows resembled otter tails. His voice spoke of the Midwest, someplace like Chicago or Milwaukee.

"What's your name, dear?" he asked me.

"Olive, sir." I smiled so he could appreciate that my teeth were straight, then shook out my hair to call attention to the color and curl.

"Exquisite," he said, whispering to his assistant, who gave a quick nod as he jotted notes on a pad.

I couldn't help but preen a bit. He remarked on the other girls as he walked along, but he only used words like "nice" or "very pretty." I was "exquisite." That had to mean something, right?

"Thank you, girls," he declared, concluding his review of our group. "The newspaper has your information, and we will be in touch in a few days."

I felt my shoulders slump at being dismissed so quickly, but I stood up straight when we passed another group on their way in. They were passable, pretty, some of them even lovely. But of all the girls, I knew I was one of the best. He said so. I took the streetcar home, exhausted but hopeful.

The next week at Klein's, I think I folded and refolded the same shirt over and over, forgetting where I had stopped. We'd gotten a new selection of serge whipcord suits, so I distracted myself with hanging and organizing them when I wasn't dodging questing fingers. After each long day in the basement, covered in new bruises, I was so exhausted that I could only think of a bowl of chicken broth and some potato before heading to bed. Until one night.

I unlocked the door to Aunt Elsie's to see a patch of white on the floor in front of the mail slot. It was a long envelope addressed to me, with the return address of the newspaper in the top corner. The flap was fastened with fancy red sealing wax. I was all thumbs as I ripped it open. Goosebumps tangoed up and down my arms as I read:

"Dear Miss Thomas:

We are excited to announce that you have won first place in the 'Most Beautiful Girl in New York' contest. We will be most pleased to see you at Mr. Christy's studio at your earliest convenience. Among the prizes you will receive are:

- *Your portrait painted by Mr. Christy*
- *Your photo in our newspaper*
- *$50 cash*

Congratulations!

The New York Statesman Examiner"

They could have heard me squealing in Hoboken.

CHAPTER THREE

HOTEL DES ARTISTES, MANHATTAN, NEW YORK CITY,

late April 1914

That morning, the buildings blended into the pale gray sky, and the sun tried to poke a ray or two over the street. At last it gave up and withdrew into the murk. Plus, the day was as windy as an old man eating prunes. I waded through the puddles to get to the building on West 67th.

"Hello, Miss Thomas," the assistant said, taking my coat. "Can I offer you a cognac or a cocoa?"

"Cocoa, please," I said, thinking cognac sounded far too fancy for a girl like me. I didn't even know what the hell it was.

"Miss Thomas, hello and congratulations," Mr. Christy said, entering the room with a flourish. He wore dark trousers and a light blue tunic splotched with red and purple. "It's good to see you. I'm so happy to be able to paint your portrait. Please, have a seat."

I plopped down in the thick upholstered chair on the platform in the center of the room. A paisley fringe blanket was tossed over the back of it.

"Lovely," he said. "Would you like some more cocoa? You

won't be able to move for a while. Might get chilly in this big loft."

"I'm fine, thanks." I grinned and spread the blanket over my lap.

"Do you mind some music? I enjoy it while I work," he said, turning and cranking the Victrola that sat in the corner.

"I love music!" I said as "That Mysterious Rag" burst forth from the disk that spun beneath the needle. It was hard to keep my body still. My legs twitched, wanting to get up and dance.

He adjusted the angle of my chin, arranging my hair over my shoulders. When he was satisfied the pose was perfect, he returned to his easel, his foot propped on a stool rung, keeping time, his ankle bobbing up and down.

"Where are you from?" I asked.

"From Ohio, originally," he said, aiming his pencil toward the canvas to begin.

"So was my father!" I said with a smile. He returned it. Humoring me, I'm sure.

"What kind of paints do you use?" I asked. I couldn't help it. When I was nervous, I talked. No, that's a lie. I talked all the time anyway.

"Oils." He put his pencil to the canvas again, ready to begin sketching.

"Did you go to school to learn how to paint? It seems very difficult," I said.

He glanced over at me, probably wondering if any of the other girls might have been less chatty.

"Yes, I attended the National Academy of Design here in New York. It was very educational. Shall we begin?"

"Oh yes. Sorry." I tried to behave myself.

He did a quick sketch, his arm moving in dramatic arcs. Then he set the pencil down and changed to paint, which he squirted onto his palette. He'd get up from time to time to change the record disk. As he worked, he cocked his head this way and that, and at last he began removing his smock.

"That will be it for today, Miss Thomas," he said. "I need to let the paint dry for a while. Can you come back on Tuesday?"

"Sure," I said. We kept this up for a week off and on as he finished the layers. And all that time he wouldn't let me peek. I wondered if I was difficult to paint, or if he thought something was missing. Maybe he'd made my nose crooked. Or made my eyebrows meet in the middle. I tried not to think about all that, sure I would turn out fine. I willed myself to remain perfectly still and stayed that way for hours each time. When at last he leaned down to the bottom corner, I figured he was adding his signature. I breathed a sigh of relief.

"Miss Thomas, you're quite a good model once you sit and let me work," he said with a chuckle. "I don't think you budged all week. Come see what I've done to you."

Gathering my skirt, I rose from the chair and rounded the edge of the easel. I hugged my arms from the chill in my bones. Then I gasped.

I was a candy box girl! My hair flowed in glowing waves, and my eyes shone with a deep blue elegance I knew I could never duplicate with any cosmetic. I looked like someone special. Someone important. The first lady, even!

"I think you mean what you've done *for* me, Mr. Christy," I said, knowing that this portrait would be my first step to making my name in this town. "I look so beautiful." My throat closed up, and tears started pooling.

He stood and gave my hand a kiss. No one had ever kissed my hand before. A marmalade-colored glow spread through my midsection, enough to brighten all of New York on such a cloudy day.

"No, dear," he said. "You *are* so beautiful. I merely told the truth on canvas."

"You're very kind," I said.

"Kind or not, I want everyone else to realize why you were the most obvious choice for this contest. In my eyes, none of the other girls stood a chance." He smiled warmly, and my heart did a little somersault.

He snapped his fingers, like he was remembering something important.

"Miss Thomas, I have two artist friends I think you should meet. One is Penrhyn Stanlaws. The other is Harrison Fisher. Penrhyn's here in the same building as me. He draws for the *Saturday Evening Post*, *The American*, and *Collier's*. Harrison does illustrations for *Ladies' Home Journal* and *Cosmopolitan*. I'm sure both of them would be thrilled to paint you. Would you like to pay either of them a visit?"

"Of course!" I blurted out.

The more poses, the more portraits, the more exposure. How better to make a name in New York? Maybe there was something big and important in my future after all. If those candy box girls could make their way modeling, maybe I could too.

Mr. Christy reached behind him to a huge breakfront he had filled with art supplies and pulled out some business cards. He wrote down the details for me on a small piece of paper. I took it and placed it in my bag, my heart pounding along with the jaunty tune playing on the Victrola.

"Thank you, Mr. Christy," I said. "For everything."

"It was my pleasure, dear. Perhaps we'll work together again one of these days." He gave me a gallant bow, and then we said our goodbyes.

Mr. Fisher's schedule was busy with sittings, so it took some time to book. When I visited him over a month later, he was as happy to meet with me as Mr. Christy had been.

"Miss Thomas, how delightful to meet you," he said, gently clasping my hands as he greeted me. "Howard tells me you won the 'Most Beautiful Girl in New York' contest. Congratulations! You are a stunner. No doubt about that."

"Thank you," I said, glancing about me at his apartment. It was a bit like Mr. Christy's, with the same overwhelming odor of turpentine. The living area was on one side, the studio space on the other. A raised platform covered with decorative pillows and a silky green-patterned blanket sat in the middle. The furniture was elegant but shabby. In a show of self-confidence or advertising chutzpah, he'd pinned several of his covers to the wall near his drawing table. I leaned in to take a look. One was a June 1913 *Ladies' Home Journal* with a group of girl graduates, another the January 1913 *Cosmopolitan* of a couple embracing, and the last was the February 1911 *Woman's Home Companion* with a girl in a beige coat and gloves holding a set of binoculars. The guy was good. His technique, like Mr. Christy's, was soft, delicate, and perfect for capturing pretty girls in pretty poses.

Harrison Fisher was not overly tall, but he seemed very grand to me. Penetrating eyes were his most noticeable feature, and they peered over a bulbous nose. His small upper lip worked its way into a full lower one, and then into a cleft in his chin. He was clean-shaven, which wasn't unusual, as more and more gentlemen were choosing to go beardless, but what I noticed most was the scent of his shave cream. It was the same type Da had used, a comforting herbal smell that reminded me of patting his cheeks when I was a girl. Mr. Fisher wore a similar paint-stained tunic as Mr. Christy had, this one a muddy gray, with trousers of the same shade.

"It's an exciting opportunity for you, isn't it?" He picked up his cigarette smoldering in the ashtray and took a hurried drag on it, returning it to burn down.

"Oh, yes. It's so thrilling in the city. So much to do and see!" I said.

"Where are you from originally?"

"Outside Pittsburgh."

"Never been to Pittsburgh," he said. "What's it like?"

"Smoky." *Awful, terrible, miserable.*

He chuckled and gestured for me to make myself comfortable against some of the pillows on the dais. When I'd found a position I could hold, he turned me toward him, my chin up and eyes down. I wasn't sure why, but I expected him to make a pass. He didn't, so I was pleasantly surprised. He was a consummate gentleman. And every hour, he checked on me.

"Miss Thomas, how are you doing?"

"I'm fine," I'd say, steeling myself against the aches and stiffness as he wielded his pastels at the paper on the easel.

"Lovely," he said when he was done. He unclipped the paper and laid it out on a table where I could see it. "I'm doing an upcoming cover for the *Saturday Evening Post*. You'd be perfect for it. Can you come back next week?"

I nodded enthusiastically. Mr. Fisher suggested I pay a visit to another friend, William Haskell Coffin, who drew for *Redbook*. I agreed.

"So, next week?"

"How about Wednesday? It's my day off," I said.

"I shall see you on Wednesday, then."

Back at Aunt Elsie's, we'd received a letter from Mamma, tickled to tears over two blessed events. Two weeks before, Mamma had given Jim and Spud and me a little half sister, whom she and Harry had named Harriett.

Plus, the previous year, my brother Jim had married his high school sweetheart, Margaret, and she had just given birth to a son—a healthy little fellow they'd decided to name James Michael Duffy Junior after Jim. As a proud new sister and an aunt with my extra income source, I prepared to spoil both of them rotten.

A few weeks later, I soaked up the sunshine on my way home from Mr. Stanlaws' studio, listening to the paperboys in rare dramatic form. They displayed their copies of the *Times* or the *New York World* or the *Statesman Examiner*, their voices more urgent than usual.

"Archduke shot in Europe!" one yelled. "Balkans a powder keg!"

"Extry extry!" another called. "Royalty shot in Sarajevo!"

In only a few days, the world went crazy. The word "war" was on everyone's lips, and rumors flew right and left on when the US would join in.

NEW YORK CITY, *May 1915*

My neck was cramped like nobody's business, but Mr. Fisher sketched away with his charcoal, oblivious. At least it wasn't long before he announced, "All right, Ollie. We're done with the sketch phase. Let's call it a day."

"Thank God. My neck is knotted tight as a Kraut pretzel." I reached my arms toward the ceiling and stretched, feeling muscles and joints popping.

I'd been posing for Mr. Fisher for about a year and often sat for Mr. Stanlaws and another artist, William Haskell Coffin, too. Mr. Fisher crossed the room to my seat and caressed my cheek.

"I adore you, you know," he said.

"I know."

"I worry about you sometimes, Ollie. You're still so young. You've matured a lot the last few months, but you're still a little naive. And you are an enticing woman. The wolves in this world will want to take advantage of that."

I smiled shyly at him as he continued.

"You must be strong and independent. Men can often be lethal, stupid creatures when it comes to getting what we want."

"Don't worry about me," I said, gathering my things. "I can take care of myself." It was true. Now that Krug and I were officially divorced, I felt invincible.

"I suspect you can," he said with a grin as I stood at the door ready to leave. I placed my hat on and did the pins up.

"Ollie..."

I turned, and he continued.

"Are you interested in the theater, by any chance?"

CHAPTER FOUR

"Who isn't?" I said as casually as I could, but my insides were like a bottle of champagne someone had just shaken and uncorked. "Why do you ask?"

"I thought so," Mr. Fisher said. "Mr. Ziegfeld over at the New Amsterdam Theatre is a friend of mine. The new season is beginning soon. I could write you a recommendation if you like."

"You scratch my back, I scratch yours, huh?" I teased him, barely able to catch my breath.

"If I can help you, I will. You know that." He took his pencil and poked me in the nose with it playfully. "You, my dear, can knock this town on its inflated backside. One look at you, and Broadway will be reeling."

Mr. Fisher turned to a small writing desk, pulled up a chair, and penned a short letter to Mr. Ziegfeld, recommending his favorite model, Miss Olive Thomas, as a perfect addition to the Follies. Folding it over, he handed it to me.

"Good luck, Ollie."

"Thank you." I kissed him on the cheek before leaving, then swept out into the street, knowing I had to try the New Amsterdam then and there. I hopped the next train to 42nd

Street and had to ask directions. A woman in a velour coat with a lynx collar was happy to oblige.

"Oh, you just head that direction, toward Longacre Square . . ." Then she stopped herself. "Oh, silly me. Sorry. It's been Times Square for a few years now. I can never quite remember. See that tall building there? The one with the skinny rectangular tower? That's the Times Building. Head toward it and you're almost there."

The hustle and bustle was exactly what I had come to New York to see. In some ways it was much like Pittsburgh—cars and wagons and people and chaos. But it was more than that. It was exciting. It was glamorous. I needed to be here, and I could sense it. It was big and important. Exactly what I had been looking for.

Theaters and their posters were everywhere I looked—Margaret Anglin was starring in a light comedy called *Beverly's Balance* at the Lyceum, and an all-star cast was featured in *Trilby* at the Schubert, with Wilton Lackaye as Svengali. There was a line out the door of the Liberty to see a new flicker called *The Birth of a Nation.* Giant billboards six stories high proclaimed the merits of Michelin Tires and Eads Gout Pills. Horseless carriages chugged and backfired down 42nd Street, dodging a plodding nag and his driver at the reins of the dependable ice wagon.

As I approached the New Amsterdam, I glanced up. The tall narrow building with the fancy front gloated above me, and the excitement pulsed in my ears. A curved arch flanked by columns greeted visitors, and an elaborate arcade below displayed the theater name surrounded by lights. A sign proclaimed that the new Follies was opening in a week.

I pulled the door open and gasped at the lobby, all sculptures and murals and thick pile carpeting. A hulking man in a double-breasted suit and a homburg with a flashy red feather approached me.

"Can I help you, miss? The stage door's on 41st Street."

"I'm not a dancer. I'm here for Mr. Ziegfeld," I said.

"Everyone's here for him. What do you want with him, doll?" His toothpick wiggled as he spoke.

"A job. Help me out?"

"He don't see nobody on Tuesdays."

"Please? I made a special trip across town. I've got a letter from Mr. Harrison Fisher, recommending me."

I reached in my bag for it, then waved it so he could see for himself.

"Harrison Fisher the artist? Ya don't say." He glanced at me like he might recognize me from one of my covers, scratched his head, and grabbed the letter. "Gimme a minute."

"Don't lose my letter!" I called after him. He retreated further into the building and I paced, waiting for him. The lavish lobby, filled with ornate moldings and curlicue sconces, surrounded me with warm light and the smells of freshly cut wood, paint, and canvas. Farther inside, a piano tinkled. Pretty girls in street clothes or lavish costumes stood and chatted; others hurried to and fro.

The big man ambled over to me again and gestured for me to follow him. He escorted me into an office, and behind a desk covered with papers sat Mr. Ziegfeld. He yelled into a gold-plated telephone he held in one hand. In the other, he clutched a stubby cigar. Another gold phone sat at the ready on his desk, and on a table in the center of the room sat a bronze bust of Ziegfeld himself.

His lush graying hair sprouted from a widow's peak, and a large hawk-like nose perched over a neat mustache. His dark eyes were intimidating, and he stared at me like a wolf sizing up dinner, not missing a thing. He wore a deep violet jacket with a diamond stickpin in the lapel, and his cologne was as bold as he was.

"Gotta go, Eddie. I'll call ya back," he said, still watching me intently. His voice was deep and nasal. I thought at first he had a cold.

"Here's the girl I told you about, Mr. Z," the big man said. "What'd you say your name was, honey?"

"It's Olive. Olive Thomas."

"Thanks, Otto," Mr. Ziegfeld said. Then to me he said, "Have a seat." He stubbed the cigar out in an ashtray.

I eased down into the wooden chair before the desk, and Otto retreated after tipping his hat at me.

"So I see Harrison took a shine to you. We've already had auditions for the season, but I had a girl drop out, and I like the way you look. So this could be your lucky day. Where you from?"

"Charleroi, Pennsylvania, originally," I said.

"That anywhere near Philly?"

"No, sir. Pittsburgh."

"How tall are you?"

"I think about five foot three, five foot four inches."

"Can you sing? Dance? Anything?"

"I'm not sure. I haven't had any training, if that's what you mean."

He rolled his eyes and turned back to his phone.

"But I love to dance, Mr. Ziegfeld. I dance every chance I get. I'll do anything for this job. Anything!"

He narrowed his eyes and looked more closely at me for a moment. "Pull your skirt up."

"Excuse me?"

"I said pull your skirt up. I need to see your legs. You don't expect me to hire you without seeing the entire bill of goods, do you?" For a minute I'd thought he wanted something else, if you know what I mean. But at that moment, I frightened myself a little; I would have given it to him.

"Oh." I raised my skirt a bit so he could see my calves.

"Higher. And stand up."

"Mr. Ziegfeld, I. . . "

"Do you want the job or not, Miss Thomas?"

I rose and planted myself next to the chair, then hiked the skirt the extra few inches.

"Now stand up straighter. And smile."

I flashed my teeth for him and turned my head a bit, like I did for my artists.

"Very nice. I'm sure we can find a spot for you in the back," he said, gesturing for me to sit down again, which I did. "You can be an extra, at least until I figure out what to do with you. We might be able to move you up, depending on how you work out. We'll start you off at fifty dollars a week. How does that sound?"

I'd been leaning forward, and I almost fell off the chair. It sounded pretty good, if you want to know the truth. I needed a cigarette.

"What would I have to do?"

"Stand there and look pretty. You seem to be quite good

at that already. I don't think you need too many extra skills at this point. We'll let you come in, study the routines, meet the cast, give you a shot, and if you've got potential, we'll go from there."

The smile on my face had to be as wide as the Dakotas.

"Show up here tomorrow afternoon about 1:00 p.m. for a costume fitting. Rehearsals are Monday morning at 10:00 a.m. sharp. Black stockings for practice. Got that?"

I nodded with enthusiasm, my throat tight.

"We'll see you tomorrow, then. We'll get you set with a costume or two."

"Yes sir."

He turned his attention back to the phone, letting me know I was being dismissed, so I hurried down the hallway and out to the street. My hands shook so hard I could barely light my Chesterfield.

Fifty bucks a week! I couldn't imagine that much money! I was only making three dollars a week at Klein's, with a little extra from my modeling. I took the streetcar to the store and crossed the main lobby, where the other girls were busy selling cheap brooches and long ropes of fake pearls to bored customers. Then I made a beeline to the stockroom, breezing past The Archbishop, who gave me hell for missing work. I'd called in sick last week to do a *Cosmopolitan* cover for Mr. Fisher and a *Saturday Evening Post* for Mr. Stanlaws.

"Miss Thomas, your absences have become unacceptable. One illness I understand, but this has become a constant problem. We at Klein's pride ourselves on our professionalism, and I simply must insist that you . . ."

Grabbing a piece of paper and a fountain pen from the

stockroom table, I wrote out a quick resignation and handed it to her. I hadn't worked a single day for Mr. Ziegfeld, but after my recent experiences posing and my triumph at the New Amsterdam, I could never return to that dreary basement. Her threats bounced off me as I turned and strutted out of the store, grinning like a fool all the way.

CHAPTER FIVE

NEW AMSTERDAM THEATRE, NEW YORK CITY, *May 1915*

The next day, I hurried in the stage door and was greeted by Otto, the side of beef in the homburg I'd met the day before. He greeted me and walked me to the backstage area. We stopped at a door marked Wardrobe, he knocked, and a harried voice yelled something resembling "Come in" over the noise of the orchestra downstairs.

Behind a giant canopy of pink marabou feathers draped on a petite blonde, a small middle-aged woman with graying brown hair and enormous spectacles was pinning flimsy fabric to the girl. She looked up, annoyed at the intrusion, until she saw Otto and gave him a little wave.

"Avis DeLuca, this is Olive Thomas, the new girl. Olive, Avis."

Avis nodded at me, sizing me up as a fresh recruit, and Otto retreated down the hall.

"Don't just stand there like a hat rack, honey. Have a seat. I'll be with you in five minutes." Her speech was garbled from all the pins in her mouth. She gestured to a chair in the corner. Pinning and tucking the blonde girl's ensemble, she stitched faster than I'd ever seen anyone sew in my life. After she dismissed the girl with a quick "It'll be ready for you by tomorrow night, Ina," she turned to me and summoned me over.

"Which number you going to be in?"

"I don't know. Mr. Ziegfeld told me I'd be an extra."

She consulted a list next to her sewing basket. "Aah, you're in the months routine. Plus, it sounds like you'll be a dove in the 'America' number. Red, white, and blue, flags—the whole shebang."

"I get the 'America' part. But . . . the months routine?"

"'A Girl for Every Month of the Year,' they're calling it. This is Lucile's costume, but I think we'll need to take it in a bit. You're shorter than Eileen."

"Lucile?"

"Lucile's the lady who designs these costumes. Her real name is *Lady* Lucile Duff Gordon. Very hoity-toity. English. She only uses top-grade stuff, believe you me. Feel this."

The delicate material slid between my fingers.

"Slip out of your clothes, okay honey? Leave your shimmy on. Step behind there if you're nervous."

A large white sheet had been strung up to allow the girls a little privacy to change. Slipping behind it, I changed out of my skirt and blouse, hanging them on a hook. Wearing only my chemise, bloomers, stockings, and garters, I pulled the sheet aside, and Avis swooped upon me with yards and yards of the silky ice blue fabric.

"All right, hold still," she said. I was too intimidated by her not to.

Avis was a chatterbox, but oh, the stories she had to tell! Of Mr. Ziegfeld and his beginnings at the World's Columbian Exposition in Chicago, the origins of the Follies, and the successes at the New Amsterdam.

Avis pinned and tucked me to within an inch of my life and then draped another shimmery piece of pale blue cloth over my shoulders like a short cape. The cuffs, neckline, and hem of the cape were all trimmed in silvery fur for more of a winter look.

The cap was a spangled blue cloche with a band of the same fur. Avis stitched me up, pausing only to restock the pins in her mouth. When I turned to see myself in the mirror, I almost fell over.

"Hello, Miss January!" Avis said, obviously proud of her handiwork.

"Which way to the stage?" I said, laughing.

CHAPTER SIX

"Say kid, don't you look swell!" the man said. His striped jacket and matching bow tie were louder than the orchestra launching into "I Can't Live Without Girls."

I was practicing walking down the corridor, trying to get used to the white lace-up boots with tiny heels Lucile wanted worn with the costume. I gave him a little smile.

"Lemme guess. Miss January, right?" he said.

"How'd you know?"

"Little bird." He tapped his ear. He stood leaning against the door of the costume department. His long face was dominated by a pair of thick-framed, perfectly round spectacles supported by one of the biggest noses I'd ever seen. He wore an undersized hat, and large tufts of hair emerged from it on both sides of his head. He squinted at me through the glasses, his face breaking into a goofy grin.

"Hi," I said, a little unsure of him.

"Hello yourself," he said. His voice was low and guttural with a curious wavering giggle at the end. He cocked his head, watching me work on my balance, then cavalierly leaned to kiss my hand. I laughed when he blew the imaginary dust off first.

"I'm Olive Thomas. I'm new."

"Good to meet ya. Ed Wynn."

"You're one of the comedians, aren't you?"

"Gorgeous and brains to match! Where ya from, kid?"

"Charleroi, Pennsylvania."

"Pennsylvania? Hey, I'm from Philly! Say, Avis . . . I got a little hole in my elbow." He held up the sleeve of a white shirt on a hanger. "Fix me up?"

"Lay it next to my sewing basket," she said. "I'll try to get to it in the next fifteen minutes."

"Honey, you all done?" Ed asked me. "I can show you around."

I looked to Avis for guidance.

"Go ahead," she said.

We'd already finished the dove costume, so I changed into my street clothes, removing the little cap and running my fingers through my hair, leaving the costume with Avis so she could work her magic. Ed jerked his head in the direction of the hall. Another crop of ladies chattered toward the stage for the next routine. As he saw them or greeted them, Ed offered asides to me on their various personalities and some of the gossip he knew.

We narrowly avoided girls in plumes and trains and not much else, and dodged some stage hands carrying large chunks of sets and scenery.

"Olive, this is Kay Laurell," Ed said, stopping short in front of a stunning redhead with a pug nose. "Kay, this is Olive Thomas," he said.

"Ziggy hired *her*?" she said, acting like she'd caught a whiff of sour milk.

"Yeah, he did. Thinking a little clearer than the day he hired you, I guess," Ed said, placing an arm around me in a protective gesture.

The girl walked away without a word. It felt like she'd spit on me.

"Who put sand in her stockings?" I said. "I don't even know her."

"One thing you gotta learn, honey. These gals get swell heads pretty fast, with everyone telling them how gorgeous they are all the time. Some of them are the nicest sweethearts I've ever met. But the others, they'll stab you in the back without a thought if it'll get 'em a lead in a routine. She's got an attitude, that one. You watch. She's always the first one to take her clothes off if it'll get her the spotlight."

Stopping in front of a tiny woman with long auburn hair and expressive eyes, Ed paused. "This is Penny, one of our best hoofers," he said. "She shakes and quivers. Penny, this is Olive Thomas."

I was at a loss. Did she have a tremor? A tic? She seemed perfectly normal. Compared to the last one, she was fun. I liked her immediately.

"Ann Pennington," the woman said, shaking my hand. "Nice to meet ya, Olive. They call me a 'shake and quiver dancer,'" she said by way of explanation, shimmying with her hips and arms so I could see her moves. "We'll get acquainted later, okay? Take care of yourself. I've got a costume fitting!" she said, dashing off down the hall.

Next, Ed waved to a gruff-looking man with thinning hair, a high forehead, and a nose like a plump cherry on top of shortcake. He wore a navy jacket with a bow tie and a straw boater.

“Whaddya want?” he asked, peering down at me. His voice was a sly mutter out the corner of his mouth.

“This is Olive. She’s new. I’m making her feel at home,” Ed said.

“How do?” the man said, doffing his hat. “William Claude Dukenfield, at your service. Stage name’s W.C. Fields.”

“How do *you* do?” I said. For all his attitude, I got the feeling he was just a big teddy bear.

“Olive’s from Pennsylvania too,” Ed said.

“Ya don’t say? Where from?” he asked, his eyes searching me for signs of recognition.

“Charleroi, McKees Rocks, Pittsburgh . . . that area.”

“Nice place, Pittsburgh. I spent a week there one night.” He leered at me. “You should watch my routine. I put the others to shame.” He gave Ed a raised eyebrow and waddled off in the direction of the stage as he pulled on a pair of white gloves.

“Bastard whacked me with a pool cue once onstage when he thought I was stealing his laughs,” Ed muttered. I tried not to chuckle.

We continued down the hall.

“And this is Marcelle,” Ed said, approaching a petite girl a few inches shorter than me. She had black eyes and delicate dark curls, and smelled of lavender toilet water. “Marcie, this is Olive Thomas. We’re making her feel at home.”

“Marcelle Earle,” she said, holding out her hand and pumping mine with enthusiasm. “It’s so good to meet you! I know we’ll be great friends.”

“Oh hell, is that the time?” Ed said, glimpsing the clock on the wall. "I'm late! Sorry gals, I gotta fly. I'll be back in a flash with more trash!" And he was gone.

Marcie took my arm as we strolled along.

"I've been here about a month," she said. "My friend Annette and I were both in *Watch Your Step*, Mr. Dillingham's production, and we decided to audition for the Follies. Done any theater?"

"No, this is my first," I admitted. "My friend Mr. Fisher, the artist, wrote me a letter of recommendation."

"You're lucky! Mr. Z already picked most of the girls for the season. But Eileen Madden got pregnant and had to drop out. Where ya from?" We rounded a corner near the stairwell.

"Outside Pittsburgh. You?"

"Brooklyn. You Irish? You look it."

"Yeah. How about you?"

"German and Puerto Rican."

"That's an interesting mix."

"Yeah, my dad moved home to Puerto Rico in '98 when the war heated up with Spain. Mom was always afraid to travel down there. Afraid she'd end up in a cannibal's pot, she said."

"My dad died when I was eight," I said.

"I'm sorry. That's so sad." She clasped my hand like it had happened yesterday instead of years before.

"Pneumonia. My mother remarried. But I'm living here now. I just quit my job at Klein's," I said.

She gasped. "I remember you now! You're the shopgirl, aren't you? The one who won the newspaper contest for the most beautiful girl in New York! Annette's sister entered that too. Boy, was she sore she didn't win! But between us, you're much prettier than she is."

"Thanks," I said.

Before we knew it, we were exchanging secrets and stories and gossip like old friends. Marcie was married to her sweetheart and glowed when she talked about him.

"His name's Arthur, and he's in the business too. We want to buy a house. Maybe on Long Island."

She was so natural, it made her easy to open up to. We spoke of our families and our fathers and our dreams for the future.

"Let me give you a tip," she said. "We can rehearse in black stockings, but onstage, it's pink every night, no matter what. Mr. Ziegfeld thinks they make our legs nice and feminine. But never—and I mean never—let him see you barelegged."

"Why?"

"It reflects badly on the *theatah* . . ." she said with a classy accent. She leaned in a little closer and lowered her voice. "I got caught on one of my very first days here. Fresh out of hosiery, and I was *skint*. I got a very stern talking-to."

"No kidding?"

"'Miss Earle,'" she said, mimicking Mr. Ziegfeld's nasal voice, "'you must never enter this theater with bare legs. It is slovenly and cheap, and we at the Follies are selling class *and* musical theater. Ziegfeld girls must always be at their best, and that includes your legs. Understood?'"

I nodded and she giggled.

"Oh, and no ragged heels on your shoes," she continued in her usual voice. "There's a cobbler over on 43rd Street who does fine work, and he'll save your life—no fooling. Invest in some quality kicks. Mr. Z has fired girls for less."

Resolving never to be stuck, like Marcie, without stockings, I stashed a bunch of extras in my drawer. And what was

Bonwit Teller for, if not for spoiling myself with a few extras?

Two of the other dancers at the theater were Rosie and Jenny, the Dolly Sisters. They were beautiful, with black hair and exotic eyes like a matched set of china dolls, so their name fit. Those weren't their real names, of course. They were from . . . I can never remember . . . Something-slavia. But it was one of those places where everybody speaks English like they're gargling spit. They were fun and loved to talk! But though I adored them, half the time I couldn't understand what the hell they were saying.

One of my favorites was a dancer named Marjorie Cassidy. Turned out her people were from Donegal. We had lots to talk about. She had jet-black hair, intent eyes under thick dark brows, and a glamorous mole next to her left eye. I was fascinated by it.

Marjorie was the one who taught me how things really worked backstage.

"Rule number one," she said, examining my first batch of flowers from an admirer. "If they only send flowers or chocolates, they're cheapskates. They just want into your pants. They get attaboys when they say they've been out with a Ziegfeld girl."

After tossing the offending bouquet into the corner with a pile of ten or twelve others given to the rest of the girls, she took the attached box of Lowney's Chocolate Cherry Blossoms and unfastened the lid, offering me one. I shook my head.

"What happens to the flowers?" I said.

"Cleaning ladies are welcome to 'em, or Marcie takes them to one of the hospitals. We sure won't use them. Too many here already. But the ones like this?" She picked up another bunch of roses, this one with a velvet box attached by a ribbon.

"These fellows mean business. They want into your family tree, or failing that, they want you to consider mistressing as a lucrative alternative to show business. Hey, not bad."

She lifted the lid, stamped inside with the Lambert Brothers cursive logo, and showed me the bauble within, a gorgeous multifaceted ruby ring.

"Is it always like this?" I asked.

Her smile told me everything I needed to know.

CHAPTER SEVEN

NEW AMSTERDAM THEATRE, NEW YORK CITY,

mid-May 1915

"Hey, it's one less of the competition," I overheard Mr. Ziegfeld saying to Gene Buck, our chief talent scout and librettist. When we had to learn a new routine, Mr. Buck was the one who taught us the lyrics and accompanied himself on the piano. He was dark-haired, dark-eyed, and very smart—intimidatingly so. If Mr. Ziegfeld had a best friend, Gene Buck was it.

"Flo, that's an awful thing to say," Gene said.

"I hated the bastard. Glad he's dead."

That month, the Germans had sunk a ship named the *Lusitania*, so the world was reeling. Mr. Ziegfeld was especially angry, being the Allied supporter he was. At the Follies, we entertained the cream of the crop of Allied sympathizers, fundraisers, and armament dealers sending their stuff to France. However, his archenemy Charles Frohman, the famous producer and theater owner, had been one of the unlucky Americans onboard who hadn't made it into a lifeboat. So Mr. Z had reason to celebrate.

The Follies was more excitement than I'd ever seen in my life. The fast pace was constant. Mr. Buck oversaw us from the audience, but our real taskmaster was the stage manager, Julian Mitchell. He shared the job with a man named Leon Errol, who'd once been a performer at the Follies. Errol and Mitchell had a contest going to see who could direct more routines.

Mr. Errol was harmless. His Australian accent turned "dance" into "dence," and "yes" into "yiss." Years later, someone showed me a comic strip of the Gumps, and forever after, Andy Gump reminded me of Mr. Errol. He never worked us as hard as Mitchell, so we liked him better.

Mitchell was an older fellow who always wore the same beige suit and brown bowler, and he sweated a lot under the lights. We knew it was the same suit. Hell's bells, we could smell it! The old geezer was deaf as a dining table, so we could complain about the rehearsals all we wanted, as long as we did it under our breath.

The tall beauties in front, the A-Team, strolled into the spotlights doing the Ziegfeld Walk, arms outstretched, headdresses precariously balanced, letting everyone admire them and their gorgeous costumes. They got center stage. We shorter girls, called "ponies and chickens," tapped or soft-shoed. The others had nicknames too.

"Squabs!" Mitchell would shout, arms up like he was directing an orchestra. "Slow your pace! That's it. One-two-three-four. Now ponies! On the beat now. One-two-three-four, five-six-seven-eight. And chickens! Very nice, girls. Keep it steady. That's it." Clapping his hands in time with the orchestra, he'd urge us on, our smiles glued to our faces, our feet just so.

We repeated the same steps over and over, in tandem, measuring our pace. Dress rehearsals were even tougher, as we had to do them in either next to nothing or elaborate getups that could be heavy or dangerous, in the case of those with long skirts or trains. We had to be constantly on guard, scanning the stage for obstacles that lay ahead. The trailing skirt in front of you, stray sequins that could make you slip, a girl who paused too long, having forgotten the steps . . . all possible hazards. And those hats! Good God. Each one must have weighed a full half ton. You ever try holding your head up straight with a hundred pounds on it? It ain't easy, and I still have the sore neck to prove it.

That trickle of sweat trailing down your spine could make you shimmy unexpectedly, causing Mr. Mitchell to halt the proceedings with an irritable "STOP!" And then we'd have to do everything again. The other girls would grow resentful and catty, and things in the dressing room could get as hot as standing under the lights on opening night.

Those spotlights were bright and uncomfortable, and when one hit the corner of your eye the right way, it could blind you for a moment. But every time the orchestra struck up a dramatic overture, I felt my pulse jump in time to the music. Nothing like the feel of the lights on my skin and the scents of sawdust and dance shoe resin to bring me the excitement I'd been craving my entire life.

Mr. Urban, our set designer, had created stunning backdrops that looked like something out of Greek mythology, with pastel colors and painted effects, including decorative urns with greenery dripping from them. The first number was a spectacular bath theme with girls "swimming" in blue lights that rippled like waves, and colossal golden elephant sculptures spouted real water from their inverted trunks. Mr. Ziegfeld loved elephants. He had lots of elephant good luck charms, but his favorite was a small jade figurine he carried in his vest pocket.

"Watch him," Rosie Dolly whispered in her guttural accent one night between acts as we watched from the wings. Mr. Z took the little elephant out and caressed it like a pet kitten. "He does dat vhen he's vorried about de show succeeding."

At one point, I had to take a note to Mr. Ziegfeld's desk from one of the squabs who couldn't make a performance because her granny was in the hospital. The outer door to his office was open, and I heard my name. I flattened myself against the wall and listened, wondering who he was talking to. It turned out to be Mr. Mitchell.

"So the new girl, Olive. How's she doing?" Mr. Ziegfeld said.

After the long pause, it was obvious Mitchell didn't want to answer.

"Not very good, Mr. Ziegfeld. But to be fair, some of these girls have been hoofing since they were in diapers. She's what, nineteen? Twenty? And she's never had a lesson."

"She has the glamour we want, though. Think you might be able to give her a little extra attention? Get her up to snuff?"

"Sure, but it might be a while. I don't use the word 'hopeless' much, but . . ."

"Jul, this organization is only as strong as our weakest girl. We're only as good as our girls make us. You. And me. And Gene. And everyone else. If she needs help, we can give her that. She has the face, and she has the body. We just need to help her with the presentation. Can you pull it off?"

Mitchell seemed more reassured after that. More confident. "Give me two weeks. I'll give you Irene Castle."

"Swell."

Mr. Mitchell wanted me to come in early for the next two weeks. I'd been practicing hard already, but it didn't compare to the extra effort I gave him. He had me repeat the same steps, but he was far more critical than he'd been in group rehearsals.

"On the beat!" he kept saying. When I tried it and failed, he'd do the steps himself and show me. Then he'd make me do it over, say "Stop!" and position my arms or my legs exactly the way he wanted. He'd stride over to me, grab my foot like it was a puppy that had piddled on the rug, and show me how to achieve the perfect point of my toe.

I bought a huge mirror and practiced at home, endlessly working my way through the steps, repeating and repeating until I could do it by rote. After about three days it got easier, but the aches and blisters didn't. Corn plasters became my constant fashion accessory, and Sloan's Liniment was my new perfume. I'd never worked so hard in my life. But if it meant one-upping Kay for the next routine she wanted, I'd do it.

Each night, when the curtain fell and the applause grew until it thundered, I went home, exhausted but still excited that I had the best job in the world.

I moved out of Aunt Elsie's that spring, got a new apartment near Lexington and 43rd, and furnished it in style with Oriental rugs, overstuffed furniture, a large brass canopy bed, ginger jars, and other exotic doodads. I even had a doorman. I sent what extra I could home so Mamma and Harry could splurge a little too. Mamma wrote me sweet letters about having the leaky roof replaced or buying a new dining room set at

Kaufmann's, and I'd choke up a little, grateful she could have nice things at last.

One night, as I grabbed a quick cigarette in the dressing room during intermission, Otto knocked on the door frame.

"Hey, doll. Mr. Z wants to see you. Says it's important."

"Important? I have to be onstage in fifteen minutes. Can't it wait?" I stubbed the smoke out in irritation.

"I guess not. Maybe he's giving you a raise, huh? I'd skip a cigarette for that."

I laughed and slipped on a dressing gown, hurrying to his office and hoping it wouldn't take too long, whatever it was.

Ziegfeld ushered me in himself. "Miss Thomas, come in. Come in!"

"You wanted to see me, Mr. Ziegfeld?"

I sank down onto the chair in front of his desk, waiting impatiently for him to tell me what it was he wanted and hoping it wasn't bad news. I'd been busting my ass for weeks with Mitchell and in front of my mirror. Having to return to modeling alone would be a slap in the face.

Reclining in his large oxblood leather chair, he planted his feet firmly on the desk. With his hands clasped behind his head, he stared at me a minute or two. I wondered if I had snot hanging from my nose or something.

"I have a proposition for you," he said.

I raised an eyebrow and leaned forward with my elbows on my knees. "What kind of proposition?"

"Mr. Mitchell tells me you've been working very hard at your extra lessons, and I wanted to let you know how appreciative I am. How'd you like to join the Frolic?"

"The Frolic?" I said, my voice squeaking.

The Frolic was an extra special revue for idle rich men up in the roof garden. It took over in the fall when the Follies was wrapping things up. Yeah, the Follies was funny and we sang and danced and told jokes, but the Frolic was far more adult. The girls weren't naked, but they might as well have been. They wore tiny coverings like balloons or these see-through bits that weren't enough to cover a fly. The moguls and millionaires sat around, ogling them and pounding their little wooden mallets on the tables. They laid out a fortune on drinks, and when the mood struck them, they spent oodles on the dancers too. Foreign ministers and diplomats, Vanderbilts and Rockefellers didn't think twice about coughing up diamonds or penthouse apartments.

Mr. Urban was the one who came up with the idea of the elevated glass platform. The girls sashayed across it and threw their garters into the audience. It was a game with them to see who could hit the greatest number of bald men. Then they divvied up their winnings on the first of the month and joked about it backstage.

Mr. Ziegfeld also made sure to toss out a raise to sweeten the deal.

"I'll bump you up to seventy-five dollars a week, honey. You'll be the most popular girl on Broadway."

I started totaling the receipts in my head. "What will I have to wear?"

"I'll be honest with you. As little as possible."

CHAPTER EIGHT

"That's what we're selling at the Frolic, in addition to lots and lots of booze. We're selling that perfect bosom and bottom of yours. That's why you'll be making so much," Mr. Ziegfeld further informed me.

Glamour, fame, nightlife, and dancing, plus all the luxuries I could send to Mamma back in the Rocks. The modeling was nice, the Follies were better, but the Frolic would grant me some real clout. What girl wouldn't jump at a chance like this? Why, the first place the big shots at the movie studios looked for new faces was the New Amsterdam. And the Frolic was their favorite place to shop.

It's something big, something important.

"Of course," I said.

"There's one thing, first."

"What's that?"

"I like to try the girls out on a trial basis for the Frolic, to see if they're good enough to bring in the big spenders."

I cocked my head, wondering what he meant.

"A private audition, shall we say."

I hadn't been in New York that long, but I wasn't stupid either. My head buzzed as he continued.

"It's a way for me to evaluate you, to see if you're up to the challenge of taking your clothes off for some of the richest and most powerful men in the world. Do you *know* the kinds of bigwigs we get here? The biggest, and with the most money to part with." He paused to take a drag from his cigar.

"This could be the biggest opportunity you get handed in your lifetime," he said. "I need to see if you're cut out for it. Some girls can't handle the pressure. They can be pretty and dance a little, but their small-town values keep them shackled up downstairs, where they choose to keep their legs stuck together at the knees. But the Frolic requires a certain . . . how can I put this delicately . . . *free-spirited* quality. I need to know if you have it."

"A private audition, then. When? Where?"

"My wife is going to be out of town for a few days. So we'll have all the time in the world. I want you to come to our apartment this weekend."

Saturday morning, after he'd collected me, the driver pulled Ziegfeld's Hispano-Suiza up in front of The Ansonia apartments, on Broadway between 73rd and 74th. The place looked like a castle from the outside, with a turret at the corner and a pointy roof like they always showed in fairy-tale books. You could smell money from two blocks away.

It took me a good twenty minutes to get out of the car. I felt queasy as I approached the doorman. He buzzed me up, and the elevator operator greeted me cheerily. I did my best to avoid making eye contact. It wouldn't do to let everyone know who I was visiting. But maybe they were used to it. Maybe they already knew. Wearing my best lavender silk with a matching bag and shoes, I'd also brought a small overnight bag, as Penny and Marjorie had warned me I'd need one.

Mr. Ziegfeld answered the door in a maroon smoking jacket, with one of his ever-present cigars dangling from his lips. "Come in, Miss Thomas, and welcome."

He took my coat, but it was hard to meet his eyes. He was at least twenty or thirty years older than me.

"He vas in love vit Anna Held for years," Rosie had told me. "He's married to Billie Burke now, but he von't be faithful to her. He's slept vit all de ingénues, and a few of de others too."

Never having seen this kind of opportunity before, I couldn't imagine myself as a home wrecker. I tried justifying it by telling myself that if Billie couldn't keep her man happy, it was her own fault. But it was a pitiful excuse. Sleeping with Ziegfeld could grant me everything I ever wanted. Regardless of the consequences, it was necessary. I distracted myself by looking around at the antiques and fancy paintings. A suit of armor stood in a corner, and a chandelier hung above us. It had probably cost more than our house in the Rocks.

He offered me a glass of Perrier-Jouët, and I downed it in one long gulp. He laughed out loud. But the bravery it supplied me gave everything a nice fuzzy edge. Taking my hand, he led me into the bedroom. A huge four-poster canopy bed took up most of the space. Beneath it was thick mulberry carpeting with a cream-colored border and a vine print.

His breath, scented with Romeo y Julieta cigars, was warm on my neck as he ran his hand over my back. Turning me to face him, he gently pulled my hair so my face was tilted closer to his, and he kissed me like he hadn't eaten in weeks. He was a far better kisser than Krug, any of the boys I'd kissed from school, or any of the fellows who'd taken me out after the show. He'd obviously done a lot of kissing.

His hands caressed my breasts through the fabric of my dress. My bones felt like overcooked noodles, but from being nervous and unsure I turned aggressive and daring, challenging every move of his with one of my own. I had to convince myself this wasn't his idea, that it was mine. As the champagne coursed through me, I responded, demanding more and more. Lifting me as lightly as he would a kitten, he carried me across the room and set me down beside the bed. I was surprised, as I thought he would have put me *on* it.

"Take this off," he said, trying to figure out the frog fasteners on my dress. I did, then leaned down to remove my stockings, but he stopped me.

"Leave them on," he said, licking his lips like a schoolboy being offered a lollipop. "And your shoes too."

I stood before him, naked except for stockings and shoes. He flung off his robe in one motion. For an older man, he was surprisingly fit. The same gray hair that made him so distinguished adorned his chest and worked its way down his middle. He stood at attention already.

"All right. Here's where you audition."

I looked up at him for confirmation, and then he erased all doubt of what he wanted by pushing me to my knees in front of him.

As we lay together later enjoying a cigarette, he announced his intention to see me more over the coming weeks.

"Miss Thomas, I want you to travel out to Long Island with me next weekend. We can go for a sail."

"Mr. Ziegfeld, I don't mean to be rude, but I've just seen a part of your body that most other people haven't. Why the formality? Call me Ollie. Everyone else does."

His laugh was a deep rumble in his gut. "Point taken. I shall call you Ollie. Everyone else calls me Flo. At the theater, I'm still Mr. Ziegfeld, though. Is that clear?"

"As a window. But I don't like the name Flo. There was a girl I hated at school with that name."

He laughed. "All right, then. What do you want to call me?"

I leaned back against the pillow and thought a moment. "Ziggy," I said.

"Ziggy it is." He kissed me again.

LONG ISLAND, NEW YORK, *July 1915*

The Long Island Rail Road took us as far as Jamaica, and we changed to an express farther east. When the train pulled into Sag Harbor station, Ziggy grabbed me and shooed me through it as fast as he could to avoid anyone he might know. His private car took us to the yacht club, where *Ziggy's Folly* lay at anchor near two other boats—the *Harvest Moon* and the *Danny Boy*.

"It's a commuter yacht," Ziggy said, obviously proud of his

investment. “Solid mahogany.” He slapped her side. “Coming aboard!” he called, and a man appeared to assist me into the boat. He was turned out in a captain’s hat, white trousers, and a smart navy blazer with brass buttons.

“This is Mr. Stone,” Ziggy said.

The man and I nodded a greeting at each other.

“Can we go bathing?” I asked.

“Maybe later,” Ziggy said. “Ed, set a course for Gardiners Island.” The sea foam bubbled around the bow and the sides of the boat, and gulls dipped and soared around us, cackling and calling to each other. I stood at the rail and pointed my face into the wind, enjoying the sea breeze and the scenery until we were proceeding at a steady clip. Then Ziggy led me below and took me over and over in the stateroom. When he was done, I collapsed and slept for hours.

When I woke up, he was gone. I threw on a robe and made my way to the aft deck. Ziggy sat at a table reading the latest fish wrap.

“Hello, darling,” he said, setting down his newspaper and stubbing out the remains of his cigar. “Sit down. We’ll have some dinner. Are you hungry?”

“Starved.”

“Good. I’ve had Chef prepare a light supper for us. Do you like French food?”

“I’ve never had French food before,” I admitted. Having graduated from some of the seedier places where I used to eat, I was still too intimidated to try any of the local lobster palaces, and too self-conscious to tell Ziggy that my favorite foods were still the five-cent butter cakes from Childs and the hash at Dinty Moore’s.

"Here's your chance. The cuisine in France is outstanding. I used to visit often when . . . I was younger." The memories of Anna Held were obviously still painful.

A dark-haired man with a waxed mustache approached with a dinner tray, and my stomach reminded me exactly how long it had been since I'd eaten. He placed the plates in front of us, and Ziggy tucked in. But when Chef lifted the lid, I cringed. Noticing me glancing down in disgust, Ziggy stopped for a minute.

"What the hell are those things?" I said.

"I'm sorry, Ollie. Let me help you." He pointed with his tiny fork, his diamond pinkie ring glinting in the moonlight. "These are escargot. Snails with butter sauce. They're chewy and quite delicious if you give them a try." He speared one for me. I reluctantly opened my mouth and he popped it in, watching my reaction as I chewed.

"Tastes like chicken." I said, then kept chewing. "Not bad, I guess."

"You see?" He nodded, satisfied with my adventuresome spirit. He continued, pointing at the bowl. "This is vichyssoise. It's potato soup."

I sipped it and wrinkled my nose. "It's cold."

"It's supposed to be, dear."

After the soup, Chef placed another plate in front of me. Ziggy pointed at the main course.

"Sole Normande. And," he said, reaching for the bottle in the ice bucket, "this is the world's most expensive champagne." He poured mine and watched as I drank. I could feel my inhibitions dropping more with each sip.

That night and the next day passed in a luxurious blur of

sunning myself and making love to Ziggy. Sure, he was older, but I was growing to care for him. And he taught me something new every day. Why, just that evening, he'd decided to teach me some French. We sat on deck, anchored in Great Peconic Bay. Waves gently patted the side of the boat.

"Now then, Ollie, when you're traveling the Côte d'Azur and you want to say hello to someone, what do you say?"

"Bon-jewer," I said.

"And what about 'good evening'?"

"*Bone-swahrr*. Ziggy, did you learn French when you went to France?"

"My first wife was French. She taught me some. Now concentrate," he said. "Say, 'I would like to go to the hotel.'"

"Huh? Oh. *Je voo-dray ah-lay ah lo-tel.*"

"Splendid, my dear. You're coming along. We'll have to travel to Paris so I can show you off one day."

"Let's go right now."

"You're not ready yet, but someday we'll go to the Folies Bergère. It's where I got the idea for the Follies. And we'll visit the Moulin Rouge and the Rat Mort . . ."

"The Rat what?"

"The Rat Mort. It's a scandalous club in Montmartre. They pay an African fellow to eat a live rat. Sounds dangerous. Rabies, you know."

"A rat? I think I'd need a few drinks in me before I'd go see that."

"Ollie," he said, pushing the French dictionary aside after we were through with dinner.

"Yes?"

"Come sit on my lap. There's something I want you to see."

Not taking my eyes off him, I pulled my dressing gown open and saw that he was already rock hard. I mounted him, pulling the flaps of his robe aside and letting him nuzzle me. He closed his eyes and buried his face in my breasts, caressing one, then the other, with his cheeks. Throwing my head back, I reveled in the feel of him. Then he took me, sitting in the chair on deck, in front of God and everyone.

CHAPTER NINE

NEW AMSTERDAM THEATRE, NEW YORK CITY, *August 1915*

The routine that grabbed the most attention was the one with the gorgeous blue waves that Mr. Urban designed. But of course the girl who got all the attention in that part was Kay, who played the "Channel Belle."

Penny and I stood in the wings, waiting for our cues, playing catty because . . . well, just because.

"What the hell is a Channel Belle?" I asked.

"Looks more like a shark to me," she said.

"I was thinking more along the lines of a barracuda."

We chuckled as Kay finished up her big number and scampered offstage after bowing repeatedly and blowing kisses to the audience. I gnashed my teeth.

After Kay's number, George White and the chorus girls had a number called "My Zebra Lady Fair," which had to be about the stupidest compliment a man could pay a woman. I was relieved I wasn't in it, since my big scene came next. Bernard Granville was a struggling artist in shirtsleeves at a drafting table, singing earnestly about how much he loved women.

"Some men are constant, and some men are true.
Some men love one girl and some men love two.
I'm an exception; that much is clear.
I need a girl for each month in the year. . ."

And that was my cue to step elegantly onstage in my shimmery blue outfit.

"I want a January Merry Maid for New Year, a frosty fairy, wary she must be . . ."

I sashayed across the stage, thinking the whole while, *Don't fuck up. Don't fuck up.*

It became a chant in my head, urging me to step lightly, just as I had practiced. The other girls entered stage left after me, also in costumes by Lucile, all in formation—a girl for when the February flurry melted away, a breezy girl and arch to worship him in March, a shower girl for April, and a flower girl for May, a rosebud girl to love him through the June days, an independent lady for July, then for August someone warm, a September girl like a storm, a brown October maiden rather shy, a November lass to cheer, and for December just a dear.

As soon as we'd taken our bows (those of us who could, without heavy hats) and the curtain fell, we all came skittering backstage, making a beeline for the dressing room to promptly change into our next getup. For me, that was the dove costume Avis had taken in, a delicate, fluttery number that represented peace perfectly. It was white chiffon over a cloth-of-silver bodice. Around the skirt, four turquoise inserts were caught at the waist by tiny chains of diamonds, and a set of ostrich plumes crossed my waist in back. In front were two diamond roses. I had to deal with Kay in that scene unfortunately, doing my best to stay out of her way as she hogged the spotlight.

After intermission, Act Two began with "I'll Be a Santa Claus to You," where Granville dressed up in a Santa Claus costume and sang to a series of the ponies dressed up in red-and-green finery:

"I'll be a Santa Claus to you, if you'll but say you will be true
I'll bring you toys; Millions of joys. . ."

Ina Claire was the pretty, delicate blonde I'd seen in wardrobe my first day at the theater. She had a scandalous number that either delighted or horrified the audience, depending on who you talked to. She wore a nun's habit as a character supposedly stashed away in some European convent, and she was completely sheltered by the nuns. The first line, *In a convent ivy-laden, lived a simple little maiden*, devolved into an outrageous story of some war in France. A bunch of Germans invaded, and our heroine got knocked up. The Protestants in the audience were whooping it up. The Catholics either got up and walked out or kept their seats, but wore expressions like someone had just punched the pope.

The last number was an advertisement for our upstairs show called *The Midnight Frolic Glide*, which introduced a new dance and persuaded everyone to come upstairs to see more. And oh, they did.

The orchestra would already be playing when the audience arrived. First, William Randolph Hearst, the newspaper mogul, would take his favorite table. Then, of course, we'd see the regulars. Millionaire Jay Gould loved to ogle the girls up close. Representing the theater set, John Drew the stage actor would sip champagne with actress Blanche Ring, and Laurette Taylor and Ethel Barrymore gossiped and ordered cocktails.

Depending on what they were hungry for, they could get fish or chicken, or for the gourmet-minded, filet mignon cocotte or grisette, spaghetti Ziegfeld, or lobster mayonnaise.

The most important part of the table setting was the knocker. If they liked the act, the patrons would pound on the table with the little mallets, and the roof garden would resound with their wooden echo.

SAG HARBOR STATION, NEW YORK, *October 1915*

The affair had continued into the fall, and so had the trysts, as often as we could manage them. In October, Billie had gone west to make a film in California, so Ziggy and I enjoyed more time away from the city. When it grew too chilly for yachting, we enjoyed escaping anyway.

As we waited for our train back to the city, he enjoyed a cigar and the *Times*, and a shoeshine boy polished his oxfords until they glowed. I read a *Photoplay*. A woman approached us, clasping her lorgnette like a magnifying glass. She was handsome, rich, and obviously intrigued.

"Shit . . ." Ziggy muttered under his breath.

"Flo?" she cried. "Florenz Ziegfeld? How are you?"

Then she saw me. Her smile froze and retreated, like she'd sucked on a persimmon.

"Sarah," he said, his voice as cold as a freshly shaken lime rickey, "so good to see you." Anyone with a brain could see he was as excited to see her as he would have been a boil on his ass. He tossed a nickel to the boy, who scrambled away with his tools.

"Who is this?" she said, focusing on me.

"This is my secretary, Olive," he said.

"Horsefeathers," she said. "This woman is no secretary. Billie knows all about your paramours, Flo. Don't think I won't be telling her about this one."

"I have no doubt you will," Ziggy said, puffing on his cigar. He calmly turned his attention back to his paper.

INTERMISSION

CHAPTER TEN

BACKSTAGE, NEW AMSTERDAM THEATRE, NEW YORK CITY,

November 1915

"Ollie, something for you in the dressing room!" Penny called as she headed to the stage.

This newest velvet box contained a small diamond brooch. In addition to it, I'd gotten an emerald necklace, oodles of roses, exotic orchids, fawning love letters, fancy chocolates, a satin dressing gown, expensive French perfume, bottles of champagne, and the pièce de résistance: the most perfect string of pearls any of us had ever seen. It had arrived by a private courier from the German Embassy, and the note said Ambassador Bernstorff was waiting for me to visit him. God, what a Prussian. He moved and acted like he had a stick up his ass. I mean, don't get me wrong. I like a man who's stiff, but not like *that*.

I'd met him at a party at the Sixty Club a couple weeks before. The Sixty Club, downstairs at the Hotel Astor, was owned by a fellow named Jack Rumsey. Rumsey loved showgirls. He loved looking at them, he loved sleeping with them, and he loved having them around. So the Sixty Club had become one of the places to see and be seen with gorgeous women. And of course the men who most wanted these women were the ones who could best afford to court them—senators, ambassadors, showmen, and millionaires. Kind of like the Frolic, but with more clothes on.

"You know," said Gladys Feldman (Gladys was one of the ponies), "my father knows something about diamonds, and he's taught me a few things." She fingered the pearls and examined them very closely. "Out on the street, I bet this strand would run you about $10,000." She handed them back to me.

"Look at them," I said holding them up, and feeling their glossiness slip through my fingers. "They're like little bits of moonlight. So perfect."

"Ollie, you can't refuse a gift like that. It would be impolite," she said, winking. "Besides, Kay will be green when she sees them."

"You're right, you know." I felt an evil little smile spread across my face. I didn't get much satisfaction in my ongoing warfare with Kay, but this was one of those times.

I thought about returning the pearls, since Ziggy was a fanatic about supporting the Allies and Bernstorff was a Kraut, but they were so beautiful. I kept them, but only Gladys and Penny were backstage with me when they arrived, and they were sworn to secrecy.

When it came to my battles with Kay, Marcie was a good confidante. She was always ready to listen. The only problem was that she did the same thing for Kay. You couldn't blame her. It was the way she was made. She was so doggone nice that she never took sides, trying to give us all good advice and get along with everyone. On the other hand, Kay Laurell was a reptile, but Marcie could never be convinced of it.

One day, Kay bumped me hard enough to send me flying during rehearsal, then apologized, syrupy as molasses. Anyone could see she'd done it on purpose. In return, I loosened the seams on her costume so the arm ripped loose when she was onstage.

The next night, my favorite pair of pink stockings had giant runs in them. They'd been fine the night before. Expecting to gloat and see me fired by Mr. Ziegfeld for wearing none, she got her own surprise when I showed up wearing one of my hidden pairs Marcie had held onto for me.

The night after that, as I hurried to the stage, holding up my long skirt and train, Kay approached me in the hallway. Two seconds later, I was sprawled out flat on the floor.

Penny reached down to give me her arm. "That was dirty, Kay. Even for you."

"What's your problem, Pennington? I didn't touch her."

"I saw your foot, you lying snake."

"I'd go get yourself checked for a pair of glasses. Your vision's going."

She tossed her mane of red hair and flounced down the hall wearing a satisfied smirk until I stopped her in her tracks by saying, "I don't know why I expect any different from a floozy like you. Everybody knows you're easier than second-grade math."

Kay turned and glared at us, but I gave her a "Who me?" smile as Penny helped me up.

"Better lay off the bonbons, Kay. Mr. Glackens will start searching for skinnier models," Penny said as Kay harrumphed away. Kay had been bragging recently about how she would be as famous as the Mona Lisa from her poses for William Glackens, a local painter. We doubted he would amount to anything. The only art anyone was excited about these days was the newfangled junk from Paris. Or so I heard. Art was for stuffy people who hung out in libraries for fun.

"You okay, honey?" Penny said, giving me the once-over and helping me place my spangled hat back on my head at the correct angle. I brushed myself off and checked the train for any tears Avis might need to fix.

"I don't understand why she hates me so much," I said, massaging a bruise that was developing on my knee.

"You don't know?" Penny said, chuckling.

"Should I?"

"It's Mr. Ziegfeld."

"What do you mean?"

"Between you, me, and this wall, Miss-High-and-Mighty was sure that since his other paramour, Lillian Lorraine, was on her way out, Mr. Z would be easy pickings for her. Then you came along and threw a giant monkey wrench into her plan. You oughta know by now, Ollie—his favorite girl always gets the best routines and the nicest costumes. Kay was sure that was going to be her. Always grabbing the spotlight, that one—whether it's on her or not! I think he gave her the Channel Belle role to shut her up. You keep doing what you're doing. You're so much prettier than she is. Just remember, you can dress a warthog in satin, but it still smells up the place."

She gave me an encouraging hug, then jerked her head toward the auditorium as the strings in the orchestra plunked out an introduction. "Yikes! That's our cue. You cheer up. That's an order." Along with the others, we swept onto the stage, all smiles as the curtain lifted to roaring applause.

My Frolic salary, in addition to my modeling work, was bringing in the cash when I wasn't spending every cent on new clothes or gifts for everyone in the Rocks or nights on the town. It was strange being one of the most recognizable women in New York. Columnist Heywood Broun wrote about me. People passing me at Gimbel's would abruptly ask for an autograph, or complete strangers would propose to me on the street. Some got down on one knee while I stood, fresh from a shopping expedition, laden with bags and hatboxes.

Ziggy had finally left Billie, which gave me hope. But then reality smacked me in the face like a cast-iron skillet. Ever been courted by a rich married man? You're nothing more than a prize to be played with and shown off, but one with little real value. No matter how much I grew to care for him, he wouldn't fully return my affections. Not the way I needed him to. We'd argue, and then we'd argue some more, but it never amounted to anything, and like a dummy, I stayed with him.

"Ziggy, I want you to divorce Billie and marry me," I'd say. "You keep telling me you're so in love with me. Prove it."

"Why are women like this?"

"Like what?"

"Why can't this be enough for you? I've given you everything you've always wanted. You're famous and glamorous, and every man in New York is ready to drop to his knees and give you more of the same. You have the world at your feet, for God's sake."

"I've never been satisfied with what I have. I always want more. And I want you. All of you. Eventually I'll settle down, and I want a home and children."

"I can't promise you that."

"Why not?"

"It's too soon, Ollie. I just left Billie. I have no idea what I'm doing. Just be patient, would you?"

Then I'd sulk, and he'd get annoyed at me for ruining our dinner or for spoiling a surprise he'd planned. He wasn't distant in bed, of course. But when he finished he rolled away, and within fifteen minutes he'd be on the phone to Gene Buck–planning, strategizing, and laying the groundwork for grander and grander numbers.

He gave me any material thing I desired, but I wanted to come first, ahead of Billie. I wasn't foolish enough to think I could ever come before the Follies. That was his life.

CHAPTER ELEVEN

OLLIE'S APARTMENT, NEW YORK CITY, *March 1916*

"Ollie—

I'm sorry, things just weren't working. Billie and I had a long talk, and we're giving it another try. I know you'll find someone far better for you than me. It might not feel like it now, but you will.

Ziggy"

That was the note he left me, scribbled on a cocktail napkin from Shanley's. And in that minute, my entire world collapsed into a miserable mess. I discovered he'd cleaned out his closet. He also packed his briefcase, all his papers, the few elephant knickknacks he'd brought with him, and the photograph of his mother he'd set on the bedside table.

The harshest part was that he'd finished with me but I still had to work with him and pretend like things were hunky-dory. So that month I discovered how much I loved the taste of gin. And each bottle down my gullet could have been engraved with Flo Ziegfeld's name.

For a month, spending late nights out at the Palais de

Danse or Maxim's helped me stay distracted, or at least as pickled as a jarful of gherkins. It was getting stale by late March, when my friend Elaine Hammerstein visited. Elaine was stunning—fair skin, black hair, and the most perfect profile I'd ever seen.

"Ollie, you have to come with us," she said, sipping her drink.

"Come where?"

"California."

Elaine had been regaling me with the latest stories of her time in the Hamptons but had also let me know that her spring trip this year would be out west. She was the granddaughter of Oscar Hammerstein, who owned the Olympia Theatre on Times Square. Her father was an opera producer. She'd shown up after the Frolic one night, and we'd been chums ever since.

I swept cold cream over my cheekbones to remove the rest of my makeup, and Elaine made herself comfortable in my slipper chair, her legs slung over the arm.

"What's California like?" I asked.

"It depends which part you visit. And when. Citrus groves are everywhere, and the scent of oranges. Eucalyptus and palm trees. Mountains on one side and beach on the other. Nothing like this nasty snow all the time until you get to the Sierras." She waved a hand at the window. "The weather is perfect."

"Who's us?" I asked.

"My friend Myra, her brother Wally, and me."

"When are you leaving?"

"Couple of days."

"Maybe a change of scenery would do me good."

"What about the Frolic?" Elaine asked with a raised eyebrow.

"The bastard left me. Let him figure out how to replace me for a month," I said. Especially after Elaine told me about the gorgeous weather, I knew California would be the perfect therapy for a broken heart. I saw the muddy slush outside and stubbed out my cigarette smoldering in the ashtray. "I'll put a trunk together."

CHAPTER TWELVE

LOS ANGELES LIMITED OUTSIDE SAN BERNARDINO, CALIFORNIA, *April 1916*

"Excited, Ollie?"

Elaine giggled as she watched me. It had been hard to contain myself. The whole trip I kept switching seats so I could see first forward, then behind us, out the big window. I'd bitten my nails to the quick, watching the terrain for days as it changed from city streets to farmland, from lush hills and valleys to prairies and wheat fields, and then to snowcapped mountains.

"Where are we now?" I'd ask, then say, "Ooh! What kind of tree is that? What state is this? It certainly is dusty. Is that corn growing in that field? Are those cows? They are!"

Elaine nudged Myra and Wally, and they all had a giggle at my expense, already traveling pros themselves. Myra's most obvious feature was her uncontrollable pale blonde hair, a curly mane like a batch of whipped buttercream. She pulled it up into a bun, but it kept escaping. Wally was a handsome college boy in his newsboy cap and knickerbockers, but he was convinced, after only a year of college, that he knew everything. Now I'm no brain, but I do know that the archduke fellow who was shot over in Europe wasn't a German.

Wally insisted he was. "Why else would Germany be in the war?"

I couldn't remember what country he was from, just like I could never remember which one Rosie and Jenny were from, but I knew it wasn't Germany.

At last, after two days of desert had drifted by, a sign along the track let us know we were in California. It was surrounded by pretty yellow flowers. A craggy peak lay in front of us. Clouds clustered at the top of the ridge like a chunky string of pearls around the neck of a Follies girl.

Elaine pointed out the coast as we got closer to it, and the smell of oranges drifted into the car as we chugged past the groves.

"This is the Cahuenga Valley," she said.

"Heaven . . ." was all I could whisper, flabbergasted at California's golden warmth and blue skies in March. "We can never leave."

At the station, we grabbed a jitney bus to the Hollywood Hotel at the corner of Highland and Hollywood Boulevard.

"All the newcomers stay here," Elaine told me as a bellhop carried our trunks up the front walk.

The hotel's owner, Mrs. Almira Hershey, was a tiny woman, no bigger than a turnip seed, but she was a force of nature in a gray housedress.

"Breakfast begins precisely at 8:00 a.m.," she proclaimed as she trundled down the corridor. "No dawdling, please. Everyone needs a good breakfast to start the day." She unlocked our room and pushed the door open so we could enter.

"We wash the sheets once a week. Strip the bed, and the washerwoman will collect them at the end of the hall. I don't make dinner. Plenty of places for a good meal in town. But no leftovers here. I don't need rats. "

She smoothed a sheet on one of the beds and plumped up a pillow before crossing to the closet and displaying the hangers inside.

"My capital rule? No liquor. And no unchaperoned gentleman callers, ladies. If I catch you with either, you'll be evicted promptly and have to find other arrangements. Do I make myself clear?" She yanked open the drapes, flooding the room with sun.

"Yes, ma'am," we all said.

"We have dances in the main ballroom on Thursday nights, and I do the supervising. Don't get any thoughts about doctoring the punch. Any hanky-panky and you're out. Are we square?"

We nodded, but I dreaded returning to that hotel. After the Follies, this was like a jail. We named it The Convent, and Mrs. Hershey was Mother Superior. At least Wally got to stay with a college friend who didn't live too far away.

"I know a great place the four of us should go for dinner. It's on a pier in Santa Monica," Elaine told us over a cocktail at the Rosslyn Hotel bar. "You'll love Nat's. It has a wonderful view, and it's fun to hobnob with the flicker stars."

At twilight, our cab pulled up in front of the marquee outside Nat Goodwin's, and we were seated immediately.

"So who is this Nat Goodwin anyway?" I said, taking a bite of deviled crab.

"He used to be a friend of Grandpa's. Did a lot of acting

on Broadway. He knows everyone in the business," Elaine said. "Belasco, the Shuberts, the Frohmans . . . I think he's from Boston originally. This place has been open, what, Myra, about two years?"

Myra nodded, her mouth full of lobster Thermidor.

"He was in the very first show at the New Amsterdam. Played Bottom in *A Midsummer Night's Dream*."

"Yeah? How was he?"

"Oh, he was fine, but the show was a flop. Papa's teased him about it for years."

Nat's, a three-story white structure, sat on a pier over the water. Two chunky pillars topped by an arcade welcomed guests. Inside, bentwood chairs sat at tables covered in white linen tablecloths with fresh flowers in vases. The inside was casually elegant, with coved ceilings, ornate gold and crystal lighting fixtures, and deep mahogany wood paneling. The first-floor dining room was separated from the raised mezzanine, where a quartet, the Versatile Harmony Four, played ragtime.

Nat made the rounds of the place, ensuring his customers were happy. Elaine pointed him out to me. His light hair was receding, revealing an expanse of high forehead. He had perfect features like a marble statue, and looming brows over blue eyes.

I picked at my chicken Marengo, too excited to eat. The whole place was full of familiar faces! That night, I'd worn my favorite plum-colored tunic dress, spangled with tiny rhinestones, and a velvet cloche the color of ripe eggplants. We'd almost finished dinner when the band launched into a jaunty version of "By the Beautiful Sea." As I looked up, I saw a slim fellow near the entrance. His hair was dark brown, slicked with pomade, his features almost pretty—dark eyes and full lips. He coolly surveyed all of Nat's like it was his throne room.

"That's Jack Pickford, isn't it?" I said, nodding in his direction. "Mary's brother, the actor?"

"Sure is," Myra said, lighting a cigarette and leaning over to offer me the flame. "He's quite scandalous."

"Scandalous how?" I watched him with more interest, inhaling thoughtfully.

"He's more famous for his drinking and womanizing than he is for his acting," Elaine said.

Evidently, seeing three gorgeous women sitting with only one man was too much for Pickford to resist. He approached our table and pulled up a chair.

"Hi, Elaine. Haven't seen you in ages. Mind if I join you?" he said, flashing a winning smile. "Who are your friends?"

We all pushed aside to make room, so Jack squeezed between Elaine and me. Nat approached and took his drink order.

"Scotch, neat." Then, turning to us, he said, "I'm Jack Pickford." He pulled a cigarette from a gold case, tapped it on the table a few times, and struck the match on his shoe. Leaning over to the vase, he snapped the stem on the red carnation and stuck it in the buttonhole of his lapel.

"Jack, these are my friends, Miss Myra Goldfarb and her brother Wallace," Elaine said. Jack shook hands with Wally and doffed his hat.

"And this is Miss Olive Thomas."

"Charmed," he said, kissing my hand.

"Likewise."

Nat brought his drink, and Jack downed it in one long

gulp. Then he took a long drag on his cigarette. We glanced sideways at each other while the others chatted.

The Versatile Harmony Four had struck up a lively version of "Pretty Baby," and Jack apologized to the others. "I hope you'll excuse us while I dance with Miss Thomas."

Then to me he said, "May I?"

He took my hand, and we glided across the dance floor. After gruff old Ziggy, Jack's youthful charm was a welcome change. He was just a few inches taller than me, with a slight build. But could he dance! His style was smooth and graceful, and his voice was soft in my ear:

"Everybody loves a baby that's why I'm in love with you,
Pretty baby, pretty baby . . ."

I smiled at him, and his eyes twinkled as he wiggled his eyebrows.

"You're a pretty thing. I hear you're in the Follies."

"You hear? From whom?"

"I know people all over," he said. "I knew you were headed out this way, so I was determined to meet 'The Most Beautiful Girl in New York.'"

"You certainly know how to flatter a girl," I said.

He leaned in closer and whispered in my ear, "I know how to do all kinds of things to a girl." The shiver traveled down my spine and along the fine hairs of my arms like the current in a live wire. Any other girl might have slapped his face. But I moved closer to him and whispered back.

"Promise?"

Our gazes locked. We didn't even acknowledge we were in

a public place. He cleared his throat and tried to appear normal to those watching. I could feel the reason against my leg.

"Where do you hail from, Miss Thomas?" he said, changing the subject, his tongue stumbling over the words.

"Pennsylvania. A town called Charleroi. You probably have no idea where that is."

"Near Pittsburgh, right?"

My eyes must have widened in shock. I'd never met anyone else outside Pennsylvania who knew of my hometown. "How did you know that?"

"We played in Charleroi once, years ago, at the Coyle Theater. Before Mary got famous in the flickers, we all traveled the country together in acting troupes—Mary, my mother, my sister Lottie, and me. We were still Smiths then. Thanks to David Belasco, the producer, we all had a name change. He said 'Gladys Smith' was too plain. So Mary took her middle name, and we all took Pickford for a surname. It's from my mother's side of the family."

"Smith?" I wrinkled my nose. "Mr. Belasco was right. I like Pickford much better. It suits you."

"I don't miss touring one bit. Months and months on the road, shitty food, and sleeping in dive hotels. In those days, *no one* would have been caught dead working in the flickers. It was the bastard stepchild of real theater. But after *The Birth of a Nation*, ordinary people finally gained some respect for what we do. Now Mary's more famous than President Wilson."

"I see that your *Poor Little Peppina* has just been released. What was it like to make?" I asked as he led me through a turn.

He snorted in disgust.

"That damned Sidney Olcott got me fired, the son of a

bitch," he said. "I was working on the film with Mary, and he was barking out orders left and right. Neither of us liked it. So I took him to task for it. 'How dare you presume to tell my sister, the world's greatest actress, what she can and can't do?' I said. I told Mary it was him or me. And she slapped me! My own sister slapped me and fired me from the picture. Do you believe that?"

"He sounds like a real peach."

"Like I said. A *son of a bitch*."

One dance turned into another, and then one more. First a maxixe, then a hesitation waltz, a tango, and the Castle Walk. And for fun, on one of the livelier numbers, we even did a Grizzly Bear and laughed the whole time. Before I knew it, the clock had struck midnight, and then 1:00 a.m.

We were one of the last couples in the place, and when Nat saw me searching for Elaine, Myra, and Wally, he hurried over.

"Don't worry, Miss Thomas. Elaine left this note for you."

He handed me a quick note scrawled on a napkin in Elaine's loopy handwriting.

"Hey, doll—We were getting tired, and you were having such a good time. I read in Photoplay *that Jack has a fancy new motorcar, and I know he would love to escort you home in it. Just please be careful with him. See you tomorrow! Elaine."*

She sure knew a budding romance when she saw one.

"I don't suppose you'd like to give me a ride home, Mr. Pickford?" I said, folding up the note and sticking it in my bag.

"Jack," he said. "I would be delighted, provided you honor me with a walk on the beach first."

My heart did a little foxtrot as he guided me toward the exit. On a bench outside Nat's, we removed our shoes, then took a wooden stairway that stretched from the pier down to the water. I held my skirts bunched at my waist. The laughing of the seagulls and the breaking of the waves provided romantic background music for our walk, and the sand was warm and giving beneath our feet. We could see a few lights in the distance from Los Angeles. From time to time, we skirted the dregs of the tide as it tickled the shore. Feeling playful, I kicked up tiny splashes at him.

Grabbing me in a sudden embrace, Jack planted a kiss on me as we stood with the foam nipping at our toes. I opened my mouth to receive him and felt my body responding right there.

"Do you have any idea how beautiful you are?" he muttered in my ear, his caress moving farther and farther forward along my middle until it reached the curve of a breast. I threw my head back, letting him kiss his way down my neck, my skin feeling singed wherever his lips had touched.

"Take me home," I whispered.

We stared at each other, our mutual intentions understood.

"I'd like to see you stop me."

CHAPTER THIRTEEN

JACK'S APARTMENT, LOS ANGELES, *April 1916*

"You enchant me, Olive Thomas."

It took me a minute to recall where I was. I remembered being at Nat's the night before, but after a few drinks, everything had gone a little fuzzy. We were tangled in the covers after making love until the sun started peeking through the drapes, then falling into an exhausted sleep.

Jack ran his fingers through my hair, inhaling its scent and kissing me over and over until he made me dizzy.

"You're rather enchanting yourself, Mr. Pickford," I said when he let me come up for air.

"Jack . . ." he whispered.

I folded him in my arms, closing my eyes and reveling in the sensation. I couldn't remember ever feeling so content. Jack ran a hand over my breast. When I gasped, he grabbed me, more roughly this time, and made me see stars. How had I stayed with Ziggy for so long? Any mooning I had done for him was over. His lovemaking was selfish and filled a need for him, but at times it had left me cold. Jack made me crave more every time he touched me.

When we lay spent among the damp sheets once more, he opened his cigarette case at the side of the bed and lit two for us. I blew smoke rings above our heads, giggling when he rated their structure and lift.

"Good thing I don't have to be on the set today," he said. "What about you? Any plans?"

"I should call Elaine at the hotel," I said. He let me use his telephone.

"Good morning, Sleeping Beauty," she said. "You know it's almost noon? I guess you're still at Jack's?"

"Yes," I said, feeling a pang of guilt.

"And you're calling to let me know you won't be returning to The Convent anytime soon?"

"Elaine, please don't hate me."

"I don't hate you, but I'm sure Mrs. Hershey will make certain to let me know what she thinks of your character, young lady," she said.

"I can't imagine staying there after last night."

"That good, huh?"

"I'll never tell." Then with a giggle, I added, "Jesus, Elaine. I saw the heavens open. Angels with harps, all of it. I swear to God."

She laughed out loud. "Don't forget to trade in your return ticket at the depot if you take a later train, sweetie."

"I won't. See you in the city?"

"I'll phone you in a few weeks. We'll have lunch at Childs, and you'll tell me all about it, you bad girl."

Jack and I stayed in bed for two whole days, pausing only for a quick bite or a swig from the whiskey bottle he'd retrieved from the liquor cabinet in the living room. Whenever I thought I could stand no more, he'd touch me again, and we'd both ignite. I wouldn't be able to sit right for a week.

He departed for an engagement on Tuesday morning, and I saw him off at the door while wearing his dressing gown, open at the neck to reveal a glimpse of leg and bosom. Clasping a breast one last time before he departed, he kissed me, then breezed down the front walk of the building. His neighbor watched us from behind the drape at her living room window, no doubt clucking her tongue.

That evening, he returned to find me in an occasional chair reading a *Photoplay*. He placed his hat on a peg in the entry hall, then approached the chair and knelt down in front of me. His breath was warm and moist in my ear, and his hands were everywhere—on my breasts, beneath my skirt, and on his trouser button. He reeked of marijuana. I wouldn't have known what it was before the Follies, but some of the musicians in the orchestra pit smelled the same. Marjorie was the one who told me what it was.

"What did you do all day?" he said against my mouth, pulling me onto the floor as he unbuttoned my dress. Then he shed his shirt and trousers.

"Slept late . . . had some lunch, then came back here." I gasped as he feasted on me like a starved animal, then took me on the living room rug as I pleaded for more.

The truth was that I'd snooped. Jack's place was obviously that of a single man who didn't give a fig for housework. It needed a woman's touch. He had two comfortable armchairs in the living area next to a brick fireplace. A wall full of built-in bookcases was nearly empty except for a stack of show business magazines (with at least one story on him featured in each, I noted). He still had many of the old playbills for the Smith family in their travels.

His closet was full of expensive jackets and trousers. He was obviously a snappy dresser. The medicine cabinet held only a package of Smith Brothers cough drops, a bottle of Fletcher's Castoria, some cod liver oil, and a syringe and length of tubing for some sort of medication.

I checked the icebox for something I could eat for lunch but gave up when the only thing I could find in it was a jar of mustard and a bottle of schnapps. We'd eaten the last of the bread and cold cuts during our marathon the last few days. The cabinets contained much of the same—a package of bicarbonate, a box of stale crackers, and a couple bottles of whiskey and rum. After taking a bath, I'd headed a few doors down to the El Rey Café for a bite. When I returned, I found the copies of *Photoplay* and lost myself in tales of Hollywood.

After we were done, I grabbed the magazine, which had slid to the floor. "I could do this, you know," I said.

"Do what?"

"This part your sister's playing—*Fanchon, the Cricket.* I could play this so easily. Plenty of girls are branching out from the Follies. I just have to figure out how. How was *your* day?" I asked.

In answer, he reached over to his jacket, which he'd tossed over the chair. He tugged a small velvet box from the pocket and handed it to me.

"Open it," he said.

When I did, I gasped. Inside was a doozy of a cigarette case. It was a silvery color, but one that shone with a special shimmer.

"What's it made of?" I asked, admiring the finish.

"Platinum," Jack said, "I love the stuff. Classier than gold, I think."

"Jack, this must have been expensive. You shouldn't have!"

"Ten thousand smackers," he said, proudly crossing his arms. "Now look at the other side."

I flipped it over and read the engraving in fancy script: "*To Olive Thomas. The only sweetheart I'll ever have. Jack.*"

"Whaddya think, baby?"

"It's beautiful." I kissed him, and he reached for me again. Stumbling into the bedroom, we didn't sleep for hours.

The next morning, I was in that blissful state between sleeping and waking, with Jack's leg slung over mine and his hand on my breast. An insistent tapping brought me to full consciousness. Unsure where the noise was coming from, I figured it had to be the neighbors downstairs, finally having the last laugh after the past few nights of our making the earth move above their heads.

Jack continued his usual *snort, snort, snore,* so rhythmic I could have used him for a metronome. Just as I was ready to toss off the sheets, march to the neighbors' door, and give them what for, the latches on the window burst open and two strange men exploded into the room and rolled on the floor, howling with laughter.

CHAPTER FOURTEEN

"You stupid bastards!" Jack grumbled, now fully awake. He grabbed his robe from the pile of clothes on the floor. "What the hell do you think you're doing?"

So he did know them. The tall one, blond with a ruddy complexion and an arrogant lift to his brows, glanced over at the other, and they both laughed uproariously. They reeked of alcohol and sin.

"We've been looking for you," the shorter one said. His dark hair was wavy, brushed to one side from a massive banner of a forehead, and his jaw was set in a bulldog's underbite. "We heard you'd kidnapped a Ziegfeld girl and brought her here. We wanted to see for ourselves."

He winked and gave me a quick once-over. I'd just sat up in bed with the covers clutched to my breasts, so I pulled them tighter.

"We got in from Tijuana this morning," said the tall one. "We got tighter than a nun's snatch!"

"Olive Thomas, this is James Kirkwood," he said, gesturing at the taller man, then the shorter. "And this is Mickey Neilan. Friends of mine."

"Drinking buddies," Mickey said, in case there was any

doubt of that.

"I can see that," I said. "You're both more souped up than consommé."

Mickey's eyebrows raised in amusement. "Say, she's a real bearcat, ain't she? You in the middle of something, Jack old buddy?"

I played along. "No, I wore him out hours ago."

This caused all of them to burst out laughing. They retreated to the living room as I searched for my clothes on the floor. I overheard them as I sat on the edge of the bed.

"Margarita wanted to know where you were, pal. Sheeesh! That señorita has more equipment than a munitions factory."

Glasses clinked, and it sounded like they were helping themselves to the last of the booze in the house.

"I was otherwise engaged," Jack said, and I could hear whispering and gloating.

"So how much more of Broadway do you have left to work through?" Mickey said.

"I'm done with that, gentlemen. Olive is perfection. The last two days have been the greatest of my life, and I plan on continuing this forever."

"You a one-woman man? I don't buy it," I heard Kirkwood say.

"Kirky, old pal, it's true. I'm a reformed fellow."

"We'll see," Kirkwood said, laughing. "The hooch too?"

"I may be reformed, but I'm not crazy," Jack said. Through the crack in the door, I saw him lift his glass, and they all toasted.

Having made myself presentable, I slipped into the living room, determined to be one of the boys, just like when Jim and Spud and I were younger.

"I don't suppose you have any of that left, do you? A girl could get thirsty, you know." I found one of the few empty glasses in the kitchen and held it up for a sampling. Jack poured in some rum, and then I lit a cigarette.

After that, we got bent as paper clips. Mickey and Kirky didn't leave for another two days. Whenever we ran out, Kirky made liquor runs to Venice or Vernon, since Hollywood was dry as the Mojave. On one of those runs, we stopped by The Convent and retrieved my trunk. I simply held my head high and let Mrs. Hershey know I'd found lodgings elsewhere. I had three men with me, so I can only imagine what must have been going through her head. Elaine couldn't stop laughing the whole time.

As much as I hated to return to New York, it had to happen eventually. Ziggy had been furious when I'd told him about my trip, but he knew he owed it to me after what he'd put me through. Jack gave me a ride to the station in his silver Phaeton, and we stopped just short of ravishing each other in the front seat when we arrived. Then I screwed up my courage and climbed aboard the train. Jack stood on the platform, and I hung out the window waving until the depot faded into the distance. I could feel a huge hole in my heart; I missed him so desperately already. The trip passed in a blur of fond memories and dreams of him that were so vivid that I blushed when I woke up.

A messy apartment waited for me when I got home. I'd

been overwhelmed with housework even before my trip, so I decided it was high time to get myself a maid. Running an advertisement in the *New York Daily Star*, I waited for just the right girl to come along. Effie Cotton appeared at my door on a Saturday, so prompt I could have set my watch by her. She handed me a sheet detailing her history, and I was impressed.

"Won't you sit down?" I said.

She took a seat politely on the couch. She wore a simple cotton shift dress, neatly ironed and sprigged with pink flowers, and a straw hat with a pink ribbon, pale against her dark skin. She'd obviously washed her dress in Lux. That familiar smell made me think of Mamma's clean laundry drying in the sun at our house in the Rocks.

It took me a minute to read the paper she'd handed me.

"You read and write?" I asked, surprised.

"Yes ma'am," she said, beaming. "The last lady I worked for done taught me."

"That's marvelous. And you're from Alabama? That's in the South somewhere, isn't it? How did you end up in New York?"

"My family moved up 'bout ten years ago so my father could find work. I been maidin' for about that long too. Mah husband, he was killed in a work accident a few years ago. I got a little girl. She stays with my parents, mainly."

"Your qualifications are very impressive. You've cared for others' children too, I see."

"Yes ma'am. You have any chi'dren?"

"Not yet, but I've got plenty of time for that, don't I?"

Effie chuckled. "Yes, ma'am."

"What do you do for transportation, Effie?"

"I take the train. It gets me just 'bout everywhere I need to go."

"It is very convenient in the city, isn't it? I'm paying a dollar a day for this job, Effie. And I may need to travel from time to time. To California, possibly. Would you have any problems being that far from your daughter?"

"I need the work, ma'am. And my parents are helpin' me raise her right. I'd just like to see her when I'm in the city."

"That's fine. It sounds like we're going to be working together for a while, then. Why don't you call me Olive?"

CHAPTER FIFTEEN

NEW AMSTERDAM THEATRE DRESSING ROOM, NEW YORK CITY, *May 1916*

Spring slogged along. I painted my face and performed my routines, but I wasn't really there. My thoughts were all of Jack. One of those miserable nights in the dressing room, I turned and saw Penny and Rosie standing in the doorway, watching me with eyes full of concern.

"You two look sadder than William S. Hart in a one-gallon hat," I said, patting my nose with a powder puff.

"We're worried," Penny said. "You've been somewhere else since you returned from California."

Rosie's head bobbed up and down in agreement. "We brought you dese, to cheer you up," she said. She carried a pretty flower arrangement in a vase.

"Oh, how sweet of you! They're so pretty," I said, taking a big sniff. "What are they?"

Rosie considered them for a minute, but knowing nothing of flowers, settled for "Red ones!"

"We heard you found a new sweetie out west," Penny said.

I lit a cigarette and exhaled, smiling up at them, my grin

growing bigger by the second until I could barely contain myself.

"You're a blasted Cheshire cat, Olive Thomas. Cough up the goods."

"Yes, tell us!" Rosie insisted.

It had been easy when Jack had been my own little secret, but now things were getting complicated. I hesitated a minute before replying.

"It's Jack Pickford, the actor," I said.

But instead of more smiles and laughs, their faces went grave.

"What?" I said.

"Ollie, are you sure about dis?" Rosie asked me.

"Of course I'm sure. He's the most amazing man I've ever met."

Penny took new interest in her shoes. Rosie shifted her weight.

"It's just . . . he has quite a reputation," Penny said. "We're worried about you is all. Will you go to Hollywood? You've got it pretty good here, you know. The rest of us will be broken-hearted if you leave."

"I don't know. I can't keep working with Ziggy now. Not after what he's done. But I want it all. With Jack I could have that—a husband, a home, children."

"I guess you're right. But please be careful. Something tells me Jack Pickford is trouble," Penny said.

"You worry too much," I said, taking her hand.

After my thoughts of flickers and my dreams of the future, opportunity came calling soon enough. His name was Jesse Lasky.

OLIVE'S APARTMENT, NEW YORK, *late May 1916*

"Miss Olive," Effie said, hearing the doorbell, "comp'ny's here."

"Thank you, Effie. Could you bring us some tea?"

She nodded. After letting in my guest, she retreated to the kitchen.

Jesse Lasky was the head of the Lasky Feature Play Company, already a recognized name in the business. They produced winning films like *The Squaw Man* and *The Virginian*. A bonus for me was that they were always searching for new talent. With these guys, I could dream big. I'd been trying to figure out how to break into movies, and this was my chance. Something big and important. Besides, I needed income when the Follies was not in session. Especially now—I was overdrawn again.

He was younger than I'd imagined he would be. His face was soft and fleshy but not overly so, and his light hair was combed to one side and smeared with pomade. Behind his small round spectacles, his light eyes were intelligent.

"Miss Thomas, it's a distinct pleasure meeting you," he said, shaking my hand.

"Likewise," I said. "I'm having Effie make us some tea."

"Tea would be nice, thank you."

I gestured to a spot on the overstuffed couch and took a seat opposite him.

"I want you to know that plenty of us in Hollywood are paying close attention to your Broadway success," he said. "I'll get right to the reason behind my visit. Several of us at my firm are eager to offer you a picture. We have a vehicle in mind we'd like you to audition for. The working title is *A Girl Like That.* Irene Fenwick is the female lead, and Owen Moore will play the male lead. Del Henderson will be directing. It's not a large part, but I'm hoping it will lead to more work for you, and I'd like for it to be with us."

"Owen Moore, huh?"

"Yes, he's popular with our audiences."

Fate was intent on throwing the Pickfords in my path, one way or another. Owen was married to Jack's sister Mary, the Queen of Hollywood.

Effie brought the tea and a plate of sugar cookies, so I smiled at her and took a sip from my cup.

"What's it about?" I asked.

"Nell is a girl whose father used to be a burglar," he began. "Harry Lee's going to play the father. He gets sick, and his old buddies talk her into helping them with a heist. She gets a job at a bank to help them with an inside job. You would play Fannie, Owen's sister. I know it's not the choicest role, but I'm hoping to work you into some other plum characters in more features."

As I saw it, Ziggy owed me a leave of absence for this role. Anytime he gave me a hard time, I laid on the guilt until he had no choice but to let me do what I wanted.

"Just so you know, my brother-in-law Samuel Goldfish and his partner Cecil B. DeMille run the production side, and Mr. Hiram Abrams is in charge of film distribution," Lasky continued. "I'm sure you've heard of Mr. Adolph Zukor. He's the founder of our company, and he has lots of plans for the future. We'd like for those to include you, if you're so inclined.

Let's see how this production goes, and we may be able to name figures for a contract."

"Then how can I say no?"

A Girl Like That was fun to shoot. I liked taking direction and running with it to create my own character. The purple fog created by the Cooper Hewitt mercury vapor lights excited me just as much as the sawdust and sandbags of the New Amsterdam.

Owen and I got along like old friends. He was pure Emerald Isle, straight off the boat, which automatically gave us a bond. He was also handsome as hell, with dark hair slicked with grease, thick eyebrows, lively blue eyes, and the devilish grin only a true Irishman can give you. Another thing—he was smooth as plate glass. Despite being married to Mary, he was a terrible flirt, always with a wink or a charming word. He confided to me that Mary was not as perfect as she appeared, and her mother was worse.

"A tigress, my dear. She hates my guts."

"But why? You're an agreeable fellow."

"An agreeable fellow who eloped with her daughter when Mary was eighteen." He wiggled those heavy brows.

"Oh, my. That might have something to do with it."

"Be careful, Ollie. Word on the street has it you and Jack are an item. He's a good friend of mine—you know that. But you need to be aware. Those women dote on Baby Brother, and they won't give him up without a fight. Lottie's the only one who's not half bad, but she's a two-fisted drinker just like me. Do watch yourself. I'd hate to see you sucked into that web of craziness that calls itself a family. Ignoring them would be like ignoring a bunch of rattlesnakes."

"Thanks for the tip, Owen."

It was common knowledge that Owen and Mary's marriage was on the rocks. I wasn't sure how much faith to put in his advice since it came from such a jaded perspective, but his hints on the set were perfect, and he told me about moviemaking. He also taught me about Klieg eye—though I didn't learn my lesson right away.

"See that light?" he said my first day. "The one like a huge pipe with a lens stuck in the end? That's a Klieg light. A carbon arc lamp, and very powerful. Whatever you do, don't look directly at one while it's turned on."

"Really. Why?"

"It'll blind you, my poor naive darling."

And wouldn't you know, it was only a few days later while we were filming on our fake bank set that I happened to glance over at one of the damned things. I won't repeat what I yelled, since most of the words had four letters, but it felt like someone had thrown sand in my eyes, and I screamed bloody murder. Especially when I realized I couldn't see when I opened them.

"Dammit, Ollie, I warned you!" Owen said, herding me to a chair and helping me into it. I heard him speaking to one of the hands.

"Hey Marty," he said. I could hear him sorting through his pocket for change. "I need you to run down to the market and get us some potatoes. A big sack of potatoes. And then stop by the druggist for some gauze."

"Potatoes?" I said, still seeing nothing but a sparkly sort of darkness. I rubbed my eyes, but Owen stopped me, saying the rubbing would only make it worse.

"Trust me," he said, speaking in a calm voice and patting my hand. When Marty got back, one of the crew offered up his pocketknife. Owen went to work on the spuds, and in a few minutes I heard him say, "Okay, Ollie. These are poultices. I'm going to put them on your eyes."

"What does that do?"

"Shush. It'll help."

I leaned back and let him pile the gauze pieces full of moist, slimy peelings on my eyes as I tried to relax.

"This is about the only thing we've found that works, other than castor oil," he said. "We'll keep doing this for four days or so, and you'll be fine."

Wouldn't you know it worked! They only needed me for one or two scenes anyway, and in a few days, my eyes were better. Unfortunately, my movie career stalled like a Model A on an uphill grade. I had hoped to do more work for Mr. Lasky, but sometimes plans change.

I waited and waited to hear something on a contract, like he had told me, but nothing happened. Jack pointed out their recent merger with Famous Players and then reminded me that after the merger Famous Players-Lasky had also dealt with a fire in the main office. Most likely, the paperwork had burned and been forgotten about. I knew then that my contract had been nothing but a pipe dream. I was stuck at the Follies for the time being, hating Ziggy and wanting out.

CHAPTER SIXTEEN

NEW AMSTERDAM THEATRE DRESSING ROOM, NEW YORK CITY, *June 12, 1916*

"Why did you want to see us?" Bessie said.

It was just after selection for the 1916 Follies season, and I'd called a few of my friends into the dressing room. Among the corsets and costumes, the Lablache face powder containers, the lip rouge, and the hundreds of feathered headdresses, Bessie Chatterton Poole, Fifi Alsop, Lilyan Tashman, Martha Ehrlich, and Kathryn Lambert all crowded into the space, where I was sitting with my new friend.

"I wanted you all to meet someone," I said, my arm around the older woman's scrawny shoulders. She was dressed in ragged clothes and shoes, and her mouth was resigned into a tight line.

"This is Ruth," I said. "She just sold me some cold cream. I wanted you all to meet her. She's been telling me some amazing stories."

Ruth obviously scared the hell out of Fifi. As a seventeen-year-old, Fifi had married a millionaire named Edward Brown Alsop, who was in his seventies. It'll come as no surprise to you that the marriage didn't last. She had seen her share of hardship since then and most likely saw Ruth as her future.

"What types of stories?" said Lil in her husky voice. Her stunning platinum blonde hair and exotic blue eyes contrasted with the matted brown hair and sad, tired hazel ones of the woman sitting before us. Ruth wasn't elderly, so maybe her body had just given out. She couldn't have been much older than forty.

Ruth paused, then reached for the glass of water I had offered her. She took a slow sip before beginning. Her lips were dry and cracked, as if every bit of energy and life had been sucked from her body.

"Years ago," she said. "I was beautiful like you. I danced in the Floradora show at the Casino Theatre. That was more than twenty years ago. We were so scandalous then, like you, so full of beauty and vigor. I want you to remember me. Save your money and marry sensibly. Don't fritter your lives away like I did. It'll only break your heart."

Martha clutched a handkerchief to her nose, sniffing and dabbing at her eyes. She and I had become instant friends, both having lost our fathers when we were young.

Ruth shared more stories with us. She'd been chums with Evelyn Nesbitt, the girl in the red velvet swing whose husband had shot and killed her lover, Stanford White. And she told us of the stage-door johnnies she had known, of the great love she'd had who'd died in the *La Bourgogne* shipwreck in 1898, and of her girlfriends who had been widowed or died young. By the time she was done, we were all in tears, and each of us paid her a nickel for the cold cream she was hawking. We made sure every jar was gone. Some of the girls even slipped her something extra.

Ruth finished her water, and I handed her an apple I'd brought with me for a snack later. She took it with a grateful half smile, then rose and winced, her shoes obviously too small.

"Bless you all," she said. I led her to the door, opening it for her onto the chaos of 41st Street, and she hugged me before she limped out for good.

When I returned to the dressing room, the girls peered over at me, all of them whiter than polar bears' pelts. Bessie was shivering, and I hugged her.

"So tragic," I said, shaking my head.

"Will that happen to us?" Martha said.

"No," I said. "Of course not. Not to any of us if we make up our minds it won't. We all have beauty and talent. Twenty years from now, *this* group of Ziegfeld Follies girls will all be famous and successful."

When they stayed quiet, I stood up. "Let's make a pact," I said.

"A pact?" said Fifi, rubbing a sleeve across her tear-stained face and leaving a smear of makeup behind.

"Yes," I said. "Remember what she said? Save money and marry wisely. She's proof. We won't be pretty forever. Let's agree to meet somewhere near here, say, twenty years from now. How about Churchill's?"

Their eyes all moved around the circle to each of the others.

"Come on," I insisted. Putting out my right hand signified the first link of an unbreakable bond. Kathryn followed. Bessie was next, then Martha, then Lil, then Fifi.

"We six ladies of the Ziegfield Follies do hereby make

this solemn vow," I said, "that on June 12, 1936, twenty years from now, we'll all meet for dinner at Churchill's Restaurant at Broadway and 49th Street. We'll compare notes about our last twenty years, and we'll tell each other tales of our colorful and oh-so-exciting adventures, our handsome husbands, our brilliant children, and our elegant homes. We'll reminisce about our Follies days, and we'll drink champagne toasts to lives well lived. Is it a deal, girls?"

"Deal!" they all said in unison.

Martha and I smiled at each other, and her face was much brighter than it had been. I'd cheered her up, and that made me smile. But frankly, if I'd known then what I know now, I would have followed Ruth out that door and bought her a drink.

CHAPTER SEVENTEEN

NEW AMSTERDAM THEATRE, NEW YORK CITY,
Summer 1916

"Ollie! Visitor!" one of the girls called.

I'd yanked off my headdress between sets and was enjoying a quick cigarette in the dressing room. Grabbing a silk robe from a hook, I slipped it on to receive company and sank into my vanity chair.

"Miss Thomas?" Blushing like a tomato in July, the man held his hat in his hand. Thin, with dark hair and a bushy mustache, he wore a pink carnation in his lapel. He kept scanning the room, obviously nervous he might see one of the girls in the altogether. He made me think of a chipmunk at a party full of buzzards. Not like the usual stage-door-johnnies at all.

"My name is Theodore Wharton," he said. "I run the Wharton Brothers Studio up in Ithaca with my brother, Leopold."

"Studio?"

"Motion pictures, ma'am," he said. "We'd be most interested in having you appear in one of our films. It's a serial. *Beatrice Fairfax*. Perhaps you've heard of it? Advice to the lovelorn reporter?"

I sat forward in my seat. Maybe I didn't need Lasky after

all. "Tell me about it."

"This would be episode ten, and you would be Miss Rita Malone, who has romantic trouble. It's a baseball theme, so we've named it 'Play Ball.'"

"When?"

"Within the next two weeks. We'd like to have everyone in town by then so we can begin shooting. Sorry for the short notice. The actress we initially selected fell through, and my brother had the brilliant idea of selecting a popular Follies girl to fill her place. You were our obvious choice."

"It sounds like a terrific opportunity. I'd love to do your picture, Mr. Wharton," I said, not thinking twice.

A week later, over Ziggy's objections, I took another short leave of absence and headed upstate to Ithaca. I checked into the Cayuga Hotel and showed up on set first thing the next morning. Mr. Wharton and his brother directed, shouting commands to us through megaphones while local townspeople watched from the sidelines.

They'd erected temporary sets at Renwick Park, covering the tops with large pieces of muslin or canvas to prevent the sunlight from creating obvious shadows in what were supposed to be interior shots.

One afternoon as we took a short break, storm clouds moved in from the west, and before we knew it, sprinkles dotted the sidewalks. In mere minutes it began to pour.

"Grab 'em!" I heard somebody say.

From the highest-paid actor to the lowly extras, everybody rushed to move chesterfields, side tables, books, and knickknacks to sheltered spots so they weren't doused. The rain soon passed, and every stick of furniture had to be put back.

It was all very relaxed. I even wore my own clothes, and they paid me $200 for the week, plus $100 for the three extra days they needed me there.

My special favorite on the set was Leopold Wharton's wife. She was about forty, almost like another mother. One day as we sat between takes, enjoying a cup of tea and talking about our lives, I happened to mention how fond I was of California.

Mrs. Wharton cooed in delight. "Olive, isn't it splendid? So scenic! I've been trying to convince the boys to move Wharton Brothers there. The weather is better, and we wouldn't be chased down by the syndicate all the time."

"Syndicate?" I had no idea what that was.

"Ah, yes. I forget you're new to all this," she said. "In the early days, when studios were springing up, Thomas Edison was incensed that we Whartons and other filmmakers were using his technology. 'It's patented!' he told them. 'It's illegal!' He served Teddy with a writ to stop using the cameras. Biograph, one of the other companies, approached Edison and they made a deal. So between those two and some of the other larger companies, they've tried to shut everyone else out of the industry. They call themselves the Motion Picture Patents Company, but everyone else calls them the syndicate. They're thugs, plain and simple. We've been lucky, but plenty of others haven't. Those brutes have destroyed cameras, frightened some of the casts and crews with guns, and even sent people to the hospital! The boys don't want to move, but I'd be far more comfortable on the West Coast."

I shook my head. I still had a lot to learn about motion pictures.

CHAPTER EIGHTEEN

NEW AMSTERDAM THEATRE ROOF GARDEN, NEW YORK CITY,

Summer 1916

"That new stage manager sure is a bastard," I said, lighting a cigarette. We'd gotten a new fellow that year, an arrogant ass named Ned Wayburn.

"That's not the half of it," Marcie said, passing me the ashtray before rubbing some Hinds Honey and Almond Cream on her legs.

"What do you know?"

"I've worked with him before, Ollie. Rehearsals during a stage call for a Winter Garden revue. I quit on account of him."

"Geez, for all Mitchell's faults, at least he made me a better dancer. This guy could give Torquemada lessons."

"We called him Neddie High-Hips," Marcie said, chuckling.

The first day we showed up for rehearsals for the new season, we knew things were going to be different. Instead of our usual straight lines of chairs, he'd set them up in a circle. And instead of letting us sit next to our best friends so we could chat, he organized us by numbers he'd selected. As the final insult, he blew a whistle at us—like we were trained dogs!

"Miss Davies, you'll be one. Miss Thomas, you will be two.

Miss Perry, you'll be three. Miss Ehrlich, four." He continued calling our names until we all had a place. Then he told us those would be our spots for the season. Thank God Kay had gone on tour with some cheap musical. But after Wayburn's torture all spring and summer, I was relieved to see the Follies end for the season. In early October, "Play Ball" was released, with talk of including me in one or two more of the *Beatrice Fairfax* episodes. Not for the first time, I considered leaving the Follies for good. But something kept me there. I couldn't quite explain it.

One night in early fall, Lawrence, the doorman, rang my apartment.

"You have a visitor, Miss Thomas."

"Who is it?"

"He says he's your fiancé." He barely got the words out before I squealed and flew downstairs, not waiting for the elevator.

"Jack!" I grabbed him in a huge hug.

"I had to come east for shooting. I decided to surprise you," he said. He handed me a bouquet of lilies and Shasta daisies wrapped in green tissue. They meant more than all the roses in the world.

"You remembered," I whispered. I'd once told him I adored the little yellow faces on daisies.

"I couldn't wait to touch you again," Jack whispered in my ear after the gate on the elevator slammed shut and the attendant pushed the lever for the fifth floor. He took my hand, raising goose pimples on my arms. "Or smell you"—he inhaled my hair—"or taste you . . ." When the doors opened, I led him to my apartment, and the months we'd been apart melted away. The lights of the city twinkled through the picture window in the living room as we kissed. And then he led me into the bedroom.

October was incredible. We went out dancing at just about every spot in New York. Rector's one night, Café des Beaux Arts the next. We had drinks at the Knickerbocker or the St. Regis, and grabbed a bite at Schrafft's or the Kaiserhof. Since Jack knew they were my favorites, we even went to Childs and stuffed ourselves with butter cakes slathered in maple syrup.

One night after dinner and drinks at the Knick, we returned to the apartment in the wee hours and made love to the symphony of backfiring cars, trucks, and shouts from the street through the open window I'd left cracked for a little air. The next morning, dawn glinted between the blinds. My head was splitting, and the eastern glare magnified it. I needed an aspirin.

I let Jack sleep and slipped into the kitchen in my robe. Effie was hard at work on breakfast, her hair up in a kerchief like Aunt Jemima.

"Mornin', Miss Olive. Got some flapjacks and bacon for you. Gonna be ready in just a few minutes."

"They smell divine, Effie. Thank you."

"Coffee's ready too."

I reached up and grabbed the aspirin bottle from the cabinet. As I was gulping three down with water, we heard a rap at the door, so Effie went to answer. Ziggy strode in with his confident swagger, cigar held aloft. He shrugged his coat off and looked at me with an expression I couldn't peg. Pity? Superiority? Power?

"What are you doing here?"

"Good morning, Ollie. Smells delicious. Mmmm . . . pancakes."

Effie's eyes grew wide, and she glanced at me for some direction. I shifted my eyes to the bedroom door and shook my head so slightly that Ziggy didn't see it. She picked up on my message.

"Mornin', sir." I heard only the slightest quiver in her voice as she gave him a smile and he returned it. Whatever he was here for, I was nipping it in the bud.

"You're not staying for breakfast," I said, with my hand on my hip. "What do you want?"

"I have some news, and I wanted to tell you myself rather than have it coming from the girls at the theater."

"What? That you've suddenly grown a spine? Why didn't you just leave me a note? It worked great last time."

"Now honey, I know you're upset. I had a reason for everything."

"That reason is your ring on the third finger, left hand." He took my arm and I shook it loose. "Don't call me honey."

"It was more than that."

"Oh yeah? What might *that* be?"

He paused for a minute, obviously trying to figure out how to say what he was going to say. Then he took a deep breath and dived in. "Billie and I spent a wonderful night together before Christmas. I found out before you left for California."

"Found out what?"

"She was pregnant, Ollie. I couldn't leave her. I'm a cad, but I'm not that much of a cad. Will you forgive me?"

I stared at him. His voice sounded distorted and monstrous.

"She had a baby last night," he continued. "A little girl. We're naming her Patricia. I wanted you to hear it from me before the news got out."

"How delightful for you," I said, having trouble getting the words out over my tongue, which had suddenly grown four sizes too big for my mouth. I didn't love him anymore, but it still hurt to hear from someone why they had left you.

The bedroom door opened, and there stood Jack in his jet-black dressing gown.

"Morning," he said, yawning and stretching before noticing the other man smoking a cigar in my living room.

If only I'd had a photographer on hand right then. I wanted to capture the expression on Ziggy's face and frame it so I could remember it forever.

"You were saying?" I said, pouring myself some coffee and gloating. "By the way, I've moved on too."

"How long?" he said. I knew that tone in his voice. The one of resentment and barely controlled temper. He turned to me.

"Since March. We met in California."

Jack was obviously entertained by the whole thing. He lit a cigarette and watched with amusement as he shook out the match and dropped it in an ashtray. Effie handed him a coffee and retreated into the kitchen.

"But . . . Jack Pickford?" Ziggy said. "Ollie, how many times have I told you about actors, for Christ's sake?"

"You're done with me, remember? I don't need your approval, and I'll love who I want."

"Love? Be serious, now."

"I'm serious as a lead pipe."

Right then, a fabulous idea bubbled up in my brain. One that would make Flo Ziegfeld sit up and take notice. Loathing him and Billie right then, I vowed to hurt him as much as he'd hurt me. Out of his view, I shifted my new opal ring to my left hand and turned the jewel palm side down.

"Jack and I were married yesterday." I held it up so only the band was visible.

"Shit!" Ziggy leaned down to pick up the cigar he'd just dropped on the rug, and I sent Jack a look that said, "Agree with me or I'll murder you after he leaves." He stared at me with a raised eyebrow and gave a little nod as Ziggy rubbed at the tiny burn mark.

"Where?" Ziggy asked.

"Not important."

"You've known him what, six months? Are you crazy? He's a drunken fool."

"Hey, don't knock it," Jack said before taking a drag of his cigarette.

"As I said, Ziggy, we're in love. It was the right time and the right place." I sat down next to Jack and took his hand, gazing at him with sappy adoration.

"How could you be so stupid? He's a playboy, Ollie."

"Playboy? The man who constantly sleeps around on his wife is going to lecture me about playboys? That's rich, Ziggy. I loved you, but I got nothing in return."

"Nothing? You got plenty!" he said. "Diamonds, furs, flowers, candy, adulation . . ." He stood right above us, lecturing down to me.

"I'm not talking about what I got from the Follies fans. I'm talking about you!"

"I told you what happened, Ollie. I can't leave Billie now. We have a child."

"So don't leave her. I got over you the minute I met Jack. We're not playing house. I want us to build a life together. Have a home and children too. All the things you wouldn't give me. I thought I only wanted money and success, but it turns out I want more." *Something big. Something important.*

"Have them, for God's sake—just don't have them with him. He's trouble."

"Sorry. You had your chance, and you blew it." I exhaled a smoke ring up into his face.

"You had a good run, old man," Jack said with a smirk.

Ziggy whirled on him with narrowed eyes and pointed a furious finger at him. His face was heaving and purple. "You shut your trap." Then to me, he said, "Ollie, I can't sell the Follies as a bunch of married women."

"That's not my problem, is it? Marcie's married. She's still there."

"You've put me in a spot."

"I guess you should have thought of that before you left me," I said. He figured he was going to come in, drop this turd in my lap, and then comfort me since I'd be so devastated. But I won. I fucking won.

"He'll make you miserable. Mark my words," Ziggy said, admitting defeat at last and stubbing out his cigar in the ashtray.

"Ziggy," I said, holding out my hand, "give me my key."

He pulled it from the pocket of his coat and handed it to me. Then he tossed his coat over his arm and paused.

Stabbing his index finger in Jack's face, he spit out his last words before leaving. "If I ever see you again, Pickford, I'll kill you." Then he stalked out and slammed the door behind him.

I giggled. I'm sure Jack was wondering how he'd become my partner in crime. Still nestled into the couch, he reached up for a big stretch. Then, cocking his eyebrow at me and smiling, he rubbed his hands together. "Are those pancakes? Who's hungry?"

CHAPTER NINETEEN

NEW YORK CITY, *February 1917*

News travels like wildfire, as they say. It wasn't long before the girls were all hounding me for news backstage. Reporters picked up the scent too, and in every interview I did, someone asked about Jack and me, and if I would care to comment about our relationship. I practiced being coy, and Jack practiced being a complete gentleman, which I think was a first for him.

It became a game, the whole "are they or aren't they?" deal. We'd have a giggle the night before a scheduled appearance, practice our newest comments, and after six or seven old-fashioneds, they'd sounded even funnier.

Penny and I were shopping at Wanamaker's one day when she piped up, "You and Jack need to come to Reisenweber's tonight at eight. I don't want any excuses."

"On a Monday?" I said. "It'll be dead."

"It most certainly will not. It will be the liveliest place in town, Ollie. So you'd better be there, or I'll take it out of your hide. You *and* Jack."

Reisenweber's sat on the corner of 58th and 8th at

Columbus Circle, and you could feel it pulsing from a distance. With its multiple floors of drinking, dining, and dancing, it was one of my favorite places in the city. Penny knew it. The first floor had a restaurant, but it was a little too snobby for me. The second floor had the 400 Cabaret with the Original Dixieland Jazz Band. They played a new music from New Orleans that was fun and exciting, with dancers hopping around like the acts at a trained flea circus. Everybody came to hear them play "Livery Stable Blues," the "Ostrich Walk," and the "Tiger Rag."

On the third floor was the Paradise Supper Club, which was a little less raucous than the 400. The fourth floor had the Hawaiian Room, where you could pretend you were visiting the islands. Some gal named Jonia and her sister swayed the hula with the South Seas Troubadours. And on top was a lovely roof garden, where you could relax and be cooled off by the breezes after dancing for hours.

Jack and I started at the bottom, working our way up, and no sooner had we gotten off the elevator at the Paradise than a group of our friends jumped out, wearing silly hats and tossing streamers and confetti.

"Surprise!" they yelled.

Penny strolled over and hugged us both.

"What is all this?" I asked.

"It's your belated engagement party, silly!"

Jack and I both burst out laughing. The orchestra lapsed into a quick, jokey version of the "Wedding March" for us, so we did a bow and a curtsey for the applauding diners nearby.

"You're a rascal," I said to Penny.

"I told you I wanted you to come. I didn't say why," she

said, winking. "Let's see your presents."

She led us over to a table where Marjorie, Elaine, Marcie, and Rosie and Jenny stood minding the presents. They all hugged me, giggling and squealing. Brightly wrapped gifts covered the table and the floor surrounding it.

"Thanks for thinking of us," I said to Penny.

"What kind of friend would I be if I didn't throw you a party? A girl doesn't get married every day, you know."

"Penny, we haven't even set a date yet," I said, keeping my voice low.

"But I thought you told Ziggy that . . ."

"Shhhhh . . ." I said. "Jack and I aren't telling anyone anything definite. We have our reasons. Trust me."

She got a devilish gleam in her eyes. "Your secret is safe with me. Do you want to open your presents now?"

"Sure." I turned to Jack. "Let's open that one first."

He handed me one of the medium-sized boxes, and we ripped the paper open together. It was full of thick white blankets with satin piping.

"Those are from Mae Murray. We didn't know what colors you were furnishing in, but white goes with everything."

"They're beautiful. Where is Mae?"

"Still wrapping up *To Have and To Hold.*"

We worked our way through the rest of the gifts, including a set of silver barware, a blue glass bowl, a jade statue, and a china casserole dish. In the middle of all the excitement, Jack pulled another velvet box out of his pocket with a gigantic star sapphire the size of a plum in it. Hell's bells, it looked like something in a raja's crown.

"Happy fake marriage," he whispered to me, making me

giggle. I gasped at the size of it.

Jack and I grabbed a booth, then ordered drinks and had a bite. The other girls were either dancing or drinking, and eventually Avis, Bessie, Fifi, Lil, Martha, and Kathryn all stopped by our booth. W.C. Fields was there, and Ed Wynn, Elaine, and Rosie and Jenny all shared hugs and presents.

When all the gifts were opened, we packed them into the car and returned to the 400, where we danced all night.

I leaned my head on Jack's chest as we slowed down for a waltz.

"I'm just curious," he said. "I know you were angry at Ziggy, but how do you expect this little joke of ours to end, exactly?"

"We'll get married, of course."

"Do you propose to all the men you marry?"

"Usually, yeah." He didn't know I wasn't kidding.

"You know, Mary and my mother will never approve of us getting married."

"Why do you need their approval?"

He either couldn't or wouldn't answer me, so we waltzed along for a while before I said anything else.

"Why *do* you need their approval?"

Early March 1917

Jack had to travel west to work on *Cupid's Touchdown* for Selig Polyscope, and I'd hoped to go with him, but Ziggy took his sweet time approving my two-week leave of absence, so I stayed behind. When the approval did come, Ziggy let Marjorie and I both go to California to test for some Hollywood roles. Ziggy thought of Hollywood as a giant promotional machine for the Follies, but he only let us girls branch out if he thought the publicity would help him.

When I arrived, Jack and I went for dinner and dancing at Nat's. We also spent nights out at the Alexandria Hotel bar. The Alex, on Spring Street, was the grande dame of Los Angeles. Actors, directors, and producers all flocked there. Crystal chandeliers hung from the high ceilings, and the columns were real marble. Elegant, ya know? They called the rug there "the million-dollar carpet" because lots of big deals got made on it. My favorite bartender in town was Eddie. He made great orange blossoms and shared bartender wisdom like how a drink wasn't really a great drink unless it had bitters in it.

The Vernon Country Club was a drive out of town, on Santa Fe at 49th in Vernon, but it was well worth the trip. Number one, Vernon was one of the few places you could drink legally around Los Angeles. Number two, the music was wonderful. It didn't look like much from outside, just a roadhouse in the middle of a field of beets. But inside, we danced into the wee hours.

The Ship Inn was an amazing place. It looked like one of those old ships in the history books. What do you call them?

A gallon. No, a galleon—that's it. A galleon built on stilts over the water at the Venice pier. They called it the Cabrillo. Even the inside looked like a ship. I felt like I was in a pirate flicker when I was onboard. The help were all dressed as naval officers, and the food was delicious. Plus, it being Venice, you could also buy booze—if you could afford it. They charged you out the nose.

I met Thomas Meighan there one night. Tom was a friend of the Pickfords who'd co-starred with Mary in *M'Liss*, and Jack had known him for two or three years. Tom was from Pittsburgh, so we had lots to talk about. He towered over me, his dark wavy hair and penetrating eyes a shifting blue-green. We chatted for hours over orange blossoms, practically ignoring Jack.

Later, when Jack drove me home, he pulled another velvet box out of his pocket. I opened the lid to find a stunning emerald ring and invited him upstairs to thank him properly.

JACK'S APARTMENT, LOS ANGELES, *March 30, 1917*

"Miss Thomas, I'll be frank. Triangle is very interested in you, and we want to make you a star. Not supporting parts like you've had, but real leading lady roles."

My first impression of Peter Underwood was of his immense lantern jaw, which arrived everywhere a few seconds before the rest of him. His hair was blond, with a fringe across his forehead like an unruly ruffle on a favorite blouse. He worked at Triangle Pictures.

I lit a cigarette and listened to his spiel, excited by the details of the pictures themselves, but not by the business end. I had one day left on my leave of absence in California, and I had no desire to return to New York, to Ziggy, and to our painful working relationship. To be honest, Triangle could save my ass.

"As you may or may not know," he continued, "Triangle is a group of companies under one umbrella name. The founders, Mr. Griffith, Mr. Sennett, and Mr. Ince, formed a triangle at its initiation, thus the name. Mr. Griffith controlled the Fine Arts label, Mr. Sennett held sway over Keystone, and Mr. Ince's properties were labeled Kay-Bee. We've experienced some staff changes over the last year, but we're still a successful enterprise, and we're obtaining new properties and signing new talent."

I'd heard the names being mentioned by the professionals at Wharton, or from the movie people I'd worked with on *A Girl Like That*, but I hadn't understood the whole production and distribution thing. I doubted I ever would.

"The first property we have in mind for you is a society-type picture. We're not sure of the title yet, but the scenario has been finished, and it's undergoing some rewrites. As I said, a starring vehicle," Mr. Underwood said.

I smiled a little wider. "What do I get to do?"

"You would be Betty Flower. Your older sister, Julia, is ready for marriage, and your mother and father are trying to find her a rich man. They want to nab her an Englishman with a title, but you get in the way of that. You're always pulling pranks or having a laugh, and you were just expelled from boarding school."

"Oh dear!" I said with a giggle.

"While the family winters in Florida, they meet an earl,

and instead of becoming interested in Julia, he falls for you." He leaned forward.

"It sounds like a hoot!" I said, slapping my knee. "I'd love to do it!"

"Good, I'm glad to hear that. If your audition pays off as we're hoping, we're offering you an exclusive contract to make pictures for Triangle, which could involve any of the labels I mentioned. Does that sound like something you'd enjoy?"

"Of course it does." I didn't tell him about not wanting to return to New York. And I didn't tell him that Lasky had told me almost the same thing he had. If Triangle worked out, I'd never have to see Ziggy again.

Underwood went over the terms of the contract with me, explaining it like I was seven years old but skimming over the important parts like its one-year length, and that it was Triangle's option to renew. All I heard was the part about getting the lead in any of the movies I was in.

They crowed about signing me and several other girls with a mention in Triangle's in-house newspaper. But then nothing. For an entire month, I sat twiddling my thumbs while they figured out what to do with me.

What happened to the flicker he'd told me about? Had it been shelved? Was it undergoing more rewrites? No one could tell me. Instead they sent me out to do ridiculous promotional photos with the other ingénues. *Photoplay* carried the photos of us frolicking in the waves with William S. Hart or examining a patient in our nursing whites. I also visited with the 7th California Infantry, and the photographer snapped me aiming a huge machine gun.

Then things got really strange.

CHAPTER TWENTY

LOS ANGELES, *April 1917*

"We're sending you to Pasadena for the day," Underwood said. "To the Cawston Ostrich Farm."

"Why am I going to an ostrich farm?" I asked, afraid to hear the answer.

"We want to take some photos of you, of course." He said it like people did this all the time.

"Why?"

"Ostriches are a novelty, that's why. They're fun, and they make people laugh. The public loves them."

"But why me?"

"You're available, Miss Thomas. And you're under contract. That means you do what Triangle tells you."

There was a trolley line not far from the farm, but I decided to take a car anyway. Homer Weatherly, the still photographer, needed room for his equipment. He packed it all up, and then he and I made the drive through downtown, up Broadway to Pasadena Avenue, past squat palm trees and orange trees, and signs for Busch Gardens and the Annandale Country Club. A little farther down the road, we saw a sign with "Cawston" in big block letters.

"Miss Thomas, Mr. Weatherly, it's so nice to meet you," said a man named Mr. Jeffreys who greeted us when we arrived. He wore dun-colored breeches and a newsboy cap over his dark hair. "Let's go see the aviary."

"The what?"

"The aviary, ma'am. That's the birds' home. Mind your step," he said, pointing out the piles that looked like dirt near the path. Homer and I followed him through the grounds, but we were careful where we walked.

Near a strangely shaped building deep inside the compound, we found several birds the size of giraffes. One of them stared at me in that funny sideways manner they have. He gazed at me with his huge dark, long-lashed eyes and bobbed his pointy pink beak. Then he cocked his head like he couldn't believe he had to pose for photos either.

"Miss Thomas, meet Leo. He's our male in this harem. Mr. Underwood wants some publicity stills of you riding him."

"Excuse me, what?"

"We have a little saddle we use and everything."

"Are you crazy? I can't ride an ostrich."

Homer was too busy doubled over laughing to say anything.

"He's very tame, I assure you," Mr. Jeffreys said.

Leo and I glared at each other doubtfully. He wasn't buying this either.

"Now, whatever you do, don't kick him in the side like a horse. He doesn't like that."

"How about I not get up on him at all? I'll just pose standing next to him."

"Because the studio—Mr. Underwood, I mean— specified

they wanted you riding him."

"Homer, do you know why we're doing this?"

"Uh . . . you work cheap, and no one else would do it."

At least he was honest.

"All right," I said with a sigh. "What do I need to do?"

At Mr. Jeffreys' signal, a bird wrangler ran out of the aviary with some heavy cords and spoke softly to Leo. Another hand ran out with a small stiff piece of leather and a stepstool for me. The bird ruffled his deep black feathers at them like he was mightily offended but allowed the first man to fit the bridle over his head. The second hand tossed the saddle over Leo's back and secured it underneath, while the bird nudged him with his head. I assumed that was ostrich for "That tickles!"

I can't think of anything more awkward than mounting an ostrich. The little saddle had no stirrups, so I pulled myself up with a prayer, hoping I wasn't showing my bloomers to every Tom, Dick, and Harry. I dangled my feet down both sides of Leo's round middle, and he reared his head up to nibble at my slipper.

"Ow!"

"Leo, no," Mr. Jeffreys said, trying to project calm. He paused as I got myself settled and Leo resigned himself to his passenger.

Homer set up his camera on the tripod on one side of the ring as Mr. Jeffreys got Leo's attention.

"Leo, walk," he said calmly, backing up a little at a time. Then he turned and ambled over to the far side of the ring.

It was the most bizarre feeling, this immense thing beneath me with his gawky waddle, flexing his skinny neck—it looked like a dandelion stem after you blew the fuzz off the top.

Leo veered to the right a bit, then stopped and tried to gnaw my shoe again.

"Cut it out," I said, wiggling my foot until he let go. I brought my foot back and accidentally jabbed him in the side.

Leo took off like a shot, and I bounced along, holding on for dear life, grasping the reins and his pipe cleaner of a neck. He didn't enjoy that at all, doing his best to make me let go. To make things worse, Mr. Jeffreys was baiting the bird, holding a lizard by the tail from across the ring, and that's what Leo was aiming for. He suddenly stopped short next to Mr. Jeffreys and grabbed his prize, his head bobbing up and down in triumph. I almost tumbled over his neck to the ground.

"Homer, please tell me you got one good shot," I said, my voice wavery and weak. I'd almost peed myself.

"I think so, Miss Thomas." He gave me an A-ok sign.

"Thank God. Leo, don't take this personally, but I want to be on the ground now."

Leo didn't mind. He was finishing his lizard.

TRIANGLE LOT, CULVER CITY, CALIFORNIA, *April 1917*

The day I finally got to start shooting, a sunrise the color of shimmery pink velvet greeted me, like the big guy upstairs was telling me I'd finally made it. It reminded me of one of my costumes at the Follies.

"Olive! Come in. Are you ready to get to work?" Mr. Underwood asked me when I arrived.

"I sure am." He was lucky I'd forgiven him for that ostrich thing.

"Then let's head out to the set."

We strolled outside onto the boardwalks that crisscrossed the property, and he told me about the other productions in progress. We passed small set vignettes showing rugs, couches, tables, and chairs, with cameras focused on the action occurring in each and directors with megaphones supervising.

"This is *Sole Mates* with Ben Turpin. That's *Her Excellency the Governor* with Wilfred Hughes over there. And across the way, that's *The Flame of the Yukon* with Dorothy Dalton and Melbourne MacDowell. What do you think of the setup?"

"It's just fine," I said. I waved at everyone. Mr. Underwood introduced me to my director Ray West, who was friendly enough. Ray sized me up, and we got right to work.

When we weren't shooting in Culver City, we filmed at the shore, which stood in for Palm Beach, where the husband hunt for Betty occurred. Eager to learn everything about moviemaking, I asked question after question. The cast members teased me about always being so curious.

"What's the name of the camera you're using?" I'd ask. "What is that process you're doing? How do you achieve that effect? Can I do this or do you prefer that?" I couldn't help it. There was so much to know, and I felt like I had to learn all of it.

They ended up changing the title of the film to *Madcap Madge*. That was how the fans remembered me for a long time—in middy blouses and tam-o'-shanter hats. I was excited until I read the review in *Variety*, which knocked me down a peg:

"In making her screen debut, Miss Thomas does not display

any great promise of ever really hitting the top of the ladder in popular favor. This is just as much due to the story in which she is presented as to her own lack of histrionic ability to create an impression."

"Lack of histrionic ability?" I said. *Bastards*. I'd show them histrionic ability. As soon as I figured out what it was. Lowering the paper with a sigh, I swore my next flicker would be my best yet. Crumpling the article in my fists, I tossed it toward the nearest trash can, then lit a cigarette and continued across the lot.

I sent the profits to Mamma and Harry, and they bought their very first car.

ACT TWO

CHAPTER TWENTY-ONE

TRIANGLE STUDIOS, LOS ANGELES, *April 1917*

"Miss Thomas, it's a pleasure to meet you," Mr. Bitzer said, holding out his hand, though I could see from his eyes it wasn't. "Today we're going to shoot some sample footage of you, and then we'll see how you'll represent on film. It's called a screen test."

Supposedly, these bits of film would measure how suited I was for other parts in Hollywood. I just didn't understand why it was necessary. Since I'd appeared on film before, they should have known already.

"But I know how I represent on film," I said.

He ignored me and readied his Mutograph.

Mr. Bitzer was D.W. Griffith's cameraman. Supposedly, he was getting a grand a week to direct me in something until Griffith returned. Assuming he ever did. Jack told me Griffith was in New York trying to negotiate his release from Triangle after seeing *Civilization* flop like nobody's business. You bet I had an attitude about this. But we were all testy in those days. Even after his campaign promise to keep us out of the war, President Wilson had still pulled us in on the Allied side, and everyone was on edge waiting to see what would happen next.

The draft boards had revved up all over the country, and the boys were getting nervous.

Mrs. Huntington, the Triangle receptionist, had seen me to the set, where Bitzer sat in the director's chair, checking the viewfinder on his camera. He was only a little taller than me, with a silly black mustache like a villain in a serial. The first thing he did after saying hello was tell me to put out my cigarette. When I pouted, he told me the film was flammable. I strolled a few yards away, dawdled over finishing it, and then ground it under my boot when I was done, smiling sweetly at him as I did.

At this point, I'd decided I had better things to do with my day and wasn't sure why I was wasting my time with Bitzer when Griffith was the one with the real say-so. It sounded like he wasn't coming back.

I allowed Bitzer to photograph and film me at various angles, but I was bored, and I wanted a drink.

"I want to run through this scene," he said, gesturing to a scenario. He handed it over and let me pantomime through it once or twice.

"Why doesn't she just leave the son of a bitch?" I pointed to the part where the main character, Lucy, fights with her spouse.

"That's not important. We only need you to read the scene as it's written."

I tried to get my head inside the character, but my heart wasn't in it. It showed.

"That was very good," Bitzer said. I knew he was lying. "Now we need to make a trip into downtown Los Angeles to the costume seamstress. Do you have a few hours to spend being fitted? We need to have your measurements on file for future productions."

"Sure," I said. But I didn't see what the point was if I wasn't going to be selected for any of Griffith's parts. Bitzer and I settled in the back of a touring car with a chauffeur in front. He put it in gear, and the car headed toward Los Angeles. He took Pico past St. Thomas the Apostle, a big mission-looking church. I wondered how long it would be before I could get my drink. As soon as we turned onto Main, I got antsy.

"Driver, stop please!" I said when we reached 5th Street.

He pulled over to the curb and glanced over the top of the front seat at me, probably thinking it was some type of emergency.

"What is it?" Bitzer asked me.

"I'm thirsty," I said. I pulled on the door handle and let myself out, ignoring his pleas.

"Keep an eye on her, Frank," I heard him say as he got out to follow me. I hotfooted it past Birkel's Piano Store, the Braly Building, the Hotel Stowell, and the Crocker Bank on the way to the Alex. Near the corner, Desmond's was having a sale on Kuppenheimer suits. But I ignored it all, intent on my drink.

By the time Bitzer got to me, I was on my usual barstool, brandishing a cigarette and flirting with Eddie, who had just whipped up my second orange blossom. Another glass sat before me on the bar.

"Come along, Miss Thomas. We have work to do at the costumers."

"It's just a cocktail, Mr. Bitzer," I said.

"Listen, if you don't do as I say and come along, any picture is off. Either you come or we're through."

I raised my hand, ready to ask Eddie for another.

"Ollie!" exclaimed a voice from the doorway.

I turned and squealed in delight to see Marjorie Cassidy. I hadn't seen her since we'd gone our separate ways after our arrival out west. We hugged and chattered away as Bitzer sighed in disgust. Marjorie caught me up on everything she'd been doing—a revue here, a limited engagement there—but said she was headed back to New York soon.

"Miss Thomas," he said, nudging me. "We need to be going."

"Mr. Bitzer, this is my friend Marjorie. Marjorie, this is Mr. Bitzer. He works for D.W. Griffith."

"Charmed," he said, barely glancing at her outstretched hand and intent on getting me to the car. "We should go," he repeated.

Marjorie gave him a quick once-over, and not knowing why he was being so rude, stood up for me. "Ollie, don't let this slob tell you what you can or can't do. You go ahead and order."

Feeling invincible after my second drink, I turned to him and said, "Go fuck yourself."

CHAPTER TWENTY-TWO

JACK'S HOUSE, LOS ANGELES, *May 1917*

"You son of a bitch! Do you think I'm stupid?" I held the newspaper up, pointing at the story of Jack and Wanda Hawley.

"Olive, please. This is silly. There is nothing between Wanda and me. Honest!"

"I know what I read." The room blurred as my eyes filled with furious tears.

"Darling, it's nothing. You know what it's like when you're on set. You're bored, and you're playing love scenes. It all seems so real."

"So what are you saying? That it *did* happen?"

He avoided the question.

"What about Louise?" I said, referring to Louise Huff, his other frequent co-star.

"Louise told me she goes the other way. But some of the others . . ."

"I knew it."

"I love you, Ollie. But you weren't here, and I was lonely."

"You weren't lonely. You were getting an itch scratched. You're in dozens of movies, for Christ's sake. Do I need to worry every time you head off to a set that you're humping someone else?"

"What about you?"

"What about me?"

"Don't tell me that with all the handsome fellows in Hollywood, you haven't wanted to bake up a little trouble with a co-star."

"I considered it maybe, but I never did anything about it like you did!"

"What about . . ." he said, moving closer.

"What about what?"

"What about when they moved in close like this?"

"Get away. I'm angry at you." I swatted at his hands.

"What about when they grabbed your skirts and pulled them up?"

"Jack, stop."

"What about when they nudged your bloomers aside and touched you under your shimmy, like this?" With his other hand he delicately caressed my breast under its silky covering, and the nipple pebbled beneath his fingers. My breathing got heavier, coming in little gasps.

He moved closer as we stood pressed against the wall. After slipping down his suspenders and unfastening his trousers with some hasty fumbling, he pounded into me right then and there. My left leg slid up his back until I finally kissed him, hot, wet, and greedy. I was angry with myself, but I knew I couldn't live without him. Our arguments always devolved into this. Even when I was in a rage, all he had to do was touch me and it would send me off like a stick of dynamite.

His voice was husky as he caught his breath afterward. "I told you, Ollie. They don't mean a thing. If one of those other actors did that to you, it wouldn't mean anything either. We're amazing together. Don't you see?"

He took a handkerchief out of his pocket and mopped up some of the mess, then did up his trousers. Tucking in the flaps of his shirt and replacing his suspenders over his shoulders, he grinned that wicked grin at me.

I let my skirts drop around my calves and gazed at him as my entire body heaved a sigh of contentment. I supposed that if co-stars were only a once-in-a-while amusement, I could handle the thought. And I could have some fun on my own lots during shooting. I couldn't wait for my next film.

In a show of independence, I found a place of my own in a house down the road from the studio and moved my things in a few days later. That week was crazy trying to get settled in. One day I heard the hasty ring of the doorbell, and some footsteps shuffled away. When I opened the door, a box sat on the porch. Great, another box. As if I didn't have enough of those right now. Annoyed, I grabbed it and took it inside. Small holes had been poked in the lid, and from inside came a strange scratching sound.

Untying the string that fastened it, I opened the cardboard flaps and was greeted by a moist nose and curious tongue. And there was the most adorable Pekingese puppy I'd ever seen. As I rubbed his silky ears and cuddled him close, I saw a card attached to the inside of the box:

"Please forgive me, darling Ollie. I saw this little fellow at a pet store downtown and knew you would love him as much as I did. I can't stop doing stupid things, but I hope this will make up for my ridiculous behavior the other night. Your Jack"

I took the puppy inside and set him on the floor. He followed me into the kitchen. I cut up the leftovers of a steak I'd had at the Ship Inn the night before and put it in a bowl Effie had unearthed that morning. Then I placed it in the corner, letting him go to work on the meat. At least I thought it was a him. I found another dish that I filled with water, so he lapped it up and promptly lifted a leg on the corner of the wall.

"No!" I said, panicking and sliding some of the packing newspaper under him. What the hell was Jack thinking? My family had never owned dogs. Hell's bells, I'd never even been near any, unless you counted the mongrel who co-starred with us at the Follies. They named him Don the Inebriate Dog, and they'd had a little suit made for him. He upstaged us every chance he got.

I took the string from the outside of the box and tied it lightly around his neck so I could take him outside on the apartment's lawn. He sniffed at bushes and flowerbeds, and tried out his high-pitched bark at birds, squirrels, and neighbors, gazing up at me for approval.

"You are a rascal, aren't you?" I said. "All rascals need good names. I don't know about Chinese things, though. Except maybe that chow mein they serve at those chop suey palaces back in New York. I could just call you Chow. Or Chow Mein. That sounds good for a little fellow like you. What do you think?"

He yapped and wagged his fluffy curled tail.

"Chow Mein, let's go inside. We have to phone your idiot dad and ask him if he's lost his mind. I've never owned a dog in my life."

He gave me another yap and seemed to be smiling at me.

CHAPTER TWENTY-THREE

MARY AND OWEN'S HOME, LOS ANGELES, *June 9, 1917*

As we neared the house, I clutched the present in my lap. It was all wrapped up in festive paper, and I fidgeted, playing with the bow.

Jack reached over and patted my hand, reassuring me. "She'll adore it. Don't worry, darling."

"I'm just nervous, that's all." Remembering what Owen had told me about these women, I'd have been nuts not to be.

I'd chosen my most demure dress, a deep navy one in a simple style with matching kid shoes, and I'd worn my hair up to seem more ladylike.

"You'll love Lottie," Jack said, speaking of the birthday girl, whose party it was. "She's the fun one. We call her Chuckie."

"Why Chuckie?"

"It was our dad's idea. Her real name is Charlotte, like our mother. But when she was born, my father thought she was a boy. They were going to name her Charles, but . . . "

"Oh, I get it. Chuckie."

We were let in by a colored maid, who Jack introduced as Nina. I could hear the guests in the living room, so we crowded in. Jack stopped to speak to some of the partygoers, and as he did, Owen handed us both a drink. He was soused.

"How are you, Ollie?"

"Nervous. How are you?"

"Desperately needing another of these. Good luck with the dragon ladies."

"Jesus, he looks like shit," Jack said as Owen moved off into the crowd.

The living room was elegant, but nothing at all like I'd imagined for a movie star. I was surprised such a wealthy woman lived so frugally. I saw Mary and her famous blonde curls in a sitting room, speaking to a petite pretty lady with silky chestnut hair wrapped in a tidy chignon. There were fewer people in here, but the same no-nonsense decor.

They both waved, and the brunette gave a big smile. Mary's face lit up when she saw her brother, then fell when it got to me. Her eyes, usually wide and blue, full of charm and spunk in her films, were now blank. She wore a dress that would have cost me a year's salary—a blue tricotine number with black soutache trim at the cuffs and hem.

We approached them, and Jack introduced me. "Mary, Frances, this is my sweetheart, Olive Thomas."

I shyly took each of their hands in turn.

"Nice to meet you," I said.

"Hello, Olive," the other woman said. "I'm Frances Marion, and I'm a scenarist. It's nice to meet 'The Most Beautiful Girl in New York.'" She winked, and I laughed.

"Your reputation precedes you, darling," Jack said with a chuckle.

"It does, doesn't it?" Mary said, taking my hand but

touching it as little as she could, like it was a rotten egg.

"I love your films, Mary. Ever since I first saw *Willful Peggy* when I was a girl," I said. *Oh shit. Nothing like making her feel old.*

"Thank you," she said. The smile didn't reach her eyes.

"Is Jack here?" I heard a smoky voice say. A woman broke from the crowd with a little yell, gathering him in an affectionate hug and smothering his face with playful kisses.

"Chuckie!" he yelled.

"You must be Olive!" she said, reaching out a hand. "I'm Lottie!" She was darker than her sister, and her large dramatic eyes were her most attractive feature. She wore a deep burgundy dress with a mink collar and shoes of the same color. The aroma of Caswell Massey's #6 and Murad cigarettes clung to her like a coat.

"This is for you," I said.

She took the gift I handed her, giving me a sideways hug.

"This is so sweet of you!" she said, ripping at the red bow on top.

When she got to the box inside, she squealed again. I'd splurged on a diamond bracelet in a bid for her to like me. She gave me another hug as she set the box on the bar.

"This is one of my favorite presents ever!" she said, fastening the bracelet around her wrist.

Right then, a little girl of about two or three crept out from behind Lottie, her face dominated by a pair of the same dark eyes as her mother.

"This is my daughter Mary," Lottie said with her hands on the girl's shoulders. I knelt down to be at the same level and smiled at her, opening my arms to see if she responded.

"Do you talk yet, sweetheart?"

"Only when she feels like it," Lottie said.

"Dat?" the little girl asked, pointing at Lottie's glass.

"This is Mommy's drink, darling. Can you say Scotch?"

Lottie knelt down and let her sniff it. Little Mary made a face and reached out to take my hand. Her baby face beamed as she looked at me.

"She obviously doesn't take after my side of the family at all!" Lottie said with a guffaw. Then she downed her drink.

At that moment, the temperature in the room dropped. An older woman marched toward us. She wore a dark dress, of the style favored by withered matrons, and her gray hair was pulled into a severe bun. No one had ever stared at me so critically in my life. Anyone would have sworn she'd just stepped in dog shit.

"Mother, this is Olive," Jack said. "Ollie, this is my mother, Charlotte Pickford."

"It's very nice to meet you," I said, smiling.

"Charmed," Mrs. Pickford said, holding her hand out for me to shake, but her glacial demeanor did not thaw one bit. Her face remained frozen and unreadable.

"Mother, see the gorgeous present Olive bought for me?" Lottie shook her arm so the bracelet gave a little tinkle.

"It's beautiful," said the iceberg, "but obviously very pricey. How does one pay for such a costly piece of jewelry?"

"I'm an actress," I said.

"I have it on good authority that your contract at Triangle pays you a pittance, Miss Thomas. So once more I ask myself what you had to do to pay for a gift like that."

"Excuse me?" I said, almost snorting Scotch out my nose.

"What are you saying, Mrs. Pickford?"

Sensing a change in the mood, Frances looked out into the living room. "Oh, there's Owen. And I haven't said hello yet. Please excuse me. Olive, it was lovely to meet you." I smiled back at her as she moved into the living room, but inside I was seething.

"Jesus Christ," I heard Lottie mutter. She slipped behind the bar and poured herself another Scotch, then opened a jet cigarette case and lit one. Jack joined her and poured himself one too.

"As warm as ever, Mother," Jack said, using the flame from Lottie's cigarette to light his own. "No 'welcome to our home' or 'thank you for Lottie's beautiful gift.' You leap right in and call my sweetheart a tramp." He crossed to a couch and sat down.

"I did no such thing."

Just as I thought they were ready to pull on boxing gloves, Mary entered the fray. "Yes, how did you pay for it? I didn't think the Follies paid *that* well, unless you count the fringe benefits, of course."

"I saved my money." It was true, for once. I'd put some money in savings. And spent it almost immediately.

Between Mary and Charlotte, I had never felt such coldness. I'd always been able to charm almost anyone, but these two were a brick wall. So that was how they wanted it. Fine, I could play along. If I could deal with a professional bitch like Kay, I could handle "America's Sweetheart." And her mother too.

Mary's like buttermilk, I thought. *Bright and sunny on the outside, but sour once you've had a taste.*

Instead of sitting in the chair she gestured to, I plopped down next to Jack on the couch, where he was already relaxing. Then I defiantly took his hand and downed the rest of my Scotch, setting it down on the table without a coaster, reveling in the determined clonk it made. The hard stare I received in return told me everything I needed to know. War had been declared.

Little Mary followed me and leaned on my friendly lap.

"I see you've met Little Mary," the elder Mary said.

"Yes," Lottie said. "She's quite taken with Olive."

"As is our Jack," Mary answered, glaring at her brother as if to say, "You idiot. How could you do this to the family?"

"So you were in the Follies." Charlotte said.

"Yes ma'am," I said, wary of what would come next.

"And the Frolic too?"

"Yes."

"You took your clothes off for money, then."

"Now see here, Mother . . ." Jack began.

"It's true, isn't it?" protested Mrs. Pickford.

It didn't matter what I said. Their minds were made up. I'd be damned if they'd condemn me like this. I was no whore, and I was ready to come out swinging at the old hag.

"Mrs. Pickford, Jack has told me he grew up poor after your husband died. Do you know the same thing happened to my mother? My father died of pneumonia when I was eight. I watched him die." I narrowed my eyes to let her know I would not be cowed. Then I continued.

"She also had three children to raise—my two brothers and me. And like you, she struggled. For weeks and weeks we lived on nothing but cabbage soup. But she managed to get food on the table. When I went to New York and became a model and joined the Follies, it was the most money I'd ever seen in my life. And I was able to help her, just like Mary was able to help all of you. I've sent Mamma money and household gifts, and pretty things she likes because I know how hard she worked to raise me. She's never judged me for what I do, and neither has Jack. I'm perfectly happy with my life. I met some nice people at the Follies, and I loved working there. Is there anything else you'd like to ask me?"

From her reaction, I could tell no one else had ever spoken to Charlotte Pickford that way in her life. She squinted at me.

"Respectable women do not take their clothes off for money, no matter how hungry they are. My son cannot marry a harlot who has been an artist's model. Everyone knows showgirls are loose. Billie Burke is a lovely woman. You had a lot of nerve trying to steal her husband."

"That's very kind of you to give me the benefit of the doubt, Mrs. Pickford." I tried not to roll my eyes. "For your information, Mr. Ziegfeld initiated our affair. He invited me to his apartment, and he took me to Long Island for rides on his yacht. But first, he introduced me to fellatio. I'm sure you wouldn't have heard of it. It's an unusual practice, where a woman uses her mouth on a man's . . ."

"Stop! I do not want to hear this. Lottie, send Little Mary to her room."

"No? The truth contradicting your judgment of me? Even though he was the one who began the affair? Come now, Mrs. Pickford. I was a showgirl, and I was paid to dance, nothing more. Mr. Ziegfeld was crazy about me. I wanted to be legitimate, and I told him that for things to continue, I wanted the sanctity of marriage. He wouldn't give me that."

"He had a wife and a child!"

"He didn't have the child yet, ma'am. Only the wife. And Mr. Ziegfeld told me sob stories of their life together, and how miserable he was. Any man that dedicated to his wife does not tell his mistress how desperately he wants to leave that wife. Does he?"

She had no answer.

"At one point, he returned home, and that was when she became pregnant. He had already left her for me. Then he went back to her. So in reality, she and I were *both* wronged."

"That's all ancient history," Jack said. "We want your blessing to marry, Mother. And we'd like it soon, so we can arrange things when we get to New York."

Charlotte was obviously horrified. "Absolutely not. This woman is the most common tramp imaginable, and I will not allow it."

"How dare you," I said between gritted teeth.

Jack patted my hand to get me to calm down.

"Why the hurry?" Mary said. "Something you're trying to keep secret?" She glanced pointedly at my middle. The nerve of her, suggesting he'd knocked me up! Didn't she have anything more original in her arsenal?

"I could have asked the same of you and Owen," Jack said, casually blowing a smoke ring.

Mary paled. Owen had told me they'd run away to Jersey City. Everyone knew she was seeing Douglas Fairbanks on the side but was keeping it very hush-hush. The only reason they hadn't divorced their respective spouses was that Mary was terrified bad press would end both their careers. I saw red when I thought of a hypocrite like her standing in judgment over me. And since Owen was a friend of mine, it made me twice as angry.

"You are not good enough for my son," Charlotte announced.

"Oh Mother, please . . ." Lottie said, lighting another Murad.

"I love your son and I want to make him happy," I said.

"No. I forbid it. Your behavior reflects badly on this family, and Mary's career will not be damaged due to your shoddy morals. You are trying to use the Pickford name to further your career in Hollywood, and that is not going to happen. You can step off our coattails right this instant."

"I beg your pardon. I'm one of the most well-known faces in New York. I don't need the Pickford name to build a career."

"Nevertheless, I refuse to sanction this marriage."

Lottie rolled her eyes. "So she was a model and a showgirl. She's one of the most beautiful women I've ever seen, Mother. Imagine how adorable their children will be. Think how those lovely grandchildren will reflect on you. Now do me a favor. Look at your son."

Charlotte reluctantly glanced over at Jack.

"If you weren't such an old prune, intent on managing Mary's career at the expense of everything else in all of our lives, you'd see how in love with her he is."

Jack's gaze was a silent plea.

"I only dream of having someone love me like that. Alf sure didn't. Why do you think we're divorced now?"

Charlotte and Mary both sat silent, digesting what Lottie had said.

"If you value your relationship with your son, you'll let him marry her. He's not Mary. He's a grown man, able to make his own decisions. And it's obvious he loves Olive. He loves you too, or he wouldn't have asked for your blessing. For God's sake, let him do what he wants. Love's all we can really hope for in life anyway." She gulped the rest of her drink.

The room was quiet, like everyone was afraid to speak.

"When?" Mary said.

"We were thinking just after the New Year," said Jack. "All Ollie's friends are in New York."

"Fine," she said. Then she sighed. A momentary cease-fire had been declared.

CHAPTER TWENTY-FOUR

ON THE WAY TO BIG BEAR LAKE, CALIFORNIA, *June 1917*

"Wind her up, Dick!" Lynn yelled.

Dick Moseley, one of the hands, cranked up the jalopy and got her going. The entire cast and crew of *Broadway, Arizona* had piled into five Model T touring cars for the god-awful trip up through the San Bernardino Mountains, fighting the potholes, the rocks, and the sand that stuck to everything. Very soon we were fighting each other too. As the temperature rose, tempers flared, and so did the sniping. Especially from the bouncing of the cars along the ridges and the tight-fitting seats.

The steep grades and hairpin turns were hell on the engines as we crossed the foothills and worked our way over the passes. Some of us had to get out and walk so the cars could clear a crest or a slope. This was the third time one of the drivers had needed to get out and recrank an engine to start one of the flivvers up. The director, Lynn Reynolds, sat next to me, and he tried to entertain me with stories of filming in some strange locations or of local lore. Sometimes he had to keep talking to distract me when I bit my nails.

"Ollie," he'd say, "those vineyards were planted by the

Guasti Indians. That's San Gorgonio. And there's Jepson Peak." He pointed at a few of the higher mountains, somehow convinced I cared for the scenery, when the truth was I was so carsick I was ready to drop my head over the side of the car and lose my lunch.

Chow had never had such a big adventure. He sat in my lap, front paws perched on top of the door frame, tail full speed ahead, panting merrily and yapping at birds and deer.

We traveled by the Mill Creek Road, passed Bluff Lake, and then emerged from the mountains near Pine Knot Lodge, where we were staying. I staggered out of the car on shaky legs from the altitude and my nausea. The area was rocky too. I had to be careful not to twist an ankle. Mamma had taught me that young ladies never spit, but by God, that sandbox in my mouth had to go. I aimed a straight shot into a crop of weeds.

"All right," Lynn said as we unstrapped trunks and equipment from the cars. "We're bedding down two to a cabin, everyone. Ollie, you and Neola are in Cabin C. I don't think I have to tell you all we don't have indoor plumbing, so everyone mind your manners. Gentleman, remember we have women present, so trek a little deeper into the woods for nature's calls, if you would. Ladies, the privy is behind that tree." He gestured down the hill a bit.

"Where am I bunking down tonight?" George said. George Chesebro was playing my love interest, a ranchman named John Keyes.

"Cabin B, George." Lynn replied. "You're in with me. I've made a list for the rest of you. We'll have dinner at the campfire in an hour or two. It's starting to get dark now. If anybody needs anything, there's a little store attached to the lodge, with a bakery and a couple of gas pumps. So you should be all set for soap or tooth powder. It has a generator, so we do have some electrical power if we need it for anything. Let's meet here for grub after you clean up a little."

The stew was delicious cooked over the open flame. Mr. Skinner owned the lodge, and he told us stories of the early days of Big Bear, of the ghost town of Bairdsville, of the prospecting days during the gold rush when his father had been a forty-niner, and of his later adventures during a silver strike at another town called Calico.

George and I cuddled up since I'd left my sweater in the cabin. He rubbed my arms to keep the circulation going, and we squeezed a little closer to the fire. For his part, Chow hunkered down on a camp blanket and went to sleep.

When George walked me to my cabin after dinner, I let him kiss me. I was tempted to let him do more, but for my temporary roommate. Shooting the next day was routine, except for the new buzz of chemistry between us.

"Ollie, turn this way!" Mr. Reynolds said through the megaphone. "Fritzi has had a nervous breakdown. She's traumatized. I need you to be dazed."

I turned and tried to pull off wounded, but the afternoon glare stabbed at my pupils from the angle of the canvas light diffuser hanging overhead, so it was really hard. Try to be traumatized with the sun in your eyes. It ain't easy. They only watered more.

The cameraman kept his Bell & Howell pointed at me, trying to pick up all my nuances of emotion.

My Fritzi was a showgirl in New York. After being

convinced by a press agent it would be good publicity, she got engaged to Mr. Keyes, then broke off the engagement. After Fritzi's nervous breakdown, Keyes returned to New York and retrieved her, then took her west to convalesce.

The sparks from the previous night flared once more as George tenderly cared for me before the cameras. Every night we gathered in the same place, eating, drinking, and talking about Hollywood. The main topic of conversation was Triangle's implosion. It turned out I'd picked a remarkably bad time to sign with them. Mr. Ince, the head, was completely out. With him, several stars defected, like Enid Bennett and William S. Hart. They'd had items in their contracts that stated all their projects would be overseen by Mr. Ince, so with him gone, their contracts were now void. We were all nervous but tried to overcome our doubts with an extra dose of Gilbey's. A couple bottles got passed around until they were gone. And the flirting between George and me really heated up.

It was harmless fun, as Jack had said. He was right. The romance was make-believe. We could resume real life when I got home. If Jack was out with his leading lady, I could do him one better. For as worrisome as his affairs were, I'd discovered his drug use was just as bad, if not worse.

I knew about the marijuana, but he'd kept the harder stuff hidden from me for a while after we became a couple. Then he hadn't bothered anymore. I joined him from time to time in what I called "magic dancing powder." I'd discovered cocaine in the days when I was dancing almost nonstop. And dance I did.

Lately, the coke had helped me to coast through any number of early morning stage calls after our late nights out. But coke wasn't Jack's only vice.

When I was still living at his place, I'd returned later than usual one night, and when I yelled I was home I heard a slight rustling from farther inside the bungalow.

"Jack?"

No answer. The bathroom door was closed, so I pushed it open, only to have it stop abruptly halfway.

"Jack? Jack! Are you all right? Answer me!" I called, banging my palm against it. The wood had an empty echo. He said something, but I couldn't make it out.

His mouth sounded like it was filled with cotton, like he couldn't form the words. When I pushed harder, a thump sounded on the other side. Slipping through the opening and stepping over the obstacle, I realized it was Jack. He sat on the floor in his trousers and undershirt, a dreamy smile on his face and slumped to one side. The piece of tubing I'd found before was tied tightly around his forearm. On the floor was a syringe, its pump on empty. A spoon and a box of matches from the Ship Café lay alongside the sink.

"Are you sick?" I said, feeling ridiculous.

"Nope, never better," he said, his voice slurred. That smile widened until he resembled that cat in Wonderland. And I sure felt like Alice right then, tumbling down the rabbit hole.

"What is this? What are you doing?" I said.

His head nodded forward, and he held up the syringe. "Want some?"

"Hell's bells," I said. I grabbed it from him and placed it on top of the toilet tank. Pulling him up, I managed to drape one of his arms over my shoulder. Then I put him to bed, where he instantly dropped off and started snoring. I watched him for a few minutes before untying the tubing. And that was how I found out Jack was on the junk.

He showed me the local people to know to keep him stocked. The Count was an immaculately dressed older fellow who supplied half of Hollywood with snow and junk. He lurked around the Sennett lot and got invited to all the best parties. I'd give him the cash and he'd hand me a small vial of white powder, which I'd hide in the pocket of my coat or my bag until I got home.

Though he'd developed a reputation as a crusader against drugs, the director William Desmond Taylor also kept us rolling in coke. Most of the books in his library were fakes. The insides were secret compartments where he hid the stuff. All it took was a visit to his bungalow on Alvarado Street for a little refresher. For anybody watching the traffic in and out, it must have seemed like he was running a lending library.

After I found Jack like that, it was harder and harder to fend off temptation when it came calling. At Big Bear, George and I snuck out of our respective cabins. He carried two blankets with us so we could snuggle. We found a perfect, secluded hillside to have a little privacy, and I really let him frost my cake, if you know what I mean. I didn't feel anything for poor George. I know that now. He was revenge. But Jack was right about one thing: no guilt.

George and I fell asleep on the grade, and the next morning, everyone on the set wondered why he was so tired and achy.

"If they think he's stiff now, they should have seen him last night," I muttered.

CHAPTER TWENTY-FIVE

THE HILLS OUTSIDE LOS ANGELES, *July 1917*

"I swear to God, if I hear one more dumb Mick mouth off, I'm going to have to punch somebody."

Those were the first words I heard from my next director, Lambert Hillyer. We were oil and water from our first meeting. Some people said he was handsome, but with his narrow nose, dark eyes, and thinning hair, he looked to me like a ferret with a comb-over. He had a whiny voice and foul breath, and I thought he was an ass. Chow couldn't stand him either and growled whenever he was near.

After I returned from Big Bear, I had to leap right into *An Even Break*. We finished the inside shots at the lot, then headed outside town to shoot exteriors. As usual, I'd driven the cast and crew nuts asking questions about every little thing.

"What type of camera is that? What's the name of this place? Did it used to be a mission? Do you think we'll see any bears?"

I never forgot Hillyer's attitude. Or let him forget how I felt about it. He soon learned not to anger a real Irishwoman. When he told me to do something, I'd consider it a suggestion and then do things my own way. What he wanted from me he had to work for. So he returned the favor by putting me through take after take just to see how angry he could make me.

I wondered if I'd chosen the wrong profession, that maybe I should consider directing instead. If for no other reason than to torture the people I didn't like. It looked even more exciting than acting, and I was determined to give it a try. It seemed big and exciting. You were able to tell the actors and actresses where to stand, what to say, and how to say it.

So I asked him if I could direct a scene or two. He snorted like a hyena with consumption and turned to his assistant. "Whaddya think, Buddy? Should we let Ollie direct for a while?"

Buddy wore a backward newsboy cap and had enough attitude for three men twice his size. He shook his head as he tittered. Hillyer joined in until they were both in tears.

"What? What's so funny?" I said.

"A woman director? I never heard anything so hilarious in my life!" Buddy finally managed to squeeze out.

"But why?" I said. "Let me do a scene and I'll prove it. How hard can it be?"

I couldn't understand why being a woman made any difference at all. I could still hear them as I retreated, grinding my teeth as I went. The next morning, I approached Mr. Hillyer when he was alone and threw myself on his good graces, assuming he had any.

"Ollie, it's not my decision. Mr. Davis hired me to direct this picture. He's paying me to do it. If someone else directs it, that's not right." H.O. Davis had been brought in from Universal after Mr. Ince left, and he was running Triangle on a shoestring budget. "Austerity measures," they called them. I didn't see him approving of a female directing, thinking it would be a waste of film.

"It's not the entire picture. It's just a scene, to help me learn about moviemaking. Nothing huge or financial. I don't expect to be paid, for God's sake."

"If it's that crucial, why don't you talk to Mr. Davis and see what he says? If he agrees to this, maybe we'll work something out."

"Oh, Mr. Hillyer, thank you!" It was obvious he expected me to fail, and that only made me more determined.

That afternoon, during a break in shooting, I visited with our scenario writer, Mr. Cunningham.

"Mr. Cunningham," I said sweetly, using every feminine wile in the book, "could I possibly borrow your typewriting machine?"

His little round head with its tiny wisps of hair blushed like an early strawberry, and he gladly let me take the typewriter and some paper to my chair under a scrub oak tree, where I set it up on a small camp table. It took me an hour of pecking out the characters, but I finished at last.

You're probably asking yourself what could have been so all-blasted important that I, Olive Thomas, two-fingered typist, would be working that hard. Well, I'll tell you. It was a petition. That's right, all official and everything. I wanted ammunition to take to Mr. Davis. I'm sure I misspelled a few words, but who really *cares* if it's "Pathay" or "Pathé" anyway? Except for Mr. Pathé himself, maybe.

I made the rounds of the set with my little paper and a fountain pen, asking everyone to sign—from my co-stars,

Darrell Foss and Charles Gunn, to the prop hands, to the stuntmen, and even to the dog wrangler. Most were happy to oblige, though they laughed as they did it—especially Darrell. He curled his lip, his thin dark mustache quivering as he fought not to laugh.

"It's what?" he said.

"A petition to let me direct part of the picture. You know, like how real government works. The will of the people."

"Good God, it'll be like the Keystone Kops. Full speed ahead!"

He scribbled his name without glancing at the result on the page. When I left him, he was holding his sides, sniggering.

After everyone on the set had signed it, including Mr. Hillyer, who obviously wanted to humor me, I took the petition to Mr. Davis. Knocking on his office door and hearing his deep voice made my knees rattle.

"Olive, come in!" he said, standing and placing his hands on his desk. He gestured to a red upholstered chair across from him. "What can I do for you?"

I sat and took a deep breath, willing the lump in my throat to melt. It didn't.

"Mr. Davis, I have a special request. It's something I'm really curious about and would like to learn to do. Mr. Hillyer told me to speak to you."

"Anything," he said expansively.

"I'd like to direct a few scenes in *An Even Break*."

His smile faded like a pair of old dungarees. "Anything but that."

"How come?"

"I hired Mr. Hillyer to direct that picture, and I hired you to act, that's why."

"But Mr. Hillyer supports me in this." I didn't tell him that Hillyer would support me only if he did, but I had the trump card in my purse.

"He does?" His voice smacked of disbelief.

"It took some convincing," I said. "Honest. The cast is also asking you to give me this opportunity." I dug in my bag for the paper and pulled it out. Laying it on his desk, I sat forward in my chair, waiting for his answer.

"You typed this yourself?"

"Yes."

He sighed. "Olive, this isn't what you want to do. Not really. As you know, Triangle is in a very tight spot financially right now. We can't afford to go wasting yards and yards of film on something shot by a woman who thinks she *might* be interested in directing."

"I'll make this film better."

"It takes hard work. It takes planning. You have to get in the thick of it all, get your hands dirty, and mentally you have to stay about ten steps ahead of the others."

"I can do it, Mr. Davis."

"Why do you think that?"

"I watch everything they do, that's why. I memorize it. I ask questions. I've gotten Buddy to show me how to work the Pathé, and on my last picture, I had Clyde Cook teach me how to run a Bell & Howell camera too. I love moviemaking, sir, the behind-the-scenes part as well as the acting. I want to learn all there is to know about it. I have ideas for techniques and shots. I don't understand why this is such a difficult decision for you, but it appears to be because I'm a woman. You don't know how angry that makes me."

I arched an eyebrow at him.

He steepled his fingers under his chin, watching me. When I finished, he sat quietly for a minute before speaking.

"You know, Olive, when we brought you on at Triangle, I daresay we were thinking only of how much an ex-Follies girl could up our prestige. Let's cut the crap. You're a beautiful girl, and it's good you're making movies for us, not someone else."

"And?"

"I'm seeing you in a new light right now. We all know you ask a lot of blasted questions, and you can be a giant pain in the ass. But I like your curiosity. I see this little petition project of yours took a lot of work. So maybe you're not just a pretty face. Let's say you're allowed to direct a scene or two . . ."

My grin grew wider and wider as he spoke.

"*If* you do, we need some rules."

"Anything!" I said.

"Mr. Hillyer lays down the rules. He is the master of that set, and you defer to him on everything."

I nodded until my head nearly bounced off my neck. It would take some doing, since I couldn't stand Hillyer, but in this case I'd do whatever it took.

"He picks the shots you do, and he has veto power to reshoot them if they stink."

"Of course!"

He chuckled and shook his head.

"All right, Olive. Good luck. Here." He scratched a signature onto the bottom of the page and shoved my petition across the desk at me.

I swept out of my chair, grabbing him in a huge bear hug and folding the paper into my bag. Then I slipped out of his office and sped back to the foothills where we'd been shooting.

Screeching to a stop in the dust of the small valley where they'd set up, I grabbed my signed petition and skipped over to Mr. Hillyer and Buddy, who was adjusting the camera.

"He said yes!" I said, grabbing Buddy and dancing a little jig with him.

Hillyer's mouth fell open.

"Better close that mouth," I said, "Lotta flies out here."

"Oh God, what have I done?" he said, turning pale. "I honestly didn't think he'd take you seriously." He sat down hard, obviously stunned.

"It'll be fun," I said. "When can I start? Mr. Davis said you get to pick the scenes, Mr. Hillyer."

"Scenes? He said you could do more than one?"

"Of course," I said.

"I'm sunk in this town," he said, holding his head in his hands. "I am so finished."

CHAPTER TWENTY-SIX

THE HILLS OUTSIDE LOS ANGELES, *the next day*

"These damned cracker boxes," Buddy grumbled, pulling the camera apart for the fourth time. "They're the worst of the bunch. Light, but not very dependable." He wrapped the black electricians' tape around and around the mechanism, then snipped it with a quick one-handed motion of his pocketknife.

The sweat poured off me. When I needed some shade, I'd go stand under a gnarled fig tree. I'd taken to directing like a pro, after a little guidance from Buddy and Mr. Hillyer. They'd taught me a few tricks of the trade they knew, like how to use the tape to fix up the Pathé when it gave us fits, and what to do when the film made that dreadful crunching noise.

Effie brought me some water every few minutes so I didn't pass out.

Once Buddy got the camera working, I hoisted the megaphone and waited for the slate boy to chalk the take.

"Okay! Places, everybody!" I let them all get settled, then yelled, "Ready? Action!"

At my signal, all hell broke loose. Everyone raced for their automobiles. *An Even Break* told the story of Claire and

Jimmy, who had big plans for Jimmy's invention. But the evil Harding Brothers wanted to steal the patent and had to be stopped. In the end, Claire and Jimmy managed to foil the Hardings, save Jimmy's patent, and ignite their love affair. Scrubbing the Hardings' plot required one of Hollywood's favorite scenes—the car chase.

Halfway through the scene, as I gestured and yelled commands to everyone, I happened to look down.

The reptile was only a yard away. When he rattled his tail at me, I let out a scream that could have melted steel.

"Snaaaaaaaake!"

I shot down that hill like a 40-centimeter shell and didn't take a gander back until I was in the arroyo and heard the gun. Mr. Hillyer stood over the thing, pointing his Smith & Wesson at it.

After I slogged back up the hill, I peppered him with questions, as usual.

"Did it bite me?" I said, checking for red spots or punctures. "Where the hell did it come from?"

"He must have been camped out in that hollow log, and we disturbed his nap," Buddy said.

"Do you think there are any more?"

"We'll check. You're okay. They don't like us any more than we like them. You got lucky this time." He winked.

"Was the scene spoiled?" I said, checking the camera to see if it had suffered any damage. It was fine. Which led me to my last embarrassing question for Mr. Hillyer: "Will you finish directing the scene?"

The cast tittered. They'd all gathered to watch the snake take one to the gizzard. Do snakes have gizzards? I still don't know.

Hillyer finished the directing, but everyone who saw my scenes said I'd done a marvelous job.

That experience satisfied my lust for directing temporarily. I decided to ask Mr. Hillyer another favor but approached him early in the morning before shooting began. He was sitting with Buddy, having his morning coffee and going over their notes.

"Mr. Hillyer, can I ask you a question?"

His eye roll told me everything I needed to know. "Another one? Your last question may end up being the death of my career. What is it now?" He pasted on a pleasant face, but I know a fake smile when I see one.

"I'd like to go scout some locations."

His eyebrows headed for the hills. "That's all? Is directing a bit too much for you now?" He and Buddy snickered. I wanted to punch them both for patronizing me.

"I'm sure I'll want to do more later. *Interior* shots."

"Fine. We'll shoot around you today." I'm sure he was thinking how nice it would be to have me gone for a few hours.

It was a pleasant hike at first. But after an hour or two, I turned my ankle in a rodent hole, hoping to God I hadn't sprained it out there all by myself. The sun baked me like a sheet cake, but I'd brought a piece of paper and wrote determined notes on it with a fountain pen I'd shoved in my skirt pocket. No telling if I'd be able to find my way back to those places a second time, but I scribbled things like "big pink manzanita, three cactus in a row, huge rock in foreground."

Dazed from the heat, I must have made a complete circle, because I think I passed the same buckeye tree four times. All the while, I kept my eyes peeled for snakes. Buddy, who carried a sidearm for protection from syndicate thugs, had given it to me for my expedition.

"Now, for God's sake, don't blow your foot off," he'd warned as he set up some empty Coca-Cola bottles on a fence and shown me how to shoot.

In the late afternoon, I found a perfect pond surrounded by pepper trees and craggy stones. I framed the scenery with my hands, changing the perspective as I'd seen the directors do. Wanting to get closer to the water, I approached the bank, my shoes making a *sklorp sklorp* noise as I slogged through the thick mud. As one slipped off my foot, I lost my balance and tumbled backward, choking and spitting out brackish water. That was it. I was *done* scouting.

"Where ya been, Ollie?" asked Stanley Reed, one of the stuntmen, when I finally trudged back to the set that evening. I was soaked to the skin. The simple dress that had seemed so practical that morning clung to me in wet clumps, my hair was damp and tangled, and I was covered in bug bites. Not only that, but the side of my left foot now had a big throbbing blister. My face was sunburned too.

"Wouldn't you like to know," I grumbled.

"Been swimming, have you?"

I stuck my tongue out at him.

"Lambert! Ollie's here!" somebody else yelled.

"Ollie, where the bloody hell have you been?" Charles Gunn asked me. I sat down in my chair and finger-combed my hair, trying to work out the knots. Seeing me in such a pitiful condition, Effie brought me a robe.

"I'ma get you a clean dress, Miss Olive. When we get home I'll run you a nice hot bath too."

"Effie, you're a dear." I closed my eyes.

"And a nice cuppa tea comin' up."

When Mr. Hillyer saw me, he doubled over laughing, a braying I found especially irritating just then. He and Buddy laughed their asses off until they saw the murderous glare I was giving them.

"Hey! It's Annette Kellerman!" Buddy said.

"What happened?" Mr. Hillyer said.

"I got a little too close to the banks of a lake," I said. "I did find some gorgeous spots, though. I'll show you tomorrow."

"You wanna tell her or should I?" Buddy said.

"Tell me what?"

"Effie went to check on Chow about two hours ago, and he's not in his spot. We all called and called, but he hasn't come out."

"Nooooo!" He must have gotten frightened when I hadn't returned right away. He usually sat under my chair on the set, waiting for me to give him chin scratches and belly rubs.

I ran to inspect some of his other favorite places: under the tablecloth where the food was set out beside a lemon tree; in the shade from Charles's Packard, where Chow adjusted his position throughout the afternoon according to the angle of the sun; or in my co-star Maggie Thompson's lap. Maggie was a sucker for dogs and teased me that one day she was going to take him for her own. I couldn't believe she might actually have done it.

"Chow!" I shouted, "Chow Chow! Come!" I was in tears by nightfall, thinking he'd been eaten by a cougar or a bear. Each new threat I imagined brought on a fresh wave of tears.

Trying to save my ravaged complexion, Effie moistened a

rag and covered my face with it. Maggie had brought three cucumbers for a snack and let me have a couple slices to put on my eyes. After that, Effie applied a thick mask of Ingram's Milkweed Cream to help the sunburn. The company was paying me a nice little sum to put my picture on the ads and had given me a year's supply, so I figured I might as well use the stuff. The combination finally helped the swelling and redness go down.

It's hard to be happy on film when your heart is breaking inside. The next day, my emoting was shit, and I knew it. For once, Hillyer took it easy on me, knowing it was all a side effect of grief for my baby. After about an hour of shooting, I heard grumbling from behind the camera.

"Cut! Cut! Dog in the shot!"

Dog?

"Chow!" I squealed, catching a glimpse of golden fur from behind Maggie's skirt. His little tail wagged furiously as he limped over to me. I picked him up and checked him over. He was coated in sticker burrs, his hair matted and clumped around each one. That also turned out to be the source of his limp. I pulled one out from between his paw pads.

"Where the dickens have you been? You're filthy!"

He gave my nose a happy lick, and all was forgiven. I squeezed him tighter than I ever had.

"I guess we both had some exploring to do, huh?"

CHAPTER TWENTY-SEVEN

SET OF *INDISCREET CORINNE*, CULVER CITY, CALIFORNIA, *August 1917*

"Ollie, this is your director, John Francis Dillon."

The man before me was tanned as brown as a hickory nut and smelled of old leather and Turkish tobacco. He wore a loose-fitting shirt, without the stiff collar still favored in the east. I now knew that for shooting outdoors, comfort took priority over everything else.

The ten-gallon hat Mr. Dillon was wearing dwarfed his head but provided a nice wide brim with some shade from the glare. And like the other crew members, he'd tucked his trousers into his dusty boots.

When I'd first arrived in Hollywood and asked Jack why so many of the directors tucked their pants into their boots, he must have thought I'd been knocked in the head with something heavy.

"Snakes," he said, like it was the most natural thing in the world. And now after my experience directing, I knew for myself that a good pair of boots was the most important fashion accessory in Hollywood.

Dillon and I sized each other up, smiling the whole time.

"Nice to meet you, Mr. Dillon," I finally said.

"Charmed, Olive." He tipped his hat.

"Dillon. That sounds Irish."

"Indeed it is. County Mayo."

"Well, what do you know? My family are Duffys. From Ulster."

"I'll be. We'll have to have a drink later and get acquainted."

"That's a brilliant idea."

"Olive, Mr. Dillon directs quite a few of our films at Triangle," Mr. Underwood said. "He's fair, he's reasonable, and he's one of the hardest-working fellows on this lot."

Dillon smiled over at him.

"But," Underwood said, pausing for effect, "Don't let that fool you into thinking that working with him will be some sort of picnic. Like I said, 'hardworking.'"

As if to illustrate that, Mr. Dillon yanked a handkerchief out of his pocket and mopped the sweat off his forehead.

"Let's get going," he said.

And just like that, we were friends. He was easy to take direction from, and we had a great time working together. He knew just what to say to get a good performance out of me. And before long we were going out for drinks after work with the rest of the cast like we'd known each other our whole lives. That was a good thing, since the Triangle stable was shrinking more every day. All the best-known talent was gone. From sitting on my can doing nothing when I first arrived, I'd been churning out a film a month. Very few others could–only Alma Rubens and me.

I let Mr. Dillon know that John Francis was a good Irish name, but that it was entirely too long a name to be saddled with and I already had one Jack in my life, so I was going to call him J.F. He was fine with that. Until I battered him with questions just like I did everyone else.

"J.F., why do we have to put all the equipment away when we break for lunch? It's an awful waste of time if we're just going to pull it out again later."

"In case anyone from the syndicate decides to stop by," he said, lighting a cigarette and leaning over to give me a light too. With his cigarette in hand, he pointed to the tripods and Pathés set up a few feet away. "All it would take is one clear photo of those cameras, and Triangle could be in scalding hot water." He paused, then muttered under his breath, "As if they're not already."

It made perfect sense.

"And all the initials on the chalkboards? What are those for?"

"For this one," he said, grabbing a board we'd been using, "it's OT EL MGC PS GC XL 25 4.5. These are the initials of the two people in the scene, you and George. See? OT for Olive Thomas and GC for George Chesebro. The other notations are all abbreviations too. Olive Thomas enters left, meets George Chesebro, plays the scene, then George Chesebro exits left. It's twenty-five feet of film, and it's shot at f.45. Does that help clear things up a little?"

"It's crystal! Thanks, J.F."

A month later, I was lounging on the set of *Betty Takes a Hand*, thinking of the next question I could ask him, when I glimpsed an older woman with a studio hand named Eugene.

She was oh so dignified, wearing expensive clothing and jewels, her hair wrapped in a topknot. I'd seen her visiting the studio before. Eugene brought her over, introducing her as

Miss Edith Hague.

"Ollie, Miss Hague asked me one or two questions I can't answer. Could you help?"

"Of course," I said, turning in my seat.

"Miss Thomas," Miss Hague said, focusing her lorgnette on the glasses sitting on a table for the thirsty dancers. "What is everyone drinking?"

"Champagne," I said.

"Is that so? Tell me more," she said, now eyeing me through the tiny lens.

I explained the scene to her, and she retreated. A short while later, Mr. Davis summoned me to his office.

"Olive, what did you tell that Hague woman the cast members were drinking?" he asked.

"Champagne, of course."

His ears glowed red, and he banged his fist on the desk. "Jesus! Do you have to tell everyone every single thing you know? She's a Prohibitionist! Now she's accusing us of plying the actors with intoxicating liquor! For God's sake, Olive, show some restraint, would you? What if she'd been with the syndicate or something? Sometimes a closed mouth is a girl's very best friend. She was just in my office threatening to contact the papers! With all I'm dealing with right now, I don't need the Women's Christian Temperance Union breathing down our necks too."

"Hell's bells," I said. "I didn't mean *we* were drinking booze. I was talking about the characters in the scene. I'm sorry Mr. Davis, I didn't realize. I'll fix everything, I promise!"

Before he could protest, I hurried back to Miss Hague and saw her deep in conversation with George Chesebro. I had to interrupt. This was important.

"Miss Hague, I'm terribly sorry, but I've given you the wrong impression about Triangle. Please come with me and I'll show you what I really meant. I'll even give you a sip."

At the word "sip," she paled. She shook her head stubbornly, positive I was tempting her to consume demon alcohol. I convinced her with the sweetest words, a smile, and a giggle or two. Cautiously, she allowed me to lead her back to the table full of glasses. When she was settled in a chair, I handed her a flute full of the stuff. It bubbled and fizzed and reeked of moral decay. She shook her head over and over until I wanted to scream at her to pull the giant stick from her ass.

"It's not really booze!" I whispered at last, like we were the only ones in on the big secret.

Miss Hague cocked an eyebrow. "Truly?"

"Cross my heart," I said, finally getting her to take the glass from me. At last she took a little nip, peering around in case anyone might be watching.

"Why, it tastes like cider!" she said, delighted at the revelation.

"Of course it does," I said. "It's sparkling apple juice. Tomorrow, if you come back, we'll have burgundy strawberry pop or Cook's Imperial lemon phosphate. See? We don't really drink. It's all acting."

Having poured one for myself, I raised it in a toast, and Miss Hague clinked glasses with me, laughing at how silly she'd been. We finished our drinks, and I took her on a tour of the lot.

"Miss Thomas, I sincerely apologize for my earlier behavior, jumping to conclusions. I'll certainly let Mr. Davis know he has no worries from my organization or from me. You're so charming. I believe Triangle has quite a discovery in you."

I could have told her that myself, the idiot.

CHAPTER TWENTY-EIGHT

BARON LONG'S WATTS TAVERN, LOS ANGELES,
September 9, 1917

"Jack, give me the shaker, will you, darling?"

He handed it to me after setting his cigarette in the ashtray. We were downing orange blossoms with J.F. and Catherine Walker, who was a wardrobe lady for Triangle. Coincidentally, she was also J.F.'s mistress.

"Ollie, have you heard the latest?" she said, lighting my cigarette.

"No, what?"

"Mr. Ince has disposed of all his Triangle holdings. He's done. Completely gone. Paramount and Artcraft will distribute the pictures from here on out." She sat, watching my reaction. Honestly, I wasn't sure what it all meant. I only knew our jobs weren't long for this world.

The Watts Tavern was out in the middle of nowhere, on 108th and Central. Lottie loved the place.

"You'll love the band, Ollie," she'd said. "Reb Spikes and his something-or-others. You simply *must* go dancing there."

I poured another drink, with difficulty, since my cigarette

holder kept shifting between my fingers and I was already full of more juice than the chair at Sing Sing.

"I'll be right back," Jack said.

"Jesus, you just went to the toilet ten minutes ago. Do I need to take you to a doctor?"

"The Count is a few booths away," he whispered.

I couldn't complain about Jack's habits tonight, since I was as high as the Wright Brothers myself. A toot of cocaine earlier had helped me stay alert, and now we were both itching for a fight.

J.F. kept whispering funny things in my ear, and I could see Jack's jaw tightening up. Ever since *Indiscreet Corinne*, he'd been convinced we'd slept together. I needed some air.

The Count saw Jack approaching and patted the seat next to him. They completed the standard negotiations, and after visiting the men's room, Jack returned in a far better mood than when he'd left.

Obviously impatient, our bartender reminded us it was time to close our tab. We paid our bill, and Jack went to get the car. Catherine and I caught up on more gossip while we waited. Mostly about the war, and what everyone in Hollywood was doing about it.

"Have you seen the Lasky Home Guard?" she asked. "It's so ridiculous, Ollie. They take prop rifles and uniforms and parade down Hollywood Boulevard on Thursday nights. As if that will keep us safe from the Hun."

As we stood between the potted palms, I saw a portly older couple, also in their evening duds, leaving the club. How had I missed them?

"Catherine, isn't that the Gordons over there?"

She peered over at them. "It sure is. We should say hello."

Mr. Gordon had been a still photographer for Triangle. The studios were throwing massive amounts of time and money into stills. The fans wanted to see shots of their favorite stars in action, and *Photoplay* and *Motion Picture Magazine* were willing to pay large sums for those pictures. He'd seen the writing on the wall and moved on to Fox.

"Everett, Lilah, how are you?" I said.

Lilah raised her cigarette in greeting. "Perfect. You? We've just been having a drink. Everett's grabbing us a cab home."

"Don't do that," I said. "We haven't seen you in weeks. We're all going to Jack's for another drink. He's bringing the car."

"Are you sure we'll all fit?"

"Sure. It's a touring car," I answered.

Jack pulled the Pierce-Arrow to the curb in front of the club. It was a tight squeeze, but we all climbed in, and he put the car in gear.

As we neared the intersection of Cahuenga and Hollywood Boulevard, Jack flew past the Hollywood National Bank and paused for a rolling stop, not noticing the truck barreling down on us from the east. He broadsided the truck, and both of the vehicles went careering off the road, we women all screaming from the backseat.

Jack let out an agonized cry. We almost flipped, but somehow he retained control. The Pierce skidded across the intersection and came to rest with its front wheels up on the curb, cattywampus from the light, the rear passenger-side quarter panel smashed in by a telephone pole.

We couldn't open that door from the impact, so I crawled out through the driver's side and assisted Lilah and Catherine out the same way. J.F. and Everett also managed to squeeze out and sat Jack down on the curb while they went to check on the truck driver. Jack and Everett were both cut. J.F. was fine.

Sometime later, J.F. returned, shaking his head. "It's not good, Jack. I had to help him build a splint for his hand out of some junk he had in the cab. I think it's broken. He's got some pretty good cuts, and I think he has a concussion. Everett's still with him to make sure he doesn't pass out. The windshield's busted too, so there's glass all over."

We saw a police car approaching from the west. It pulled to a stop at the curb, and the cop got out. He was a burly, blond fellow with no neck—a big Swede—the kind it would be dangerous to cross. I doubted our movie business status would help us either. The local police hated "movies," the film people who, in their eyes, had brought Hollywood to this new low.

"Shit," J.F. whispered.

"Evening, everyone, I'm Officer Carlson," the policeman said, doffing his hat to us ladies, who were clustered next to the damaged vehicle. We nodded at him.

"Evening, officer," J.F. said, taking charge.

"Who can tell me what happened?" Carlson pulled a paper pad and a pencil out of his pocket and took notes about the accident.

Everett had assisted the truck driver over to where the rest of us stood. The front of his overalls was spangled with tiny bits of broken glass and blood.

"Yeah, I can," the man said.

"Could I have your name, sir?" Officer Carlson asked him.

"Wilbur Baker, officer. I'm driving a load of vegetables down to Long Beach." He took out a ragged handkerchief and mopped at the blood on his face.

"Could I get your version of the events, sir?"

"I was just moseying along in the truck"—he pointed at the vehicle across the road—"and this fella done come out of nowhere—BAM!" Jack and I jumped and looked nervously at each other.

The policeman surveyed the intersection and turned to us. "And who was driving the sedan?"

"I was," Jack admitted. The cop took a few steps toward him. When he got closer, his nose perked up.

"Sir, you smell like you just stepped out of a distillery. I'm not going to ask you if you've been drinking because I can tell you have, and I don't want you to lie to me. Do you realize how dangerous it can be to drive in your condition, Mister . . ."

"Pickford," Jack answered, with all the confidence he'd developed from using his name like a suit of armor. He didn't see why anything should change now.

"Pickford? Jack Pickford the actor?"

"Yes sir, that's me," Jack said, smiling. The truck driver appeared disgusted that the accident might be shrugged off by a cop who enjoyed flickers.

"That's too bad," the officer said, making more notes on his pad.

"Why's that?" Jack said.

"Well, it will be a terrible reflection on your sister when the papers learn how I had to drag you to jail this evening. Please put your hands together, Mr. Pickford. I'm placing you under arrest."

"For what?" Jack protested.

"Reckless endangerment, sir."

The bracelets clinked as he locked them over Jack's wrists. I held my head in my hands, dreading the call to Mary and hoping the cop couldn't tell he'd had anything besides gin.

We spent the rest of the wee hours at the police station. After taking their statements, the police released Lilah and Everett. Then they took the cab home they should have caught hours before. When I stopped pacing and collapsed into a hard wooden chair, Catherine held my hand and tried to comfort me. J.F. negotiated with the police.

Jack was eventually released on his own recognizance and would have to appear in court later. "They took my cigarettes," he grumbled. I was grateful they hadn't confiscated anything else, like a small package from his pocket. He must have consumed all of it in the toilet.

I tiptoed around him for the next few days as he shopped the ads and the dealers for a new car. He decided on a Stutz.

Mary made everything disappear, like magic. And do you know? That truck driver never had to worry about transporting vegetables ever again.

CHAPTER TWENTY-NINE

LIMOUSINE LIFE SET, CULVER CITY, CALIFORNIA, *October 1917*

Ever been scared out of your wits? I mean genuinely had the piss frightened out of you? But loved it just the same and screamed for more? That was filming *Limousine Life*. Before this, the most excitement I'd seen was riding the Drop-the-Dip at Coney Island with Ed Wynn, Marcie, and her husband. Never having been on a roller coaster before, I didn't know what to expect. By the end of the ride, I was squealing and begging to ride it again and again.

I loved cars and I loved speeding. Unfortunately, my driving record reflected this. Tickets, dents, and more tickets. But I loved that in my next flicker, I got to speed on camera.

This was one of those perfect California mornings that the companies still filming in the east would have killed for. The golden light was perfect, and the breeze whispered through the eucalyptus trees. Since he didn't think I'd be able to pull off my big scene, driving a car into a fence, J.F. had brought in three limousines for it. After all, he'd heard about my driving record, just like everyone else in town.

In *Limousine Life*, my character Minnie Wills, the belle of Three Oaks, Iowa, traveled to Chicago, and though she was warned by her sweetheart at home about the cads in the big city, she took up with a roué by the name of Moncure Kelts. Lee Phelps played Moncure, and he saw his main job as making me giggle at the worst times, costing us a mint in linear feet of film. We were supposed to be getting romantic when I destroyed the fence.

"Places, everyone!" J.F. said.

The slate boy scribbled a messy number on his board and yawned as he clacked the halves together.

"*Limousine Life*. Take one."

"Action!"

I started up the old girl and gave her a little rev before letting out the clutch too fast. We lurched forward and stopped. Lee winced.

"What?" I said.

"Nothing," he muttered.

"Eyes this way, Ollie!" J.F. called. Then, realizing the shot was a dud, he said, "Cut!"

"Easy does it," Lee said. "Don't be impatient, just do everything slowly and deliberately."

The makeup mistress poked her head in the car window. "You forget who you're talking to," she said, chuckling. She gave me a quick buff with the powder puff before retreating to the sidelines, along with the rest of the crew.

"Places . . ." J.F. said. Everyone took their marks.

"*Limousine Life*. Take two," said the slate boy after chalking the new number on the board.

"Action!" said J.F.

"Slowly and deliberately . . ." I whispered. Letting out the clutch, I pressed more intently on the gas. As I got more confident, we were able to concentrate on the scene. The cameramen followed alongside in a truck, and J.F. stood in the bed of it, calling commands through the megaphone as he held on for dear life.

"Remember to smile, Ollie! Things are going swimmingly! Kelts is nothing like you thought he'd be. Quite a fellow, not a scoundrel at all! Let him cuddle you a bit. That's it! Let me see that coquettish expression! Stay in character. You're a flirt, you're enjoying a day out, and you're loving the drive. Nice!"

No sooner were the words out of his mouth than Lee nuzzled my ear in the most perfect way as the road forked. Closing my eyes for a fraction of a second, I imagined it was Jack next to me and thought of what we usually did when we were together. It was only the slightest twitch at the wheel. But it was enough to send us off course and directly into the back of a wagon carting barrels of beer toward Los Angeles.

"Hell's bells!" I said, trying to swerve, but I only succeeded in wedging us directly under the wagon, to the savage sound of ripping metal. At least I got us stopped before we were completely swallowed by the rear of the thing. The seals popped, and beer frothed all over the rear of the wagon and the hood of the car. An Irishman with a mug could have made short work of the mess, but as it was the limo now reeked of hops.

In his terror, the driver stared at us like he'd been violated. The horse had squealed and leaped forward, but now he turned his head and stood skittishly, waiting for directions. It took five men to dislodge the auto and two more to negotiate with the driver for the value of his cargo. When they did get us unstuck, we were minus a radiator.

J.F. sighed when he saw the first limousine limping away

toward a mechanic's place with some help from the crew. Lee and I had already settled ourselves in the front seat of the replacement when J.F. approached us.

Running a hand through his hair, he leaned over the driver's side door at me. "Ollie, you know we have a job to do. This is an easy scene, and driving is not as difficult as you seem to think it is. You put your foot on the gas pedal and use that stick when you want to go faster, you use that brake pedal to slow down, and you use this steering wheel to go the direction you want. Sounds simple, right?"

"Of course."

"Good. For this take, I'd like you to remember that Triangle has no budget for more limousines. I had a hard enough time trying to find these. I need for you to make this work, or Mr. Davis will use my guts for guitar strings. I am the director, and I am the one who's responsible if you mess this up. Do we understand each other?"

I nodded with new determination, placing my hands in their sporty driving gloves firmly on the wheel. Firing up the limousine once more, I pulled away from J.F. as he crossed himself and mouthed a small prayer.

"Places!" he called.

"*Limousine Life*. Take three," the slate boy mumbled after scribbling another chalk number onto the board.

"Action!"

As a group, the observers crowded in behind me as the Cadillac moved forward. Everyone wanted the best view they could get of the carnage they were sure was going to occur.

Up in the truck alongside, J.F. tried a calmer approach, treating me like a temperamental filly that might buck any minute.

"Okay, Ollie, steady as she goes. You're doing great! Now I want you to accelerate a bit, so don't go crazy. Just a little faster."

"Jesus H. Christ," I heard from the passenger seat.

"Now what?" I said, eyes forward and accelerating just like J.F. wanted.

"We've got company, that's what."

"I know. J.F.'s right there."

"Now check behind him."

Over my left shoulder, I saw a copper gesturing at us to pull over. J.F. saw him too, and I could see him mouthing curses before hollering a furious "Cu-u-u-u-t!"

I steered the limo to a rutted spot near a shallow ditch and looked up innocently at the policeman when he strolled over to my window.

"Afternoon ma'am. I'm Officer Mueller."

"Yes, officer?"

"Miss, did you notice how fast you were going?"

"Yes, sir. But I was under orders to go a little faster."

"Orders?"

"Yes. That's my director." I gestured to J.F. a few yards away.

"Your what?"

J.F. had gotten the driver of the truck to brake at last, and he had climbed down from the bed and was tramping toward us, his megaphone at half-mast. It was obvious he was trying to keep a lid on his temper at the cop for ruining this take.

"He's our director, sir," Lee cut in. "We're making a flicker, officer."

"You're movies?"

"Yes, sir," we said together.

"So you're filming a flicker?" the cop asked J.F. when he

stomped up.

"Yes, officer. I apologize if we broke any traffic laws, but Olive isn't a great driver, and I had to work with what I had."

"Thanks for the vote of confidence, J.F.," I said. I smiled up at the cop.

"Couldn't you have someone else pilot the vehicle if she isn't a good driver?" Officer Mueller said.

"No sir, we can't. Olive's character is the one who needs to be driving in this scene, you see. We had hoped it wouldn't be as much trouble since we were out of downtown. The traffic in Culver City isn't as bad."

"You got a point," Mueller said, scratching his head with his pencil. Then it evidently dawned on him. "Olive? Say, are you Olive Thomas?"

"I sure am," I said with a smile.

"Whaddya know? Olive Thomas! My wife loved you in *Madcap Madge*."

"We'd be mighty grateful if you could just ticket us or whatever you need to do so we can continue shooting, sir," J. F. said. "The daylight is very important to our schedule."

"Tell you what," Mueller said. "You let me stay and watch, and I'll forget all about this."

"Honestly?" I piped up.

"Sure. I've always wondered how these things work. The wife won't believe it. Which flicker is it?"

"It's called *Limousine Life*," I said. "Here." I took his ticket pad and autographed it in broad strokes across the top page. He beamed at me before retreating to the side-lines. J.F. took his place in the truck bed once again. Putting the Cadillac in gear, I reversed it away from the culvert and kept going until J.F. told me to stop.

"Take four," said the slate boy. *Clack*.

"And . . . action!"

This time, I let out the clutch with precision, keeping my foot steady on the gas. The truck followed alongside.

J.F. resumed his narration through the megaphone. "Doing good, Ollie, slow . . . steady . . . we're coming up to the fence, so get ready. Now approach it from the left . . . steady . . . and . . .VEER!"

I jerked the steering wheel, shattering the fence and creating a mass of splintered white matchsticks in my wake. The momentum carried us a couple more yards until at last I downshifted and braked. The Cadillac came to rest in a cow pasture, only a foot from a Holstein heifer. Her big brown eyes followed me for a second, then she resumed chewing her cud.

"Cut!"

"I coulda turned you into steak, you know. Just a few more feet . . ." I said. I climbed out and gave her a slap on the rump. At the applause from my impromptu audience, I took an elaborate bow as J.F. laughed and shook his head.

CHAPTER THIRTY

OCEAN PARK, SANTA MONICA, CALIFORNIA,
November 25, 1917

"OLLIE GETTING SHIPPED OUT STOP WAS HOPING TO SEE YOU BEFORE I LEAVE STOP ANY WAY YOU COULD CATCH TRAIN EAST EARLIER STOP LOVE JIM"

Here I was in a tent overlooking the ocean, and Western Union had handed me this awful telegram. It seemed strange to be looking at the Ship Inn across the water as I read the news.

The organizers for the Eagles festival had built a huge platform near the bath house and covered it with bunting and streamers. The bath house itself was a work of art—a Far-Eastern-looking thing with domes and minarets and rounded windows and arches. Each tower flew its own individual stars and stripes.

The audience was gathering, the hum of their conversation competing with the noise of the waves. Then the orchestra struck up a tune, "If the Girlies Could Be Soldiers," and a cheer rose from the crowd.

"Hell's bells," I said, sinking onto a box full of bond forms. I was dressed as Liberty, in a fancy red, white, and blue costume.

"Ollie, what is it?" My co-star glanced up from his *Santa Monica Herald*. I didn't even remember his name, fer crying out loud. I'd been at this liberty bond thing for weeks.

"Dammit. My older brother's getting sent overseas. He has a wife and a little boy. Can't they find some single boys who can go instead?"

"There is a war on, you know. You said he signed up."

"It's already been hard enough to plan my visit east for the holidays, between the crazy shooting schedules and the war. I'd planned on spending a few weeks in Pennsylvania for Christmas, then on to New York to see Jack. He's shooting *Jack and Jill* there. Now with all this extra publicity Davis wants us to do, I can't get out of these events. Too many people are depending on me."

"Did you get the same song and dance I did? That it's something your public wants? Seeing their sweetheart being all-American and patriotic?"

I nodded, clutching the wire in disbelief. War rallies, bond drives, personal fundraising appearances . . . they all had to be done. Plus, nearly all the other talent at Triangle was gone. Alma and I were the only ones keeping things afloat until the boat sank altogether.

"They couldn't have waited one more week until I was home? I just want to say goodbye to him."

"How about letting the papers know?" he said.

"What would that do?"

"You're a celebrity, Ollie. Use it to your advantage. Let them know how hard you're working to drum up support for the war effort, and how cruel it is that your beloved brother has to go just before your arrival in the east. This is the thanks you get?"

"That's crafty," I said.

"We're stars," he said. "Celebrity provides certain fringe benefits."

Sure enough, he was right. I sent a telegram to Jim, telling him to hold off as long as he could, letting me take the consequences. In the end, I didn't have to worry. His departure was postponed a few weeks—long enough for me to get in and Jack to arrive from New York so we could spend the holidays with everyone.

Jack's train arrived an hour after mine. Harry came to pick us up at the McKees Rocks depot. He proudly showed off the Model T he and Mamma had purchased, and we oohed and aahed. We'd had a porter collect our trunks, so he loaded them wherever they fit.

Instead of taking us straight to the house, Harry decided to show Jack the sights, such as they were.

"That's the Enterprise Hotel," he'd say, or "That's the hospital sitting up on the hill. That's the Norwood Pavilion. Lotsa dances there." And a few minutes later, "There's the O'Donovan Bridge. And there's the P & LE yard. That's where I work."

Jack was bored the entire time, casually smoking his cigarette and then tossing it out of the car near the river. We pulled up in front of the house, and even through the snow the improvement was obvious. With the extra cash, Harry had gotten the place painted. It was now a cheery pale blue with a shiny red door, and the front step that had been crumbling for years had been repaired.

Harry loosened the straps holding the trunks fast to the rear of the Ford, and he and Jack each grabbed a handle to bring one inside. They made another trip and got the second one.

Inside, a fire snapped cheerily in the hearth, and the mantel was lined with evergreen boughs. Mamma was in the middle of her weekly baking. I could smell meat too, sure it was pot roast. The new dining room suite was set for dinner with an ironed tablecloth and new china in an ivy pattern.

"Ollie!" she cried, pausing in her dough rolling. She turned and gathered me in a huge hug. Harriett stood on a stool at the counter, covered in flour, holding a cookie cutter, which she was intently pressing into some dough. When she saw me, she squealed and ran forward, grabbing my leg.

"How are you, Mamma?" I said, wrapping my arm around Harriett's shoulders. Mamma had recently gotten over the flu, but her color was good. I think it was the heat from the stove.

"Couldn't be better," she said, wiping her hands on her apron.

"Mamma, this is Jack."

He stepped out from behind me, holding his hat in his hands.

She gave him a warm smile, then folded him in her arms. "Welcome, Jack. We're happy you're here."

"Nice to meet you, Mrs. Van Kirk." He appeared shocked at the hug. It wasn't surprising, considering most of the women in his life except Lottie were ice queens. He stood, still as a scarecrow, making no move to return the gesture.

"Ollie, I've put you two in Harriett's room, and she's in with us," Mamma said, giving no sign she'd sensed Jack's discomfort at us sharing a room with my half sister's things. "I'll have dinner ready in an hour or two."

Jim and Margaret arrived before dinner, bringing another pie. Jimmie ran to hug me too, and climbed up on my lap, playing with the beads on my dress. Conversation before dinner was stilted and awkward. Jack answered in monosyllables, quite unlike his usual chatty self.

"These zeppelins and their air raids . . . it's up to us to take care of them now that we're in it," Harry said. "Ernie Twitchell told me he read about some attack they made in September. Huge fleet headed to London. Tried to attack the city."

For once, I was more interested in Harry than Jack. "What happened?" I said.

"The Brits counterattacked, of course. Harassed them for hours. Wouldn't let up. They won't be able to keep it up forever, though. They need our help. That's why it's so important that Jim and all the men like him go over."

Jim acknowledged the compliment with a shy smile and a nod. Margaret patted his hand and looked over proudly, but with tears in her eyes.

Dinner was the roast with turnips and yeast rolls, and mincemeat pie for dessert. The top of the pie was covered with Harriett's cookie cutter designs. Pot roast was Harry's favorite Sunday evening dinner, and it had always been one of mine too. Jack picked at his, even though I kicked him under the table, letting him know he was being rude. As a final slap in the face to me, he refused Harry's offer of an after-dinner whiskey with him and Jim. He'd never refused a drink, ever. He sulked in our room instead, stretched full-length on the bed. I slipped in after helping Mamma with the dishes.

"What is wrong with you?"

"I want to go home."

"One night with my family and you want to leave?"

"You didn't even last a few hours at Mary's," he joked.

"Don't you dare compare my family to your mother the hydra, who called me a slut to my face, or your high-and-mighty sister who expects everyone to bow and scrape to her. My family are decent human beings, and they've been nothing but kind to you since you got here."

He rolled over, pushing Harriett's dolls out of his way. I heard a sharp crack and looked over. The one she'd named Lucretia lay on the floor, her china face cracked and broken beyond repair.

"Jack, you've ruined it!" I held the doll up for him to see.

He shrugged. "Buy her another."

"I can't just 'buy her another.' She loves this doll. How could you be so careless?"

But he had closed his eyes, and in a few minutes he was snoring.

On Christmas, he sat near the tree, drinking nog with us and smoking like a fiend. We were all still worried sick about Jim, but Mamma and Margaret tried to make everything special for the children.

I'd come laden with gifts. For Jim, everything he'd need overseas: four extra sweaters, razor blades, paper and pens for writing home, chocolate, thick wool socks, and lots of cigarettes. Plus a uniform driving suit of tan whipcord for when he got back. For Margaret, an entire set of china to replace the cheap stuff they'd gotten for their wedding. Once, while we'd been shopping downtown at Horne's, she'd mooned over a delicate pattern decorated with a border of violets. I'd bought them a service for eight along with matching silverware and glassware.

For Spud, I'd bought a new Hudson seal coat, along with

two silk shirts and a pair of silver cufflinks.

For Mamma, I'd splurged on one silk dressing gown in citron, a peach one with Chantilly flounces, and one of tea rose shot silk. Also, a platinum toilet set and two pretty perfume bottles I'd found at Nordlinger's in downtown Los Angeles.

For Harry, I'd gotten a book on railroading and a smart striped necktie from a men's specialty store that had recently opened in Hollywood. And I'd had three new hats made, thanks to measurements Mamma had sent me.

For Harriett, I'd bought two new china dolls, along with lovely clothes for them, and a tiny tea set with table and chairs. I'd also had a dollhouse from Horne's delivered to the house not long after our arrival. She sat in the center of it all like a little angel, her hair pale and downy, her blue eyes alive with wonder at everything. I hoped the gifts would make up for Lucretia's injury.

Little Jimmie was surrounded by Christmas loot too. For him, I'd splurged on the largest stuffed bear at Kaufmann's, a brand new model train, an erector set, alphabet blocks, and a tricycle, which he peddled in delight around the cramped living room.

He was the sweetest boy I'd ever met—the image of Jim as a tot—golden hair and blue eyes with big ears that stuck out from his head like the lamps on an old Buick.

While Jack sulked on the couch, Jim and Margaret sat around the new dining table with Mamma and Harry and Spud, watching as the children and I played with their new toys on the floor. They kept up a continual stream of baby talk, climbing over me like they were mountain goats claiming their territory. Then we would tumble to the floor in a giggling mass, and I'd tickle them until Jimmie announced very matter-of-factly that he'd messed his diaper.

Margaret laughed her bubbly laugh and led him off to get cleaned up. She was a loving, capable mother, patient and tender. I could only dream of being like her when I had my own kids someday.

When they returned, I sat down with the rest of the family. Mamma was holding Harriett, so I planted Jimmie on my lap and bounced him up and down. From time to time, I'd plant a kiss on his little blond head. Soon he reclined on his own and fell asleep sitting up, still clutching his big bear. He'd named him Wilson.

"After the president," Jim explained. We watched Jimmie sleep nestled up to his bear, and then the talk turned serious, and Christmas bittersweet.

"What time do you have to be at the train?" Mamma asked, turning to Jim.

"About nine," he said, clasping her hand.

"Damn the Hun," Mamma said, taking us all off guard. She'd never cursed before, but we all knew exactly what she was feeling. No one was sure why the war had been necessary, but we all knew that without American help the French and British were sunk.

"So where is this you're going?" I asked.

"Paris Island, off the coast of South Carolina," Jim said.

When it was time to say goodbye, we accompanied him to the station. Little Jimmie watched the proceedings with eyes as big as Klieg lights. Margaret and I both held Jim tightly, unwilling to let go, and so did Mamma. Harry shook his hand, and when that wasn't enough he hugged Jim as he would have a natural son. Spud hugged Jim too, clapping him on the shoulder as he had done when they were boys. His eyes filled with tears, but he tried to be brave.

"We Duffys are tough bastards," Spud said. "Those Krauts don't stand a chance. Even so, keep your head down."

Jim nodded. As children, Spud and I were the fearless ones—climbing trees and sledding down the tallest hills. Jim had been the sensitive one, given to writing bad poetry and painting bowls of flowers with cheap paints purchased with his paperboy money. The war made me see him in a new light, as a brave man putting country first.

My brother and his wife were perfect together. They were intelligent, quiet, and full of love for each other. Jim and Margaret had met at school, and their courting was done at the library—a dull, dreary place, the dusty corridors piled full of shelves of mildewy books. Jim tried explaining the attraction of books to me once, the knowledge and adventure and other worlds contained in them, but I couldn't see it. I wanted to see the world itself, not some version of it in a book. I couldn't understand what was romantic about stiff chairs, crumbling pages, and Mrs. Harrison, the stern librarian whispering, "Sshhh!" in her sober black dress and high collar with a perfect cameo on it. Why spend time in a morgue when I could be dancing and drinking?

Even so, watching them made me crave what they had—a relationship of respect, sweet, quiet kisses, and being mother and father to little Jimmie. It seemed like something much bigger, and far more important, than what I had with Jack.

Jack moped the entire two weeks we were there, leaving our room as little as possible and walking alone to Riley's

Bar, where he could drink as much as he wanted without the family seeing. Then he'd stumble home at some odd hour and throw pebbles at the bedroom window so I'd let him in.

On January 2, he had Harry drive him to the depot, where he booked a ticket for New York. Repacking his trunk at the house, he said very little. Harry drove him back later to catch the train.

"I'll see you when you get there," Jack said. "Stay as long as you want." Then he kissed my forehead and boarded. I was left to explain to my family that he wasn't always an insensitive ass—he was just tired from overwork.

With all that had happened in the last month, I asked myself, *Why couldn't I have met a man like one of my brothers?*

CHAPTER THIRTY-ONE

HOTEL MCALPIN BAR, NEW YORK CITY, *January 7, 1918*

"Ollie, let's get married tomorrow," Jack said, sipping his Scotch.

Tom Meighan, the Pickford family friend, had arrived from Los Angeles that week, and we'd taken him out for a whirl, Jack and me.

"Tomorrow?" I said. "Don't be silly. We haven't planned anything."

"I want to marry you. Mother and Mary have given us their blessing, so we might as well go ahead and make this legal."

"Like hell they gave their blessing. Lottie wore them down," I said.

"Tom, would you like to be our witness?"

"I certainly would," Tom said, studying the both of us. "You two could make some beautiful babies. What do you say, Ollie?"

I downed the rest of my Bronx cocktail in one gulp and peered at them. Tom reached over and lit my cigarette.

"Where should we go?" I said.

"Why not just drive to the courthouse? We'll use our real names to throw reporters off our scent. And it's less trouble.

We'll go to the Knickerbocker for some drinks afterward, then back here for the fun part." Jack winked.

"I'll phone Marjorie. She's in town too," I said. "Last week she told me she's taking a leave of absence to work on a revue. She'll want to come."

Tom held up his whiskey in a toast. The next morning, we all took a cab to the courthouse in Manhattan. We filled out the license as John Charles Smith and Oliveretta Duffy, and Tom and Marjorie stood up for us. The clerk signed the bottom, and a little while later, we were officially man and wife. Jack slipped the ladies in the office each a fifty-dollar bill to ensure their silence to the trades and the newspapers.

Afterward, we all headed for the Knickerbocker bar and uncorked about a hundred bottles of champagne, sharing them with the other patrons but keeping mum on the reason for our excitement. That night, Tom left us to hop his train west, Marjorie headed home to study her lines, and Jack and I checked into the McAlpin. You bet your ass we celebrated.

Though Charlotte and Mary had given a halfhearted blessing to us getting hitched, relations were still strained. When we returned to California, Jack moved us into his apartment at Mary's house on Fremont Place. We called it The Compound, a cheerless term that conjured up thoughts of a penal colony, and it sure felt that way to me. We had a separate entrance, but I still felt like a caged rat. If it hadn't been for Effie's company, I'd have lost my mind. It was a farce of false cheerfulness and play-acting every time we saw them. But what better way to perfect my craft than blowing air kisses to two of the women I detested most in the world?

CULVER CITY, CALIFORNIA, *January 1918*

"Ollie, will you hand me that green ball of yarn next to you? This one's getting a little spare," Alma Rubens asked.

Alma was a kick. She was gorgeous—dark-haired, dark-eyed—and she was seeing Franklyn Farnum, who was twenty years older than she was, so we had plenty to talk about on that score. And she loved magic dancing powder. Every time we had to do one of our ridiculous publicity junkets, we'd have a little snort in the ladies' toilet beforehand. After that, she could knit like nobody's business.

I handed her the yarn and thought of about a thousand places I'd rather be. Then I remembered Jim in the trenches and stayed put. Still needing the good publicity, Mr. Davis kept nagging us to do our wartime duty. We stayed busy either knitting socks for our brave boys overseas or staging war rallies so the fans would buy war bonds. Unfortunately, my sewing skills were lacking, so bandage rolling and public appearances were usually the extent of my volunteering. But to her credit, Alma was trying for the fifth time to show me how to do an inset gusset. And of course I wasn't getting it.

As we worked, a thin, slight fellow with blue eyes, brown hair cut into an awkward shape, and the most strangely shaped cauliflower ears I'd ever seen approached me across one of the wooden walkways.

"Good morning, Miss Thomas," he said, doffing his hat. "I am Herbert Howe from *Motion Picture Classic* magazine. I spoke to Mr. Davis about an interview. I'm pleased to meet you."

"Are you? Pleased to meet me, I mean." I recognized the name. He was famous for savaging movie folk. Alma gave a little wave and retreated, knowing she wouldn't be able to stop laughing.

"I suppose you've read what I've written about vaudevillians in the past," he said, obviously annoyed at my smart mouth.

"Some of it."

"So you know I'm not necessarily fond of them."

"Yes, but actors are no more alike than reporters are," I said. "We're all different. Just like you reporters. Some girls are out for nothing but gold however they can get it. And then there are girls like me who are just trying to make our mark in the world. I happened to get lucky."

"I'll be completely honest with you, Miss Thomas. I've found most of the Broadway and film types I've met to be crippled intellects," he said.

"And I think most entertainment reporters are judgmental hacks. But that doesn't stop me from talking to you, since some of you aren't. Hacks, I mean. I'd be a hypocrite if I said *you* were judgmental but then refused to meet with you because I think you're a hack." To show him I was willing to chat, I gestured to Alma's vacated chair.

He nodded and chuckled as he took it. I'd scored a point.

"You're quite outspoken, Miss Thomas. You must have taken Hollywood by storm when you arrived," he said.

"I'm just curious. I like meeting new people and learning new things, especially what those people might teach me. I don't have a lot of education, but it doesn't mean I'm not intelligent. When I arrived on this lot, I knew the names of every man, woman, dog, and prop in about two hours. On account of my movie *Madcap Madge*, everyone called me Madcap. Or Pep. Lambert Hillyer, the director, liked Miss Inquisitive."

"Miss Inquisitive, eh?" Howe said. "What sorts of questions were you asking him?"

"Ummm . . . things like 'What do you do that for?' 'Why can't I weep real tears instead of glycerin ones?' 'Why do some actresses smell an onion when they want to cry? Onions make me sneezy, not weepy.' I must have terrified them with all my questions."

He scratched down some notes.

"It took about four weeks until I could do just about anything on this lot—act, build sets, or tame wild animals." Then I added as an aside, "Or directors."

"Why the great thirst for knowledge?" he asked.

"Well, I'm only a Follies girl, really. I could turn out to be a nobody in pictures, so I've always figured I should know how to be a carpenter if it comes to that."

Mr. Howe nodded. "So has your mettle paid off then, Miss Inquisitive?"

I lit a cigarette and offered him one. He shook his head, so I inhaled deeply before beginning. "Of course! The scenario editor, Mr. Cunningham, gave in and let me sit at his typewriter. I helped him on a play. When we headed to the foothills to shoot, I asked them if they'd let me direct. Of course they said no. You've never heard a bunch of men laugh so much. 'Why not?' I asked."

"What happened then?" Mr. Howe asked, leaning forward in his chair. I told him of my petition, my short tenure as a director, and the rattler that scared the ever-loving shit out of me. By the time I got to the story of location scouting and my runaway dog, he was in tears, he was laughing so hard.

"But he's here, obviously," Howe noted, wiping his eyes and laughing.

I reached under my chair and cooed at Chow, rubbing him under his chin and giving him scratches on his fluffy gold head.

"He returned in the morning, coated in sticker burrs," Then to Chow I said, "Rough night, huh, pal? Probably out knocking up some poodle."

Chow flipped onto his back in a plea for a belly rub, and I obliged. He panted happily, his little face full of love. Effie had roasted some chicken snacks he loved, so I tossed him one and he gobbled it up.

"Chow's a movie star like me. He even had a special appearance in *An Even Break*."

"So I'm sitting with two celebrities instead of just one," he said. "These are delightful stories, Miss Thomas. Do you have any others to share with your fans?"

I thought a second. "Well, recently we needed a bunch of girls to complete a dancing sequence. Our director, Mr. Dillon, wanted to bring in a dance instructor to drill them. I said, 'What are you doing? I used to be in the Follies, for God's sake.'"

Howe continued the constant scratch of his pen.

"I had the girls repeat the same steps over and over until they had them down. Mr. Dillon was so grateful, he said he'd show me more about moviemaking. But it meant staying after hours. Was I willing to do that? Of course I was!"

"Did he teach you anything useful then?"

"Yes, he did. He showed me the microscope they use to balance the depth field for scenes, and he demonstrated the blue glass that directors keep on a chain around their necks so they can see how a scene will appear in black and white. He also explained why we have to wear such heavy makeup."

"I'm curious about that myself," Mr. Howe said.

"We use something called orthochromatic film. It makes our skin tones register much darker, so the makeup people smear us with white so we look ready to be embalmed, like this." I gestured to my face.

"Or . . . this is interesting." I walked over to one of the sets under construction. Surrounding it, four wooden markers had been pounded into the ground in a square shape. String had been stretched and tied between each stake. "They do this to show us the boundaries of the set," I said, pointing. "If we walk outside this area, our legs won't show up when the film's released, so we have to stay within the string. Ingenious, don't you think?"

"Yes, it is," Howe said. "You know, I wouldn't mind speaking to Mr. Dillon myself."

"It shouldn't be too hard," I said. "He's shooting *A Prisoner for Life* over at Universal."

Mr. Howe gave me a wave and took his leave. J.F. later told me what they talked about.

"No doubt about it," J.F. said he'd told Howe. "That girl has a businesswoman's head. I think she'll be able to direct someday, but never tragedies. Ollie would speed up Lady MacBeth and have her doing a foxtrot and a handspring. She's a joy-of-living optimist, and an intelligent one."

That J.F.—a girl's best friend. I told him he'd flattered me far too much.

CHAPTER THIRTY-TWO

56 FREMONT PLACE, LOS ANGELES, *late February 1918*

Shooting exteriors was always harder for me. I was never sure how much my makeup would melt off during the day or if my sweat stains were showing. But with interiors we always had the hot lights on us, so it was a trade-off. After the Follies, I guess I was just used to working inside.

I was exhausted from being outside all afternoon, and all I could think of when I got home that night was a drink and a bath. Jack was in a mood. I'd seen him testy before, but this was ridiculous.

"What's wrong with you?" I said, pouring orange juice and gin into the shaker for an orange blossom.

He just shook his head and ignored me. *Great, the silent treatment*, I thought, retreating to the couch with my glass. Restless, he crossed to the bar, poured himself a Scotch, and lit a Murad. Then he collapsed on the couch next to me with his head in his hands.

"Jack, what the hell is it?"

He pointed at the letter on the coffee table in front of him and downed his drink.

I picked up the paper and studied it. It was from the State

Department in Washington, DC, and informed him that as a Canadian citizen during the current situation in Europe, he had two choices. He could remain in America and volunteer for the armed forces, or he could return to Canada and be drafted. Either way, it meant he was going to war, and it would throw a huge monkey wrench into his movie career and our life together.

"What should we do?"

"We?" he snapped. "It's me they're worried about."

Talk about a knife to the ribs. I downed my drink in one gulp and slammed the glass on the table. It came pretty damned close to breaking.

"I *am* your wife, remember? How do you think I'll feel worrying about you the whole time? We won't get to see each other for months! Don't be so selfish, Jack. This will be rough for both of us, whether you think so or not."

He rose and poured another Scotch, and we looked warily at each other.

"I'm sorry, honey," he said after a few minutes. "That was awful of me, wasn't it?"

We deliberated for a week and finally decided that the American tack was wisest. It wouldn't interfere with him working when he got home—if he did get home. And he could choose from among his possible assignments.

Thinking he'd have a better chance on a seagoing vessel or in the air than in the trenches, Jack signed up for the new aviation section of the navy, hoping he could get a desk position and avoid combat altogether.

On March 11, I bawled all morning. The sky followed suit, pouring buckets. Jack was scheduled on the California

Limited east to Chicago, and then he'd connect to another train that would take him to the Brooklyn Navy Yard. I lost count of everyone who met us at the depot, but Mickey Neilan was one of them.

"Come on, Jack," Mickey said, leading him toward the men's toilet. I found out later he'd provided moral support and an extra toot so Jack could steel himself. William Desmond Taylor entered the station and approached us, his elegant carriage unmistakable, even from that distance.

He handed Jack a book from his library. "For the road," he said, winking at Jack and Mickey. "This one's on me."

Then, approaching like a Bedouin chief herding a tribe through the desert, Mary led a procession of family members toward us, including Charlotte, Lottie, and Little Mary. In the midst of a series of emotional goodbye hugs, I stood aside as they once more dominated the scene, fawning over their precious Jack.

As a conductor shouted the name of his train, Jack and I clung to each other, hugging and kissing like our lives depended on it. The stress of the last two months had been too much, and I slid to the floor in a faint.

Jack, Mickey, and Mr. Taylor all summoned help, and they held the train until I came to and Jack and I could have a final kiss. He hung out the window, and I waved from the platform until he disappeared from view. Then Mickey helped me back to the car, where I dropped my head into my hands and sobbed.

CHAPTER THIRTY-THREE

56 FREMONT PLACE, LOS ANGELES, *May 1918*

"So I says to ole Reg Barker, I says, 'You better watch the angle for that shot or you're gonna have too much glare on her face. See where your reflector is? For God's sake, have him move it back,'" Owen said.

I handed him a whiskey and poured another for myself. Then I lit a cigarette. "So what'd he do?"

"Oh, he moved it, of course. He knew I was right. I may be a lousy drunk, but I know what I'm talking about. I've been in flickers long enough, haven't I?" He took a snuff and gave a small burp. He'd been telling me about *The Crimson Gardenia*, some little throwaway he'd been working on for Rex Beach.

I plopped down next to him on the couch, tucking my foot under me. "You're not lousy, Owen. Just a drunk."

"To the inebriates," he said. I held up my glass, and he clinked it. Then he sighed.

"So how's everything going? With . . . you know . . ." I nodded toward the main house.

"You know, of course, that Her Highness has requested I vacate the royal bedchamber," he said. "My place has been usurped by a pretender to the throne. But sshhh . . . no one must know that part." His voice was slurred.

Owen had come for a visit to our apartment at The Compound. While Jack was in the service, we had only my income, which had been spotty from Triangle's financial problems. So we'd had to economize. Jack had convinced me that staying here was the smart thing to do, so I said okay, despite my better judgment. The house was lonely with no Jack, especially with the two vipers on the other side of the wall. Owen and I both felt out of place.

Lottie had her own adjoining unit too, where she lived with Little Mary. When the boredom got too much, I'd go next door and Lottie and I would toss back a couple and gab about men, acting, and life in general. Of my two sisters-in-law, Lottie was the more likable, but she was also just like Jack. Everyone knew about her problems with booze and, even by Hollywood standards, her round heels.

"Now, about this scenario," I said. Owen had said he'd stop by to help with my emoting. Mr. Davis had said he wanted to see me work on it, since *Betty Takes a Hand* hadn't been as much of a success as they'd hoped. With some effort, *The Follies Girl* could be my best work yet.

"I think your emoting is top notch, Ollie dear," he said, gulping more Bushmills. "Hell, you're married to Jack, aren't you? That would make any sane person emote more than usual."

"Thanks. Unfortunately, Mr. Davis's approval is the one that really counts," I said, poking him.

"Davis has been brought in to clean up a mess, dear. He knows very little about filmmaking."

"He used to work at Universal. He must know something about it."

"Applesauce. All those moneymen in New York, like Harry Aitken? He's doing what they want. He's a cog in a machine. A machine that has been running for too long with no lubrication, if you know what I mean," he said, rubbing his fingers together.

Mr. Aitken ran Triangle's financial workings in New York, approving or vetoing everything we did with the stroke of a pen.

"So what did you come over for, if you won't help me work on my sobbing and cringing?" I teased him.

"I needed the company. Jack's in the east, Mickey's up in Frisco, Kirky's in San Diego, and I'm in a state."

"Got it," I said. "So, another?" I waved the bottle over his glass.

"What a perfect figure of a woman you are, dear Ollie."

A key in the lock gave us pause. Mary and Charlotte rarely if ever intruded on us in our own quarters. But there Mary stood, her eyes blazing, America's Sweetheart nowhere to be found.

"What the hell are you doing here?" she demanded of Owen.

"Just having a drink, sweetness," he said, raising his glass.

"You're always having a drink," she said to him, then turned to glare at me.

"What?" I said. I wasn't sure why she was so angry with me. Other than for marrying her brother and ruining her life, which was her usual reason.

"What is he doing?" she said.

"He's helping me practice my emoting," I said, pointing at the scenario on the coffee table.

"Yes, he's famed as a dramatist," she said, her voice full of disgust. "Get out."

"Calm down, dearest," he said. "Ollie's improving daily. Show her, Ollie."

I burst out laughing. Owen was the only person I knew who

spoke to Mary the way I wanted to.

"Ahhh . . . the nuances in that laugh. Happiness and joy, tempered with sarcasm. She's absolutely perfect," he said, downing his drink. "Perfect."

"Get out of this apartment."

"Now, dear heart, no need to overreact," he said, pulling himself off the couch. "It's a casual visit. Not like the ones you've been making to Mr. Fairbanks."

"You bastard! I'm not overreacting. I want you gone."

"Fine, I'm going, I'm going." Owen slurred his words. He pulled himself up and almost did a header into a potted palm.

"You too!" she said, pointing at me.

"What? Jack and I live here, remember?"

"No, Jack lives on base at the Brooklyn Navy Yard. *You* live here due to my good graces. That ends now."

"Mary, I—"

"Get your stuff and get out. You're a disgrace to the Pickford name. I've known it from the beginning."

After Effie and I collected as much of our stuff as I could, I overnighted at the Alex and found her a room not far away. Then I called a realtor, who began collecting lists of properties to show me. It took a week to find something I liked, but I moved us into a place on Sunset and wired Jack about our change of residence. I wasn't sure how the hell I would pay for it.

CHAPTER THIRTY-FOUR

SAN DIEGO, CALIFORNIA, *June 1918*

During *The Follies Girl*, my correspondence with Jack was constant. After we wrapped, the newspapers had a photographer come in and snap a picture of me at my writing desk to show me pining for him.

"Dear Jack—

I miss you more every day. I loved the earrings, sweetheart. Thank you so much! I've begun a new picture, working for Frank Borzage again on The Vital Spark. *I get to play a dual role as mother and daughter, and I even get to masquerade as a boy. It takes place in Paris. I think it's my best work so far. We're shooting at the exposition grounds in San Diego, so I'll give you my temporary address here.*

How do you like Brooklyn? Have you met the Dodgers yet? You must let me know if you hear of any shows worth seeing while I am in New York. Hope to squeeze in a visit to you soon. I kiss you ten times and give you big hugs. I miss you desperately, dear.

Your Ollie
c/o U.S. Grant Hotel
San Diego, CA"

Two weeks later, a reply arrived.

"Dear Ollie—

The cufflinks were a fantastic surprise, and they're so smart. You shouldn't have, though. I have nowhere to wear them for a while. Things at the yard are dull as dishwater, but I'm managing. Brooklyn is boring compared to Manhattan. The boys and I grab the ferry across the river to have fun when we get a minute's leave. I am sorry Mickey and Kirky aren't here to enjoy it with me, but I'm sure they're keeping everyone in California hopping.

How are you, darling? How is The Vital Spark *coming? Hoping for a visit from you soon. Can't wait to see you.*

Love, Jack"

GRAND CENTRAL TERMINAL, NEW YORK CITY, *July 1918*

The flashbulbs cracked and hissed in greeting as I stepped off the train. "Miss Thomas! Miss Thomas!" the reporters called.

Jack held his usual bouquet of daisies for me, smiling slyly as I strolled toward him across the platform. He was cocky he'd been able to get leave.

Giving me a big kiss for the benefit of the newspapermen, he leaned over to my ear and whispered, "I've been hard as a chunk of granite all week. Something you could see to for me?"

We let ourselves be photographed and gave them a few comments before grabbing a cab to Mary's New York brownstone. She let Jack use it when she wasn't in town. How would she feel knowing we'd be there after she'd just kicked me out?

Inside, our clothes hit the expensive Turkish rugs near the door. He held me against the door frame, gasping in my ear as I clasped him through his trousers and sent his hat sailing across the room. Then he undressed me until I stood before him in chemise and stockings. He wore only an undershirt, boxer shorts, and sock garters.

As he reached down to pull off the garters, I shimmied the rest of the way out of my underwear, and he could wait no longer. So we did what we did best right on the couch—with the important distinction that I'd barely gotten going by the time he was done and snoring. The rest of the week continued in the same vein. For the first time ever, I was relieved to head home to California. And a new co-star.

LOS ANGELES, *August 1918*

"Miss Thomas! Miss Thomas!" Jake Anderson of the *Tribune* said. "Did you have fun in the east?"

Stepping into the bright Los Angeles afternoon, I waved at the reporters. They stood on the platform waiting for me, their pens poised for the latest scoop on my time in New York. My newest gift from Jack glinted in the sun. It was a frothy creation of gold and blue diamonds that jingled like sleigh bells when I moved my arm.

"Yes, I had a fine time," I said. "I bought a splendid new wardrobe, and the best part of it is that Jack is coming west soon." I smiled fetchingly when referring to Jack. Why hide it? They knew what we'd been doing— drinking, dancing, wrecking cars, or fucking. It's what we always did.

"How were the Broadway shows?" Mike Dorsey of the *Santa Barbara Journal* asked.

"Very entertaining! But you ought to see Jack in his uniform! So handsome and distinguished." They all snapped the expression on my face, attempting to capture my devotion.

"He's in the navy now. Did you meet any submarines?" joked Guy Rowell of the *Orange County Sun*.

"Maybe. Jack told me about the navy yard. But not too much! That would be a breach of security!" I said with a giggle. "It was nice to find him in such good spirits."

"I suppose the styles are all military at present?" asked Eddie Francis of the *Santa Monica Herald*.

"Oh, yes! Brass buttons and epaulets! And now I have the cutest motoring cap—just like Jack's!"

The performance ranked as one of my best. We were the picture of wedded bliss, even as things were starting to fall apart.

CHAPTER THIRTY-FIVE

LOS ANGELES, *August 16, 1918*

"That's quite a dress," Mickey said.

"Thanks. Let's get going." We piled into Mickey's navy-blue Willys-Knight for the trip to the Alex.

My dress was a robin's-egg blue with a mink collar, and I wore a broad-brimmed hat of the same color, accented with a bright pink ribbon band. The blue brought out my eyes, so I wore it for all sorts of fancy occasions.

By now Mr. Lasky's brother-in-law, Mr. Goldfish, had changed his name to the more respectable-sounding Goldwyn. He'd put together a tribute to Sid Grauman, the theater impresario, and everyone who was anyone in Hollywood was going to be there. The banquet was at the Palm Court Ballroom inside the Alex, all stained glass, potted palms, and crystal chandeliers.

"Ollie, you wouldn't believe everything Sid's done!" Mickey said. "He started up in Alaska, prospecting during the gold rush."

"Yeah? How'd he do?"

"Not bad. He took the money he made and started buying up theaters from Juneau all the way down to northern

California. He lived through the quake. Destroyed all his businesses in Frisco, so he decided to try his luck farther south. Hit it even bigger here."

When we pulled up in front of the Alex, Mickey held out his arm so I could take it. Times like this, you could almost mistake him for a gentleman. The first time Mickey and I had been alone together, I discovered he had more hands than an all-night poker game. But after our rocky beginning, we were now chums. Once we'd come to an understanding of boundaries, we were fine. While Jack was out of town, Mickey escorted me to these types of events. Since Jack was out promoting *Mile-a-Minute Kendall*, Mickey was my date.

"Champagne?" A waiter asked me.

"Of course!" I eagerly thrust out my glass.

Blanche Sweet sat on my left, all silky hair and bee-stung lips. Everyone called her by her last name, since she was wholesome as a jelly roll. She'd made a big splash about four years earlier in Mr. Griffith's *Judith of Bethulia*. We compared notes on the pheasant since neither of us had tried it before. The best thing about Blanche? She couldn't stand Mary either. They'd worked at Biograph together, and Mary got all the attention and the plum roles. We had lots to gab about.

Blanche and Mickey were seeing each other on the sly, since Mickey was still married to his wife Gertrude. They'd worked together on two films in 1917, and Blanche had told me later their chemistry was instant. She knew how to keep a secret, like a spy, but Mickey had a big mouth. If he didn't watch his step, Gertie was going to sue him for divorce.

Three other speakers gave speeches for Mr. Grauman, and then it was my turn. Mr. Davis had asked me to compose a short piece about California in honor of Mr. Grauman, who had invested so much of his life and his fortune here. I'd tried to sum up all my feelings in one tidy package.

I stumbled to the podium clutching my notes like I had rigor mortis, my knees knocking. It was one thing to be Ziegfeld's prize attraction and know that you held a room in the palm of your hand because you were beautiful. It was another to appear on film, only to read in the notices later how awful you were. But to speak in front of nearly a hundred people in person, hoping to sound intelligent when you'd quit school at sixteen, was something else. As the polite applause faded, I took a deep breath and cleared my throat. Someone clanked a spoon against a glass to call for quiet.

"Good evening, Ladies and Gentlemen. As a tribute to Mr. Grauman, who has found his greatest successes in this beautiful state, Mr. Davis has asked me to give you my impressions of our home. This is a piece I wrote, which I've named 'My California.'"

Everyone clapped, including Mr. Grauman, who carefully avoided the cigar clasped between two fingers.

Dear God, don't let me fuck this up.

"'My California is a scenic wonder of warm golden sunshine and pounding surf. It stands between the cool, glorious Pacific Ocean and Death Valley, one of the hottest, driest places on earth. When I arrived on the train, two golden lines of poppies stood with open arms to receive me.

"'From its choking dirt roads stretching into the foothills to the Santa Anas that whip my clothes around me, from the herbal fragrance of the coastal sage, to the snakes that make friends with me when I have my turn behind the camera . . . California is my home.'" This brought a titter from the audience, especially J.F., a few tables away. And a glare from Lambert Hillyer, seated across the room.

"'It is the place I fell in love. Not just with my husband, but also with the beach at Santa Monica, where we took our first walk in the waves. And with the pepper trees that provide us with pleasant shade when we're working. And with the scent of the citrus groves, promising us fresh lemonade when we're through shooting.

"'It is the land of rolling hills, majestic mountains, and clear lakes. It is the land of sea lions and coyotes, of little wild deer and brown pelicans. It is the state where I have been adopted like a child and the state I love like a mother. It is My California.'"

I was so surprised at the noise that I almost didn't recognize it after all this time—thunderous applause, like the kind I used to get at the Follies. I almost expected to hear knockers on the tables.

"Bravo!" I heard from the crowd. Mr. Grauman was suddenly at my side, clasping my hands and with tears in his eyes.

"Miss Thomas, you definitely tugged at my heartstrings, young lady. Mr. Davis better hold on to you!"

When the event was over, a gaggle of friends and co-stars told me I'd spoken for them far better than they could have, and they congratulated me on such a great speech. Mickey gave me a big hug and a kiss on the cheek for a job well done. Blanche, Mickey, and I strolled out of the Palm Court Ballroom and into the bar to celebrate. We were getting tighter than last year's pants when I saw an old friend sipping cognac nearby.

"Julian!" I called, waving.

"Ollie!"

In a single sleek motion, he was on his feet and standing

beside us. Julian Eltinge was a wonder of a man, a strapping six-foot fellow who happened to masquerade as a woman onstage. Julian was celebrated in his New York revues and even had a theater named after him, but he was living on the West Coast now. I hadn't seen him since my time at the Follies. We chatted a few minutes, and I introduced him to Blanche and Mickey.

"Ollie, I'm not living far from here. Would you all like to join me for tea this weekend?"

"We'd love to," I said.

After about eight bottles of champagne between the four of us, we ended the evening by singing an off-key chorus of "K-K-K-Katy" and staggering out of the lobby to our cars. Afterward, I nursed one of the worst hangovers I'd ever had but smiled when I thought about my speech.

"Somebody please tell me why I'm going to fucking *tea*," Mickey said when he showed up at the door on Sunday. He was soused, as usual.

"Because maybe I can teach an old dog new tricks," I said. I gave him a broad wink and grabbed my handbag before we headed down the driveway. I'd selected an afternoon frock of deepest royal blue and a Juliet cap of woven shanks of silk interspersed with spangles. Our brand new canary-yellow Locomobile sat in the driveway.

"Nice car," he said, leaning into the leather seat.

"I bought it for Jack as a present for when he gets out of the service. Spent oodles of my profits from *Betty Takes a Hand*, but I couldn't resist. It's been weeks, though. He's stuck in Brooklyn for the time being. It doesn't hurt to keep the thing tuned up and in good running shape, right? We'll just take it out for a spin."

He was obviously skeptical. He'd seen my driving too.

"I'm sorry Blanche couldn't join us," I said.

"Yeah, she had to meet with her agent. Probably better this way. I think Gertie suspects something."

"That's too bad. Julian will cheer you up, though. He has some crazy stories to tell."

Mickey grumbled under his breath that Julian had to be a fruit. "Why else would any regular fella wear women's clothes?" he said. "It ain't normal, I tell ya."

"You might think that, and it might even be true, but don't you dare say it out loud, Mickey Neilan," I said. "He's punched out men for less than that. He escorted plenty of lovely ladies when he was in New York. So keep your trap shut."

I tore down Sunset, narrowly missing a stray dog that picked that moment to cross. It yelped in panic as the Locomobile careered past, leaving clouds of dust in its wake. The remnants of the *Intolerance* set loomed at the corner of Sunset and Hillhurst, becoming more and more decrepit as the months wore on. Large chunks of the Wall of Babylon were now missing, but the giant elephants still sat, their trunks raised in halfhearted salute as we flew by.

"What's his house number again?"

He glanced at the cocktail napkin on which Eltinge had scribbled his address. "It's 2329 Baxter," he said, watching the surrounding homes for numbers. As we drew near, he gasped. "It's a bleedin' monastery!"

He was right. The house sat up on its own hill, with a half-enclosed second-floor balcony accented by three arches hemmed in with a cast-iron banister. In between each arch stood an exotic twisted column. Sitting toward the rear of the building was a small turret, and behind that was a rectangular tower. The entire place was topped off with red terra-cotta roof tiles. An Oriental gardener, who was caring for the palms out front, waved as the Locomobile climbed the steep driveway.

In my excitement, I pressed too hard on the accelerator, and the car leaped to the right. Mickey yelled as his side slammed into a stone retaining wall holding back a bed of thriving bougainvillea.

"Hell's bells!" I yelled, making our presence known right away. If Julian had been wondering when we'd arrive before, he wasn't now.

"Dammit!" I said. I'd just gotten the blasted thing out of the shop after denting it before I left for New York. At this rate, Jack might never get to see it.

I put it in reverse in time to see Julian dashing outside. He fought not to laugh. We stood examining the crumpled metal slash on the passenger side, and Mickey massaged his neck. The gardener assessed the damage to the wall and the plants.

"You okay, Mickey?" Julian said.

"Yeah, I'll be fine."

"I've got a hot water bottle inside. We should keep that on your neck for a while. Wu Ming, what do you think?"

"It not too bad, Mr. Julian. Can be fixed. Very easy."

"Thank you. I'll try to get some help for you next week. We'll rebuild it." He patted the gardener on the shoulder. "After all that, I'm sure you've worked up quite a thirst, Ollie my dear." He put a protective arm around me, and he and Mickey chuckled at women drivers.

"I'm so sorry, Julian."

"Don't worry about it. Come on, you two. Let's have some tea. I found the most delicious lemon biscuits at the little Italian market down the road."

As he led us into the house, Julian turned to me. "Ollie, have you heard the latest? I got it from someone in the know that if this influenza business gets much worse, all the studios may have to declare a temporary shutdown."

CHAPTER THIRTY-SIX

LOS ANGELES, *October 1, 1918*

Julian wasn't far off the mark. Just over a month later, Mickey showed me what he was reading as we sat on the terrace eating breakfast. I'd just wrapped up *The Glorious Lady* when whispers of a shutdown started.

"Says they aren't filming any new pictures," he said.

"Jesus. That flu is everywhere," I said.

No one knew what caused it. Some had named it "The Grippe," or "The Spanish Lady," but mostly it was just the Spanish flu. People were now wearing cloth masks whenever they left the house. Stores were forbidden from having sales, and funerals were limited to fifteen minutes.

"Look at this," Mickey said, passing me the front page.

"'The National Motion Picture Industry of manufacturers and distributors has voted to begin a four-week shutdown due to the recent influenza pandemic,'" I read. "Shit."

Mickey and I stared at each other. Everyone knew about Triangle's financial troubles and the austerity measures. It was another reason why we'd been shooting in San Diego instead of Culver City—Triangle had leased out space to Mr. Goldwyn's new outfit since they needed the money. With the way this was going, Triangle wouldn't survive the flu.

All the studios were asking their actors and actresses to forgo salaries during the length of the shutdown, hoping the ticket-buying public would avoid the cinemas and keep the flu from spreading. In the hardest hit cities like Philadelphia and Boston, large events were cancelled by order of the municipal health departments.

I wondered how smart it would be to take the train east for Thanksgiving but decided to go anyway. With the time off during the shutdown, I wouldn't find a better time for visiting Mamma and Harry and the family. Harry said he'd pick me up at the depot.

He'd brought Harriett with him, and they both wore cloth masks over their faces. She was dressed in a shearling coat over a butter-yellow pinafore and wore a huge bow in her hair. She reached up, demanding a hug. So I picked her up and blew raspberry sounds into her neck as she giggled.

"How is my baby sister?"

"Good!" She pulled off her mask. "Mamma and Harry got me a new doll for my birthday!"

I played along. "What did you name her? Where is she?"

"Her name is Mildred. She's at home, serving tea with my other dolls."

"We'll have to join her, won't we?"

She squealed and clasped her hands even more tightly around my neck. I never wanted to let her go.

"You are growing, dearie. I'm afraid you're getting far too heavy for me to carry anymore."

"Just a little longer," she said, nestling into my neck. "You smell pretty."

"It's called Narcisse Noir. Jack bought it for me."

Smothering her face with kisses made her giggle even more.

"Jack busy filming?" Harry asked me after pulling down his mask. It was obvious that after Jack's behavior last visit, Harry was relieved he hadn't come. But he would never say it.

"Yeah," I lied. The truth was, he'd really got himself neck-deep this time. I'd just found out he was sitting in the brig at the Brooklyn Navy Yard. Even Mary and Charlotte's clout might not work this time.

CHAPTER THIRTY-SEVEN

ANN PENNINGTON'S APARTMENT, NEW YORK CITY,

early December 1918

"Thanks, Penny. You have no idea how much I appreciate this," I said. I dropped my little carpetbag with a thud and set Chow's dog carrier down next to it. Unfastening the catch, I opened the door and he skittered out, snuffling and sniffing the unfamiliar scents in her place. He looked up at me hopefully.

"Don't pee," I said.

I pulled off my astrakhan coat, and Penny hung it up for me. My rose-colored *duvet de laine* suit was rumpled from traveling. Even in my time doing double-duty at the Follies and the Frolic, or the past year acting in a movie a month, I hadn't been this tired.

"I'm making the davenport up for you," she said, picking up a second blanket and waving it over the other already in place. "You can put your stuff over here." She pointed at a small occasional table between the couch and an armchair. "I'm sorry it's not much. Between the Follies and the Scandals, work has been steady, but you know—always newer, sweeter faces out there competing for some of the same jobs. And I'm not getting any younger." Penny took whatever work she could—she loved to dance. After being one of Ziegfeld's starring attractions, she now divided her time between the Follies and George White's Scandals, a competing revue.

"You don't have to apologize. This is so generous of you." Generosity had always been Penny's best quality. When she found out the pickle I was in, she had insisted I come to live with her in the city. So many of my Follies friends were in and out of town, off to film in California or Fort Lee or some other far-flung location. Penny said she was staying right where she was, and her place was mine as long as I needed it.

It had become all-important over the last month to be near Brooklyn. I still hadn't been able to decide if it had been a slap in the face or a blessing that Triangle had finally let me go. At the end, with creditors hounding them, Mr. Aitken, the company head, had fired Mr. Davis and supervised every penny coming in and going out himself. I was ready for it to be over, and I was unemployed for the first time in years.

Out of guilt, I kept paying Effie with money from a little modeling work I'd picked up. I told her she had a job waiting for her as soon as we were on our feet once more. She took the break to spend some much-needed time with her daughter.

Funny, but now that the armistice had been declared, the war was just beginning for Jack. I'd tried to enjoy the holiday with my family, but I couldn't ignore the problem anymore. I'd hopped the train east at the end of November, but Jack still wouldn't come clean about what had happened.

The Graham Avenue #5134 took me east on Sands Avenue, toward the yard. The street was packed with stores for buying navy uniforms, but there were also plenty of bars and cathouses with their gaudy red lights outside. God only knew what Jack had gotten up to here.

The Brooklyn Navy Yard was still going full steam then, but the war effort was winding down. It sat on Wallabout Bay, just off the East River, a couple hundred acres worth of cranes, dry docks, and flapping flags. The noise was unbelievable. Pounding, clanking, blasting, welding. Red brick buildings were stationed around the yard, their smokestacks churning out blue-black soot. *Just like home*, I thought with a sinking feeling.

The brig was a rough-hewn red stone building. It had arched windows on the bottom floor finished with white bars. Jack was cooling his heels there until they could figure out what to do with him. I'd go through all the security measures, men in military uniforms gently prodding me with questions to see why I was visiting. They just wanted to be sure I wasn't slipping him any files or contraband, and we'd sit on opposite sides of a big wooden table with a guard standing watch. For most of that time, we'd hold hands or make stupid small talk, but no matter how I tried to get him to tell me about his case, he wouldn't.

Finally one day, I gathered my things and got ready to leave.

"Where are you going?"

"If you won't say anything to me about what you did, what's the point in staying?"

"Ollie, I'm in big trouble."

"Yeah, that's obvious, Jack. Wives don't visit their husbands in jail unless something is very wrong. I won't sit in this damned chair one more minute if you don't tell me what's going on."

He sighed. “They’re accusing me of helping rich boys get out of service at the front, and they say that I was setting a senior officer up with girls. For money.”

“Were you?”

“Ollie . . . ssshh . . .” He nodded over his shoulder at the guards. “They listen to my conversations! They want to send me to Leavenworth!” The panic in his voice was unmistakable.

I rolled my eyes. “But were you?”

“I wasn’t, and Mother and Mary are going to prove it. Mother is hiring me a military lawyer. She’s going to fix everything.”

“Still doing all the cleaning up for you. That’s swell. How old are you, anyway?”

The next morning, I picked up a paper and the full story stared me in the face with the headline:

PICKFORD BEING INVESTIGATED IN NAVY SCANDAL

He’d brought shame on himself, on the armed forces, on his films, on me, and on the fans who loved him. But most of all, on Mary. And that was something his mother wouldn’t tolerate. I got the story in bits and pieces from his lawyer and from Charlotte, but usually from the papers. As usual, Jack clung to his innocence, even when confronted with the truth. Once more, the Pickford name served as a reliable suit of armor.

According to the service, Jack had been a go-between for a Lieutenant Benjamin Davis, who liked attractive young women, and he was also willing to sell spots in cushy desk jobs to the rich, who didn’t want their precious sons being sent into harm’s way.

Charlotte phoned me when she checked into the Knickerbocker. She hated my guts, but she knew she owed me updates of what was going on with Jack. "Our lawyer says that Jack must tell them everything he knows," she said. "They'll go easier on him. We should know more soon."

"Thank you, Mrs. Pickford," I said as sweetly as I could while making faces at the phone. Penny giggled as she handed me a large whiskey. I hung up and took it gratefully.

"Here. You look like you can use this," she said.

"Thanks," I said. Chow sat in my lap, and I petted his head as he dozed.

"Hey, have you heard anything from any of those producers who sounded interested?"

"One or two. I suppose I'm terrified of jumping into a bad situation like I did with Triangle. Waiting for the perfect opportunity to come along, I guess."

"Well, here's to perfect opportunities."

"I'll drink to that."

CHAPTER THIRTY-EIGHT

ANN PENNINGTON'S APARTMENT, NEW YORK CITY,
December 1918

He held his hat in his hand, and his knock had been extremely confident for someone so young. Myron Selznick was doing a sales pitch, and he got right to the point.

"Miss Thomas, I think it would behoove you to listen to what I have to say."

"Be-what?"

"Behoove. It means . . . never mind. But you should listen."

He had to be at least a year or two younger than me, but he explained he could make me an even bigger star than Triangle had.

I sized him up. He wasn't tall, but he had an extra dose of self-confidence to compensate for it. I could have sworn he was six feet. Dark hair was slicked away from a high forehead, and his bulbous nose was accented by a doughy face, chin cleft, and round wire-framed glasses.

"But you're just a boy," I said.

"My age is not important. With my support, you'll have all the financial assistance and promotion you need to go far."

When I didn't respond right away, he continued.

"My father, Lewis, is quite respected in the film business. He was forced out of Select Pictures when he didn't see eye to eye with Adolph Zukor. I learned everything I know from him. I'll have his guidance and that of my brother, David, to help me. I apprenticed for my dad, and I also served as a studio manager for Norma Talmadge. Believe me, I've been watching and I know what I'm doing. I'll be twenty-one soon, and I'm celebrating by forming my very own motion picture company. We're building a brand new studio in Long Island City, and we have offices at the Astor Trust Building on 5th Avenue. I'm getting everything into shape right now."

I had to give the kid credit for all the name-dropping.

"Miss Thomas, you have real star potential, and I believe I can help you get there. I will make you *far* more famous than your sister-in-law."

Now *that* caught my interest. It would be nice to bring The Empress down a peg.

"Do you have any plans you can tell me about? I mean, what should I expect if I sign with you, Mr. Selznick?" I didn't want to seem too eager.

"Most certainly!" he said, obviously pleased I was willing to hear him out. "My mother is fronting us the cash to go big with this. I have some terrific projects in mind for you—respected plays that have been successes in the past and new material from the best scenarists working today. The most pressing thing for us to do is to get your name out there. I want to put up huge billboards in major cities—New York, Chicago, Pittsburgh, and Buffalo. I'm picturing two or three in New York—we'll have one facing the New Amsterdam! Everyone who remembers you from the Follies will want to go straight from the theater to an Olive Thomas picture. Visibility is the name of the game with Selznick. Your name in lights. As a bonus, Selznick Pictures will provide you with a clothing allowance to purchase splendid frocks for your public appearances, since we're planning quite a few of those. What do you think?"

I swallowed hard and thought for a second. Then he did something I didn't expect.

"Good doggie," he said. He leaned down and gave Chow a pat on the head.

I was charmed.

"I think I want to read your contract," I said, grinning at him. He didn't even look old enough to shave, but his enthusiasm trumped that of the other studios that had been sniffing around after Triangle went bloomers-up.

His excitement was contagious, like he could see something in me I couldn't. Something big and important.

"Where ya from, Mr. Selznick?"

"Pittsburgh."

"You don't say."

We all sat in the Selznick living room and read over the contract together—Myron, his father Lewis, brother David, and mother Florence. It was then I fully realized that working with the Selznicks would be a family affair. Myron's mother watched him, beaming with pride. She was sweet—a dumpling of a woman, and like her son, her biscuity face was interrupted only by the cleft that dimpled her chin. Her name was the one included on the contract, since Myron wouldn't turn twenty-one until October 5 of the next year. David sat and gazed at me like a dog entranced by a pork chop. I tried not to laugh. When you've been in the Follies long enough, you know that look.

"'Two years beginning January 13, 1919 . . . $1,000 per week,'" I said.

"Yes, Olive. I told you. You'll have the full support of Selznick behind you, and that means we'll pay you what we feel you are worth."

"'And $1,250 per week during the second year . . .'" I read out loud.

"Don't forget the fringe benefits. Read clause two under paragraph five."

"'Clothing allowance and monetary advances . . .'" I said.

"Due to unforeseen circumstances you may encounter, Selznick is willing to forward you portions of your paycheck in a pinch. Say you find the most gorgeous mink coat you simply must have," he said.

"I have a mink," I said, mentally inventorying my closet.

"Sable, then. Let's say you see a sable you must have. Or you're at Tiffany's and want to buy yourself something shiny. Contact my office, and we'll make the arrangements."

"You'd advance me that much?"

"We aim to keep you happy."

"That's a lot of happiness," I noted.

"All you need to do is submit your bills for clothing, hosiery, shoes, hats, and accessories. They'll be covered, and we'll issue a payment. We want our biggest attraction to be impeccably turned out at all times."

He read over my shoulder. "I have the option of renewing for another year on January 16, 1921 with the same terms and conditions, but your salary will be $2,250," he said, sweetening the deal yet again. "We'll let you know about renewing in writing on or before July 1. It's all in paragraph seven," he said.

"And you want me to star in eight pictures a year?"

"Yes, that's correct."

"I sure will be hopping for that $1,000 a week, won't I?"

"Your public loves you. We need to give them as much of you as possible."

"Won't they get sick of me?"

"I don't ever see that ever happening, Miss Thomas," he said softly, his face flushing.

"Call me Ollie, for God's sake. You're going to be my boss, right?"

With the stroke of a pen, I was under contract to Selznick Pictures. The next day I rented a new apartment for the occasion.

CHAPTER THIRTY-NINE

MANHATTAN, NEW YORK CITY, *December 23, 1918*

Most cities had lifted their quarantine restrictions about the middle of November, but the flu was still spreading in certain areas. I developed a raspy sore throat and started coughing into a handkerchief three days before Christmas. Blowing my stuffy nose did nothing. I was god-awfully achy, and when I woke that next morning I knew something was wrong. My forehead was on fire, and my legs didn't want to move.

Thank God I'd been able to bring Effie back on the payroll. Getting myself up and dressed was almost impossible, even with her help. I stabbed at the elevator button to reach the lobby, and once I arrived I collapsed at the foot of the front desk clerk. The concierge had Sam, the Negro doorman, call a cab right away. They propped me up on a bench in the corner, and I trembled with fever. At last the cab arrived.

"All Saints Hospital," Sam told the driver. "And step on it, y'hear? Miss Thomas is real sick."

"No . . . not hospital . . . no . . . hospital . . . please . . ." I mumbled. All I could think of was Da's blue-gray face and that smell of Lysol.

As he pulled the car to a stop in front of All Saints, the cabbie told me his name was Earl Steuben and he was a flicker fan. He recognized me from *Madcap Madge*, and he babbled on, saying that if he lived through the flu, someday he'd be able to tell his children how he'd carried Olive Thomas into the hospital. He tenderly held the flat of his hand to my forehead, telling the orderly I was feverish.

"Let me see if we have any beds," the orderly said, obviously at the end of a double shift.

"Mister, do you know who this is?" Earl Steuben protested. "This is Miss Olive Thomas, the actress."

The orderly told someone named Miss Ottewell. In my daze, I could hear them talking. Together, they found two litter bearers to move me upstairs and into a ward, and the staff monitored me for a week. In my worst delirium, I had nightmares of Da and the way I had seen him die, choking on his own fluid. I was convinced I would see him soon and prepared myself for the worst. But somehow I surprised everyone by fighting off the pneumonia that usually followed the flu.

I couldn't remember much but the moans and the coughing and dying all around me. Every few minutes, orderlies came with a litter and removed someone who had been alive less than ten minutes before. They cleaned and disinfected the area and changed the sheets, then brought in another to take the place of the dead person.

Private rooms were nonexistent. Beds were jammed wherever they would fit. But the corner they gave me filled with all the flowers from friends and relatives. I spent my time coughing, crying, and trying to sleep, lying in bed staring out the window at the snowy skies, the dirty roof next door, and the advertisement for Wissner Upright Player Pianos painted on the wall two buildings away. Penny brought me some copies of *Photoplay*, saving me from complete boredom, and she promised she would get word to Jack about my condition. The air in the mask over my face was like a swamp. Yeah, it kept my germs from infecting others, but I desperately wanted some fresh air.

A courageous group of carolers braved the plague in the wards to spread some Christmas cheer to the patients. I rolled over and pulled the covers over my head, still miserable.

On Christmas Eve, a man approached my bed. He had hair the color of a copper penny and a spray of freckles. Most of his face was hidden by his white cloth mask, but his brown eyes twinkled, and he introduced himself as Millard Fillmore Warner.

"Call me Phil," he said. He explained that Jack was still stuck in the brig but wanted to send me his love. My heart took off like the elevator at the Algonquin on its way to the penthouse. He'd gotten Penny's message! Phil pulled a velvet box from his pocket and drew it open for me. The insignia inside was for H. Healy in Brooklyn. A diamond necklace nestled inside.

"He gave me this too," he said. He placed a buff-colored envelope on the sheet. I opened it while he glanced away.

"Dear Ollie—

I'm sorry you're feeling so low. Please forgive me for being such an oaf. I could not convince them to let me visit, even though I told them you were ill. I hope this small offering will improve your spirits.

Merry Christmas, darling

Your Jack"

Since the necklace was so pricey and the hospital didn't have a safe, Phil offered to keep it in his safe-deposit box at Metropolitan Bank uptown. That sounded like a smart idea, so he took it with him. Unfortunately, Phil was visiting family on Christmas Day. No necklace, no Jack.

The next week, I felt a calming presence and peeked out from under the covers to see Jim standing over my bed. He was thinner than I remembered, but all his limbs were still there. No eye patches, no crutches, and no bandages. His blue eyes crinkled at the corners as he smiled, and auburn whiskers covered his chin.

"Jim . . ." I whispered, holding out my arms. "Oh God, Jim, you're home. You're alive." He set his bag down.

"I came straight from the boat. Mamma wired that you were in this awful place. Are you contagious? How do you feel?"

He hugged me awkwardly from the chair next to the bed.

"They tell me I'm on the road to recovery, but it sure doesn't feel like it, cooped up here. Oh God, I missed you. How are you?"

"Never so happy to be back home in the States. How long have you been sick?"

"Just before Christmas," I said, coughing into a handkerchief. The coughs didn't hurt as much now, but my breastbone and diaphragm still ached like someone had hit me with a sledgehammer. I pulled my mask up over my face and tossed my handkerchief into the nearby laundry receptacle. Effie, bless her soul, had brought me a stack of them, laundered and folded next to my bed.

"Where the hell is your husband, what's-his-name?" Jim

said, glancing up and down the ward. "He should be with you."

"Jack," I said, trying to hide the sadness in my voice. "Still on base." I was too embarrassed to say, "In the brig," in case Jim hadn't seen any of the news stories. Jim was a war hero, for Christ's sake. Jack had been labeled a coward and a disgrace only several months into his service. I relaxed against the pillows as Jim leaned forward in his chair.

"My big brother, a soldier. I worried about you so many nights. Was it awful?"

He was quiet for a long time.

"It was bad. We were at Belleau Wood. I'm not sure how I'm supposed to go home to Margaret and Jimmie and be normal after this. I don't feel normal at all."

I took his hand, and both of us had tears in our eyes.

"I thought I'd never be clean again, with all the mud and the lice, and the . . ." He stopped short. "But here I am. Same old Jim, same old uniform. Like nothing happened, huh? The cold seeped into your bones in those trenches—I can't seem to get warm, no matter how long I sit next to a roaring fireplace."

"Oh, Jim," I said, clasping his hand. "I'm just glad you're home. What are you going to do now? Do you know?"

"I was going to ask you if you know anyone who might hire a vet like me."

"Actually, I have some connections," I said.

CHAPTER FORTY

LOS ANGELES LIMITED NEAR SALT LAKE CITY, UTAH,
January 1919

"All the way to Los Angeles, miss?" The conductor startled me out of my daydream by asking for my ticket.

"Yes, thanks."

He punched it and handed it to me after a second glance. I was used to it by now—they were all convinced they knew my face but couldn't place it. Turning my attention to the sagebrush sailing by, I thought of my next film, *Upstairs and Down*, ready to film at the Brunton Studios in California. Oh, Myron had told me upfront that they were finishing a new studio in Long Island City, but something he'd neglected to tell me was that until it was finished, he had no place to shoot. That meant traveling to wherever we could book useable space. This time, it was California. But he had plenty of other locations in mind, and I had a feeling the schedule was going to be exhausting. He was also using the Biograph space in the Bronx and getting ready to take over the Universal plant in Fort Lee, New Jersey. Before I left, Lottie sent me a telegram that Jack was in the hospital in Los Angeles for his appendix. So I hurried putting my trunk together.

Mary wanted Jack shooting wherever was farthest from me. Jack was just excited to return to work after the scandal. The lieutenant behind all his troubles was court-martialed. Jack turned state's evidence, spilling his guts about the entire affair. As usual, Charlotte and Mary saw to his defense like bulldogs, got him released, and paid a mint to the papers to have the story go away. The secretary of the navy recommended a dishonorable discharge and said Jack wasn't fit to be kept in the service. But I developed new respect for Charlotte, the old battle-ax, when she copped a letter from President Wilson's chief of staff, Joe Tumulty, recommending Jack be given a regular discharge instead.

"Mr. Pickford has a new picture coming out—*The Brood of the Bald Eagle*," Tumulty told the press. "As far as the American government is concerned, he is far more valuable in his role as a star in propaganda films than he was in his clerical role."

The film was never begun, but no one bothered to tell Tumulty or the navy.

"What a bunch of saps!" Jack commented later, a cigarette in one hand and a Scotch in the other.

It took everything I had to walk into another hospital, but I rushed directly to Room 302, gagging on the smell of disinfectant. The only thing I found there were cards and flowers piled on any surface they would fit and nurses stripping the sheets off the bed.

"I'm sorry. Mr. Pickford has checked himself out," a pretty blonde nurse told me.

"But I told him I was coming . . ." I said, fuming.

"You're Mrs. Pickford, aren't you? I recognized you from *Madcap Madge*. He left you this."

She handed me a note scrawled on a pharmacy receipt in Jack's spidery handwriting. *"Ollie, get to the Pavilion at Fiesta Park and ask for Chauncey Ford at the main desk,"* I read. *"I have a surprise for you. Love, Jack."*

I should have been excited about the surprise, but I was only annoyed. He'd been in the hospital, for crying out loud. He might not have recovered completely.

I picked up a few of the cards and didn't recognize any of the names on them. Most of them read something like this: *"Dear Mr. Pickford. My name is ___, and I live in ___. I am your biggest fan. You are the handsomest man in the movies, and I wanted to send you these flowers to help you feel better . . ."*

Thanking the nurse, I turned on my heel and left, flagging a cab outside.

"Pico and Grand," I said, crawling into the rear of the car.

"Going to the auto show?" the cab driver asked over the seat at me.

"Yeah, I guess I am."

"Heard they got some real beauties this year. If I had a million dollars, I'd buy one of those nice Peerless things they got."

I kept my mouth shut, knowing that was probably just what Jack had gotten. Slipping the driver a little extra to help him save for his Peerless, I climbed out when he pulled up to a stop at the grounds. He was a nice enough fellow.

The auto show pavilion was dressed up like a showgirl in her gaudiest finery, with bunting and banners hung all over. At the front desk, they summoned Mr. Ford right away, and he escorted me to the Pierce-Arrow booth, where Jack stood smiling, his arms outstretched next to a silver machine that had been polished to within an inch of its life.

"Ollie, isn't she fantastic?"

"You bought a Pierce?"

"Not just any Pierce! Nine-thousand simoleons! I got it for you! Lottie and I saw her a week ago, and I insisted on buying her. It's a Model 48. Got a T-head inline six-cylinder engine, 525 cubic inches, 142-wheelbase chassis." I doubted he knew what any of that stuff was—it just sounded great coming from the salesman.

"Aluminum body, and this part is why I had to leave the hospital early. I wanted to surprise you. Monogrammed there on the door. See? *OTP*, for Olive Thomas Pickford. I warned everyone they could clean her up, that type of thing, but your exquisite derriere had to be the first to sit in it or I'd rip up the contract."

"It's nice," I said, somewhat overwhelmed by the whole thing. It was just a car, after all. We had so many. And we'd had to store them at Mary's while I was staying at Penny's and he was rooming at the government's expense.

Shooting at Brunton wasn't bad. Oodles of companies shot flickers at their place on Melrose, and they had enough equipment for all of us. They had enclosed stages and huge banks of arcs and Cooper Hewitts. Jack was filming at Brunton too, so we were able to have lunch together. Every night, I prayed that my last few Triangle films would see distribution, or we'd be selling one or two of those fancy cars to pay the bills.

CHAPTER FORTY-ONE

LOS ANGELES, *March 10, 1919*

J.F. wanted to see the Pierce, and I wanted to get out of the house. The weather was perfect. Balmy and warm, and the breeze off the Pacific tickled the palm tree fronds so they hissed and crackled.

"Niiiiice!" J.F. said, circling the Pierce and whistling.

"It's mostly the monogram that's impressive," I said.

"I'll have to get one of these," he said, crawling into the front seat and placing his hands on the wheel. "Hop in!" he said gleefully.

"Scoot over," I said. "I'm driving."

I'll admit I was distracted, thinking about the situation with Myron. We hadn't meant for it to happen, but we'd drifted into an affair, and now we were like toast and honey. His mother was just as close as my own, his brother David was a special friend, and his father Lewis had become another father to me.

Myron and I rendezvoused at the Algonquin in New York or at the Alex when we were both on the West Coast. We'd check in separately, then visit each other's rooms. So far, no one was suspicious. Myron had visited me often at the hospital, bringing me flowers and candy and pots of nutritious chicken soup that Florence had cooked up. He was even pressuring me to divorce Jack and marry him.

We'd rounded a corner when a group of children playing in a front yard all raised their heads like a flock of prairie dogs. One of them scampered into the street in front of me after his ball.

"Ollie, you're going a little fas—look out!" J.F. yelled.

I slammed on the brakes and jerked the wheel, but we still hit the boy.

"Oh, good Christ! What have I done?" I said. I stumbled out of the car, but my knees crumpled under me. J.F. raced to the boy's side and tried to figure out how badly he was injured.

"Where does it hurt?" I heard him say. The boy was stunned, obviously, but still tried pointing.

The children in the yard craned their necks, frightened and whispering.

J.F. took charge. "Have one of your parents fetch the doctor!" he cried. "Hurry now!"

One of the kids scurried away. I crawled over to J.F. and the boy and slipped off my scarf, placing it under the boy's head.

"I'm so sorry, sweetheart," I said. "We're calling a doctor, and you're gonna be fine. Everything's gonna be okay." I think I was saying it more to convince myself.

"It hurts," he said.

"I know," I said, clasping his hand.

"What's your name, son?" J.F. said.

"Chester."

At long last, an ambulance pulled up a few yards away from us. Two litter bearers in white coats dashed over, carefully placing

Chester on the stretcher and checking his vital signs.

"Could be internal injuries. We need to take him to St. Elizabeth's," one of them said when they had him in the ambulance. He held two fingers to the boy's wrist.

We traveled behind it and sat in the waiting room for hours. I paced and smoked like crazy. Couldn't believe I was in another goddamned hospital. J. F. phoned Myron, who was in town negotiating with Brunton. He joined us in the waiting room, and when I told him I needed to leave he blocked my way.

"Oh no, missy. You're staying right where you are."

"Myron, I'm exhausted."

He lowered his voice and pointed. "Then you'll grab a nap in that chair. If you act caring and concerned, we might be able to repair the damage this accident will do to your career. You cannot go home until that kid leaves the hospital. Got it?"

I sighed and plopped into one of the chairs in the waiting room, uncomfortably making conversation with Chester's parents. It sounds crazy, but I think they were more excited to meet me than they were worried for their son. Of course, I signed autographs for them, hoping to lessen some of the guilt, but my chest was so tight it felt like I was wearing an over-laced corset.

I spent four days in that waiting room, gradually getting stinkier and more exhausted until the doctors finally declared Chester's situation stable and let him go home. So Myron let me go too.

Two weeks later, we headed to New York together. Three days after we arrived, he summoned me to a lawyer's office with the words, "It's important, Ollie. And for fuck's sakes, take a cab. Nathan Burkan. He's at 1431 Broadway."

The cab pulled to a stop in front of a brown brick building in the garment district, and I took the stairs up.

"I'll announce you," said a secretary, a graying woman in her forties with multiple chins and a bosom like a pillow.

Myron was seated in one of the chairs in front of an imposing oak desk, smoking smelly cigars with two men I didn't know. One chair remained vacant.

"Ollie, come on in!" he said, rising. Behind the desk sat an older man in a navy suit with a full head of gray hair. He put his hand out to shake mine. I shook it halfheartedly.

"Nathan Burkan," he said.

"Ollie, Nathan's an entertainment lawyer. He's going to help us with this Chester problem."

"Lovely to meet you, Miss Thomas," Mr. Burkan said. "Won't you have a seat?"

I sat. "Chester problem?"

"The kid you hit," Myron said. "His bills have been hefty, and his parents are hopping mad. The kid fractured his collarbone and he had some internal injuries. We need to nip this in the bud so it doesn't damage your worth with the public."

"Okay. What are *we* doing?"

"Everyone already knows you're a lousy driver," Myron said. "The story of the boy hit the papers, but we need it to disappear. The faster it goes away, the less the public will make of it. Nathan's going to help us with that."

"How?"

"That brings me to my next introduction. This is Mischa Ryzhkov. He's going to be your new chauffeur." The bohunk clutched his hat, holding out his hand.

"My what?" I sat for a minute, unable to say anything.

"Miss Thomas," Mr. Burkan said, "I've had discussions with Myron and with Chester's parents. Their main worry is that you're still driving. They see you as a reckless speeder, and they're worried about the safety of other children. Unfortunately, your reputation precedes you."

"My reputation?"

"The drinking, Miss Thomas. Since you are married to Jack Pickford, people will always assume the worst about you. You're movie stars of course, but you're not beloved like his sister is. Take Jack's problems in the service, for instance. To the public, he is a drunken rogue, and Chester's parents are worried about that influence on you. I promised them we would get you a chauffeur."

"But my driving is getting better. I like seeing the sights," I said.

"Forgive me for saying so, but Chester's injuries are proof that you're not getting better. This measure is absolutely necessary. The alternative is that Chester's parents sell their story to the papers, keeping your name in the news that much longer. Olive Thomas, careless! Olive Thomas, a speeder! All a prosecuting attorney has to do is bring up your record of tickets, multiple wrecked luxury cars, the accident when Jack was jailed for drunkenness two years ago, and Chester's injuries. If that happens, I won't have much to do in the courtroom."

"But I like driving—"

"Ollie," Myron said, "if you don't do this, your career will go into a major skid. I can't help you. You're not used to this since you haven't been in pictures long, but I saw it when I was working for my father. The public is fickle. My main concern is keeping Chester's parents happy and preventing them from suing you or Selznick Pictures. This will keep them quiet. Let Jack worry about his own neck. For me, this is the best course for you."

"Hell's bells," I muttered under my breath. Then I turned to the bohunk. "What was your name again?"

"Mischa."

"Is that Russian?"

He nodded.

I cocked my head. "Are you a Bolshevik?"

"No, madam. I left my country to get away from the Bolsheviks. My family was of the nobility. I escaped to Paris last year and then decided to try my luck in America."

"It's nice to meet you then, I guess. Can you drive?"

"I was a driver for Prince Michael, the Czar's brother."

"Then I guess you're hired."

March 24, 1919

I was tickled to see that *The Vital Spark*, one of my last Triangle pictures, was going to see release. But now they were calling it *Toton the Apache*, which had to be about the stupidest name ever, and I told Myron so.

"They don't have Apache Indians in France, do they?" I said. "Why the hell did they change the name to something so ridiculous?"

"Actually, Ollie, this name is pronounced 'Apahsh,'" he said. "It's a type of criminal in Paris. They also named a dance after it."

That was news to me. The distributors had flooded the market with ads in newspapers and *Photoplay*. Hoping for a success, I bought myself a silver fox neckpiece for my favorite coat, then promptly came down with the damned flu once more. This time, Mischa drove me to the hospital in style. Myron threatened me, so I had to go. And I lived through the same hell of coughing, hacking, and not being able to breathe for weeks. I was still weak as a kitten when I got home.

After this second bout, Myron was struck by the fear of God and telephoned me, telling me to come to his office right away.

"What's all the fuss about?" I said.

"Ollie, you have to understand," he said. "At this point in my production career, you *are* Selznick Pictures. I can't afford to lose you or the box office receipts you generate. I've conferred with several insurance agents, and I've taken out multiple policies covering you for $300,000."

I put him off for as long as I could, pleading lingering exhaustion, until he called me a few days later, completely out of patience.

"I'm going to give it to you straight," he said. "If you die of the flu or in a car accident, or if you push up daisies any other old way, not only will your death sadden me beyond belief, it will also bankrupt me. Now come down to my office to sign these fucking papers. I mean it."

When he laid everything out in dollars and cents and I realized what a huge hole my death could cause, I got more agreeable about the insurance and the dough. Mischa took me to Myron's office and helped me climb the stairs. Myron settled me down with a cup of tea, added honey and lemon, and tucked an afghan around me and into the corners of the chair, nice and cozy. We signed the forms, and he breathed a little easier when it came to his starring attraction, me.

Why couldn't I have met Myron three years ago? He was far better for my career, my publicity machine, and my ego than Jack. I didn't know if he could dance and he wasn't as great in bed, but any relationship had trade-offs, didn't it?

That said, all Jack had to do was wink and I'd come running. He knew the hold he had on me was too strong to break. For all his faults, I was still in love with him and expected to see the earth shaking or volcanoes exploding every time we crawled in the sack. I'd never experienced that with anyone else. He was like a sickness with me, but we fought worse than Punch and Judy when we were together.

CHAPTER FORTY-TWO

NEW YORK CITY, *early April 1919*

"DEAR OLLIE STOP SHEET MUSIC SALES FOR UP-STAIRS AND DOWN THEME OFF THE CHARTS STOP GOOD JOB STOP LOVE MYRON"

He was right. *Upstairs and Down* turned out to be a real humdinger, along with its snappy theme song.

Audiences loved me as snotty Alice Chesterton, one of the new breed of what everyone was calling "baby vamps." They were modeled after the vamp characters like Theda Bara, but they were younger and more innocent. They lured men into bad situations by flirting and manipulation rather than by being downright evil.

I'd just finished shooting scenes for *The Spite Bride* in San Francisco and had time for a visit to New York. Myron said he had something to show me, so he met me at the station and had his driver take us to Broadway between 45th and 46th. The Astor was advertising *East Is West* with Fay Bainter, the Lyceum had David Belasco's production of *Daddies*, and the Loew's was featuring May Allison in *Island of Intrigue*.

But the billboard he'd told me about dwarfed the signs for them all. It must have been over thirty feet long and thirty feet wide. The letters in *Upstairs* ran up on a diagonal, and each sat on a step of a stairway rendered in lights. Each stair flashed one at a time, showing upstairs movement.

"That one?" he said, pointing. "It faces Zukor's office. I know someone inside who told me that when it lit up the first time, he had kittens." The triumph in his voice was unmistakable.

"Myron, it's incredible!"

"Wait!" he said, "We're not done yet. Gerald, the next stop I mentioned, please. Thanks."

Gerald continued on, and another sign about the same size came into view at 42nd and 7th— a little less elaborate, without the flashing steps, but still making a statement among all the others.

A third billboard squatted not far away. Myron had done what he'd promised—my name in lights in Times Square. He also let me know about the other boards they'd put up in Buffalo, Chicago, and Pittsburgh.

At a small newsstand near the New Amsterdam, he jumped out and bought a copy of *Variety* and a *Wid's Daily* theater manual. Then he hopped back in the car, flipping pages.

"Listen to this! '*Miss Thomas makes a jolly-looking Baby Vamp, as she is termed by her acquaintances of the country club set. She has a real girlish appearance, and romps through her part, carrying the audience with her*'!"

I leaned my head on his shoulder as we read together. Next he passed me the *Wid's*.

"Page thirteen," he said, smiling.

"'Baby Vamp' has become a household word," I read out loud. *"No community is complete without one or two innocent-eyed, wiser than their years young women who steal men from their mature sisters. The baby vamp received her name and her first boost to fame in* Upstairs and Down. *This is the part filled by Olive Thomas in the picture, and she makes full use of 'the baby stare,' kittenish mannerisms and the plea, after she has been caught in some bit of trickery, 'But you know, I'm only a child.' Miss Thomas is entertaining even if she isn't appealing, the part forbids that, and the plot is so arranged that she is kept in the foreground most of the time...'"*

He pulled a bottle of champagne from the seat next to him. "Gerald had to drive to four or five bars to find a place that would sell us this," he confided. Something called the Wartime Prohibition Act was putting a crimp in everyone's lives. The government said it needed the grain for feeding the soldiers, and booze wasn't as easy to get anymore. Champagne was as good as gold. He popped the cork, spraying the both of us with bubbles. We took turns chugging on it.

"Didn't I tell you, Ollie? Didn't I tell you I'd make you a star?" he said, taking another pull and passing it to me.

Gazing at his face, I leaned in for a kiss. He responded, and before we knew it, we were groping each other in the rear seat of the limousine. Myron slipped Gerald an extra fifty bucks before we got out at his apartment. We continued upstairs, celebrating my success the only way we knew how.

CHAPTER FORTY-THREE

ASTOR TRUST BUILDING, MANHATTAN, NEW YORK CITY,
April 1919

"Ollie, come in! I want you to meet someone."

I'd stopped by Myron's office at 42nd Street and 5th Avenue to comb through some more paperwork. It turned out to be a happy coincidence.

The Astor Trust Building sat like an upended white brick, with big arched windows overlooking 5th Avenue and the library across the street. The doors inside were fancy metal, sculpted with fish and wacky sea creatures. I had the elevator operator take me up to the eighth floor.

Myron was behind his walnut desk, and in front of him sat a woman in a blue serge day suit with her back to me. She turned when I came in.

"Frances!"

"Olive!"

"Ah . . . you two have met," Myron said. "Perfect."

"It's so good to see you!" Frances said. "It's been ages!" She rose and took my hand. I took hers, and we each sat in one of the chairs facing the desk.

"How are you?" I said.

"Wonderful," she said. "I'm a newlywed."

I had to admit she glowed. "Congratulations! When?"

"Back in February. But let's talk about you. That's why I'm here."

"Ollie, Frances is one of the world's best scenario writers," Myron said. "She's written some of the most popular stuff in Hollywood, and plenty of it was for Mary. *Fanchon, the Cricket*; *Rags*; *Poor Little Rich Girl* . . . Mary trusts her to create tremendous stories, and now Frances is going to be writing a scenario just for you."

"Bully! What will it be about? Who will I be playing? When do I start?"

"Well, she has to write it first. But this film should speak to your public, and I want them to fall in love with you over this role. This will be your signature picture, Ollie. We're going to promote the hell out of it. Billboards in the big cities and large ads in the major dailies. In Pittsburgh, we can milk a 'local-girl-made-good' theme."

"Frances, this is so exciting! How did you get into flickers? How do you succeed as a woman in this business? What's it like writing scenarios? What a career you must have!"

Frances laughed and turned to Myron. "You weren't kidding, were you? She *is* curious."

I had a good feeling about Frances Marion.

After we chatted with Myron all morning, Frances asked me if I'd like to have lunch. We agreed on Childs, both having a hankering for butter cakes.

Over chicken croquettes, butter cakes, and fresh fruit salad, she mapped out a possible creation. "So Ollie, you've had some work as a baby vamp. I read that interview with E.V.

Durling that you did. You know, the one where you talked about the baby vamp being more dangerous than the Bolsheviks? That was a spot of brilliance, dear. We should capitalize on that. You were gorgeous in *Upstairs and Down,* a comely little coquette and a lot of trouble for any fellow unlucky enough to be attracted to you. Alice Chesterton was an almost perfect part, but I'd like to create someone more likable for you. Since you also love playing girls in middy blouses, I say we should carve out that little niche just for you."

"I like that idea. Anything coming to mind yet?"

"I'm seeing a baby vamp. Maybe from the South. From someplace like . . . Florida. We'll need a typical Florida sort of name for her hometown. A little citrusy. How about Orange Springs? That'll work. A town so small, they don't even have a saloon to close."

"Now that's small."

"We'll give her a good name. Something flavorful. Sunny. No, too clichéd. Maybe more ladylike, like Genevieve. But her friends will call her Ginger. That's the kind of fun character we want you to project." She took a bite of fruit salad.

"Great so far. Then what?"

"She'll have a boyfriend too. He'll be a tiresome braggart, and she'll get bored with him. We'll have Ginger misbehave a bit, so her father . . . someone prominent . . . a senator...will send her to a boarding school. Somewhere far away."

"Switzerland?" I said excitedly.

"No, that's too far. It needs to be in America. Not *too* far from home. How about New York? We'll send her to school in New York State and contrast the palm trees with some snow." She gestured with her fork, a chunk of banana emphasizing her point.

"Now, near the boarding school, we'll have a fellow who rides by on a horse from time to time," she said. "Richard . . ."

"Channing?" I offered, glimpsing the bottle of Channing's catsup sauce that sat on our table.

"Channing . . ." Frances thought a minute. "Yes! That will work nicely. We'll have the girls at the boarding school enjoy some ice skating and fun outdoors," Frances said. "Ginger sees Richard Channing riding by on his horse, and she lies to him about her age . . ."

"She sneaks out to meet him . . ." I added.

"Good!" Frances said, pointing her fountain pen at me. "Ollie, you're a natural at this."

We talked for hours, and by the end of lunch we'd hashed out a plot. Frances promised to go home and perfect it. With the real work out of the way, she regaled me with tales of her youth. She was originally from San Francisco and told me about her first job in a peach cannery.

"It lasted all of about a week," she said, chuckling. She had also tried working as a telephone operator, but that hadn't been successful either.

She'd happened into a position as the assistant to a photographer named Arnold Genthe, become his model, then stumbled into writing. She'd married twice and talked casually about her husbands, Wesley and Robert. But she'd divorced young, just like me. Twice.

"Wesley and I were both artists in our own right," she said. "But I'll caution you never to wed another artist. If you're both starving for your principles, no one can afford to pay the rent."

"I'll remember that," I said, sipping my tea.

"Robert was the antithesis of Wesley. Money, status, but we had nothing in common. He divorced *me*." She let out a little sigh and shrugged. "Lived through the quake. I'd just bought a new Easter hat. I was so proud of that thing. I was with Wesley at the park. We were getting ready to go home when we felt the shaking."

"What happened to the hat?" I joked.

"Oh, I saved it, but life sure was different after that."

She also told me of her short stint in France as a war correspondent.

"All two months of it," she said, joking. "But it felt like I was doing my part too."

It struck me how similar we were. Having other jobs we hadn't liked, finding modeling by accident, then getting into the pictures and succeeding in a man's world. Marrying young, and then divorcing.

"I admire you, Ollie," she said. "You stuck to your principles and wanted something better than Pennsylvania. You have a real fire in you. I have so much respect for that. We're alike in many ways, you know."

"I noticed that too," I said, popping a piece of pineapple into my mouth, "but I bet you're a better driver."

Frances laughed a real belly laugh, causing me to like her even more. She also shared stories of her new husband, a preacher named Fred Thomson. "I never thought I would marry a third time," she confessed, "but Fred has shown me how different it is when you find the right person."

I saw the deep love in her eyes as she talked about him, and I wondered when things had changed with Jack. Or if they were never good but I'd been too stupid to notice.

When we finished our meal, Frances reached for the check, but I grabbed it first.

"Don't be silly," she said, peeling it from my fingers. "Myron told me you're overdrawn again. Scenarios provide a nice comfortable living for me. I've got this."

"Thanks, Frances."

"I'll phone as soon as I'm finished with an update," she said, pointing at the notes she'd made. "It should take a couple days to pound out the first few bits of it. But I think you'll be pleased when I'm done. And then I'll move on to the next one. Myron wants me to concentrate my efforts in your direction, so I'm all yours for a while."

Myron always knew best.

Frances and I said goodbye outside Childs with a hug, agreeing to talk soon. As Mischa drove me home, I thought about Myron.

His suggestions had been invaluable so far in everything from roles to finance. His generous policy of cash advances had saved my hide more than once. For all the money coming in, it never went far enough. I hated balancing a bankbook, and it showed. I wasn't sure how my account could be overdrawn so often, but Myron's generosity had gotten me through some hard times. And then I'd always gone and bought some expensive new trinket for Jack or me to feel better. Now I'd added gifts for Myron and his family too. I wasn't sure which way was up anymore.

CHAPTER FORTY-FOUR

GREAT NECK, LONG ISLAND, NEW YORK, *mid-May 1919*

"What's the name of this place again?" Jack said, squinting through the window at a cluster of maple trees as we rounded a corner.

"Idylhurst."

"I hope things out here are livelier at night than they are now," Jack said, "or I'll rename it I-dull-hurst."

"Give it a chance, for God's sake. We're supposed to be relaxing. On vacation. We don't need things to be lively," I said.

The key had been left for us at the Wolf Realty Office, so Mischa drove us there to pick it up. It was a short drive from there to our summer home, owned by the stage actor Raymond Hitchcock. I hoped the time together could help us repair our fraying marriage.

"There it is, Mischa," I said, pointing.

The house sat at the intersection of Middle Neck Road and Clover Drive. It was a two story, with a distinctive roof and a central turret over the front porch. Set into the turret was a decorative clock, and at the very top, a widow's walk. The windows were trimmed with shutters.

For the last few years, the railroad had begun snaking out

to Great Neck, and now it was popular for summer retreats and retirement. Though the drive out from Manhattan was full of ash heaps and gaudy billboards for Horlick's Malted Milk and Post Toasties, the destination was a fine reward.

Jack poked the key in the front door lock and ushered me inside with a big bow. I walked through with a giggle, cradling the bottle of champagne we'd brought to christen it. We'd had to pay a bartender on 43rd a pretty penny for it, under the table. Chow followed us in after christening the front lawn in his own way. The furniture was draped in sheets now that Mr. Hitchcock was living in Florida, so I pulled them off and opened the windows to relieve the stuffiness. The breeze added a whiff of salt and marsh grass to the place.

The kitchen was full of the latest in technology, including a General Electric icebox. I ran my hand over the stove, thinking my cooking skills hadn't progressed much since my marriage to Krug. Effie had the summer off to visit cousins in Alabama, but I was determined to cook something. The kitchen had a glorious view down a little hill, and the terrace was set with Westport chairs and small tables for dining outside. Two white ash trees provided a little shade. Jack inspected the empty liquor cabinet, filling it with the stash we'd brought along. Then he shook up some Bronx cocktails.

Upstairs, I pulled off the sheets that had draped the beds and dressers. Mr. Hitchcock's taste ran to the classics. Since Manhasset Bay was nearby, he'd arranged collections of seashells on the windowsills and hung prints of sailboats and windblown dunes on the walls. Above one of the fireplaces sat a bottle with a miniature ship inside.

I rejoined Jack in the parlor, and he handed me a drink.

We would have three gorgeous months together. No twelve-hour days on the set, no threats from the US government, and no Mary and Charlotte interfering in our lives. Just us, though Myron's presence lingered, along with God knows who for Jack. We clinked glasses.

The silver Pierce was parked in the wide curving driveway that lay before the house. Jack and Mischa unstrapped our trunks from the rear of it, dragging them up the wide veranda with its four steep steps. Then they grabbed the rest of the baggage—shoes, makeup case, and my copies of *Photoplay* to keep up with news of the business. After they were done, Mischa took his bag to the servants' quarters to get settled in.

We'd picked up some lamb chops and a sack of potatoes at the market in town, and I'd found some mint growing wild in the garden. Pulling a frying pan off a hook on the kitchen wall, I pan-fried the chops with a mint sauce like Effie had always done. My baked potatoes didn't come out too terrible. Jack had brought some of our phonograph records, and we'd been delighted to find a Columbia Grafonola in the living room. He cranked the lever and played "Take Your Girlie to the Movies If You Can't Make Love at Home."

We sat on the floor, eating the food picnic-style, enjoying the bottle of champagne we'd brought with us, and tossing bits of meat to Chow, who gobbled them up, then fell asleep under a footstool. When dinner was finished, I began collecting the dishes to wash, but Jack summoned me with a whisper.

"Come here," he said. He poured us both more champagne, but I was feeling flirty and frisky already.

I scooted closer after taking another sip, and we kissed. Our tongues danced with the bubbles, and our hands clung together. He pushed me down on the rug, then pulled my skirt up. Freeing himself from his lightweight summer trousers, he took me on the rug of our new living room. Knowing the season was ours to do whatever we pleased, I hung on for the ride and felt myself falling with him.

The season was one big round of parties and groups of friends staying over when they were in town. The afternoons were full of rummy and orange blossoms on the terrace, and the nights were crammed with drunken croquet and swimming in Little Neck Bay at 2:00 a.m.

One lazy Saturday morning in July, I had just made pancakes that were on the rubbery side. They still tasted good with maple syrup, though, so I was congratulating myself when the phone rang. Jack picked it up in his usual cocky manner, figuring it was Mickey or Kirky. A minute later, he tripped over his words, and I heard, "Hold on Jim, I'll put her on. Ollie, phone for you. It's Jim." He handed me the handset.

"What a surprise!" I said into the mouthpiece.

My enthusiasm was met with a long silence. This was not like him.

"Jim?"

"Ollie, I'm sorry to bother you on your vacation. Myron gave me the number. It's . . . it's Margaret. She's . . . dead." His voice broke, and I could hear him trying to restrain his tears.

Covering my mouth with my hand, I sat down hard in an armchair. "Oh my God, no! Jim, I don't believe it. She was always so healthy. Was it the flu?"

"No. We're not sure what happened."

I hadn't heard a voice so full of sorrow since Mamma's after Da's passing all those years ago. "We discovered she was expecting a few weeks ago, and we were so thrilled. I went to wake her this morning before breakfast, and she was dead. The doctor thinks it might have been some sort of heart trouble. No one knew. I didn't know. Oh God, what am I going to do without her?"

"How's Jimmie doing?" I asked.

"Sad. Confused. Scared. Like me."

The thought of Jimmie so frightened made my heart physically hurt. I needed to be in the city right now.

"Jim, I'll be there as fast as I can."

"Oh Ollie, could you? It would mean so much to us."

"Of course I'll come. We all loved Margaret. I couldn't imagine you and Jimmie being alone during all this."

"Mamma and Harry are on the train. Spud is on his way too. I'll have our neighbor meet you at the station," he said.

"Don't worry about that. I've got a chauffeur. I'll have him drive me in."

He paused. "I have to . . . make the arrangements."

"Be strong for Jimmie," I said. "I'll be there soon."

As soon as the line disconnected, I sat numb for a minute.

"What is it?" Jack said, approaching from the kitchen and holding two Bronx cocktails. He eyed me with a raised eyebrow.

"It's Margaret. She's gone."

"Who?" He took a casual sip from his drink, and in a flash I saw him with new eyes. He'd met her three times, for God's sake.

"My sister-in-law," I said through clenched teeth.

"Oh, yes. Gone? Where?"

"She's dead." I swept past him on my way up to the bedroom. He stood saying nothing, offering no comfort. I don't think he knew how. At last, he dragged himself up the stairs and stood, like a block of marble.

"I'm going to Long Island City," I said.

"What? For how long? We're on vacation!"

"That's all that matters to you? That I'm interrupting our holiday?"

"No, but . . ."

"You'll survive without me. My brother needs me, and so does my nephew. You keep inviting everyone over and getting bent every night. You'll all have a marvelous time."

"But Ollie, I . . ."

I narrowed my eyes until they were icier than the berg that brought down the *Titanic*. He got the point. As he stood, unsure how to react, I grabbed hangers full of my plainer frocks in darker colors and tossed them into a trunk, along with my toiletries, some shoes, and a turban or two.

"Take care of Chow while I'm gone," I said, giving my baby a quick belly rub. And then I hurried to the car. Mischa put it in gear, and I gave him directions to my brother's house in Long Island City. After I'd gotten Jim his studio job, he and Margaret had moved there to be close to it.

Jim let me in. "Jimmie's napping," he said. His eyes were sunken purple hollows. I had never seen them so lifeless. Even after his return from the war.

A few minutes later, Jimmie shyly appeared at the corner of the kitchen doorway, dragging his bear, Wilson.

"Auntie Olive!" His voice changed from a childish whisper

to a squeal of delight, and he darted toward me with his arms open. I held him close, inhaling his little boy scent of talcum powder, mud pies, and metal toy soldiers.

The cheery dishes with violets I'd bought them only two Christmases ago sat in heaps in the sink, unwashed since the death of the lady of the house. I set to work on them, then fixed Jim and Jimmie some sandwiches. Jim barely touched his. We sat together on the couch in the parlor, Jim and I reminiscing about the good old days and Jimmie falling asleep in my lap. I put him to bed, and Jim and I stayed up late talking until he got too tired. I could have packed my entire Follies wardrobe into the bags under his eyes. The next morning, Mamma and Harry arrived, and then Spud.

Harry had quite a few more gray hairs than he'd had on my last visit, and his eyes had lost much of their cheer. From the constant worry for Jim in the war, he and Mamma had been blindsided by this tragedy. Mamma had adored Margaret, as we all had. She mopped away tears when she thought no one could see. Jim sat at the kitchen table, almost unable to move or function. He sat, staring straight ahead.

"Daddy's sick," Jimmie whispered to me.

"Yes he is," I replied.

"Where's Mommy? She should be taking care of him."

"I know, sweetie, I know."

"Some men took her away. She was sleeping. She didn't wake up or anything!"

I knelt down and said, "Let's go outside and play for a little while. You and me. Would you like that?"

He nodded and led me by the hand to his spot in the tiny yard. Margaret had turned it into a pretty garden with roses, peonies, and hollyhocks.

We sat on the ground, and he motioned for me to come see the tiny battle theater, including trenches and fortifications, he'd created for his tin soldiers under the leaves and stems of the flowers.

"It's the Battle of Big Flowers. Those are the Germans." Then pointing at one of the opposing line, he said, "This is Daddy."

"That's impressive," I said, hugging him closer to me.

"What's wrong with him?" he blurted in frustration.

Jesus. What did you say to a kid whose mother had just died? I sighed before answering, not sure how good I might be at this type of thing. Communicating with children, I mean. Other than playing with them.

"Your daddy is very sad right now, Jimmie."

"But why?"

"Did they tell you about Heaven, and what happens when we go there?"

"They teach us in Sunday school," he said.

"Good. Well honey, your mommy is in Heaven now. When you saw her sleeping, she had really gone to be with Jesus and the saints and everyone."

"But why?" His face fell.

"I think God thought she was extra special, and he wanted her up in the sky with him."

"But Daddy's sad. And me too. And she wasn't hardly old at all."

"Yes, I know. It's not very fair when he decides to take someone we love, is it? Your dad and I and Uncle Spud lost our dad when we were little, like you. But God must have wanted him a lot. You see?"

He gave a halfhearted nod.

"Will you promise Auntie Olive something?"

The head shaking increased, the little blond cowlick slipping to and fro as it did.

"You must be a very brave boy, and that means being very good right now. You have to eat all your spinach, and brush your teeth without being asked, and maybe go to bed without a story or a drink of water. You hug Wilson and go right to sleep, okay?"

He continued nodding.

"If you're scared of monsters, think of me. I'll be right there with you. But I'll be invisible. It'll be our secret. Your dad misses your mom very much, so he's going to be sad for a while. You must hold Wilson very tight, and think of Auntie Olive, and be good for your dad until he feels better. Will you do that for me?"

"Yes, Auntie Olive."

I kissed the top of his head and pulled him close. Christ, I needed a smoke.

That night after Jimmie was in bed, I spoke with Jim, knowing it would be hard for him to decide anything in the shape he was in. We sat next to each other, both of us unsure of what to say or do.

"Jim, if you need something, for God's sake let me know. A maid to care for Jimmie, money for the funeral, absolutely anything. You call me."

He nodded, but the life in his eyes was gone. I grabbed him in a huge hug, and we stayed like that for almost an hour, Jim crying his eyes out and me rocking with him as his sorrow poured out. I knew if I had been through all he had in the last two years, they'd have stuck me in the booby hatch by now.

At the wake, Jim was catatonic. He sat in the front row, gazing at the peaceful face of his wife, who now resembled a wax doll in a gunmetal-colored box. Jimmie sat next to him in his Little Lord Fauntleroy outfit, tiny legs not reaching the floor.

Jim's voice shook as he delivered Margaret's eulogy, mumbling certain words and choking on others—happy thoughts about her love of flowers and baking and children, and how she always saw the good in people. He sank into his seat afterward, relieved to have it over with. At the graveside, I took his hand.

The mourners returned to the house afterward, and most brought offerings of food—corned beef and cabbage, stew, and shepherd's pie—and whispered over their plates of food in the parlor. Mamma and I stood at the sink, doing dishes and remembering the good times, especially birthdays and Christmases, when I'd come home loaded with gifts.

"Ollie, I wish you wouldn't spend so much money on us all the time."

"Why, Mamma? I like spoiling you. You worked so hard for so many years."

"Yes I did. And we appreciate everything. But you need to save something too. A rainy day could come, and you might need every dime."

"I enjoy picking out presents for everyone."

"You need to listen to me. The year I was born was a scary time. A panic, they called it. I don't know about how all that financial stuff works, but times were tight for lots of folks. It could happen again. You and Jack with your fancy cars and jewelry and such . . . it's wasteful, honey. Out of love, I ain't said anything before now, but Jack worries me."

It terrified me to hear the same thing out of her mouth I'd fretted about myself.

"I love him, Mamma."

"I know that, honey. But that boy has a lot of growing up to do. If Da was still alive, he'd have tossed Jack Pickford over his knee and walloped him a long time ago. Harry's not like that, but he's got his reservations too."

I stood there a full five minutes before answering, and she took hold of my arm, her hand still wet from the dishes.

"I don't know what to do, Mamma."

"How do you mean?"

"About Jack. I've been having an affair with my producer."

"You what?" Her jaw dropped, and I continued.

"He's been so good for me. And Jack has been . . ." I shrugged my shoulders.

"Is this that Jewish fellow you told us about? Myron?"

I nodded, tears blurring my vision.

"I know it's not who your father and I would have picked for you, but it sounds like he's got his head screwed on the right way, which is more than I will say for the fellow you married. From what you've told us, Myron sounds crazy about you . . ."

"He wants me to leave Jack."

"I daresay a few of us want that, but it's your life."

"I feel so stupid. I can't decide what I want."

"I think you know what to do, but doing it scares the heck out of you. You gotta decide if you want to keep being miserable with Jack and using presents to cover it up or if you want something better. Your married friend from the Follies—what'd you say her name was?"

"Marcie?"

"Yeah. She found herself a good one. One who isn't spoiled rotten 'cause his sister's the Queen of Hollywood. Plenty of nice men would love to marry my Ollie. You just have to find one. Maybe this Myron fellow is him."

"I'm going to give it a little longer and see how things go. Jack has his problems, but he can be so wonderful, Mamma."

She pursed her lips, letting me know I was only trying to convince myself.

When I returned to Great Neck a week later, Jack greeted me with an emerald necklace and another apology. "Penny said I was being insufferable and took me into the city so I could buy you this," he said. Handing me an orange blossom, he lit us both cigarettes.

"I'm sorry I was such a Philistine, darling."

CHAPTER FORTY-FIVE

IDYLHURST GROUNDS, LONG ISLAND, NEW YORK,
August 18, 1919

"Say cheese, Ollie!"

Another flashbulb hissed. A photographer was strolling the grounds of Idylhurst, taking snaps of everyone. We had two reasons to celebrate that night—it was Jack's twenty-third birthday, and on Friday he'd signed a new contract with Goldwyn.

Jack had snared this position all on his own, and he was terribly proud of himself. He'd be working in California. I was still in New York under contract to Myron, but with no full-time studio yet, I could be working anywhere within the next few months. That included California.

Chairs were arranged in circles, torches sparkled on the lawn, and streamers hung between the tree limbs and across the rose arbor. Caterers from the city served canapés and savory meat pies, and I'd insisted on hash. A birthday cake sat at a place of honor on a table on the terrace. Multiple tiers were frosted with vanilla icing, Jack's favorite. We'd also stocked up on the finest caviar and champagne, now that we could get it again. With the exception of hooch, the scarcities of the war were becoming a memory, and now everyone was discussing the peace talks in Paris and what should be done with the Kaiser. We'd also hired a quartet, the Tuneful Troubadours. They were playing a sweet, soft version of "After You've Gone."

At first, it was only going to be a small party, but as more and more friends discovered they were in town for the season, the invitations multiplied.

Out in the garden, Tony Moreno was deep in discussion with Charles Winninger, and Tom Meighan was talking to Elaine. She'd signed with Selznick too and was filming *The Country Cousin* in Fort Lee. Mickey was arguing with our lawyer, Nathan. No surprise. Mickey would argue with anybody. Chow patrolled the grass for stray hors d'oeuvres.

Across the lawn was the Follies bunch. Jenny and Rosie Dolly were laughing with Marjorie and Mae Murray, who was hot off the success of her *Delicious Little Devil* for Metro. Bessie Poole stood with W.C. Fields, chatting with Penny, who was doing a little shimmy to the "Darktown Strutters' Ball." W.C. was already three sheets to the wind, after finishing off our precious bottle of Old Grand-Dad.

"Last Thursday," I heard him braying, "that audience was colder than a penguin's tootsies. Did you see 'em, Penny?"

Myron arrived just then, with Florence, Lewis, and David in tow. Myron guided me by the arm into the house and we stood together in the darkened kitchen, leaning against the door to the dumbwaiter.

"Ollie!" Jack called, "I have to try to find some whiskey! Fields is drinking us out of house and home!" He jangled the keys as he headed out to the Arrow.

"Let Mischa drive you!" I yelled after him, but it was too

late. I heard gravel spraying in all directions as he flew down the driveway.

As soon as Jack took off, Myron nuzzled me, and his hand slipped beneath the skirt of my silver chiffon summer frock and into the area between my thighs.

"I need you, Ollie. You have no idea how lonely I've been without you the past few weeks."

I peeked out the kitchen window, and seeing no one approaching the house, led him into the first-floor guest bedroom. The shades were all down, and Myron flipped the lock. We pulled at clothes—a necktie went flying along with a shirt, and then a dress fell, followed by trousers, chemise, and undershirt. It would be hell if anyone caught us. But it only made things more exciting.

Not wanting to risk the squeaking of the bedsprings, I yanked out the desk chair and Myron pulled me onto him. We were a mass of writhing hands and slippery bliss until the finale rippled over both of us in satisfying waves, and I bit my lip to keep from crying out.

I tossed him a guest towel, then took another and cleaned myself up with it.

"Ollie? Are you in there?" Mae said in a soft drawl. She knocked, then the door shook in its frame. "What are you doing?"

"Nothing," I said, trying to sound breezy. "Just going to the toilet!"

"Oh," she said. "We wanted to say goodbye. I'm a little tired."

"I won't be a minute," I called. Pointing to the closet, I gestured to Myron to go into it and quickly pulled my clothes and shoes on.

"Wait five minutes after I leave," I whispered. I kissed him and slipped out, then followed Mae outside.

Later that night, after everyone left, Jack cornered me in the kitchen like Myron had done. And like Myron, he kissed me and touched me the way I liked to be touched. I followed him into the guest room, and he promptly passed out. His snores echoed through the darkness. First thing Monday morning he hopped the train out to California to begin filming *Little Shepherd of Kingdom Come*.

CHAPTER FORTY-SIX

QUEENS COUNTY FAMILY COURT, NEW YORK CITY,
August 1919

In August, Jim telephoned and begged me for a huge favor. It had to have been the hardest thing he'd ever had to ask anyone in his life. But he couldn't care for himself or anyone else in the shape he was in. I agreed right away, though I had my doubts about us being any better as guardians for Jimmie. Half the time, being with Jack was like being with a ten-year-old.

The bailiff's voice echoed off the spare wooden pews and marble floors of Courtroom A. "Oye, Oye, Oye. All rise. The court of the Honorable Melvin J. Corrigan is now in session."

Jack and I stood at one table, with Nathan acting as our attorney. Jim stood at another table with his attorney and Jimmie, all of five years old. In an effort to look extra respectable, I'd worn an ivory duvetyn suit and boots of the same color. I'd made Jack wear his best charcoal gray suit and a striped tie I'd gotten him two Christmases before.

"In the matter of the guardianship of James Michael Duffy Junior, who has brought this case?"

"I have, Your Honor," Jim said.

The judge peered at the file, skimming some of it. "James Michael Duffy Senior?"

"Yes sir."

"How say you?"

"Your Honor, my wife Margaret died last month. It has been difficult for me to care for a young son and deal with my incredible grief. My job as a cameraman for the Selznick studio sometimes requires me to travel to shooting locations. My sister, Olive Duffy"—he pointed at me—"now known as Olive Thomas Pickford, is an actress in moving pictures. She earns a lucrative living and can give Jimmie all the things I can't as a single father. My employment grants me only limited means compared to Olive's income. I would like Olive and her husband to share custody when I am forced to be out of town or am unable to tend to Jimmie."

"So you have not remarried, sir?"

"No, Your Honor. I haven't even considered it. It's far too soon."

The judge glanced around the room until he saw Jack and me at the other table. "Mrs. . . . Pickford," he said, referring to the file. "You are a motion picture actress."

"Yes, Your Honor." *Obviously not a fan, this guy.*

"And this is your husband?"

"Yes sir. Jack Pickford," I said.

Did I see his nose wrinkle? Or was it my imagination?

"Do you have any experience with children, Mrs. Pickford? Nurturing them and providing for their upkeep? I know what a hedonistic lifestyle you movie people lead." He hissed the word "hedonistic."

"Yes sir," I said. "I was the middle child, so I helped to attend to our younger brother William when he was little. I helped my mother to feed him, change his diapers, bathe him, get him dressed, and put him to bed. Our father passed away when we were young, so it was important that we all pulled together to keep our family strong. I have a younger half-sister, Harriett Van Kirk, as well as our niece, Little Mary Rupp. That's Jack's sister Lottie's girl. She's also quite fond of us and loves to visit with us when we are in California."

"So you have experience with children. What about your husband?"

Not unless you count being one, I thought.

"No, Your Honor. But Ollie is a terrific teacher," Jack said, trying to crack a little joke, but the Mount Everest in the black robe would not be moved.

"And what does the child think of this arrangement?"

We all turned toward little Jimmie, who was picking at the varnish on his chair.

"Son," Judge Corrigan said, not unkindly, "do you love your aunt and want her to help care for you?" He didn't ask about Jack, which was a little strange. I guess he knew who would be doing most of the work.

Jimmie's eyes were as big as the wheel rims on a Packard. Jim leaned down and gave him a little nudge, whispering in his ear. Having just lost a tooth three days before, Jimmie spoke up in his lisp. "Yeth, Your Honor."

"Do you have anything else you'd like to tell the court?" the judge said.

"I miss my mommy something terrible, thir. But I know my daddy's had a hard time since she died. And my Auntie

Olive and Uncle Jack are nice when I visit. I love my dad, and he loves me. But he says I'll be able to have lots more toys at Auntie Olive's, and I'll get to go to college and have all the things Daddy can't afford. And that sounds all right to me." Another nudge. "Your Honor."

He looked up for approval, like a little gentleman.

A few more witnesses spoke up on our behalf, including Mamma, Tom Meighan, and Kirky, who happened to be in New York for the week.

"Your Honor," I added, "We want Jimmie to have all the material things his heart desires, but also all the love and closeness of an extended family. I hope you will consider that in your judgment. Thank you."

Judge Corrigan sat scribbling notes with a fountain pen before speaking.

"Then it is the opinion of this court that the interests of the minor, James Michael Duffy Junior, would best be served in the care and custody of Mr. and Mrs. Pickford when his father is forced to be away. This custody hearing is official according to the laws of the State of New York. This case is dismissed."

Jimmie sat in his chair, his eyes filling with tears. Jim knelt down next to him, and they hugged each other. Jack and I waited a moment, and then Jim turned and hugged me so tight I thought he might crack a rib.

"It'll be okay," I said, touching his cheek. "Someday it will feel better."

His eyes held the first bit of hope I'd glimpsed in months. "I love you, sis."

"I know. Love you too."

Jimmie ran over to me and grabbed my hands. "You get to be my new mommy now, Auntie Olive!"

NEW YORK CITY, *August 1919*

Jim had to leave right away to film *The Country Cousin* with Ralph Ince, Mr. Ince's brother, so Jack and I cared for Jimmie. Those few weeks flew by in a blur of trips to the zoo, Fatty Arbuckle flickers, and visits to as many toy stores as we could find. I bought him a new train set and a toy sailboat, which we floated in the pond at Central Park. One bright morning, Mischa drove us to the Jersey Shore and we played in the waves, bought saltwater taffy, and built sand castles. Another day we went to Coney Island and rode everything at least twice. We ate fairy floss candy that stuck to our noses and gobbled down hot dogs and chocolate ice cream sodas.

At night, I put him to bed in his new room, which we'd had painted a very big-boy shade of blue. We'd decorated it with trains, which he loved, and even an engineer's hat, which hung at a cocky angle from the bedpost. I'd read to him from *Tarzan* or *Tom Sawyer* and then bring him a drink of water before snugly tucking him in. Chow had taken to sleeping at the foot of his bed, pleased to have a young master who also enjoyed getting into mischief. They'd become best friends.

"Auntie Olive," he'd say.

"Yes, Jimmie."

"Thanks for being my new mommy."

"You're welcome, pal." I kissed his forehead and turned off the lamp, thinking this was what I had been waiting for my whole life. If only he could be mine for real.

As summer progressed, I'd have to make a difficult decision. I'd be out-of-pocket for weeks, and Jack was stuck in Hollywood for the time being. I needed to think about schooling for Jimmie.

The only option appeared to be a boarding school near New York, so we could see each other as much as possible. It was good our place in the city was across from Central Park, but I also wanted him to romp and frolic with kids his own age. I'd heard good things about a woman from Italy named Montessori who had established a new way of teaching children. Now one of these schools had opened in Tarrytown. I'd checked with Jim and he'd given it the okay, realizing it was a far better school than he could afford.

It was a sunny summer morning after oatmeal and toast when I told Jimmie we were making a little trip.

"Where are we going?" he asked.

"Westchester County," I said. "It's not far. And it's very pretty."

"But why?"

Knowing I would go to hell for fibbing to him, I said, "Auntie Olive has some business."

I dressed him in his best shirt with a little bow tie and nicest pair of short pants. Gotta hand it to the kid—he knew he was being fed a line of horseshit.

"Mommy said we don't wear nice clothes to play. So we're not going to play, are we?"

I looked down at my Tailleur suit of goldenrod-colored serge and sighed. He was sharper at six than I was at sixteen.

"No, Jimmie, we're not. We have something very important to do. Auntie Olive needs to find a school for you."

"You're sending me away?" his eyes pooled with tears.

So this was what parenting was all about. Maybe I'd need to think about it a little harder.

"Honey, it's not like that. Don't you want to run and play tag outside in the fresh air, and swim, climb trees, and go sledding in the wintertime? Those are the fun things most little boys do. If you're not in school, you'd have to go with me to all the places I film, and that won't work. You'd be very lonely, for one. I'd be working most of the time. And second, New York City isn't the kind of place for a little boy. You should do more than ride the elevated railway, visit Coney Island, and go to Central Park. Wouldn't you rather make friends and play soldiers and Germans with them? Or cowboys and Indians?"

He thought a minute. "Cowboys and Indians is fun."

"Sure it is. Sitting on a movie set all day is boring. Trust me—I do it all the time. You only see the flicker after we're all done filming it. Half the day, we sit around twiddling our thumbs."

He seemed skeptical. "What about Chow?"

"You can see Chow anytime you want. I'll bring him when we visit each other on weekends. Honestly, Jimmie, when you see this place, you'll change your mind about it. I've seen the pictures, and it's very nice. You trust me, right? We're pals, you and me. And I wouldn't let anything bad happen to you. I can't replace your mom, and I won't even try. She was the sweetest lady in the world. But I love you with all my heart, and I'm going to take good care of you, I promise."

"Cross your heart and hope to die?"

"Cross my heart, at least." I took my fingers and struck a cross between my breasts.

"All right," he said, his drawn-out sigh proving that a flair for drama ran in the family.

"Look at you," I said, "Sadder than limp celery. If you promise to be a good boy, I'll have Mischa drive us to Schrafft's for an ice cream soda later."

He let out a whoop like Sitting Bull if he'd been poked in the backside with a knitting needle. When he beat me to the front door and stood impatiently pulling at a thread on his jacket, I knew all was forgiven.

Ever ridden with a six-year-old? It's like a monologue that never ends. It could concern every topic from the weather, the scenery, the billboards, and the wildlife to any strange unrelated thought that might creep in along the way.

As Jimmie babbled about everything from the roadside ads for Ingram's shaving cream to what General Pershing's dog must be like, Mischa kept the Arrow at a steady speed and chuckled from time to time at the chatter.

Mischa had taken Broadway until it turned rural and veered north through Yonkers, Hastings, and Dobbs Ferry, and we took the scenic route through town, noticing the multiple posters for an eager fellow named Carl Loh, Realtor.

The tall spruces appearing along the road outside of town let us know we were close to the school. Shrubs and flowers in neat beds lay in front of a red brick half wall that announced "The Children's Place." Mischa followed the drive up to an impressive building of the same red brick.

He helped us out of the car, and we entered the front lobby. It had a black-and-white tile floor like a checkerboard and a staircase that stretched up to the second-floor landing.

A woman with a spectacularly large bosom listed toward us in the way top-heavy women do. She wore an afternoon suit of a dusky peach color that matched her flushed complexion. A ruched blouse frothed out of her jacket, and an emerald brooch hid between the ruffles.

Her voice was a pleasant burble, the sound of someone who loved her job, like liquor splashing over the ice in a lowball glass. "Hello! Hello! I am Mrs. Perkins! Welcome to The Children's Place. Miss Thomas, I recognize you from your films," she said, taking my hands and clasping them. "It's a delight. And this must be James."

"Jimmie," the boy said with all the crotchety bad humor of his father at that age.

I nudged him to let him know his ice cream soda was riding on better manners.

"Sorry," he said. "I go by Jimmie, ma'am." He glanced at me for approval, and I gave him the nod.

Mrs. Perkins took us on the grand tour so we could see the neat navy spreads on the beds and the tidy organization of the rooms in separate wings for the boys and girls. The playrooms were big and full of a wide variety of toys. A girl cuddled a china doll in an armchair a few feet away, and two boys played with a cast-iron fire engine and a windup drummer boy. When she took us outside to the grounds, we saw kids doing all the things kids do. Jimmie craned his neck to get a better view, and I could tell he was intrigued.

"Would you like to see our dining area?" Mrs. Perkins asked.

"Of course," I said. "You like to eat, don't you, pal?"

He nodded enthusiastically, and we entered the cafeteria

to see the kids enjoying spaghetti and meatballs for lunch. In a corner, some of the children were playing a piano and plunked out an off-key version of "Camptown Races," one of Jimmie's favorite songs. He nodded to the music, mouthing, "Doo dah, doo dah . . ."

"We want the children to eat balanced meals," said Mrs. Perkins. "And we also like to liven up mealtime by letting them amuse themselves with music. It's been conducive to better study habits too."

"Do you have chocolate cake?" Jimmie suddenly asked with concern. He loved Effie's chocolate cake.

"Why yes, we certainly do. We vary sweets with fruit and also let the children enjoy at least two hours of outdoor playtime if they choose. Or they can use the library. It's well-stocked with books they are welcome to check out, either for their classes or for personal use."

"We sure are impressed, aren't we, Jim?"

He nodded, apparently still more concerned with the chocolate cake and the ice cream soda. At the end of the tour, he was satisfied enough that I went ahead and registered him for the upcoming term. The next week, we moved him in.

REPRISE

CHAPTER FORTY-SEVEN

FOOTLIGHTS AND SHADOWS SET, NEW YORK CITY

October 1919

"Action!"

"Okay Olive! You're angry!" the director, John Noble, said into his megaphone. "You put in all that work, and then the ungrateful bastard left! Show him how angry you are!"

It wasn't a baby vamp role this time, but I did get to play a showgirl. My character, Gloria, was engaged to a man she didn't love. When a dazed explorer, Jerry, stumbled into her apartment, she nursed him through his tropical fever. Then, he recovered and wandered off, not remembering anything, only the face of the woman who had nurtured him while he was sick.

"But how did he get into my apartment in the first place?" I asked. "Did he have a key? Did he break in? Was the door ajar?" The rest of the crew either couldn't or wouldn't answer. But they all grinned in spite of themselves.

I pantomimed annoyance. My co-star, Alex Onslow as Jerry, gazed up at me. In a few minutes, a fire was supposed to engulf that part of the set.

"Jerry! You've combed the city and you've finally found Gloria! There she is! That gorgeous face you remember! But she hates you! She's not buying it! She huffs off! If nothing will work, you're going to get plastered! Head for Eddie's Bar and a double Bushmills! Stand by with the matches, firebugs!"

Noble gave the signal when he was ready, and with a whoosh, the scenery went up in flames where the matches had been struck. Alex and I moved into an adjoining area, the small fire burned itself out, and the two of us married after reconciling, when Gloria realized Jerry was in love with her. It was the standard goody-goody ending, but I was beginning to see that real life often didn't work out that way.

From *Footlights and Shadows* I moved straight into *Glorious Youth*. I could barely think straight enough to put a trunk together. Effie kept asking questions about what she should pack for me, but I didn't have a clue. Between that and trying to plan for Christmas, I was a nervous wreck. We were going to be shooting exteriors in New Orleans, so on the fifth of De-November, we caught the Piedmont Limited to Atlanta and I slept half the trip.

We were about an hour out of Charlotte when the train began to rock. The trees that flew by the windows were bent sideways by the force of the wind. The fat swollen raindrops hit the window like bullets, each one making a sharp snap against the glass.

Between us, we had three decks of cards, and the rest of the crew had some checkers and dominoes. After we finished five hands of pinochle, one of the hands took me for twenty-five bucks at canasta. We finally rolled into Atlanta about 10:30 p.m., but as we collected our gear to change trains a

Negro porter climbed aboard and alerted us to the bad news.

"Dreadful sorry, folks," he said, "Ain't nobody goin' nowhere."

"What is it?" Helen Gill said. She was playing Lola Ainsley.

"Lotsa floodin'," he said. "Been rainin' for a week. Chattahoochee's crested in about three or four places. Bridges out in a few others. Gonna be at least three days, they're sayin'." He shook his head.

The Reverend shook his head. Charles Craig was one of our co-stars and played Reverend Bluebottle. "The Reverend" was now his official nickname.

"What a cock-up," Crauford Kent said, groaning. He was playing David Montgomery, my husband in the movie. He was at least ten years older than me, with deep dark brows over sad-looking eyes. But he was the least sad person I'd met in a long time. His British sarcasm kept me in stitches.

We'd get another train eventually, but no one had any clue when that would be. So we crowded into the station with our equipment, knowing we were stuck for the foreseeable future. I tried to send Myron a telegram, but all the lines were down.

"Well, girls," said Crauford in his elegant English accent, "guess we're stuck in Atlanta. Let's make the best of it. What does one do in Georgia, anyway?"

"Drown, evidently," I said, watching the water continue to rise.

"Nonsense. We shall find something fabulously entertaining and oh-so-southern to do while we're in town. Anyone keen on peaches? Isn't that what they're famous for here?"

"Come to think of it . . ." someone said.

"If we're bored, it's our own blasted faults. Let's go suss out something to do. Reverend? Care to join us in breaking a few commandments?"

Craig tippled from a small flask and nodded, raising it to show he was in for finding some fun. The crew would have to hold down the benches while we were gone, but several hundred dollars' worth of cameras, costumes, and equipment could not watch themselves.

They warned us not to go far from the depot, in case the weather changed. But we pooh-poohed that. That water wasn't receding anytime soon. We craved escape from the depot, so went in search of a place to kick up our heels.

The rain had soaked us to our skins but changed from a downpour to a drizzle while we were sloshing through the streets. The air stayed as thick and moist as a wet wool blanket. It felt like we were swimming in it, our clothes hanging limply on us, and hordes of mosquitoes moved in for a snack. I noticed how thirsty I was when all of the streets near Terminal Station were crowded with billboards for Coca-Cola.

"Look over there! That's more like it!" Crauford said, two blocks from Peachtree Street.

We glanced in the direction he was pointing and saw a sign saying Cobb Dancehall. As he sloshed ahead, we fought to keep up. We had just crossed the street to the box office when the attendant slid down the shade.

"I say, you have some customers, my good man," said Crauford, knocking on the glass.

"Sorry sir," drawled the fellow peering out from under the shade. "Closing time is ten thirty."

"But we're abominably bored. We've only just arrived on the train from New York. If we can't dance, what is there to do in this veritable cauldron of vice?"

"Ain't much, sir. Try the Alhambra down the street. They're open until midnight." He pointed in the direction we'd come.

"You heard what the man said, ladies. Shall we go?"

Helen grabbed the Reverend and I took Crauford's arm, and they escorted us two blocks to the east. But when we arrived, the Alhambra disappointed us too. Signs told us that due to the rain, massive ceiling leaks had caused a temporary closure. They were to reopen the next week.

"Fat lot of good that does us now," Crauford said with a sigh. "Back to the station, then?"

By then, our enthusiasm had waned a bit.

"I'm hungry," Helen grumbled.

"Me too," I said. "Maybe we could find a café that's open."

"Ollie dear, we're not in Times Square," Crauford noted. "If you'll notice, it's deader than a Topeka graveyard here."

"There has to be someplace," I complained.

"Then I suppose the center of the universe right now is the depot."

We nodded and tramped after him, our shoes squelching from the rain. Inside the entrance of the depot, we noticed a hot dog vendor we'd ignored the first go-round.

"Frankfurters, ladies?" Crauford asked.

"Do we still have to call them liberty sausages?" I asked.

"Hmmmm . . . the war is over. I'm not sure. What do you think?"

"I think . . . lots of mustard, no relish."

"How do you not *relish* the green stuff, my dear?"

"It's disgusting," I said, pulling a dime out of my pocketbook and handing it to the man behind the cart.

"No onions, either?"

"I taste them for days afterward."

"I could make a very crude remark about Mr. Pickford right now, but I am a gentleman. Helen, what's your poison?"

"Load mine up. Everything."

"Good girl."

The vendor ladled on all sorts of stuff and passed the wiener to Helen. The Reverend ordered his with lots of ketchup and nothing else.

"We must be a sight," Crauford said. "Like a pack of drenched muskrats feasting on . . . whatever muskrats eat, I suppose."

"Only you, Crauford," The Reverend said with a chuckle. "The rest of us have held up pretty well." He had very little hair to worry about. One wipe to the top of his bald head with a handkerchief and he was a picture of clerical dignity.

"Aren't these fun?" Crauford circled a display set up near the booth. The racks were full of strange masks covered in feathers, glitter, and interesting designs. Donning one with painted peaches over the eye holes, he fluttered his lashes at us, pantomiming his heart out. "Who am I?" he said, stretching his arms out wide, then advancing upon us with fingers bared like claws.

"Theda Bara!" we crowed.

"Indeed," he said, pleased with his performance.

Placing one with turquoise blue plumes over my face, he adjusted the cord around my head. The vendor watched us to see if we'd filch any of his masks.

"You're Princess Beloved in *Intolerance*!" Helen said with a laugh.

"What a shame we're not going to be in Fat City during Mardi Gras. What a load of fun that would be!" Crauford said, paying for his mask.

"What's that?" I said, nibbling the end of my dog.

"Mardi Gras? Surely you're kidding, Ollie."

"No, what is it?"

"Fat Tuesday, my naive darling. You weren't raised Catholic?"

"Episcopalian. Why?"

"With so many French and Italians and Irish there, the Catholics celebrate by stuffing themselves with pancakes on Fat Tuesday before Lent begins. You know, with the fasting and all that. They have parades and floats and sensational parties. And everyone wears these monstrosities."

The mask vendor glared at him.

We paid for our wieners and bought a few of the masks. Jimmie had recently become fascinated by Africa, with its lions and monkeys and elephants, so I bought him one with the face of a lion. Wearing our masks, we rejoined the crew and played cards and dominoes until Atlanta woke up and we could get breakfast. Two days later, the water finally receded enough for us to board our connecting train and continue west.

When we arrived in New Orleans, we checked into the Monteleone Hotel. As Crauford was the only one of us who'd traveled to the city before, he knew all the most interesting places to see and the most divine restaurants to visit, so we sampled the gumbo at the Commander's Palace and sucked up bowls of étouffée at Antoine's. He told us frightening stories about Marie Laveau and Madame LaLaurie, and we heard lots of lively music like the band at Reisenweber's had played.

When we weren't filming, we drank chicory coffee and ate beignets until I thought I'd explode.

"No!" I said, waving Crauford away as he dangled another one of the donuts in front of me. "Crauford, my costumes are starting to feel like sausage casing. I can't possibly eat one more."

"They're amazing little things, aren't they? So scrumptious." He took a bite and closed his eyes in bliss.

"Between these and the red beans and rice, I think I could stay in New Orleans forever." If it hadn't been for Jimmie waiting at home, I might have. These days, I had less and less to go back to. My life was a wreck.

CHAPTER FORTY-EIGHT

OLIVE'S APARTMENT, NEW YORK CITY

December 25, 1919

Under the huge fir, we opened gifts with Jimmie. He loved his new Lincoln Logs, plus he had a large stuffed toy dog, a chemistry set, and soft, cuddly pajamas. Jimmie sat tucked in the crook of my arm, and we watched Jack open his gifts. Effie served us all glasses of eggnog topped with nutmeg.

"Mistah Jimmie, you take this one," she said, handing him the smaller glass with no liquor in it. He took a huge gulp and smiled, ending up with a huge yellow splotch on his nose.

Jack ripped open the fancy papers to reveal the lounging robe I'd splurged on, running his hand over the fine silk.

"Now this one," I said, pushing another gift in front of him.

He slid the decorative bow off the velvet box and opened it, revealing the shimmery black cufflinks. Next he unwrapped the obsidian tie tack, a billfold of black snakeskin, and a platinum pinkie ring.

"Your turn, darling," he said, sliding a stack of packages toward me. Reaching for the Tiffany's box first, I opened the lid to a real stunner. It was a cuff bracelet, composed of a series of curlicues. They were inset with diamonds and sapphires. Gasping in delight, I pulled it out and fastened it on my wrist, moving my arm to and fro, watching the jewels catch the light at various angles and sparkle like icicles. Really expensive icicles.

In addition to the cuff, he'd bought me a new hair clip of emeralds, a fourteen-carat gold twenty-piece vanity set, a kolinsky robe, and a stone marten stole.

I finished my eggnog and reached for a piece of stollen. Effie had brought some Christmas goodies out on a silver tray for us, but we'd been so busy opening gifts that we'd barely touched them. The nog did its work before too long. Filming and travel the last few weeks had been exhausting, and I found myself nodding off with my back against the couch. Jimmie crawled into my lap and teased me, playing with my eyelids and kissing me on the cheek.

"Come on, darling," Jack said, "I'll put you to bed."

"No, it's still early," I protested. "I'm fine."

Jimmie pulled me over to his logs spread out on the floor, and we began building a big cabin. Jack crossed to the bar and poured himself a Scotch, the nog not having quite the kick he needed.

A knock sounded at the door, and I stood to get it since Effie was in the kitchen whipping up more eggnog.

"I'll get it," Jack said. He was closer to the door, so I let him. I took a seat on the couch so I could stretch my legs a little.

"Hi . . ." I heard a soft, feminine voice say.

"This isn't a good time," Jack whispered, retreating from the door and ready to close it. I felt every nerve in me tense, knowing what he was up to.

"Who is it, darling?" I asked. I stood up, ready for a

confrontation. I shepherded Jimmie toward his room, putting my index finger over my lips and indicating we'd talk about it later. He slouched off.

I pulled the front door open to reveal the world's biggest floozy standing in the corridor.

I had never seen hair that color, even at the Follies. It was the color of corn—not blonde and not gold. Yellow. And the rouge! Her cheeks were redder than a baboon's ass. Her dress was a step up from street-corner hooker, but not much. She couldn't have been any older than nineteen.

"Visiting on Christmas, honey? You're just like Santa Claus, aren't you?" I said to her. Then to Jack, I said, "Kinda young, isn't she? Aren't you going to introduce me to the little sugarplum?"

She eyed Jack, then me, and then him again, crossing her arms with annoyance.

"So I guess you're married," she said to him, snapping her gum in disgust and turning to leave.

"Did you forget to mention that part, sweetheart?" I said to Jack. "I'm sure it just slipped your mind, right?"

The girl snorted and sashayed away.

"Don't ever come near my husband again, Blondie. If you do, I'll pull all your hair out by the roots. Try me," I called to her.

I closed the door. Jack tried to open his arms to hug me, but I crossed the room.

"Don't you fucking touch me."

"Ollie, she meant nothing. I swear to you."

"Yes, yes, I know. It didn't mean anything. We've had this discussion before."

"I can't help myself."

"Yes, I see that." I went into the bedroom and grabbed a pillow and blanket off the bed, then threw them at him. "Here. You're sleeping on the couch."

It took me hours to get to sleep. I would think of Myron and wonder if I was being fair, since I was doing the same thing as Jack, but Jack had chosen the most whorish creature he could find. Drifting off, I'd dream of the two of them together in our bed and wake up panting, my heart racing like the champion at the Kentucky Derby.

On New Year's Eve, we were expected at a Sixty Club ball. I didn't know how the hell I would get through the week. For the next five days, I spent time with Jimmie, buying him more toys and playing with him in his room, but I couldn't avoid Jack forever. So I was itching for a fight the night of the ball.

"Now what are you doing?" I asked, powdering my nose and dabbing Narcisse Noir on my wrists and behind my ears.

I fastened the cuff onto my wrist, enjoying the gift but hating the giver. My dress was a gorgeous violet-blue silk with a hobble skirt embroidered with blown glass baubles, tiny pearls, and rhinestones. I wore blue slippers in the same shade.

"Let's not quarrel tonight," he said. "Jimmie might hear. We have to worry about him now too."

I snorted. "Now you worry about Jimmie? I wish I'd never told Jim we'd take him on. We're terrible role models, and I'm ashamed he has to see us arguing all the time. Especially when your date shows up at our door on Christmas night."

"Me? What about you? Did you think I wouldn't hear about you and Myron? Or what about his brother?"

"David? Are you crazy?"

"Oh, but I was right about Myron, wasn't I? Don't even bother denying it."

"All right, I won't. You never do. Myron has been better for me than you ever were. He cares about me and about my career."

"I married you, didn't I? If you remember, that's what you wanted when Ziegfeld threw you over for his *wife.*"

The perfume bottle I lobbed missed his cheek by inches. Narcisse Noir dripped down the wall, the shards of glass lying in a ragged pile on the rug. The reek was overpowering.

"Typical showgirl," he said, shaking his head.

"You son of a bitch."

"Let's go," he said, turning and stalking out of the bedroom.

When we entered the living room, Effie greeted us with small tumblers of eggnog. A valiant effort on her part, but both of us were in foul moods.

"Effie, I broke a perfume bottle near the vanity. Could you do what you can with the mess?" I said. "We'll be back a little after midnight."

"We'll be back *well* after midnight," Jack said. "Or maybe not at all."

"Please serve Jimmie his dinner in another hour or so," I said, ignoring him, "and put him to bed by eight thirty."

"Yes, Miss Olive," Effie said with a nervous smile. Her favorite charge sat surrounded by new toys, and Chow nibbled the stray crumbs from Jimmie's gingerbread. She picked up the little Pekingese and let him lick her nose. "C'mon Chow. Got a bone for you in the kitchen."

Though I pulled it from him four times, Jack kept grabbing my arm, guiding me downstairs, wanting the world to know the Pickford marriage was sound. Effie had phoned for Mischa, and he waited for us in the lobby, opening first the doors of the building for us, then the car doors.

"Hotel Astor, please Mischa," I told him. He nodded and aimed us toward Times Square.

The Hotel Astor was one of the most beautiful buildings in Manhattan. It reminded me of pictures I'd seen of the buildings in Paris. Very tall, very classy, with potted palms, marble floors, and carpets that must have cost a fortune.

When we arrived, an orchestra was playing "I'm Forever Blowing Bubbles." Jack found us a table near some Follies members, and I caught up on all the latest dirt from Broadway.

"Let's dance," he said through clenched teeth.

"Not now, I'm having fun," I said. I started speaking with Eddie Cantor, who'd joined the Follies the year after I left.

Jack found the nearest blonde showgirl and began leading her across the dance floor in a scandalous tango, grinding into her hips with every step.

"Ollie, *bubbeleh!*"

I turned at the sound of a familiar voice. It was Fanny Brice, one of the greatest stars of the Follies. She was gone my first year but returned in 1916. She had popularized "Second Hand Rose," "Rose of Washington Square," and other wonderful songs. Her wavy brown hair was tucked under a turban, emphasizing her nose and long jaw. Her face was even more animated than usual.

Fanny and I had a kinship. We'd both had been divorced, and both of us had challenged Ziggy. Fanny was famed as much for her personal life as for the lushness of her voice. She knew the heartbreak of being married to a scoundrel, as Nicky Arnstein had put her through the wringer. We chatted for a few minutes, and she noticed the cuff on my arm.

"*Oy vey*, Ollie! That's some *tchotchke*."

"This was one of my Christmas presents. Do you like it?"

She fingered the filigree finish and let out a low whistle.

"I'd hang onto that fella if I were you. Where is he?"

"Sulking. We got into another fight before the party."

"Sulking about what?"

"Not being able to bang anyone he wants."

Fanny cocked her head. "You don't say."

"Tangoing with the blonde," I said, nodding at the spectacle across the room.

"Forget everything I said. Buy yourself jewelry. You don't have to put up with a *putz* like that."

"I keep saying that, but . . ." I said with a sigh.

"Tell me all about it," she said, patting the chair next to her and settling in for a long tale.

"I honestly don't know what to do, Fanny. I love him, but he's driving me crazy. The booze, the drugs, the affairs . . ."

"You know what they say, honey. What's good for the goose . . ."

"Oh, believe me, I've been indulging too, but only because he convinced me he didn't care. There's something about him that keeps me coming back. Like a big idiot."

"It's awful to love a bastard. But a big *shvanz* only counts for so much, honey."

"I know. I've been seeing Myron on the side. He wants me to divorce Jack."

Her brows lifted and she grinned. "Discovering the wonders of the tribal persuasion, are we?"

I blushed and laughed.

"Someone gave me some wise advice years ago, Ollie, and I'm going to share it with you. Men are like dogs. If they can't eat it or fuck it, they'll piss all over it. You're too pretty to be a fire hydrant. Number one, concentrate on your career. And number two, lose your canine friend over there."

CHAPTER FORTY-NINE

LOS ANGELES, CALIFORNIA

January 6, 1920

Heeding Fanny's advice, I threw myself into my next role, that of Ginger, the girl Frances and I had created over lunch. I waded my way through the colorful piles of middy blouses and skirts, trying on one tam-o'-shanter after another. Interviewer Helen Rockwell was having her photographer, Clarence Barney, snap a few photos for her article. She wrote for various papers but lately had been penning plenty for the *Morning Telegraph* and *Exhibitors Trade Review.*

"Miss Rockwell, I'm so excited about this part," I said. Ever since *Madcap Madge* for Triangle, I've longed to do more schoolgirls. I disliked myself as a wife and mother, and I loathed myself as a fisher maid in *Out Yonder*. I haven't been satisfied with any of my celluloid selves since Madge. That picture was three years ago, and my fans have never stopped asking when I'll play a schoolgirl again. That one picture remains their favorite. They haven't forgotten it after all this time. Now Mr. Selznick has agreed to let me shorten my skirts, put a bow on my hair, and romp to my heart's content."

"But how do you look at a middy blouse and get excited? We're women. Don't you want to appear as a woman?"

"Sure I'm feminine, but I'm also a big kid. I'd like to create a certain role in pictures, if you know what I mean. Mary Pickford is the kid. Connie Talmadge is the flippant, flighty wife, Dorothy Talmadge is a hoyden, and Nazimova is exotic and mysterious. My Jack plays boys. I'm nothing at all. No fixed position. I don't mean anything definite to anybody."

Miss Rockwell nodded.

"I'm going to try my hand at schoolgirl roles, and if the public likes them, I'll keep doing them. Kind of a Booth Tarkington girl, I guess. It'd be nice to be the feminine version of what Jack is in his boyish way. I'd like my audience to know me as something specific. Can I confide in you Miss Rockwell? Off the record."

"Of course," she said, setting her pad aside.

"I have very high hopes for the scenarist Mr. Selznick has hired for me. Frances Marion is an amazing writer and a good friend. I believe the baby vamp is my niche. She's writing material that will truly appeal to my fans. I think she's going to write some plum roles for me. Let's go down the hall now." I led her to another room, and we almost stumbled over a projector.

"This is a lot of fun," I said pointing at it. "I ran Charlie Chaplin last night. New films arrive every day. I project them up on the wall and entertain my friends."

"Do you screen *your* new pictures?" Miss Rockwell asked.

"Good heavens, no. I hate my pictures. What's the use of pretending I like them when I don't? When they show me one of my pictures in the Selznick projection room, no one will sit next to me. I pan myself so hard, they get sick of listening. I think I'm awful."

"That's very humble of you, Miss Thomas. It's also wrong. It's nice to meet someone who fails to enthuse about herself but loves Dorothy Gish, and raves about Connie and Norma Talmadge."

"Sometimes I'm not so bad," I said, "but I always think my face is funny, or my hair isn't right, or my tears seem fake. I've got some photos if you'd like to see."

At her nod, I opened a breakfront that contained books, papers, and other mementos and pulled out a photograph album.

"This is a scene from *The Spite Bride*. This is Claire Du-Brey. She's lots of fun! And this is Robert Ellis. He's an excellent actor and a charming person. He's been on the stage for eighteen years. This is my dog Chow Chow on the set. We filmed at two of the theaters in downtown Los Angeles and also in San Francisco."

We turned the page, and she noticed I was holding my thumb over my own image in one of the other photographs. She lifted it and smiled at me as I giggled.

"Miss Thomas, I think you'd let me view this entire album with your finger over your pictures on each page."

CHAPTER FIFTY

SET OF *THE FLAPPER*, WINTER SPRINGS, FLORIDA

March 1920

Not much will make you crankier than hot sun and glare in your eyes. Except finding out your bitch of a sister-in-law got married and you weren't even invited to the wedding. The biggest event in Hollywood history and I had to hear it from Frances.

"Dear Ollie—

Isn't it exciting? Mary and Douglas have wed, and Hollywood is rejoicing at the news. It was just natural for America's Sweetheart to marry America's Hero. Sorry you couldn't make it. I missed you, and so did Fred.

Love,
Frances"

"But darling," Jack said, trying to make me feel better, "you were on location. We knew it would be hard for you to get away. Besides, you didn't miss much. Fairbanks is such a giant phony. Always 'on.' I don't even like being in the same room with him."

I was comforted by the fact that Myron had been correct about Frances. She understood my dream to represent a certain character to my movie going public—the Baby Vamp. She explained that a new term had been coined for these young ladies who were not quite women and not quite girls. They were breaking rules and carving out a new, more liberated niche in society. She called them flappers. And the name of *Sixteen* had been changed to *The Flapper*, to my delight. Frances had been right.

Due to the tension at home, I grew closer to my co-stars, especially the girls who played my boarding school chums. Katherine Johnston was dark-haired and full of fun, always ready for a dance or a smoke. My favorite was a girl from Montreal, Norma Shearer, who was there with her sister Athole.

Norma had so much ambition but very little confidence in herself. Though she was petite and slim, her arms and legs were full, so they did not photograph to her best advantage. And as we'd talked one night, I noticed one of her eyes was a little off-kilter. She held her head at an angle to minimize it. She and Athole both had striking blue eyes, but something told me Norma was self-conscious about her features.

When she told me she'd been rejected from the Follies, we shared a chuckle, but I could tell it still stung.

"I was doing okay until he asked to see my legs," she said of Ziggy. "That ended things right there. They're huge"—she gestured to her muscular calves—"and I'm knock-kneed to boot." She lifted her skirt to show me.

"Ziggy knows what he wants, I suppose," I said, lighting a cigarette.

"And I wasn't it. You're so pretty, Olive. What was it like, having men make fools of themselves over you like that?"

"Surrounded by flowers and diamonds . . ." Athole added dreamily, grabbing a light from my smoke.

"It was pretty special," I admitted.

"I've always dreamed of living in rooms full of flowers . . . drinking champagne, with a wolfhound or two at my feet," Athole continued. "We used to have a life like that at our Grosvenor Street house. Luxury, leisure, and everything we wanted handed to us. Those were the days, eh Norma?"

I'd gotten used to Ath's rambling by now, since Norma had told me her sister was unstable. Two years before, their father had lost his business, and they'd gone from rich to poor all faster than a chorus girl on a bender. Their mother left their father, and that same year Ath spent time in a mental institution. I adored them both, but it was hard to listen to Ath sometimes. She rambled on about God knows what, and her moods ran the gamut from ecstatic to miserable. No one really knew how to help her.

"We'll be lucky to get a toehold in this business, Ath," Norma said. "But the Selznicks have been wonderful to us. Ollie, are they always this generous?"

"Always," I said. "They've become my second family. I don't know what I would do without them."

"Me either," Norma said. "Ath and I are grateful for anything that comes our way. But I'm determined to succeed. What will happen to Mother and Ath if I fail?"

"You're going to do fine," I told her. "You're beautiful and you have talent."

"I'm funny looking," she moaned.

"Oh, you are not," I said. "So your legs are a little broad and your eye . . ." I stopped abruptly, thinking, *Oh shit.*

"Go ahead, say it. I know. My eye has a cast to it. I'm going to get medical help for it, but first I had to find the right doctor, and now I have. One in New York fits the bill, I think." She lowered her voice a bit. "Promise you won't say anything?"

I nodded, realizing she was sharing a secret.

"When I took this part, I talked them into picking up Ath too. I told them we needed better clothes, so they gave us $100 to do it. I'm going to use it for my surgery. I have an appointment booked during that two days we have off between here and Lake Placid. I found an express to take us into the city."

"What about the clothes?"

"My mother is a talented seamstress. Didn't I tell you that?" she said with a wink.

"But what if you haven't recovered by then?"

"I'll pull the bandage off during the day and wear it at night if I have to. You won't tell on me, will you Ollie?"

"Of course not. You've got guts. You need them in this business. I think you're going to go far."

"Everyone keeps telling us we won't go anywhere. 'Blue eyes photograph white on film,' they say," Ath said.

"Malarkey. My eyes are blue," I said.

"Yes, but yours are dark blue," Norma said.

I patted her hand. "I see you being bigger than Constance Talmadge. You have an elegant way of carrying yourself. Not like me. I'm sort of a maniac—go-go-go all the time. You'll be able to test for those classy parts I can't. Queens and empresses and ladies with titles. Not like my baby vamps."

"But you have so much fun playing them!" she said. "Sometimes dignified is good, but I'd rather have fun like you. Heck, I'd rather *be* you."

"No you wouldn't," I told her. "My life is pretty complicated, believe you me. Keep doing what you're doing, Norma. It's going to happen, and then I'll say I knew you when you were only an extra."

Two weeks later, we packed up and left Florida for our next shooting location in Lake Placid, New York, for the winter scenes at Ginger's boarding school. Everyone wondered where Ath and Norma were. They'd made up an excuse about visiting a sick relative in New York.

On the train, Myron rattled on and on about Lake Placid being the home of the abolitionist John Brown. "His farm is in this area somewhere," he said.

I nodded and politely "mm-hmmed" as I read over the rest of the scenario.

"Dad brought us up here for a vacation a couple years ago," he continued. "Wait until you see the Lake Placid Club. Founded by the originator of the Dewey Decimal System."

"Why Lake Placid?" I said. "Nobody's even heard of the place."

"Scenery, Ollie! It's spectacular. And so much to do! Imported skis, tobogganing runs, and the best part is that Dr. Dewey had separate rinks constructed for skating, curling, and hockey. Wait 'til you see it."

The first day of shooting was long and full, with frequent breaks near the fire pits to defrost our frozen fingers and toes. Norma and Ath had returned and were greeted by squealing, hugs, and kisses from the other girls. Norma's cast was gone. Not only was her eye better, but she also carried herself with more grace and confidence. That evening, everyone gathered for a sing-along in the great room, curling up near the fireplace with warm apple cider and hot chocolate. Everyone grumbled about the Volstead Act, already into its third miserable month of existence. I would have killed for a toddy right then—something stronger to fight off the cold.

The next day, Myron took the train into the city to take care of some business. I returned to my room later to find a postcard from Frances, who'd left for Europe two weeks before:

Madrid, Spain

Ollie dearest— *April 7, 1920*

I hope everything is going fine. So disappointed not to have seen you before I left. Am working out a story I am sure you and Myron will like and snapping lots of pictures so the foreign sequence will be well interpreted. They talk about their French and Spanish girls. They ought to see our American Ollie!

Love to Myron,
Frances

Smiling, I blew my nose once more, tired of it being numb and running all the time. My fingers were frigid, and it took an hour next to the fire to defrost them. A week later, a depressing letter from Selznick Pictures let me know my account was overdrawn again and they had advanced funds to cover the shortage. The good news was they were also sending me a check for $250.

Myron wired after another two weeks, and the telegram was delivered to me on the set:

"CHECKS DEPOSITED FOR SALARY TO WEEK ENDING MAY EIGHTH STOP WIRE WHETHER YOU WANT ME TO DEPOSIT ANY MORE MONEY STOP LOVE MYRON"

What would I do without Myron? He was not only my lover but my banker, my mentor, and my friend. I sent off a quick wire to him to let him know that things upstate were going all right. But the past few weeks, I'd been having second thoughts about the affair. My correspondence with him had been less often, and what I sent was less wordy. Jack and I had dealt with so many obstacles tossed in our way by the studios: his mother, his sister, the American government, or the Kaiser. He had his faults—huge ones—but he loved me and I loved him, even if it had been half-hearted the last few months. Fanny's advice hung in the back of my mind like an old dress I'd consigned to the rear of the closet. I knew it was there, but I wasn't sure about wearing it again.

One afternoon, we had to shoot a scene with the whole flock of a hundred extras tobogganing down a steep hill, which resembled a thick white woolen blanket someone had spread down the grade. When the girls heard, "Action!" the deep impressions of sled blades cut through the snow in hundreds of striped patterns.

But many of the girls had never been on sleds in their lives. The sleds veered, then careered into each other, and the girls ended up like rag dolls tossed into the snow at the bottom. It was a disaster.

"Phone an ambulance!" our director Alan Crosland yelled, trying to run through the knee-deep snow to reach everyone.

Two crew members ran to the lodge and had the staff grab as many first aid supplies as they could carry—mercurochrome, iodine, alcohol, bandages, and whatever wood they could find to make splints. I counted a lot of broken bones.

When I found Norma and Ath, they were lying together, tangled up like a skein of bright yarn. Norma was okay, with only a few big bruises and a cut or two, but Ath had been pulled underneath her sled, and everything we touched caused her to cry out in pain.

"Mr. Crosland!" I cried out. "Ath's hurt pretty bad."

"We've got ambulances on their way," he said.

Between Mr. Crosland, the ambulance driver, the crew, and one or two of the nurses who had traveled to the scene, they rated the severity of the injuries and decided who would go first. Ath was in the second shipment to the General Hospital of Saranac Lake.

By the time we got to the hospital, the doctor on duty was examining her broken arm, busted collarbone, cut-up ear, and what turned out to be a sprained ankle. Plus all the cuts and bruises. They told us it would be at least three hours before we'd be able to see her.

"But she's my sister," Norma said.

"I'm sorry, ma'am. They're working their way through the girls as fast as possible. Fifty girls were injured, and your sister was one of the worst," the head nurse said.

"Come on, Norma, I have an idea," I said.

"What?"

"Trust me."

I wheeled out of the parking lot in Mr. Crosland's borrowed Cadillac, hoping no one would tell Myron they'd seen me driving. As we rounded a corner, I saw a flower shop and pulled into a spot on Main Street.

"Saranac Flowers? Ollie, what a sweet gesture," Norma said.

We scooted inside to get out of the cold, stamping our feet and rubbing our hands to lose some of the chill.

"May I help you?" said the older lady at the counter. She was placing some larkspur and stephanotis in a vase, and her gray hair was escaping a little at a time from her topknot.

"Do you have any pretty arrangements for hospital patients?" I asked her.

"Of course. Do you have any favorite varieties?"

"All of them."

"Beg your pardon?"

"All of them. I want every flower in your store put into an arrangement and sent to Saranac Lake Hospital." I fingered one of the flowers in a vase on the counter.

"How many arrangements?"

"How many can you make?"

The woman must have thought she was hearing things. "Ma'am, using every flower I have in the store would be very expensive. I'm sure that . . ."

"That's what we want. Every bloomin' blossom in this store needs to go in a vase and get sent over. Norma, Ath's not allergic to anything, is she?" I lit a cigarette and blew a smoke ring toward the ceiling.

"Not that I know of."

"Good. Then every last bloom."

The clerk cocked her head at me, still unconvinced.

"Madam, do you read the papers?" Norma said, getting into the act and leaning on the counter.

"Why yes, of course."

"Are you aware that a troupe from Hollywood is in town

shooting a movie called *The Flapper*?"

"I think I did hear something about that, yes."

"We are in the cast, and many of the other girls were injured today while we were shooting a scene." She pointed to the bruise and scratches on her forehead to make a point.

"Oh dear. Nothing too serious, I hope."

"Mostly broken bones, sprains, cuts, that type of thing," Norma said.

"I want to help these girls recuperate. They will wake up to your beautiful flowers when they come to," I said.

"Then let me write up a sales ticket, Miss . . ."

"Thomas. Olive Thomas."

As our shoes clicked across the linoleum, Ath's eyes fluttered open, and a big smile crept across her face when she saw us. Three huge arrangements took up a corner of the room.

"The nurse read the cards to me. Ollie, you're certifiable."

"Nah," I said. "I just like flowers. The other girls got plenty too." I took her hand. "Norma will be here in a few minutes. The poor dear hadn't eaten, and she was famished. She went to go grab a sandwich at the café down the street."

"I'm so worried."

"What in the world for? You're getting excellent care."

"That's the problem. I imagine how much this excellent care is costing us."

"Don't worry yourself about that. Why don't you get some rest?"

When she drifted off to sleep, I took the stairs to the billing office and wrote them a check for the entire amount. When Norma asked me about it, I slipped her a little too, since they'd be minus Ath's salary for what was likely going to be a few months. She couldn't speak for about an hour afterward except to stammer thank-you after thank-you.

Darling Mine was due to begin shooting in two weeks, so I had to hop the train to California when we were finished. Norma and Ath and the others threw me a party before I left.

Things with Jack had been strained at New Year's, but we were still communicating. The telegraph wires between New York and Hollywood had been buzzing for weeks.

CHAPTER FIFTY-ONE

LOS ANGELES, *April 1920*

Our last parting hadn't been on good terms. Jack knew how close Myron was to replacing him. But we kissed for the benefit of the newspapermen on the platform. Mischa got behind the wheel of the new Packard for the ride to the house on Wilshire that Jack had rented us.

We relaxed in the living room with a cigarette. Jack poured us each a glass of some bootleg gin he'd gotten a hold of, and we leaned into the overstuffed horsehair.

"So how have you been?" he said.

"All right. We're starting *Darling Mine*. Myron thinks it's going to be huge. I met my co-stars the other day. They're nice guys."

"Who's directing?"

"Trimble."

"He's a horse's ass."

I sighed. "I like him."

"Guess that says a lot."

"Oh, for Christ's sake, Jack. We just sat down and you're already picking a fight? What the hell is wrong with you?"

He stared at me like I was invisible.

"You don't have to say everything you think as soon as you think it, you know," I continued. "And you don't have to work with Trimble. I do. So stuff it, already."

He shook his head and took a long drag on his Murad. "So how are things going with Myron?"

"Perfect. How are things going with . . . who is it this week?"

"Fuck you."

"You know what? I'm leaving. I don't need you, or your drugs, or your whores, or anything else, Jack Pickford."

"We just got here, like you said." He jiggled his glass so the ice tinkled merrily. Then he turned and gave me a look that chilled me, his smile pearly white and dangerous. That was it.

"Put away those dice, you bastard," I said. I picked up a gorgeous jade-green glass bowl that was sitting on a side table and smashed him over the head with it. A trickle of blood slithered down his cheek from his hairline where glass fragments had cut into his scalp.

"You bitch!" In an instant, he was on his feet, grabbing both my forearms. He wasn't large, but he was larger than me, and that was all that mattered. I couldn't free my hands, but I still used them to beat on his chest as hard as I could.

"Effie!" I yelled. "Effie!"

I heard her bustling down the hall before she appeared, and her imminent arrival intimidated Jack enough that he dropped my arms.

"Ever'thing okay, Miss Olive?" she asked. Her voice shook a bit.

Jack had pulled out his handkerchief and was using it to mop up some of the blood.

"Thank you, Effie," I said, trying to pretend for all our sakes that everything was fine. "We should go now."

"No. I'll go," he said. "I'll be at the Athletic Club."

He strode across the room in three steps and slammed the door behind him, leaving Effie standing speechless, her mouth a little O of surprise. I sank down on the couch, shaking all over.

THE WILSHIRE HOUSE, LOS ANGELES, *April 30, 1920*

"Ollie . . . I'm sorry . . . I'm so sorry. Oh God, don't you understand how much I love you? More than anything on earth, don't you see? I'm sorry I was so awful before. Please forgive me. I'm torn up about you and Myron. I want things to work, Ollie. I'll do absolutely anything. I love you."

My little clock showed it was close to 3:00 a.m. It was obvious he'd been drinking, but it sounded like he'd taken something else too.

"Jack . . . do you know what time it is?"

"Way too early?" he asked, obviously knowing the answer.

"Yes. Let's talk tomorrow. I promise I'll listen, but I'm exhausted. I have shooting in three hours."

"You promise you'll talk to me?"

"I promise. Now go to sleep."

"I'm at the Athletic Club, darling . . ." he managed to get out before I put the receiver back.

I've never had much trouble sleeping in my life. But when I hung up, I had lots of time to think. About Myron, about my marriage, about my future and where it was going. Jack deserved a fair shake, but I didn't know where to draw the line. I had little Jimmie to consider now too.

All I wanted was to return to New York and Myron and Jimmie. My confidence was completely shaken, and Jack had become more of a drinking partner than a spouse. Lately, all we had done was fight. I was tired of him, tired of his family, and tired of feeling like shit all the time. My revenge on Ziggy appeared to have backfired on me.

When was my career going to take off like Myron had promised? I'd had some success, sure. But something was keeping me from being as big as Mary. Maybe it was Jack. Maybe it was me. I'd already been through one divorce with Krug, but I didn't know if my reputation or my emotions could handle another one.

I scribbled out a note to Myron, pleading to film my next project, *Mary's Ankle*, in the city so I could get away from Jack and from California. Unfortunately, the response was not encouraging.

ALL ARRANGEMENTS HAVE BEEN MADE TO DO YOUR NEXT PICTURE ON COAST STOP TO DO IT IN NEW YORK WOULD UPSET PRODUCTION SCHEDULE AND WILL CROWD ME FOR STUDIO SPACE AS BIOGRAPH LEASE EXPIRES NEXT WEEK AND I DO NOT TAKE POSSESSION OF PARAGON FOR ANOTHER MONTH STOP AWFULLY SORRY OLLIE BUT IT WILL BE IMPOSSIBLE TO DO IT HERE STOP MYRON.

Shit.

Between insecurity over my acting, worries over my marriage, and concern over the example we were setting for Jimmie, I was a wreck. Myron saw beauty and charm and dollar signs, but I pictured everyone else laughing at the amateur. They could see what a phony I was compared to Mary. I'd come so far but felt like I could return to shopgirl status any minute. No matter how much Myron tried to reassure me, I was shaky all the time and couldn't explain why. I needed a vacation, but the stream of telegrams kept arriving, notifying me, alerting me, hounding me.

Myron was coming west to negotiate some space at the Brunton studio, and he'd be staying at the Alex, so he'd phone when he got settled in. I beat him to the punch. He'd been lounging on the couch in his suite with his feet up when I got there.

"Ollie," he said, setting his paperwork aside and standing to give me a hug. "I was just going to call you."

"I wanted to talk to you, but it couldn't wait."

"Did you get my telegram? The rushes are terrific. It's going to be such a great picture."

"Yeah, it is." I sat down hard on the occasional chair, unsure how to proceed.

"Ollie, what is it?"

"Myron, I need a break. I've been working nonstop for you since I signed, and I'm exhausted."

"Huh?"

"I need a rest."

"Impossible. We've got you booked solid for the next three months. You're our cash register. You know that."

"Myron, I'm so tired. Look at me." I looked down at my hands, which were shaking. "I need a break, and I need it now.

Please let me get away for a little while. To Europe maybe. I've never been."

"Ollie, I've told you this. Selznick Pictures is built on you. You're the one who brings in the majority of our ticket sales right now. We need you working to be able to pay the other stars and get their pictures done. We lost the Talmadge sisters to First National, for God's sake. We need you working."

"Myron, I need a vacation, and I'm taking one."

"How long?"

"End of August and into September."

"I don't want you to go."

"Too bad. You'll have to hold things together until I get back."

He ran a hand through his pomaded hair and glared at me. "If you were anyone else, I'd sue you for breach of contract."

"If I were anyone else, I wouldn't be under contract."

"The minute you return, we're shooting, Ollie. And I'm not talking some little la-di-da shoot. You're working off this debt. Every penny of it. Maybe I should suspend you while you're gone."

"Suspend me? Are you crazy? I've earned a holiday, Myron. I've busted my ass for you the last year and a half."

"And like I said, you're going to keep doing that. How about I suspend your clothing allowance? And maybe that pesky policy about cash advances too. You've been enjoying a lot of oranges and crushed ice on the train. "

"You bastard. That's in my contract."

"So is the working part."

"I'll have Nathan make mincemeat of that contract."

"Guess you're in a tight spot, then. How will you pay a lawyer with no money coming in from the son of a bitch who signs your paychecks? And the one who signs for the money you need when you're overdrawn? You got another notice today. You wanna see it?" He crossed to the desk and waved another bank slip at me.

My head throbbed, and the blood pounded in my ears. So here he was: the greedy Myron everyone in Hollywood had known existed but me.

"This isn't over," I said, grabbing the notice and slamming the door behind me.

CHAPTER FIFTY-TWO

LOS ANGELES, *June 1920*

In the early summer, *Everybody's Sweetheart* was under way. Since Myron and I had hit an iceberg, I tried to get along with Jack. Jack said he hadn't been feeling well, so against his protests, I forced him to see Dr. Charles Gros in Los Angeles. I'd suspected something unusual when he hadn't been interested in sex lately. No matter how I tried to entice him into the sack, he would not be budged. He'd claim fatigue or a headache or something else. The real cause was much worse.

As I sat in the waiting area with a copy of *Variety*, Jack opened the door to Dr. Gros's examining room with a sheepish expression on his face and gestured for me to join them. The doctor was an older man of perhaps sixty, with kind brown eyes and a bit of a potbelly contained by a brown belt and suspenders beneath his white coat. His beard looked like something the cat coughed up.

"Mrs. Pickford, I wanted you to be present for this discussion, as it involves you too."

Does this ever sound good coming from a doctor?

"I hate to tell you this, but your husband has contracted syphilis from a previous liaison."

"A previous what?" I asked, unable to hear another word but the terrifying one.

"I'll need to check you for signs of the disease too."

"You son of a bitch," I said, turning to Jack.

As you modern types like to say, my life was circling the drain. If anyone found out about this, my career would be over. I felt like Jess Willard had just clobbered me in the solar plexus. For his part, Jack sat there, not saying a word, as ridiculous as a two-legged stool. A poster on the wall taunted me: "You kept fit and defeated the Hun. Now set a high standard. A CLEAN AMERICA! Stamp out venereal disease!"

"I'll show you the technique for treating yourselves so it will be familiar to both of you. This condition does not have to be lethal if you dose yourself regularly," Dr. Gros said. "The regimen takes up to three years to be effective. So you must use this solution whenever the chancres appear on your . . . extremities . . ." he finished, attempting to be delicate for my sake.

He removed a blue bottle from a glass cabinet. It had a skull and crossbones on the label. This was no Milk of Magnesia he was handing out.

"Remove two of the tablets," he said. "You'll notice the danger markings on the label for your protection. This mercury"—he gestured to the bottle—"is a lethal substance if consumed. It should only be used topically—or in layman's terms, on the outside of your body. Do I make myself clear?"

We both nodded.

"Place them in a glass, like so," he continued. "Then pour about eight ounces of alcohol over the tablets. Stir, and it will be ready to use when the mercury dissolves. Use a washcloth you designate specifically for this purpose, and cleanse the affected area with the solution. Do not reuse the washcloth on other parts of your body. Mercury can damage them too."

All the oxygen had drained from the room.

"I need some air," I gasped, slipping out the door of the clinic and down to the street. In an alley around the corner, I vomited my breakfast into a rusty garbage can. Moving away from the stench, I took several deep breaths of car exhaust.

When I returned, the doctor's eyes were full of sympathy.

"Come in, Mrs. Pickford," he said. "I was just telling your husband about the four stages of the disease that have been identified."

He let me sit down before he continued. "As I was saying, the four categories are primary, secondary, latent, and tertiary. Your husband is still in the primary stage, so it's good we have discovered it now. He has very few symptoms other than a lesion or two. Do you happen to know the last time you . . . had relations?"

The bile rose as I opened my mouth to speak. I closed it, just in case. "It's hard to answer," I said. "We've been apart so much lately." Anyone who'd bought a newspaper since Jack's unceremonious dismissal from the service would know why. "It's been a while . . . since we . . ." My voice faded off. "Jack said he wasn't feeling very good, and we haven't . . . you know . . . for a month or two, I guess."

"That could be extremely beneficial to you in not contracting the disease, Mrs. Pickford. It's possible you may not be infected. For her protection, Mr. Pickford, I must demand that you use a prophylactic device when you have relations from now on."

Dr. Gros had taken a book down from the shelf and was thumbing through it as he spoke to me. It appeared he was verifying the facts he was sharing.

"Do you want to have children?" he asked.

"We do," I said. "I love children."

"I'm afraid it's out of the question if you're infected. The disease is passed from mother to child through the birth canal. This may result in blindness or a whole host of other deformities for the infant. If Mr. Pickford is the only one of you who is ill, it's still a risk for you with no prophylactic. I don't recommend it."

One of my dreams was now in tatters. I'd fallen in love and lassoed myself to Jack because I wanted a husband, children, and a home. Now I had the husband, but we'd never be able to have children. And with the crazy cross-country nature of our relationship, we could rule out a permanent home for the foreseeable future. Our marriage might never be normal.

"You said Jack is in the primary stage now," I said, needing clarification. "How long does that usually last?

"Anywhere from a year to twenty years," he said.

My head spun.

"So which of them was it?" I said, turning to Jack, who had barely uttered a word during the entire appointment. "Which sweet little ingénue or seductive vamp was it who gave you this? It was that little bitch at Christmas, wasn't it? *Wasn't it?*"

"Olive, you know I . . ."

"You what?" I said. "Who were you fucking after telling *me* I was the only sweetheart you would ever have? Which whorehouse in Tijuana did you go to?"

"Mrs. Pickford, this is no time for recrimination. Mr.

Pickford could have picked up the disease from anyone. It didn't have to be a prostitute."

"What about showgirls or two-bit actresses? Or yellow-haired tramps?"

The doctor was at a loss. He opened his mouth and closed it again, like an over-inflated goldfish.

"The mercury should be effective if you use it as I've directed," he finally said.

"Is mercury the only option?" I asked.

"A fellow in Germany has created something he's named Salvarsan, but it's still in the early stages of use. Call me a traditionalist, but I believe this is the way to go. However, you're always welcome to seek a second opinion."

He tapped his prescription pad, then ripped off the slip and handed it to Jack. "Now, Mr. Pickford, you must fill this immediately and begin with the treatment, for your own good and that of your wife. Mrs. Pickford, if you step into the room next door, my nurse will administer the test. We should have the results in a few days."

Doctor Gros shook hands with Jack, and the next few days were one long fight. Fighting in the lobby of the doctor's, fighting on the train, or fighting at the druggist's.

The call came a week later. Somehow I'd avoided the pox. I breathed a sigh of relief, but *Everybody's Sweetheart* was still filming, so I hopped the train to New York once again.

CHAPTER FIFTY-THREE

NEW YORK CITY, *circa late June 1920*

This reunion was even stranger than the last. Jack waited for me to approach first. I kissed him on the cheek and held my face close to his for the photographers, but the rest of me stayed removed. The distance was almost too much to bridge.

We put on a good front as usual for the snapping of the cameras, and Jack took my arm and led me off the train platform to the car, where Mischa waited for instructions.

"Home please, Mischa," I said.

He nodded and steered us into traffic. The silence screamed between us.

"Where are we going, Jack?" I finally said.

"When?"

"Right now. The future. Ever."

"I guess that's up to you."

"No, it's up to you. This is our *last* chance. I'm asking you to grow up and be a man, instead of acting like an overgrown kid all the time. We have Jimmie to think of now, and since we can't have our own kids, we need to do right by him. Do right by Jim too, since he trusts us. I want us to be a family. This coast-to-coast thing won't last forever. If we are together, we can dedicate ourselves to each other, and to this marriage."

Jack was quiet.

"I'm saying dump the drugs and the floozies and be with me. If we're going to save this thing, we need to do it. Otherwise, we're just wasting our time. Let's decide once and for all what we want. We never had a genuine honeymoon, you know. We never got a chance to focus only on each other for a week or two and really be in love. Let's see if it works."

"That sounds like a good idea. Where should we go?"

"How about Europe? France is so cheap right now with the inflation since the war. I'd love to see Paris. Maybe we could see England or Italy afterward. There's supposed to be lots to see, right? Ruins and things?"

"Let's do it. Mother wants me to drum up business for the Jack Pickford Motion Picture Company in Europe so United Artists has something else to sell. Since the war ended, Europe's a huge market. Mary and Doug's trip was proof of that."

Mary and Doug had gone to Europe for their honeymoon. We heard stories of crowds of fans nearly crushing them and tearing lace, feathers, and fabric from Mary's dresses. They had been famous before, but since they'd founded United Artists Studio with Charlie Chaplin the year before, they were the King and Queen of Hollywood.

I'd just begged Jack to save our marriage, and all he could think of was running an errand for his mother, for a company that was his in name only. I couldn't help it. I snorted a little and lit a cigarette.

"What?"

"Nothing."

"Tell me, Ollie."

"The company is named after you, but your mother is the one telling you to go get publicity? That's funny, you know," I said, inhaling.

"Why is it funny?"

"How old are you now?"

"Don't patronize me. My production company is going to be my ticket off Mary's coattails. Laugh all you want, but I'm going to be as big as my sister someday."

"Whatever you say, Jack."

The next day, Mischa drove me to an appointment with Dr. Choate, my family doctor. The doc had me change into a paper gown and gave me a physical, making sure I was fully healthy after fighting off the Spanish flu twice.

"What's the trouble, Miss Thomas?" he asked, sitting down on the little stool next to the examining table.

"I've had trouble sleeping lately, doctor," I told him.

"Is that so?" Dr. Choate said. "Blood pressure's fine," he said, unwinding the cuff from my arm. Then he shook down a thermometer and placed it under my tongue.

"It's 98.6," he said with satisfaction after a minute or two.

He asked me questions about other illnesses, female issues, and the happenings in my life. I explained I was under enormous pressure from Myron to produce more pictures, but that we'd temporarily called a truce. Instead of the closeness we'd shared two Christmases ago, a strange wariness had taken hold between Myron and me. We still hadn't agreed on terms for a contract. At this point, it was good just to have my option picked up.

I told Dr. Choate about our custody arrangement with Jimmie and how it had changed my thoughts on marriage and family, stressing the tension it had brought with it. I couldn't tell him about the affair with Myron or my constant worries about the syphilis. I was too ashamed.

"Sounds like you're dealing with a lot lately," Dr. Choate said. "Motion pictures not turning out to be quite what you thought they were?"

"Oh, I love my job," I insisted. "But I'd also love to be in one place for a while. I guess I didn't realize all the traveling it would involve. I know every tree and hill between Los Angeles and New York."

He chuckled. "Perhaps you could take some time off?"

"Actually, I've already thought of that," I said. "Jack and I are planning a trip to Europe."

"When?" he said, now much more interested.

"August possibly, maybe September."

"How do you like that! The wife and I are traveling to Paris about the same time."

"We're stopping in Paris," I said. "But we're thinking about maybe Rome or London too."

"Good. Travel is good for the soul, and for expanding our horizons. But it sounds like you simply need some good rest, Miss Thomas. So for that, I'm going to prescribe a sleeping potion for you." He scribbled the medication name on his little pad.

"Thank you, doctor."

He reached up to a medicine cabinet across the room and grabbed a blue bottle from it.

"Now for this medication, take two of these pills," he said, demonstrating. “Place them in a glass and pour some water over them. Stir, then drink the solution. This should help you drop right off.”

Relieved, I snatched the prescription from his fingers.

“See you at the Eiffel Tower,” I joked as I left the office.

FINALE

CHAPTER FIFTY-FOUR

RMS IMPERATOR, NEW YORK HARBOR

August 12, 1920

"Miss Thomas, Mr. Pickford, I'm Edward Stockbridge, *New York World*. Might we film a bit of footage?"

"Of course," Jack said, smiling into the camera.

We let the reporter and his cameraman shoot us as we leaned against the railing, the very epitome of relaxed stardom. Later, the wire services would send stills all over the country, showing us enjoying our holiday.

My boarding outfit was a black silk number with a fox collar and pleated skirt, two-tone pumps, and a turban. Jack wore a dove-gray suit and hat, as well as spats. We knew reporters watched the docks for celebrities, so we'd come prepared, the perfect Hollywood couple. On the surface. However, the reality was much different.

All we'd done since boarding was bicker. The honeymoon story had been circulated far and wide, but it had been a futile gesture. I doubted our marriage would see out the trip. Part of me thought it sounded like the greatest thing in the world, finally cutting the cord with Jack. The other part of me felt deep black dread for what might happen to my career without the ever-present Pickford publicity machine cataloging our every move.

"Where's our cabin?" I asked when we boarded.

"First class," Jack said proudly. "C Deck."

A huge group of friends and relatives saw us off. The suite was so full of flower arrangements, we could barely move. I told the steward to add a few to the other tables as decorations for the dinner service, and he gratefully relayed my message to the captain.

It wasn't completely obvious how gigantic the ship was until we'd promenaded around her a few times. She had a black hull and buff-colored funnels that chugged out plumes of thick smoke. Our suite had a separate bedroom and salon plus a sofa bed, original oil paintings, plush carpeting, clusters of lights, and a room just for our trunks. The headboard of the bed was a three-paneled mirror. A small desk was handy for writing postcards home. The salon had a couch, an armchair, and a wardrobe, and also a window with a view of the ocean. We had a full bathroom with a marble basin for washing up.

After the departure festivities, we returned to the suite for a rest, dripping confetti. Frances had sent us a quick departure note and a huge spray of pink lilies.

"Ollie—

*I just read the most amazing book—*This Side of Paradise *by a new writer named Fitzgerald. This Rosalind role is absolutely perfect for you, and I'm going to speak to Myron about getting the rights to production. See? Flappers! They're the baby vamps of the new decade!"*

All my love,
Frances"

The idea for *This Side of Paradise* was a good one, and I needed to stick with Myron, if only for my career. If the squabbling with Jack kept up, another divorce would be in the works soon.

The first few days of August, I'd been preoccupied by negotiations with Myron, along with a new film, *Jennie*, that had started shooting. Myron had also gone public with the roster of shows I'd star in next season. The *New York Times* had promptly published the list of my upcoming films: *Nobody*, *Keep Him Guessing*, *The Girl with the Faun Ears*, *The Magdalene of Mudville*, and *The Fib*. As Myron had threatened, I'd be working my fanny off when I returned.

I changed into an indigo-blue silk dress for dinner, and Jack wore a tuxedo he'd recently had custom-made at one of the top tailors in Los Angeles. We climbed the main staircase, which stretched from F deck up to A deck. Lacy metalwork supported the banisters. On the top landing hung a portrait of the king. Someone said they'd replaced a painting of the Kaiser that had hung in that spot for years, which was good. I didn't want to see the old bastard after all the pain and suffering he had caused.

"She was a German ship for Hamburg-Amerika," an Englishman behind us said. "They took her as war reparation and gave her to the British. Now she's a Cunarder."

Jack took my arm as we entered the first-class dining room, and the maître d' sat us next to a couple who owned a department store chain in Washington State. On the other side were an older man and the woman who was obviously his mistress. They said they were from San Francisco. I knew that expression the girl wore. Hell, I'd been her once. A little too much décolleté showing, and she was hanging on the old man's words like he was the Delphic Oracle. What had the old coot promised her . . . a plum theater role? A feature film? Marriage?

Dorothy Gish, one of our longtime friends, was also on the crossing with her mother. Like Jack, they were going abroad to drum up publicity for new films. We gave them a little wave from across the room.

Our friend Lois Meredith was making the voyage too. We'd met her through Owen. He'd starred with her in *Help Wanted* five years before.

We studied the menu, but everything was too hoity-toity for me. "Do you have any hash, or even a simple roast chicken?" I asked the waiter.

"No madam, but I think you'll find the quails Richelieu to be a very tasty substitute. The preparation is quite simple."

I agreed instead of creating a stink. Jack decided on the galantine of capon with Oxford sauce, whatever the hell that was. Since Prohibition was in effect, we had to wait until the ship was safely out of American waters before we could order wine, so we settled on a Viognier, to be served the minute we hit open ocean. As soon as the all clear was given, Jack ordered twelve bottles for the table, and we all got more bent than a bunch of pretzels.

When someone brought up Prohibition, the businessman, whose name was Monty Porter, mentioned he'd already found an outstanding bootlegger. "Although the guy charges more than a new Packard costs!" he said with bluster. Then he lowered his voice. "Know how to make gin? It's easy! Mix three parts grain alcohol, one part distilled water, and juniper oil to taste . . ." He spoke slowly, and everyone grabbed cocktail napkins and took notes.

Jack and I were still at each other's throats, so feeling guilty, I surprised him with a birthday party on the high seas. I'd met with the headwaiter and the chef beforehand while Jack was busy playing cards and smoking cigars with the other first-class men.

Chef had prepared a feast of seared foie gras, duck à l'Orange, oysters Rockefeller, green beans almandine, exotic cheeses, and bottles and bottles of champagne. The cake was a work of art—five tiers, with liqueur between the layers. The booze had also been added to a sweet chocolate sauce served alongside. The dining room had been hung with streamers, and the other diners wore party hats and blew their noisemakers to celebrate too.

"Thank you for the party." Jack leaned over and kissed me, nuzzling my neck. It wasn't romantic—it was just from the dose of junk he'd thrown together before dinner.

We were having a grand time, but then Jack made some smartass remark about my co-star in *The Flapper*, William Carleton, suggesting we'd had an affair, and everything lit up like a forest fire. Even if I hadn't slept with him, it was a shitty thing to do, bringing it up in front of all these people. What about the rumors of him out at the Hotel Clark's bar with Molly Malone, his co-star in *Just Out of College*?

I took more interest in my dinner than I did in Jack, and he was irritated at me too. When he didn't get the attention he craved, he was like a five-year-old. So he set about entertaining our tablemates, pouring an unending stream of champagne, and when that ran out he ordered more.

Dorothy stopped by to say hello, and she could sense the tension immediately. “Everything okay?” she asked.

“Fine,” I said. “Jack’s tight as an outsized belt, as usual.”

“Ollie darling,” she said, “Stop by for a nightcap, will you? Dump him and come sit with Mother and me,” she said. She took my arm and attempted to guide me away from Jack.

“Dorothy, I’d love to, but I’m not feeling myself,” I said. I feigned a headache later and retreated to our suite, willing myself not to cry.

When I was a shopgirl in Pittsburgh, how could I ever have imagined buying drugs for my husband, the junkie? Or having to deal with the clap? Or my husband’s sleeping with not only one other woman, but a whole chorus line? The sleeping draught was in my bag. It would be so easy to drink the entire thing and go to sleep. No more pain, no more frustration, no more Jack screwing up both of our lives. I pulled out the little bottle and thought things I’d never considered before.

The door closed and Jack staggered in, his ridiculous hat wobbling on his head. “I missed you,” he said, slurring his words.

“Did you?” I said, tilting my chin up. “You seemed pretty cozy with that lady from San Francisco to me.”

“Ollie, why do we do this?”

“Do what? You accused me of having an affair. You’ve had dozens of affairs. You’re an immature boy who has no idea what he wants, and I’m an immature girl who can’t believe I married you. What a pair of idiots we are.”

“I love you, Ollie,” he said.

“That’s not enough of a reason for a marriage,” I said.

“Why not?” he said.

"Honestly, if I'd have known how miserable you would make me, I could have stayed with Ziggy for that. Or Myron."

"I make you miserable?" he said. His eyes were dark and pained, like a cocker spaniel's.

"Sometimes."

"Sometimes?"

"Most of the time," I admitted.

"I'm better for you than them. You know I am," he said, kissing me. Even in his condition, he knew what worked to turn me from a raging cougar to a purring pussycat in a few quick seconds. Pulling up my skirt, he felt beneath it. His hand was relentless.

"Stop, Jack. Stop it!" It wasn't going to work this time.

I put every ounce of energy into my slap. He was so stunned, he stopped, giving me time to slip away from him as he rubbed his cheek.

That night, I barred the door to our trunk room with a chair under the knob. I curled up with a blanket on the floor and got the worst sleep of my life.

CHAPTER FIFTY-FIVE

CHERBOURG, FRANCE, *August 20, 1920*

The harbor in Cherbourg reminded me of the time Spud and I had kicked over an ant nest when we were little. If possible, the place was even more bustling than the dock in New York. The ships lined up along the docks belched out thousands of passengers, who then waited impatiently in the same taxi lines we did. The salt air was a tangy contrast to the odor of dead fish, stevedore sweat, and rotting vegetables in the alleys behind the seaside cafés.

Eventually we did find a cab, which took us to the train station, and we hopped the sleeper car to Paris. It was a quiet trip, with each of us giving the silent treatment to the other. The scenery out the window flew by—cows, hillocks, apple trees, and farmers with their wagons. We grabbed another cab at the Gare St. Lazare. After loading up our trunks, our driver, who told us his name was Gustave, leaned over the front seat for instructions.

"The Ritz," Jack told him.

After fighting the chaos on the streets of Paris, the driver pulled up in front of the Ritz Hotel. Long vertical windows on the second floor seemed to look down their noses at anyone not wealthy enough to afford the joint. A nodding bellhop loaded our trunks onto a cart and patiently stood by as we checked in.

"Mr. and Mrs. Jack Pickford," Jack said, leaning on the desk and watching the desk clerk for signs of fawning. He loved the compliments he got, the exaggerated courtesies, and the power his name carried. It was obvious the clerk enjoyed registering two Hollywood stars. We weren't royalty, of course, but we were the closest thing the Americans could offer.

"What's your name?" I said, leaning across the counter toward the clerk.

"Jacques, madame," he said.

"Ever been to Hollywood, Jacques?"

"No, madame," he said, handing Jack the guest register to sign and smiling at me, "but I do enjoy ze fleekers."

"You should visit sometime," I said.

Brandishing the pen like a magic wand, Jack signed his name and handed the book to Jacques. Then he glared at me. It was fine for him to flirt, but I was not allowed.

"Aah, Monsieur Pickford, *un* telegram for you."

He reached behind him to a series of cubbyholes and handed Jack the slip. We both watched as Jack read.

"Shit."

"What is it?" I asked.

"It's Owen. He's been in an accident in England. It says an air crash."

"Oh God. He mentioned his trip to me. Is he okay?"

"It doesn't say. He's at a hospital in London."

He got very quiet as Jacques handed him the room key.

"Hubert, please see Monsieur *et* Madame Pickford to their room and assist them with their bags. *Merci.*"

"*Oui*, Monsieur Chabert." Hubert nodded and followed us into the elevator.

"What the hell was that?" Jack said.

"What the hell was what?"

"The flirting with the desk clerk, that's what."

"I wasn't flirting. I was being friendly."

"You weren't just being friendly. I saw you, Ollie."

"Oh, for Christ's sake, Jack." I blew out a breath. "Can we not do this now?"

"When am I supposed to do it, exactly?"

"Never," I said. "You flirt with everything in a skirt. I say boo to a desk clerk, and all of a sudden I'm the whore of Babylon? Gimme a break."

Hubert's eyes were huge as he tried to ignore the battle being waged in front of him. The elevator doors opened to everyone's great relief, and he ushered us down the hall, unlocking our room. Jack handed him a generous tip before he retreated.

"Classy," I said, admiring the room.

The heavy velvet drapes blocked too much of the afternoon sun, so I pulled them open wide and allowed light to flood the room. I unlatched the window to fully enjoy the view of the Place Vendôme and realized what Ziggy had told me was true—Paris had its own fragrance. From the bakeries removing fresh bread from the ovens to the elegant cologne worn by Frenchwomen out promenading the avenues, from the reeking fish markets to the flowers in the Luxembourg Gardens, from the mildewy tinge of the Seine to the tobacco drifting from the outdoor cafes and the dog shit from mongrels out strolling with their masters. The last made me think of Chow, now stuck at home with Effie.

Jack sighed.

"What?" I said, lighting a cigarette.

"I have to go," he said.

"Go? Go where?"

"To England. I have to check up on Owen."

I said nothing.

"I swear to you. It's the only reason, Ollie. I'll grab a flight and be back before you know it. I just want to make sure he's all right."

"Then go." I blew out a frustrated mouthful of smoke.

"He was my brother-in-law for nine years. I need to do this."

Anything I said would sound spoiled and selfish. I cared for Owen too, but we'd only just arrived in Europe, and I was hoping to save our marriage. Every time I tried grabbing at a chance, it seemed to drift away.

I watched from the window to the sidewalk below as Jack lit a cigarette and scrambled into a taxicab to Le Bourget Airport. Then I made myself a drink. After three more drinks, I fell asleep on the couch.

Despite the next morning's hangover, I decided to go sightseeing. I was in the City of Light, for Christ's sake. After cleaning myself up, I had the concierge call me a cab, and I watched eagerly out the windows at the bakeries, cafés, posters for Chocolat Suchard and Pernod, and old men playing boules in the park. First, I took the elevator to the top of the Eiffel Tower. At the Île Saint-Louis, I visited Notre-Dame, and though I wasn't Catholic, I lit a candle for Da inside.

The next day, after a café crème and a croissant or two, I strolled along the Rue du Faubourg Saint-Honoré, visiting the most popular salons. At the House of Lanvin, I was pinned, prodded, and draped for hours. Continuing on to Vionnet, I purchased six of her draped pieces.

The ladies at the House of Chanel twittered around me, telling me it was such an honor to fit the great actress Olive Thomas. To make the trip even more worthwhile, I ordered two fur coats, one a fantastic combination of ermine and seal, and the other beaver.

When the fittings were over, I explored Paris, sticking my nose into nooks and crannies I'd have missed otherwise. At Les Halles, I dug up a bauble or two I knew Mamma would love, a couple small toys for Jimmie and Harriett, a necklace for Penny, and a keepsake bracelet for Frances. While I strolled beneath the plane trees, absorbing the sights and smells of Paris, I realized something: Jack was gone, and I was fine. I was perfectly fine. I wasn't falling apart without him, I didn't miss him, and I actually dreaded his return. I knew what I needed to do.

That night, I had the operator connect me long distance to New York. I planned for the future and arranged my ducks in a nice, neat row. Then I prepared the sleeping solution Dr. Choate had prescribed and slept like a baby.

CHAPTER FIFTY-SIX

HOTEL RITZ, PARIS, SATURDAY, *September 4, 1920*

"Morning, Ollie," Jack said, slurring the words.

Assuming it was breakfast, I had opened the door, expecting to see my favorite waiter, Etienne. Instead Jack stood there, unshaven and with deep shadows beneath his eyes, his stare glazed. He was wearing the same suit he'd left in days ago.

"You look like shit," I said.

"I missed you," he said simply. "Owen's fine. It wasn't a serious crash."

"Good. Glad to hear it. I had a dandy time while you were gone." I left him at the open door.

He followed me, but his movements were slow and uncoordinated.

"Don't act this way," he said.

"When we get to the States, I'm filing for divorce. I've already spoken to Nathan, and he's recommended a good divorce lawyer. I'm tired of this nightmare. I'm tired of the fighting, the drugs, the affairs, the clap, all of it."

"No, please. I love you."

"No you don't. You love sex. You love booze. You love drugs. You love yourself. But you don't love anything else."

"Can we at least go out one last time? I just got here. I'd like to spend a little time with you before we separate for good."

"What's the point? You want to go down to the Pigalle to buy drugs. You can do that by yourself. You don't need my help."

"Ollie, we talked about seeing Italy while we were in Europe. Let's go somewhere exotic."

"Exotic? Fine. We'll go to the Rat Mort tonight. It's exotic. Ziggy told me about it years ago, and I want to see it while I'm here. Other than that, this tour is over. It was pointless to begin with. I don't know why I thought it might make a difference. I won't force you to get another room tonight because the papers will pick up on it right away, and that'll ruin your publicity tour. We don't need Mary reading about all this yet. She and Charlotte will finally be rid of the cheap little showgirl who ruined their precious Jack. But keep your distance from me if you know what's good for you." I threw him a moistened hand towel from the bathroom. "Clean yourself up."

Instead of taking it, he shuffled past me to the bathroom and showered. Then he cooked up another dose of junk.

I knew one thing. I didn't want to be anywhere near him on the trip home. Since it would be five days, I intended on finding an attractive gentleman onboard ship to help me forget ever knowing Jack Pickford. I still had to get through the flight to England first.

When he finished and lay almost comatose on one of the beds, I got ready to go out and opened the medicine cabinet to find my Narcisse Noir.

I hadn't drunk all my sleeping draught the night before.

It sat reassuringly on the counter, waiting for me if I needed it. I was tempted to stay in, to rest and relax, but it was Paris, for God's sake. I was going to kick up my heels and have some fun, not be some shrinking violet.

That night, I wore my white dress with lace appliqués, a lacy slip I'd bought at one of the French lingerie boutiques, pink garters, white stockings, and my new white shoes, purchased at one of the stores on the Rue Montaigne. Jack dozed in one of the armchairs, so maybe I could leave him to sleep it off. I'd have more fun alone.

As I pulled the door shut, the telephone in our room jingled. Quickly reinserting the key, I hurried to the phone and was surprised to hear Rosie Dolly on the other end.

"Ollie!" she squealed.

"Rosie honey, how are you? *Where* are you?"

"I am in Paris, darling! In three days I vill drive to de coast to break de bank at Deauville. I saw Mae at de Moulin Rouge, and she told me you vere on your vay over on de *Imperator*. She said you vere at de Ritz and so I am calling! Jenny and I vould love a visit vit you!"

Of course, the phone woke Jack, and he began pulling himself up. So much for leaving him behind.

"Are you free tonight? I'm going to the Pigalle." I glared at him. He slipped into the bathroom, and I heard him cleaning himself up.

"Oh, dis is too bad," Rosie said. "Tonight, ve are having plans at Fouquet's. Some friends have invited us for dinner. I vas hoping perhaps for lunch tomorrow?"

"Hell's bells. I wish I could, but Jack and I are leaving tomorrow. We're catching a flight to England and then sailing home. I'll call you when I get to New York, all right?"

"Goodbye den, dear. À bientôt, Ollie!"

"'Bye, Rosie."

Jack glared at me.

"I'm going," I said. "Come if you want, but don't expect us to be a couple while we're out. We're not."

A cab took us to Montmartre, and I avoided Jack as much as possible. That got much easier when we ran into an acquaintance from his time in the service, Lieutenant G.A. Ray, at the Casino de Paris. He was working at the embassy now, he said. Fred Almey also showed up. He was Myron's man, keeping tabs on me and others in the stable.

Even more strangely, my friend Florence Wufelt was strolling along the Rue Caulaincourt. Florence and her husband Clarence had lived near us when we'd rented the house on Wilshire, and she and I had kept in touch. Clarence was some bigwig at the Los Angeles Athletic Club, but I'd never understood exactly what it was he did. Florence was tall and gangly, towering over Jack, me, and even her husband, who stood six feet tall.

Au Lapin Agile was a pink stucco cottage with green shutters and a spindly green fence outside hemming in the small garden at the corner of Rue des Saules and Rue Saint-Vincent. The boeuf bourguignon and tarte Tatin there were delicious, especially with a glass of Beaujolais. And another glass. And another.

While we ate, Florence talked about Toulouse-Lautrec. "We own several of his prints," she said. "Such a sad life, Ollie."

"What happened?" I said, lighting a cigarette.

She told me about the artist who became famous for his

pictures of what she called "the Paris demimonde"—the dance hall girls, bartenders, club-goers, and prostitutes.

"He could have sat in that very chair," she said.

"To tortured geniuses, then," I said, clinking glasses with her.

Lieutenant Ray, Almey, Florence, Jack and I continued on with our merrymaking. At Zelli's on the Rue Fontaine, we ran into three more of Jack's friends— Fred Nelson, Cyril Gray, and Wilfred Graham. I had no idea how they all knew each other and didn't care. They were friendly enough, and we were all having a jolly time. There were gigantic mirrors hung inside, which made the place look even bigger than it was. And a grouping of caricatures hung along one wall, celebrating patrons of the past. A mass of streamers hung from the ceiling, and the colored fellows in the jazz band put on a rollicking show.

When Jack tried to grab my hand, I pulled it loose under the table. We put on a good front for our friends, laughing and acting frivolous, but my head was splitting from the stress. All I wanted was to be far away from anyone with the last name of Pickford.

"Olive, have you ever tried absinthe?" Florence said. "The name in French is *la fée verte*—'the green fairy.' Clarence and I sampled it when we were here before the war."

"What a charming name!" I said. "What is it, exactly?"

"They distill a plant called Artemisia, or 'wormwood' in England. Tastes a bit like licorice, but it's illegal in France now. For a time, though, it was quite popular."

"Illegal? What for?"

"Some people claim it causes insanity. About fifteen years ago, a man in Switzerland killed his entire family. His two children, for goodness' sakes! And his wife was expecting. Can you imagine?" She downed the last dregs of her wine and gestured to the waiter for another. "I'm so glad you're in Paris, Ollie dear. I always knew you would love it. Wasn't I right?"

"It's perfect," I said. "I only wish I was in a better mood for enjoying it."

At her raised eyebrow, I nodded toward Jack. She nodded, placing a comforting hand on my arm.

From the Lapin, our group continued to Le Café de L'Enfer on Boulevard de Clichy, called Hell by the locals. Surrounding the entrance was a monstrous sculpted mouth with sharp teeth, letting all of us think we were entering the jaws of Hell. The theme continued inside, where spiky stalactites hung from the low ceiling and gargoyles hid in niches in the walls and ceiling. The doorman wore a red costume with horns and a forked tail and leered at us like Satan.

"Enter, and be damned!" he said with an evil laugh.

We ordered cognac for the whole table, and the waiter shouted to the bar, "Six glasses of brimstone!"

"Ollie!" Cyril yelled over the raucous noise. I found myself staring at his blonde hair, which was mussed from being jostled at the front door.

I leaned toward him.

"Have you heard the story they tell about the fellow at Café Boum?" he said.

"What about him?"

"It's said he was a tourist. He ordered the very best meal on the menu—snails, a filet du boeuf Godard, potatoes Anna, clafouti, and a glass of the most expensive brandy. He received the bill, but as he had spent every last franc on drugs and high-priced courtesans, he flipped it over and scribbled, 'I regret I cannot pay the tab, but I will give you as little inconvenience as possible.' Then he blew his brains out."

"No!" I said, covering my mouth as I gasped.

"It happened. Honest." His eyes were full of mischief.

"You're pulling my leg, Cyril."

He cocked an eyebrow and kept smiling.

Wilfred joined in then. Pointing at my drink, he said, "Have you tried an ether and brandy yet, Ollie?"

"No," I said, sipping my cognac. "Is it what I think it is?"

"Madame Rapette's serves it. It's a sublime cocktail of the two of them mixed."

"Ether? Isn't that what they use in operating rooms so you fall asleep? It sounds dreadful. Isn't it dangerous?"

"Oh it is! Frightfully so! But it's a still, quiet sort of wooziness. It was an American, Madame Harvard, who first made it popular. She was a regular patron at Madame Rapette's for years."

"What happened to her? Where is she now?"

"Oh, dead of course. Some sort of nerve problem. I heard she died stashed away in an asylum. So it's probably not anything you want to do a lot of, eh?" He guffawed, slapping his knee. *"Garçon!"*

The waiter brought more cognac and kept it coming until I needed some air.

"How about we head over to the Rat Mort?" I said.

"Isn't that a little savage for our Ollie?" Florence said.

"Someone told me about it years ago. I've always been curious."

I lit another cigarette and joined Florence and Cyril near the exit.

The Rat Mort was on the Place Pigalle, near another club called L'Abbaye de Thélème. There were striped awnings out front, with an arcade and a sign to draw more people in. Ziggy had taught me enough French to know that *ouverte toute la nuit* meant open all night. It seemed to me that if they were looking for customers, they couldn't do better for advertising than that. We ordered more cognac and a bottle of Burgundy. Lieutenant Ray flirted shamelessly, asking me endless questions about show business and placing his muscled hand on my knee under the table.

"Have you heard the history of this place, Ollie?" he asked.

I shook my head, which was a mistake, considering the amount of booze I'd had. I closed my eyes so the room would stop shimmying.

"A group of artists and writers used to frequent the place across the street, the New Athens, but they got into a disagreement with the owner one day, and they all came here instead. The place had been painted that afternoon, and the plaster on the walls was still wet. One of them sat down and said, 'Good God, this place smells like a dead rat.'"

"No!" I couldn't help but giggle.

"That's what they say. Anything wrong with Jack?" he said as Jack inched his way to the toilets in the rear.

"Damned if I know. Or care," I said. Ray had lovely soft brown hair and eyes the color of deep mocha coffee, and I think I got lost in them for a second. "Jack Pickford and I are through. I'll be contacting the trades when we get home, but you're the first to hear."

"That's wonderful news, Ollie!"

"It is? I can't imagine why."

"Because I've been wanting to do this all night," he whispered in my ear. He leaned over and kissed me, gently prying my lips open with his tongue. Hidden by the tablecloth, his hand slid over the top of my knee and continued its way up my stockinged leg until it reached my inner thigh. The exotic pulsating rhythms of the house band echoed like tribal drums. Our tongues danced little curlicues to the music, and my head spun. Just as my breathing came in heavy gasps, Ray removed his hand. We pulled apart just as Jack returned from the john. It was all very scandalous. Jack was in improved spirits, full speed ahead like a Model T in a Keystone Kops short—obviously from coke this time.

After the kiss ended, Ray gazed at me with undisguised lust, and I gave him a coy smile. He winked at me as an African man strode to the center of the place, where a group of tables and chairs had been pushed to one side. The audience watched as he stripped down to a tiny cloth wrapped around his hips and privates. An assistant rushed to the center of the room under the spotlight and held up a cage that contained a huge sewer rat. At first the audience's response was a half-hearted gurgle, but then the noise gained in strength and intensity until they were shouting and stomping their feet in anticipation. The band beat drums and clanged cymbals too. The other man faded into the crowd as the African took center stage.

His smile broke across his face like the beam of a flashlight in a dark room. He deftly unfastened the catch on the cage and took the rodent by his slimy pink tail. The creature raised himself up to examine the fingers that held him, confused by what was happening.

"Does he eat it whole?" I whispered to Cyril.

"He can't, can he? He'd choke to death. He'll have to bite it."

"I'm not sure I can watch." Terrified, I put a hand up to shield an eye. But I kept the other focused on the show. Like everyone else, I couldn't pull my gaze away.

The Negro smiled even more broadly and opened his jaws wide, like a big bear trap. His teeth flashed blindingly white as he held the rodent dangling above his gaping mouth. As he lowered the rat, the audience held its collective breath. Then it disappeared. Until the screeching started . . . a terrifying noise of panic and pain. And then nothing.

We heard the sickening crunch of bone as the tail slipped in bit by bit after the rest of it and the African chewed. Blood spurted out of his mouth, down his chin, and over his oiled chest and torso. Still we sat, completely speechless.

The applause grew until the entire place thundered—hands clapped, feet stomped, glasses banged on the bar, canes banged on the floor, and the help rattled the pots and pans in the kitchen.

After it appeared he'd digested his snack, the black man bowed and the assistant brought him a glass of red wine, presumably to rinse the taste out of his mouth. I didn't blame him. I would have downed the whole bottle.

CHAPTER FIFTY-SEVEN

THE RITZ HOTEL, PARIS, SUNDAY
September 5, 1920, 3:00 a.m.

Back at the hotel, the mood in our room was quiet but hostile. I clutched my aching head, regretting the wine and especially the cognac. I desperately needed some aspirins, but I was determined to finish my letter to Mamma. In a few hours, we were boarding a flight on one of those newfangled airplanes from Le Bourget to Croydon, and then after a few more days in London, we were going to embark on a ship home from Southampton. Separate staterooms, if I had anything to say about it.

I sat at the antique desk with a lamp focused over my letter, but Jack whined I was interrupting his sleep. With an arm over his eyes, he moaned pitifully.

"Ollie, you know I can't sleep with that light on. Couldn't you please come to bed?"

"Maybe if you hadn't done all that coke, you'd be able to sleep," I snapped. My headache had caused me to cut the letter far too short.

"Mamma dear: Well and having a nice time. Leaving

Europe September 11. I will cable you from the boat and tell you all the news when I arrive. Ollie. Love to all."

My head still splitting from the drink and the stress, I flicked off the light so Jack would stop complaining about it. I padded into the bathroom and felt around in the medicine cabinet for the aspirin, then downed a few and searched for my sleeping draught pills. Remembering I hadn't finished the previous night's portion, I found it on the counter and drank the leftover fluid, praying for relief from the pounding in my skull.

As soon as it had passed my lips, I knew something was wrong. Oh my God, the burning! I dropped the cup, not able to recognize the shriek being torn from my middle. I felt something searing my mouth, like it was on fire. My windpipe—my vocal cords— my guts—none of them wanted to work properly. I panicked and remembered Dr. Gros telling us about the mercury.

"Jack! Oh God, Jack!" I tried to scream, but all that came out was a strangled wheeze. I banged on the wall to get his attention.

He plodded into the bathroom, seeing the broken tumbler on the floor. His mouth fell open at the horrible realization I had swallowed what was in it.

"Treatment?" I mouthed, pointing at the glass pieces. When he nodded, I fell to my knees on the floor, mindless of the shards, supporting myself with my arms.

"Oh my God, no!" he said.

He ran to the telephone, frantically dialing until he reached someone.

"Please help!" he screamed. "This is Mr. Pickford in Room 312. My wife has taken poison! We need your help right away! Hurry! It's an *emergency!*" He got me into the bedroom and helped me lie down across the bed.

"Darling, the manager is sending up some milk and eggs right away. He says they'll coat your stomach." I draped myself over the edge and moaned. I had never felt such god-awful searing pain.

It was so late, the hotel kitchen was locked. It took forever for the waiter to arrive.

"Monsieur, the ambulance has been called," I heard him say. "It should arrive soon."

Jack fed me the milk and eggs, but all that happened was I puked up everything but my intestines. It only hurt more, bringing the mercury up to do more damage. It hissed as it hit my skin. I flinched as it burned my cheeks and chin, moving my face to and fro until the waiter took a soft, moist rag and absorbed it.

Two men in white coats hurried into the room, placing me on the floor where they had a clear space to spread out. Then they tried pumping my stomach, but the fucking tube hurt so badly going in I fought them all the way. After deliberating with Jack, they decided on the American Hospital in Neuilly.

"*Madame* will receive excellent care and be able to hear English spoken," I heard as they placed me on a litter. I drifted in and out of consciousness.

We arrived as daylight was breaking over the distant treetops, but I was too delirious with pain to know much beyond that. They found me a bed, and Jack must have kept a vigil by my side, because I sensed his musk of toilet water and fear. Sometime after we arrived, someone had evidently found a Doctor Wharton and introduced him to Jack. Urging Jack to the corner of the room and conferring in whispers, the doctor gave him the bad news. I could hear them, though they thought I couldn't.

"Mr. Pickford, I want you to prepare yourself. The outcome of this cannot be any other way. Your wife will not survive. She may last a few days, but mercury is a lethal substance, and it will kill her. It will attack all of her organs, and eventually they will stop working. Her bloodstream has absorbed the mercury, and it will travel through her body. It will pass to her kidneys and is doing severe damage, even now. All we can do is make her comfortable in her final hours and pray for her release from the agony she must be in."

"You mean . . . she . . . I . . ."

"I mean your wife is going to die. I hate for that to sound harsh, but you would only resent me for trying to spare your feelings at a time like this. You must be strong for her."

That was the one thing I knew Jack was completely incapable of. He'd never been strong his entire life. What was the need? Not with Mary and Charlotte to fight all his battles for him.

"Mr. Pickford! Mr. Pickford, please!"

I realized the inhuman wailing I heard had to be from Jack. He slammed and kicked the wall, and his moaning was like nothing I had ever heard before. I couldn't hear words, just curses and pleas to God, more brutal pounding to a door, and finally, a chair being tossed.

"Mr. Pickford, please! Nurse! Nurse!"

I couldn't see much—my vision was fading—but the flutter of white I saw must have been a nurse with a syringe in her hand. I assumed she gave him some sort of shot, calming him down. He must have collapsed to the floor, and between all of them, they got him out of the room because the noise faded to nothing. It made me see just how unequipped Jack was for real life.

As I came to that realization, my eyes finally open for the first time in years, an ironic thing happened: all the light in the room faded, even the bright lights over my bed. I let out a silent cry as I sat up in a panic, unable to scream in fright anymore. My vocal cords were completely burned away.

All I could do was inhale more air, becoming more and more frightened. My lips still tried to form words. They were dry and cracked from the corrosive liquid.

"*Huuuuurts . . .*" I managed to mouthe. *"Bliiiind . . ."* The only noise that came out was a strange panting sound.

"I know, dear." It was Owen. I didn't even know he'd arrived, but he was over his injuries and speaking softly to me. "Jack's in a bad way, Ollie. But I'm here." He patted my hand and leaned closer, humming Irish ditties to make me smile. I drifted off to a fitful doze, exhausted, but my body was not ready to go yet. I lingered for five long hellish days. Not fully alive, but not dead either. I thought of Jimmie and Mamma, and my brothers, and little Harriett, and my sweet boy, Chow. I remembered the ragtag woman. What was her name? Oh yes, Ruth. She'd told us to save our money and marry wisely. I'd certainly blown that chunk of advice, hadn't I?

Hell's bells. Every part of my body was on fire. Couldn't I just go? The newspapers must have caught wind of my condition at home, and visitors from the States who happened to be on the continent stopped by the hospital to offer flowers, liquor, memories of me, and hopes for recovery.

One afternoon, I heard a familiar Slavic-sounding voice and felt a hand in mine. It was Rosie Dolly, and she spoke softly to me, telling me stories of our days at the Follies.

She'd brought me some flowers. "Red ones," she said,

crying softly. With no sense of taste, I couldn't smell anything either. But her hand was so soft. I clutched it to my cheek and fell asleep like that. When I woke up, she was gone.

It was later in the day when an unfamiliar pair of shoes clicked across the floor. I knew it was afternoon since I could feel the heat of the sun move across my legs under the sheets. Dorothy Gish's familiar voice told me she'd brought me a bottle of brandy, and she apologized for not knowing at the time that I couldn't drink it. She sat with me for close to an hour, also reminiscing about the good times and holding my hand.

My body shut down, bit by bit, until the day I felt nothing more and I knew it was finally over. Jack and Owen brought my body home on the *Mauretania*, and Owen had to coax Jack away from the rail when he threatened to jump.

I floated through a cloudy sort of space and saw a bright light that drew me toward it. The light turned out to be a bustling office, and the angel or whoever she was asked me lots of questions about where I wanted to spend my afterlife. Somehow, I'd pictured Heaven as less of a bureaucracy, but it was the same as a county registrar's office.

"Miss Hostetler," the lady behind the counter said when I asked her name.

"Are you dead?" I asked.

"Of course I am," she snapped, grabbing a ghostly white clipboard. "We all are."

I gulped.

"Name?"

"Olive Thomas."

"Stay or go?"

"What?" I wondered if I was allowed to smoke, then realized I had no idea where my cigarettes were or if they even existed in this place.

The clerk popped her gum. "Stay or go?"

"I'm sorry, I . . ."

"Are you satisfied with your final passage into the heavenly realms? Or do you need more time below to complete unfinished business?"

"Unfinished business? What's that?"

"Were you murdered, the perpetrator not found, and you're assisting the police in the investigation from beyond? Are your loved ones unable to cope with your death and need your continued presence during their grieving process? Are you unusually fond of a special spot that makes you unable to leave it?"

She waited, chewing the tip of her pen.

"The last one, I guess."

She checked off a blank on the form.

"Location of special spot?"

"The New Amsterdam Theatre, New York, New York." I suppose I could have stayed at Nat's place, but my memories of Jack were tainted now. I belonged at the old girl.

She nodded. "Funeral?"

"I'm sorry?"

"You have the option of remaining behind to view your own funeral before being sent down. It's included in the package deal."

"Sure." Who'd miss something like that?

She told me to choose something to wear and sent me down to the New Amsterdam a couple of weeks after that.

My service was on September 28 at St. Thomas Episcopal Church. From my comfortable perch in the Great Beyond, I watched the proceedings, still unable to believe it all.

Long before 10:00 a.m., throngs of friends and fans packed the streets leading to the church on 53rd Avenue. So many of the girls had come—Marcie, Bessie, Fifi, Mae, Lil, Rosie and Jenny. Seeing their faces streaked with tears broke my heart.

An all-male choir sang, and about four thousand people were jammed in like kippers in a can. All the familiar faces. Over here were Mamma, Harry, Jim, Jimmie, Harriett, and Spud. Over there were Penny, J.F. Dillon, Elaine Hammerstein, Ed Wynn, Fanny Brice, and Marjorie Cassidy. Ziggy wouldn't come and everyone knew it. He had a mortal fear of death. Even the mere mention of it sent him into a black depression. He'd sent flowers—one of the biggest, most elaborate designs. It was a good thing he hadn't come, though. He once said if he caught sight of Jack he'd kill him, and I believed it.

Delores, an extra who'd recently done herself in by jumping in the Los Angeles River ("Not enough parts, but plenty of bills," she told me) sat down next to me, and we watched the spectacle together.

They couldn't give me an open casket due to the chemical burns to my face. But how they decorated! Lilies and orchids as far as the eye could see.

As I gazed over the thickest part of the crowd, my eyes came to rest on the floral arrangements. One was inscribed with "60," obviously an offering from the Sixty Club. The one that most genuinely brought tears to my eyes wasn't the biggest or fanciest but the one that said the most: "Our pal Ollie," it read. Delores put her arm around me then and leaned her head on my shoulder.

"Everyone loves you," she said in wonder. "I think twenty people showed up for mine. One nice arrangement, maybe. This is unreal. Who's that?"

The blackened eyes and newsboy caps signaled the stalwart daredevils who had shown me the tricks of the trade.

"Harvey Perry and the boys. Stuntmen."

It all passed in a blur. The choir sang "Abide With Me" and "Hark, Hark My Soul," but I couldn't remember the rest. If you've never attended your own funeral, I highly recommend it. You don't have a lot to do in the afterlife unless you like harp lessons. Only you, watching from a distance, can tell who's there because they truly loved you, or who thinks it gives them cachet for showing up.

Harry, Owen, Tom, Myron, Alan Crosland, Gene Buck, William Skelton, and Harry Carrington, our old landlord from Wilshire, were my pallbearers. But bless 'em, they had problems even getting me out of the church. With all the fans jostling the coffin, their job was almost impossible. The police had to jump into action so they didn't drop me. The women in the crowd were dropping like flies, fainting right and left.

"Doesn't anyone have any smelling salts? This is getting ridiculous," I said after the seventh one hit the ground outside.

They say fame does strange things to people, and that sure was front and center at that church. Women driven bats by what had happened to me ripped at the floral arrangements as they passed. It was a wonder anything survived to head to the cemetery, but they still needed twelve cars to get all the flowers to the crypt.

Mamma, Harry, Jim, and Spud had a terrible time trying to reach the car after the service. Jimmie and Harriett were sad and terrified. When the family got separated by the crowd, the policemen were finally able to herd them back together. But it was like watching someone try to guide an ocean wave in the correct direction, with the head lieutenant as Moses.

CHAPTER FIFTY-EIGHT

So now you know how it all ended for me. I'm seeing out my days at the New Amsterdam in this silly green outfit. No one even knows my name. Today, when anyone says the word "flapper," people think of Clara Bow or Colleen Moore, Louise Brooks, or even Joan Crawford. I was dead before the "Roaring Twenties" even revved up.

Ziggy died of pleurisy in 1932. I wonder if he even watched his *own* funeral. Probably no, based on his record. But who could resist that much adulation?

Sadly, Myron took to alcohol after I shuffled off the mortal coil. He watched as his brother David eclipsed him, and then personal problems and booze caused him to join me in 1944. He was only forty-five.

Penny kept dancing for a long time, until arthritis began to get the better of her. She lived out her years on welfare in New York until she passed away of a stroke in 1971.

Owen died of a heart attack in 1939. If you ask me, Mary never deserved him. And he never deserved to be treated like a second-class citizen in his own marriage.

J.F. had a heart attack in Los Angeles in 1934. He was only forty-nine.

Kay Laurell, the warthog in a wig, died of pneumonia in London only seven years after I bought it. Not soon enough for me.

Lucky little Norma Shearer became the toast of Hollywood, just like I said she would, playing queens and empresses. It didn't hurt that she nabbed producer Irving Thalberg for a husband. As one of the most powerful men in Hollywood next to Louis B. Mayer, he put her on the map. Ath wasn't as lucky. She married a director named Howard Hawks, but she was in and out of hospitals the rest of her life.

Charlotte Pickford, the frigid old witch, finally met her maker in 1928. Lottie followed her, way too young, from a heart attack in 1936. Mary, unfortunately, lived a long life—but a lonely, reclusive one. The alcoholism that ran in the Pickford family claimed her too. The public forgot her, and silents became as extinct as dinosaurs. Mary's entire family was gone, and even Douglas Fairbanks left her. The only ones she had left were her bottle of gin and her third husband, Buddy Rogers. I didn't know him personally. But anyone who could put up with her for forty-something years deserves a medal, if you ask me.

My family all lived long lives except for poor Harriett. She was killed in a car accident in 1931. She was only sixteen years old. Chow passed on that very same year to the great doghouse in the sky.

Effie lived long enough to see the beginnings of the Civil Rights movement, and she became a grandmother many times over. She died in her sleep in 1963, after listening to Martin Luther King's speech on the radio.

Jack remarried twice after me. And both times to Ziegfeld girls, strangely enough. Both pretty ladies, of course, but they couldn't be me, could they? And we all know that's what he was going for. Marilyn Miller was a dancer. Boy, could she dance! I watched her from up in the rafters here at the theater. A regular Pavlova, she was. Ziggy took a shine to her too, but she had to lock her dressing room door to keep him out. Before Jack, she'd been completely in love with Frank Carter, an actor who'd been in the Follies too. But he'd been killed in a car crash.

How was that supposed to work? Two people who married, both wishing the spouse was someone else. It had to fail. They were wed in 1922 and divorced in 1927. So much for that, I guess.

Mary Mulhern was his next Ziegfeld conquest. After only a few months, Jack hit her the first time, and kept hitting her. I guess the stress of seeing his body fall apart and his mind in tatters was too much for him. He'd needed help from either the wife or the ever-present sister to walk, stand, or move. He even used a wheelchair on the bad days. The pox does that to a person, you know. Eventually.

Jack and Mary (Mrs. Pickford #3, I mean) were in the process of a nasty divorce when he traveled to Europe in 1932. And wouldn't you know, when his body gave out in January of the next year, it chose to do so with a great flair for drama and irony in Paris, at the American Hospital in Neuilly—the scene of my own last breath. It was hard to watch him go, but I was torn. He'd hurt so many people, between his insensitivity and his refusal to admit fault for anything he ever did. My starlet friend Delores held my hand, and my tears alternated with wry observations of his character (or lack of it).

The worst part of everything? Mary didn't even bury us together. When Jack went, she had him buried at Forest Lawn in California. I was furious, and still am. My bones are moldering away in a decrepit concrete box in the Bronx. Nobody's cared for the damned crypt for almost a century.

I suppose this is the part where my reminiscences are supposed to turn deep and profound. But those who knew me then and those who know me now know that's not me. I'm not a smart person. Not smart enough to wax philosophical, anyway. Was it fate that took me? Even when I was alive, I didn't think you could change anything that was going to happen to you any more than you could change what had already happened.

Jack and I being together was like a forest fire. He was spectacular and dangerous, and more than a little destructive. And I was only a girl playing with matches—no idea of the risks. The more I gave, the more he took, until there was nothing left of me to consume.

Do I blame him? Well, yes and no. If he hadn't had the clap, I'd still be speaking to you from a higher plane, but I wouldn't have gotten here quite so early.

On the other hand, what kind of numbskull doesn't pay attention to what she's drinking? I let that pounding headache blind me to the danger signs right in front of me, and after the mercury, that headache looked like a walk in the park.

One of the saddest times I remember from my afterlife was June 12, 1936. Wanting to make my reunion date with the other Follies girls, I slipped through the outside wall to see who would show up. Though I was chained to the theater by some sort of invisible tether, I could sometimes move between the place and the nearby spots I used to frequent. I hadn't figured out what the secret was, but once in a while I could walk through an exterior wall and keep going.

Churchill's was long gone, thanks to Prohibition, and the Paradise Cabaret was the closest thing to a replacement. Kathryn trudged into the restaurant alone, everything about her gray and lifeless, like a sad little raisin. She'd dressed up, of course, but it was like trying to drape wrapping paper over a dead leaf. No point. Not long after Kathryn sat down, a younger blonde woman joined her.

"Miss Lambert," she said, "It's lovely to meet you. I'm Madelin Blitzstein, *Every Week* magazine." She held out her hand for a shake, then pulled up a seat and gestured to the bartender. She wore a scarlet snood over blonde hair and a smart skirt and blouse with a tailored jacket.

"Double whiskey and tonic," she said, "and whatever Miss Lambert is drinking."

"Call me Kathryn. Gin." She raised her glass so the bartender could see its clear consistency.

"So tell me about your reunion," Miss Blitzstein said, obviously enthusiastic for a good story.

"This is it," Kathryn said. In addition to the extra weight she was now sporting, she also carried an extra helping of cynicism wherever she went.

The reporter regarded the half-empty cafe, certain she must be missing the punch line of the joke. "When you phoned the magazine, you said you had a scoop on a reunion of Ziegfeld girls." She sounded infinitely disappointed.

"That's the thing, Miss Blitzstein. I do. Six of us were supposed to be here this evening. Perhaps you've heard of some of us."

Miss Blitzstein appeared ready to put away her writing pad and leave until Kathryn said something that captured her attention.

"First, Ollie. Olive Thomas, the actress. Remember her?"

"Vaguely," the younger woman said. "My mother was a fan."

"Do you know what happened to her?

Miss Blitzstein furrowed her brow, thinking. "It was somewhat scandalous, wasn't it?"

"She drank her husband's syphilis medication in 1920. Some people said it was suicide, but they didn't know our Ollie at all. It was purely accidental. Ollie would never have killed herself."

"So Olive Thomas was supposed to attend?"

"Yes." Kathryn lit a Lucky and inhaled deeply before answering any more questions.

"Who else?"

"Ever hear of Martha Mansfield?"

"She was an actress too, I believe."

"Yes. She used to be Martha Ehrlich in her Follies days. Ever seen a movie called *The Warrens of Virginia*? From 1924. A period drama. You know, petticoats, hoop skirts, all of that frilly nonsense. Some thoughtless ignoramus tossed a cigarette in her direction and that was it for Martha. She went up like a torch."

I knew all of this, having listened to the newer girls at the Follies while I wandered around in my ghostly state. It still hurt to hear the story.

"Lilyan Tashman," Kathryn said, moving on to the next unfortunate.

Miss Blitzstein's face fell. "I loved her work," the reporter murmured.

"Lil was special. Incredible cat's eyes, and a body to match. A stunningly gorgeous woman. She was a lesbian, of course—we all knew it, but everyone kept it under wraps. She married Edmund Lowe, who was also a . . . homosexual. But they were good together. They had an . . . agreement for their marriage. Lil was always on a diet. She watched her figure religiously, living on lettuce leaves, carrots, and water. We always worried about her, since we thought she simply couldn't be getting enough nourishment that way. But she and Ed threw parties that haven't been equaled in Hollywood since."

"So what happened to Miss Tashman?"

"She got some sort of abdominal cancer. It ate her away. She was only thirty-seven." Kathryn dabbed at her eyes with a handkerchief she'd pulled out of her purse. Then she took a deep breath and continued.

"Bessie Poole was a society girl, from old New England money. We don't understand exactly what happened with Bessie. Toward the end of her life, she was living with Lillian Lorraine, another old Ziegfeld girl, at the Dorset Hotel. God knows we all loved to kick up our heels and have a good time. Bessie liked all that, and she liked her drink too. Texas Guinan's place, Chez Florence, was her favorite place to go.

"She and Lillian went out one night and supposedly she got into a fight with two men at the club. What that fight entailed is anyone's guess. She felt crummy when they got home, and the next day they phoned a doctor. She was sent to the hospital and died that day. No one ever gave a definite reason. The doctors mumbled something about 'heart disease,' but that was a load, wasn't it?" She took another drag on her cigarette and continued.

The reporter's expression had gone from annoyed to amused to saddened. I think at this point it was approaching horrified as she scribbled some notes.

"And Fifi. Poor Fifi," Kathryn said.

Miss Blitzstein glanced up from her note-taking, eyes a little dazed from having so much grief thrust upon her all at once.

"Fifi?" she asked.

"Fifi Alsop. Delightfully pretty, but very naive. She'd already been married and divorced by the time she joined us at the Follies. She was seventeen and the old codger was in his seventies. When he got tired of her, he locked up all his money and property and deeded it to his sons from a previous marriage. She fought the drink, but she was so depressed about Edward's double-crossing that she couldn't cope. The money gave out, what little she had. I sent her what I could, but she was fighting demons I couldn't help her with."

"What happened?"

"She was living in this complete dive—the Stillwell Arms. There's an ironic name for you. She was anything but well at that point, and she tried to end it all several times. Ever used veronal?"

The reporter shook her head at the continuing procession of heartbreak being paraded before her.

"It was only a year ago. If only I'd been able to do something," Kathryn said, her voice breaking. "It was as if Bellevue had a revolving door for Fifi. They'd clean her up and dismiss her, and she'd return a few weeks later in worse shape than before. The very last time, she'd gotten kicked out of the Stillwell. She had no ID on her when they found her. All those days alone on a block in the morgue, and nobody knew who she was. The mortician finally found my number buried deep in her coat pocket."

Kathryn raised her glass into the air. "To Fifi. And Ollie, and Martha, and Bessie, and Lil."

Then she downed the rest of the gin in one gulp. I couldn't help it. I lowered my head into my hands and bawled. So much wasted talent and beauty. What the hell had gone wrong with us? We weren't only *like* Ruth—some of us had turned out even worse.

We were so gay, and so stupid, and so convinced our entire lives would be just as they always had been—full of glamour and luxury and dreams. It only took one schmuck with dark, dancing eyes and a silver tongue to derail things for me.

But when I reminisce about my life (the first one, not this last ninety years of strangeness, mind you), I wouldn't have lived it any other way. I couldn't have. You can't change the way you're made, can you? It was all worth it—the late nights, the parties, the jewels, the orange blossoms, and the making love 'til dawn. When you're young, that's really all that matters, isn't it?

THE END

AUTHOR'S NOTE

Like many old movie fans, much of my interest in Hollywood history was ignited with Kenneth Anger's *Hollywood Babylon*. In my case, I'd checked it out from the now-consigned-to-history North Village Library in Austin, Texas. As a twelve-year-old, I was particularly intrigued by the story of Olive Thomas.

That fascination lay dormant for many years. What rekindled it was another book, *Loving Frank* by Nancy Horan. Her narrative was so beautiful and vivid, I felt as if I was watching a movie. I wanted to create that with characters of my own. But who? I wanted to write about real people as filtered through my fertile imagination. I wanted to research the living bejeezus out of every person in the story, every building, every theater, and all the other factual items I could find. And then Olive called my name, saying, "Hell's bells! What about me?" So here we are.

Almost everyone in this book actually existed. Here are those who didn't: Otto, Myra and her brother Wally; Buddy, the cameraman; Effie; Mischa; and Peter Underwood. All added something to the story, and any liberties taken with historical facts were for dramatic purposes where the story necessitated it.

I've attempted to draw Olive's life as faithfully as I could. I researched through censuses for information on her family. For those who say her father was a steelworker, I'll guide them to the 1900 census, where Michael Duffy was listed in Charleroi with his family, and his profession was listed as "brick mason." I had a friend who managed to see information for his death on file at the Pennsylvania State Health Department, and advised me accordingly.

I discovered that Jack and Olive's ship, the *Imperator*, actually changed names to the *Berengaria* in April 1920, but because this is such a well-known fact of Olive lore, I left it as is.

Many still argue the circumstances of Olive's death and her relationship with Jack. I realize that I can't please everyone with my conclusions about them, but I tried to write this book the way I'd always imagined her life, warts and all.

BIBLIOGRAPHY

Olive and Jack were difficult to pin down, since they alternated traveling cross country constantly, and I encountered conflicting information from multiple sources. Literally every book that included information about them differed. So I had to find a happy medium with facts. With the exception of a very early census record or two, and a WWI draft card for her brother, these are all secondary accounts of her and/or Hollywood in general:

BOOKS

Agreen, Bernadette Sulzer with the McKees Rocks Historical Society. *Images of America: McKees Rocks and Stowe Township.* Charleston, SC: Arcadia Publishing, 2009.

Beauchamp, Cari. *Without Lying Down: Frances Marion and the Powerful Women of Early Hollywood.* New York: Scribner, 1997.

Bitzer, G.W. *Billy Bitzer: His Story.* Toronto: Farar, Straus and Giroux, 1973.

Brown, Karl. *Adventures with D.W. Griffith.* Toronto: Farar, Straus and Giroux, 1973.

Brownlow, Kevin. *Hollywood, The Pioneers.* London: William Collins Sons & Co, Ltd., 1979.

Brownlow, Kevin. *The Parade's Gone By.* Berkeley: University of California Press, 1968.

Carter, Randolph. *The World of Flo Ziegfeld*. New York: Praeger Publishers, 1974.

Creason, Glen. *Los Angeles in Maps*. New York: Random House, 2010.

Dangcil, Tommy. *Postcard History Series: Hollywood Studios*. Charleston, SC: Arcadia Publishing, 2007.

Earle, Marcelle, with Arthur Homme, Jr. *Midnight Frolic: A Ziegfeld Girl's True Story*. Basking Ridge, NJ: Twin Oaks Publishing Company, 1955 (renewed 1980).

Eyman, Scott. *Mary Pickford, America's Sweetheart*. New York: Donald I. Fine, Inc., 1990.

Fields, W.C. *W.C. Fields By Himself*. Englewood Cliffs, NJ: Prentice –Hall, Inc., 1973.

Haver, Ronald. *David O. Selznick's Hollywood*. New York: Alfred A. Knopf, 1980.

Heimann, Jim. *Out With the Stars: Hollywood Nightlife in the Golden Era*. New York: Abbeville Press, 1985.

Lahue, Kalton. *Dreams For Sale The Rise and Fall of the Triangle Film Corporation*. Cranbury, NJ: A.S. Barnes and Co., Inc., 1971

Lorant, Stefan. *Pittsburgh The Story of an American City*. Lenox, Massachusetts: Kingsport Press, 1980.

Quirk, Lawrence J. *Norma The Story of Norma Shearer*. New York: St. Martin's Press, 1988.

Standiford, Les. *Meet You in Hell: Andrew Carnegie, Henry Clay Frick, and the Bitter Partnership That Changed America*. New York: Crown Publishing, 2005.

Torrence, Bruce T. *Hollywood: The First Hundred Years*. New York: Zoetrope, 1979, 1982.

Vivian, Cassandra. *Postcard History Series: The Mid Mon Valley*. Charleston, SC: Arcadia Publishing, 2004.

Vogel, Michelle. *Olive Thomas: The Life and Death of a Silent Film Beauty*. Jefferson, NC: McFarland Publishing, 2007.

Whitfield, Eileen. *Pickford*. Toronto: MacFarlane, Walter & Ross, 1997.

Williams, Gregory Paul. *The Story of Hollywood: An Illustrated History*. Austin, Texas: BL Press, LLC. 2011.

INTERNET

Big Bear History. Accessed March 9, 2010 and subsequent visits. <http://www.bigbearhistorysite.com/big-bear-historical-photographs/big-bear-lodges-photo-album>

Long, Bruce. Taylorology 33. September 1995. March 8, 2010 and subsequent visits <http://www.taylorology.com/issues/Taylor33.txt>.

Naureckas, Jim. New York Songlines. March 25, 2010 and subsequent visits. <http://www.nysonglines.com>.

Tryniski, Tom. Old Fulton NY Post Cards. June 25, 2012 and subsequent visits. <http://fultonhistory.com/Fulton.html>.

GoogleNews Archives. January 13, 2011 and subsequent visits <https://news.google.com/newspapers?hl=en>.

Media History Project. February 13, 2012 and subsequent visits. <http://mediahistoryproject.org/fanmagazines/>.

Family Search. February 10, 2010 and subsequent visits. <www.familysearch.org>.

Ultimate Imperator. February 12, 2011 and subsequent visits. <www.freewebs.com/ultimateimperator/welcome.htm>

VIDEO

Online

The Serial Squadron. "Olive Thomas first screen performance in BEATRICE FAIRFAX Ep. 10: "Play Ball!"" 30 March 2010. Online video clip. Youtube. Accessed on April 4, 2010. <https://www.

youtube.com/watch?v=JyF5wYJaAGI>

Jamon2112. "Hollywood - Ep 2: In the Beginning" April 16, 2014. Online video clip. Youtube. Accessed April 20, 2014. <https://www.youtube.com/watch?v=CpO6aiTjldk>

Jamon2112. "Hollywood - Ep 3: Single Beds and Double Standards" April 16, 2014. Online video clip. Youtube. Accessed April 20, 2014. <https://www.youtube.com/watch?v=WKAq6trYuYs>

Jamon2112. "Hollywood - Ep 4: Hollywood Goes to War" April 18, 2014. Online video clip. Youtube. Accessed April 20, 2014. <https://www.youtube.com/watch?v=yLtXuGded04>

Jamon2112. "Hollywood - Ep 8: Comedy - A Serious Business" April 19, 2014. Online video clip. Youtube. Accessed April 20, 2014. <https://www.youtube.com/watch?v=qwfA7suKAng>

DVD

Olive Thomas: Everybody's Sweetheart prod. Hugh Hefner. Image Entertainment, Milestone Film & Video. DVD, 2005.

The Flapper. Dir. Alan Crosland. Perfs. Olive Thomas, Theodore Westman, Jr. 1920. DVD color tinted. Image Entertainment. Milestone Film & Video. Print from the George Eastman House. DVD, 2005.

VHS

Hollywood: A Celebration of the American Silent Film - The Pioneers. Dirs. David Gill and Kevin Brownlow. Perf. James Mason, Lillian Gish, Dolores Costello, Blanche Sweet, Jackie Coogan. Thames Television, 1979. VHS. HBO Home Video, 1998.

Hollywood: A Celebration of the American Silent Film - The Autocrats. Dirs. David Gill and Kevin Brownlow. Perf. Agnes DeMille, Gloria Swanson, Henry King, Paul Ivano, James Mason. Thames

Television, 1979. VHS. HBO Home Video, 1998.

Hollywood: A Celebration of the American Silent Film - Trick of the Light. Dirs. David Gill and Kevin Brownlow. Perf. Viola Dana, Byron Haskin, Allan Dwan, Colleen Moore. Thames Television, 1979. VHS. HBO Home Video, 1998.

THANKS

- Jonathan Pettit—(R.I.P., friend) For his in-detail knowledge of the nuances of Olive and her life.
- Caroline Kaiser—For turning a good book into a great one with her edits!
- Ian Koviak—For his lovely book design. I didn't know my words could look so GORGEOUS!
- Michelle Vogel—For her book on Olive, which provided a host of wonderful details and a filmography.
- The Mennonite Thrift Shop in Edmonton—For their collection of donated Hollywood books that formed the basis of my research library.
- Martin Turnbull—For being the inspiration and encouragement I needed to do this solo!
- Faithful readers Margaret Lesh and Deb Mieszala—For giving me some wonderful pointers.
- The Edmonton Writers Group—Your feedback is always spot-on!
- My buds at absolutewrite.com—For six terrific years of camaraderie and tough love.

- My friends at the Surrey and Santa Barbara Writers Conferences—For their support and solidarity.
- Susannah Kearsley—For the kind words. They meant a lot!
- Sarah Baker, Hugh Hefner, et al.—For releasing *The Flapper/*Olive documentary on DVD.
- Nancy Horan—For her lightning bolt of inspiration, *Loving Frank*, and helping me discover my perfect genre.
- Kevin Brownlow—For igniting my passion for silent movies.

BOOK CLUB QUESTIONS

1. Why do you think that, of all the places she'd been, Ollie picked the New Amsterdam to haunt?
2. Why were the Pickfords so resistant to Ollie? Was it that she'd been poor? Or a showgirl? Or both?
3. How different do you think Ollie's life would have been if she'd never entered the contest? Do you think it would have been happier?
4. Why do you think Ollie stayed with Jack despite all their troubles? Was it just love, or was there something else involved? Her career? Fear of scandal?
5. Initially, she says she wants to do something big and important. Do you think she has any ideas of what that will be?
6. Why do you think Ollie's story has so resonated with silent film fans, even all these years later?
7. Why do you think Kay Laurell and Ollie hated each other so much?
8. Knowing what eventually happened to Ollie's group of Ziegfeld girls, contrast this with the fame that the Follies represented at the time. Do you think all the glamour was worth it in the long run?

9. Is Jack actually a sympathetic character? With his sister and her career dictating his entire life, do you think he had any chance to develop into a healthy, independent man? Do you think choosing Ollie was his first opportunity to rebel against Mary?
10. Did you have a favorite supporting character? Why did you choose that person?

CONTACT

Want to know all the latest news from Laini?
Let's keep in touch!

lainigiles@yahoo.com

www.lainigiles.com

4gottenflapper@twitter.com

sepiastories.wordpress.com

THE IT GIRL AND ME

If you liked *The Forgotten Flapper*, look for Laini's new book, *The It Girl and Me*, coming in 2017!

WOMEN'S CELL BLOCK
HALL OF JUSTICE, LOS ANGELES, CALIFORNIA

January 1931

Rumor has it that when confronted with a patrol of bluecoats ready to bivouac outside his cabin near Fredonia, Kentucky, my Grandpappy, Will Henry DeBoe, gave their captain such an earful that they turned tail and spent the night elsewhere. Yes, they had guns, but he had a tongue sharper than Robert E. Lee's saber. Kentucky was a border state, but there was no doubt where Grandpap's sympathies lie. When Nathan Bedford Forrest invaded a few years later, Grandpappy saluted and tacked his Stars and Bars to the cabin wall. His was one of the few places that wasn't burned to the ground.

It seems far-fetched, I know, but my daddy swears up and down that it's true. Even though he wasn't born until twelve years after the war ended. My point being—we DeBoes don't scare easily. Then or now.

Mama comes to visit me, but I try to talk her out of it, because those vulture newspapermen camped outside on the front steps snap her picture. The neighbors already saw the police arrest me. That's the kind of celebrity she doesn't need. Not after what happened with Daddy. She's getting older, and I had hoped that at my age I'd be helping her instead of being such a burden.

"Daisy, honey," she said, last time she came to visit. "Cain't you make some kind of plea bargain? So's they can get you out of here?" She sniffed into her handkerchief and tucked it back into her pocketbook.

"Fraid not, Mama," I said. I took her hand across the visiting room table. "I done what was right, here. I ain't a thief. The judge is going to realize that, and so is the jury."

I'd been sitting in clover with this job—secretary to the world's most famous movie star—traveling the country, making decent money, trying to keep Clara Bow in line, until a minor squabble turned into an arrest. Mine.

Now, here I sit in the L.A. County Jail. Money, publicity, and the power of Paramount Pictures was going to trump a poor Kentucky girl with the best of intentions. I'm fresh out of aces.

Made in the USA
Lexington, KY
07 August 2019